W9-BHA-574

SWEET FORGIVENESS

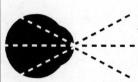

This Large Print Book carries the
Seal of Approval of N.A.V.H.

SWEET FORGIVENESS

LORI NELSON SPIELMAN

THORNDIKE PRESS
A part of Gale, Cengage Learning

GALE
CENGAGE Learning·

Farmington Hills, Mich • San Francisco • New York • Waterville, Maine
Meriden, Conn • Mason, Ohio • Chicago

GALE
CENGAGE Learning·

Copyright © 2015 by Lori Nelson Spielman.
Thorndike Press, a part of Gale, Cengage Learning.

Thorndike Press® Large Print Women's Fiction.
The text of this Large Print edition is unabridged.
Other aspects of the book may vary from the original edition.
Set in 16 pt. Plantin.

LIBRARY OF CONGRESS CATALOGING-IN-PUBLICATION DATA

Spielman, Lori Nelson.
  Sweet forgiveness / Lori Nelson Spielman. — Large print edition.
     pages cm. — (Thorndike Press large print women's fiction)
  ISBN 978-1-4104-8362-1 (hardback) — ISBN 1-4104-8362-2 (hardcover)
  1. Television personalities—Fiction. 2. Mothers and daughters—Fiction. 3. Forgiveness—Fiction. 4. Large type books. I. Title.
  PS3619.P5434S94 2015b
  813'.6—dc23   2015024657

Published in 2015 by arrangement with Plume, an imprint of Penguin Publishing Group, a division of Penguin Random House LLC

Printed in Mexico
1 2 3 4 5 6 7 19 18 17 16 15

For Bill

"To forgive is to set a prisoner free and discover that the prisoner was you."

— Lewis B. Smedes

CHAPTER 1

It went on for one hundred sixty-three days. I looked back at my diary years later and counted. And now she's written a book. Unbelievable. The woman's a rising star. An expert on forgiveness, how ironic. I study her picture. She's still cute, with a pixie haircut and a button nose. But her smile looks genuine now, her eyes no longer mocking. Even so, her very image makes my heart race.

I fling the newspaper onto my coffee table and instantly snatch it up again.

CLAIM YOUR SHAME
By Brian Moss | The Times-Picayune

NEW ORLEANS — Can an apology heal old wounds, or are some secrets better left unsaid?

According to Fiona Knowles, a 34-year-old attorney from Royal Oak, Michigan, making amends for past grievances is a crucial step toward achieving inner peace.

"It takes courage to claim our shame," Knowles said. "Most of us aren't comfortable demonstrating vulnerability. Instead, we stuff our guilt inside, hoping no one will ever see what's hidden within. Releasing our shame frees us."

And Ms. Knowles should know. She put her theory to the test in the spring of 2013, when she penned 35 letters of apology. With each letter, she enclosed a pouch containing two stones, which she dubbed the Forgiveness Stones. The recipient was given two simple requests: to forgive and to seek forgiveness.

"I realized people were desperate for an excuse — an obligation — to atone," Knowles said. "Like the seeds of a dandelion, the Forgiveness Stones caught the wind and migrated."

Whether the result of the wind or Ms. Knowles' savvy use of social media, it's clear the Forgiveness Stones have hit their mark. To date, it's estimated that nearly 400,000 forgiveness stones are in circulation.

Ms. Knowles will appear at Octavia Books Thursday, April 24, to talk about her

new book, appropriately titled THE
FORGIVENESS STONES.

I jump when my cell phone buzzes, telling
me it's four forty-five — time to go to work.
My hands shake as I tuck the paper into my
tote. I grab my keys and to-go mug, and
head out the door.

Three hours later, after reviewing last
week's abysmal ratings and being briefed on
today's riveting topic — how to apply self-
tanner properly — I sit in my office/dressing
room, Velcro curlers in my hair and a plastic
cape covering my dress du jour. It's my least
favorite part of the day. After ten years of
being on camera, you'd think I'd be used to
it. But getting made up requires that I arrive unmade, which for me is akin to trying
on bathing suits under fluorescent lights
with a spectator present. I used to apologize
to Jade for having to witness the potholes,
otherwise known as pores, on my nose, or
the under-eye circles that make me look like
I'm ready to play football. I once tried
wrestling the foundation brush from her
clutches, hoping to spare her the horrifying
and impossible task of trying to camouflage
a zit the size of Mauna Loa on my chin. As
my father used to say, if God wanted a

11

woman's face to be naked, he wouldn't have created mascara.

While Jade performs her magic, I shuffle through a stack of mail and freeze when I see it. My stomach sinks. It's buried mid-stack, with just the upper right corner visible. It tortures me, that big round Chicago postmark. *C'mon, Jack, enough already!* It's been over a year since he last contacted me. How many times do I have to tell him it's okay, he's forgiven, I've moved on? I drop the stack on the ledge in front of me, arranging the letters so that the postmark is no longer visible, and flip open my laptop.

"Dear Hannah," I read aloud from my e-mail, trying to push aside all thoughts of Jack Rousseau. *"My husband and I watch your show every morning. He thinks you're terrific, says you're the next Katie Couric."*

"Look up, Ms. Couric," Jade orders, and smudges my lower lashes with a chalk pencil.

"Uh-huh. Katie Couric minus the millions of dollars and gazillions of fans." . . . And the gorgeous daughters and perfect new husband . . .

"You'll get there," Jade says with such certainty I almost believe her. She looks especially pretty today, with her dreadlocks pulled into a wild and wiry ponytail, accenting her dark eyes and flawless brown skin. She's wearing her usual leggings and black smock, each pocket stuffed with brushes and pencils of various widths and angles.

She blends the liner with a flat-tipped brush, and I resume reading. *"Personally, I think Katie is overrated. My favorite is Hoda Kotb. Now that girl is funny."*

"Ouch!" Jade says. "You just got slammed."

I laugh and continue reading. *"My husband says you're divorced. I say you've never been married. Who's right?"*

I position my fingers on the keyboard.

"Dear Ms. Nixon," I say as I type. *"Thank you so much for watching* The Hannah Farr Show. *I hope you and your husband enjoy the new season. (And by the way, I agree . . . Hoda is hilarious.) Wishing you the best, Hannah."*

"Hey, you didn't answer her question."

I shoot Jade a look in the mirror. She shakes her head and grabs a palette of eye shadow. "Of course you didn't."

"I was nice."

"You always are. Too nice, if you ask me."

"Yeah, right. Like when I'm complaining about that snooty chef on last week's show — Mason What's-His-Name — who answered every question with a one-word reply? Nice when I'm obsessing about ratings? And now, oh, God, now Claudia." I turn to look at Jade. "Did I tell you Stuart's thinking of making her my cohost? I'm history!"

"Close your eyes," she tells me, and brushes shadow over my lids.

"The woman's been in town all of six weeks, and already she's more popular than I am."

"Not a chance," Jade says. "This city has adopted you as one of their own. But that's not going to stop Claudia Campbell from attempting a takeover. I get a bad vibe from that one."

"I don't see it," I say. "She's ambitious, all right, but she seems really nice. It's Stuart I'm worried about. With him it's all about ratings, and lately mine have been —"

"Shit. I know. But they'll rise again. I'm just saying, you need to watch your back. Miss Claudia's used to being top dog. There's no way the rising star from WNBC New York is going to settle for some rinky-dink spot as the morning anchor."

There's a pecking order in broadcast journalism. Most of us start our careers by doing live shots for the five a.m. news, which means waking at three for an audience of two. After only nine months of that grueling schedule, I was lucky enough to advance to the weekend anchor, and soon after, the noon news, a spot I enjoyed for four years. Of course, anchoring the evening news is the grand prize, and I happened to be with station WNO at just the right time. Robert Jacobs retired, or, as rumor had it, was forced to retire, and Priscille offered me the position. Ratings soared. Soon I was booked day and night, hosting charity events throughout the city, playing the master of ceremonies at fund-raisers and Mardi Gras celebrations. To my surprise, I became a local celebrity, something I still can't wrap my head around. And my rapid rise didn't stop with evening anchor. Because the Crescent City "fell in love with Hannah Farr," or so I was told, two years ago I was offered my own show — an opportunity most journalists would kill for.

"Um, I hate to break it to you, sunshine, but *The Hannah Farr Show* ain't exactly the big leagues."

Jade shrugs. "Best TV in Louisiana, if you ask me. Claudia's licking her chops, mark my words. If she's got to be here, there's only one job she's going to settle for, and that's yours." Jade's phone chirps and she peers at the caller ID. "Mind if I take this?"

"Go ahead," I say, welcoming the interruption. I don't want to talk about Claudia, the striking blonde who, at twenty-four, is a full — and crucial — decade younger than I am. Why does her fiancé have to live in New Orleans, of all places? Looks, talent, youth, *and* a fiancé! She's one-upped me in every single category, including relationship status.

Jade's voice grows louder. "Are you serious?" she says to the caller. "Dad's got an appointment at West Jefferson Medical. I reminded you yesterday."

My stomach turns. It's her soon-to-be ex, Marcus, the father of her twelve-year-old son — or Officer Asshole, as she now calls him.

I close my laptop and grab the stack of mail from the counter, hoping to give Jade the illusion of privacy. I thumb through the pile, searching for the Chicago postmark. I'll read Jack's apology, and then I'll compose a response, reminding him that I'm happy now, that he needs to get on with his life. The thought makes me weary.

I land on the envelope and pull it loose. Instead of Jackson Rousseau's address in the upper left-hand corner, it reads, *WCHI News.*

So it's not from Jack. That's a relief.

Dear Hannah,

It was a pleasure meeting you last month in Dallas. Your speech at the NAB Conference was both captivating and inspiring.

As I mentioned to you then, WCHI is creating a new morning talk show, *Good Morning, Chicago*. Like *The Hannah Farr Show*, *GMC*'s target audience will be women. Along with the occasional fun and frivolous segments, *GMC* will tackle some weighty topics, including politics, literature and the arts, and world affairs.

We are searching for a host and would very much like to discuss the position with you. Would you be interested? In addition to the interview process and a demo tape, we ask that you provide a proposal for an original show.

Sincerely yours,
James Peters
Senior Vice President,
WCHI Chicago

Wow. So he was serious when he pulled me aside at the National Association of Broadcasters Conference. He'd seen my show. He knew my ratings were down, but he told me I had great potential, given the right opportunity. Maybe this was the opportunity he was alluding to. And how refreshing that WCHI wants to hear my idea for a rundown. Stuart rarely considers my input. "There are four topics people want to watch on morning television," Stuart claims. "Celebrities, sex, weight loss, and beauty." What I wouldn't give to host a show with some controversy.

My head swells for all of two seconds. Then I come back to reality. I don't want a job in Chicago, a city nine hundred miles away. I'm too invested in New Orleans. I love this dichotomous city, the gentility mixed with grit, with its jazz and po'boys and crawfish gumbo. And more important, I'm in love with the city's mayor. Even if I wanted to apply — which I don't — Michael wouldn't hear of it. He is third-generation "N'awlins," now raising the fourth generation — his daughter, Abby. Still, it's nice to feel wanted.

Jade punches off the phone, the vein in her forehead bulging. "That jackass! My dad cannot miss this appointment. Marcus insisted he'd take him — he's been sucking up again. 'No problem,' he told me last week. 'I'll swing by on my way to the station.' I should have known." In the mirror's reflection, her dark eyes glisten. She turns away and punches numbers into her phone. "Maybe Natalie can break away."

Jade's sister is a high school principal. There's no way she can break away. "What time is the appointment?"

"Nine o'clock. Marcus claims he's tied up. Yeah, he's tied up, all right. Tied to his ho's bedpost, doing his morning cardio."

I check my watch: 8:20. "Go," I say. "Doctors are never on schedule. If you hurry, you can still make it."

She scowls at me. "I can't leave. I haven't finished your makeup."

I hop from my chair. "What? You think I've forgotten how to apply makeup?" I shoo her away. "Go. Now."

"But Stuart. If he finds out . . ."

"Don't worry. I've got you covered. Just be back in time to get Sheri ready for the evening news or we'll both catch hell." I point her petite frame toward the hallway. "Now get going."

Her eyes dart to the clock above the door. She stands silent, biting her lip. Suddenly it occurs to me: Jade took the streetcar to work. I grab my tote from the locker and fish out my keys. "Take my car," I say, extending the keys.

"What? No. I can't do that! What if I —"

"It's a car, Jade. It's replaceable." *Unlike your father,* but I don't say this. I tuck the keys into her palm. "Now get out of here before Stuart comes along and finds out you skipped out on me."

Her face floods with relief and she captures me in a hug. "Oh, thank you. Don't you worry, I'll take good care of your ride." She turns to the door. "Stay in trouble," she says, her favorite parting line. She's halfway to the elevator when I hear her call, "I owe you one, Hannabelle."

"And don't think I'm going to forget it. Give Pop a hug for me."

I close the door, alone in my dressing room with thirty minutes to spare until pre-show. I find a compact of bronzer and brush it over my forehead and across the bridge of my nose.

I free the snaps of my plastic cape and pick up the letter, rereading Mr. Peters's words as I meander past the sofa and over to my desk. There's no question the job's a fantastic opportunity, especially given my current slump here. I'd be moving from the fifty-third to the third largest television market in the country. Within a few years, I'd be a competitor for nationally syndicated programs like *GMA* or the *Today* show. No doubt my salary would quadruple.

I sit down behind my desk. Obviously, Mr. Peters sees the same Hannah Farr everyone else sees: a happily single career woman with no roots, an opportunist who'd gladly pack up and move across the country for a better salary and bigger assignment.

My gaze lands on a photo of my father and me, taken at the Critics' Choice Awards in 2012. I bite my cheek, remembering the swanky event. My dad's glassy eyes and ruddy nose tell me he's already had too much to drink. I'm wearing a silver ball gown and a huge grin. But my eyes look vacant and hollow, the same way I felt that night, sitting alone with my father. It wasn't because I'd lost the award. It was because I *felt* lost. Spouses and children and parents who weren't drunk surrounded the other recipients. They laughed and cheered, and later danced together in big circles. I wanted what they had.

I lift another picture, this one of Michael and me, sailing on Lake Pontchartrain last summer. A shock of Abby's blond hair is visible at the frame's edge. She's perched on the bow to my right, her back to me.

I set the photo back on my desk. In a couple years I hope to have a different picture on my desk, this one of Michael and me standing in front of a pretty home, along with a smiling Abby, and maybe even a child of our own.

I tuck Mr. Peters's letter into a private file marked INTEREST, where I've stashed the dozen or so similar letters I've received over the years. Tonight I'll send the usual thanks-but-no-thanks note. Michael doesn't need to know. For, as cliché and terribly outdated as it sounds, a high-profile job in Chicago is nothing compared to being part of a family.

But when will I get that family? Early on, Michael and I seemed completely in sync. Within weeks we were speaking in future tense. We spent hours sharing our dreams. We'd toss out possible names for our children — Zachary or Emma or Liam — speculate on what they'd look like and whether Abby would prefer a brother or a sister. We'd scour the Internet for houses, sending links back and forth with notes like, *Cute, but Zachary will need a bigger backyard,* or *Imagine what we could do in a bedroom this size.* All that seems like ages ago. Now Michael's dreams are focused on his political career, and any talk of our future has been tabled for "once Abby graduates."

A thought occurs to me. Could the prospect of losing me trigger the commitment from Michael I've been hoping for?

I pull the letter from the file, my idea gaining momentum. This is more than a job opportunity. It's an opportunity to speed things along. Abby's graduation is only a year away now. It's time we start making a plan. I reach for my cell phone, feeling lighter than I have in weeks.

I punch in his number, wondering if I'll get lucky and catch him in a rare moment of solitude. He'll be impressed that I'm being courted for a job — especially in a big market like Chicago. He'll tell me how proud he is, and then he'll remind me of all the wonderful reasons I can't leave, the most important reason being him. And later, when he's a chance to reflect, he'll realize that he'd better seal the deal, before I'm snatched from his clutches. I smile, giddy with the thought of being sought-after both professionally and personally.

"Mayor Payne." His voice is already heavy, and his day has just begun.

"Happy Wednesday," I say, hoping the reminder of our date night might cheer him. Last December Abby started babysitting every Wednesday evening, relieving Michael of his parental duties and allowing us one weeknight together.

"Hey, babe." He sighs. "What a crazy day. There's a community forum at Warren Easton High. Brainstorming session on school violence prevention. I'm on my way over there now. I hope to be back by noon for the rally. You're coming, right?"

He's talking about the Into the Light Rally, to spread awareness about child sexual abuse. I lean my elbows on the desk. "I told Marisa I wouldn't be at this one. Noon is cutting it too close. I feel awful."

"Don't. You give them plenty. I can only make a quick appearance myself. I've got meetings all afternoon to discuss the escalation in poverty. They'll run through the dinner hour, I suspect. Would you mind if we take the night off?"

Poverty issues? I can't argue with that, even if it is Wednesday. If I hope to become the mayor's wife, I'd better learn to accept that he is a man of service. After all, it is one of the things I love most about him. "No. It's okay. But you sound exhausted. Try to get some sleep tonight."

"I will." He lowers his voice. "Though I'd prefer to get something other than sleep."

I smile, imagining myself wrapped in Michael's arms. "Me, too."

Should I tell him about the letter from James Peters? He's got enough to worry about, without me adding a threat.

"I'll let you go," he says. "Unless there was something you needed."

Yes, I want to tell him, *I do need something. I need to know that you'll miss me tonight, that I am a priority. I need assurance that we're heading toward a future together, that you want to marry me.* I take a deep breath.

"I just wanted to give you a heads-up. Someone's after your girlfriend." I say it with a lighthearted, singsong voice. "I got a love letter in the mail today."

"Who's my competition?" he says. "I'll kill him, I swear."

I laugh and explain the letter from James Peters and the job prospect, hoping to convey just enough enthusiasm to sound a little warning bell in Michael.

"It's not exactly a job offer, but it sounds like they're interested in me. They want a proposal for an original story idea. Kind of cool, right?"

"Very cool. Congratulations, superstar. Another reminder that you're completely out of my league."

My heart does a little jig. "Thanks. It felt good." I squeeze shut my eyes and plow on, before I lose my nerve. "The show premieres in the fall. They need to move quickly."

"That's only six months away. Better get a move on. Have you scheduled the interview?"

The wind is knocked from me. I put a hand to my throat and force myself to breathe. Thank God Michael can't see me.

"I . . . no, I — I haven't responded yet."

"If we can swing it, Abby and I'll come with you. Make a mini-vacation of it. I haven't been to Chicago in years."

Say something! Tell him you're disappointed, that you were hoping he'd beg you to stay. Remind him that your ex-fiancé lives in Chicago, for God's sake!

"So, you wouldn't mind if I left?"

"Well, I wouldn't like it. Long-distance would be a bitch. But we could make it work, don't you think?"

"Sure," I say. But inside I'm thinking of our current schedules, where even in the same city we can't seem to carve any alone time.

"Listen," he says, "I've got to run. I'll call you later. And congratulations, babe. I'm proud of you."

I punch off the phone and slump into my chair. Michael doesn't care if I leave. I'm an idiot. Marriage is no longer on his radar. And he's left me no choice now. I have to send Mr. Peters my résumé and an episode proposal. Otherwise it'll look like I was being manipulative, which, I suppose, I was.

My eyes land on the *Times-Picayune,* peeking from my tote. I lift the paper and

26

scowl at the headline. CLAIM YOUR SHAME. Yeah, right. Send a Forgiveness Stone and everything will be forgiven. You're delusional, Fiona Knowles.

I knead my forehead. I could sabotage this job offer, write a crummy proposal and tell Michael I didn't get the interview. No. I have too much pride. If Michael wants me to pursue the job, dammit, I will! And not just pursue it, I'll get the offer. I'll move away and start fresh. The show will be wildly popular and I'll be Chicago's next Oprah Winfrey! I'll meet someone new, someone who loves kids and is ready to commit. How do you like me now, Michael Payne?

But first I need to write the proposal.

I pace the room, trying to drum up an idea for a killer rundown, something thought-provoking and fresh and timely. Something that would land me the job and impress Michael . . . and maybe even make him reconsider.

My eyes return again to the newspaper. Slowly, my scowl softens. Yes. It might work. But could I do it?

I pull the newspaper from my tote and carefully tear out Fiona's article. I move to my desk drawer and suck in a deep breath. *What the hell am I doing?* I stare at the closed drawer as if it's Pandora's box.

Finally, I yank it open.

I fumble past pens and paper clips and Post-it notes until I spot it. It's tucked in the very back corner of the drawer, just where I'd hidden it two years ago.

A letter of apology from Fiona Knowles. And a velvet pouch containing a pair of Forgiveness Stones.

CHAPTER 2

I draw open the pouch strings. Two small, round ordinary garden pebbles tumble onto my palm. I run my finger over them, one gray with black veins, the other ivory. I feel a crinkle within the velvet fabric and pull out the accordion-pleated note, like a fortune in a cookie.

One stone signifies the weight of anger.
The other stone symbolizes the weight of shame.
Both can be lifted, if you choose to rid yourself of their burdens.

Is she still waiting for my stone? Have the other thirty-four she sent been returned to her? Guilt chokes me.

I unfold the cream-colored piece of stationery and reread the letter.

Dear Hannah,

My name is Fiona Knowles. I sincerely hope you haven't a clue who I am. If you remember me, it's because I left a scar on you.

You and I were in middle school together at Bloomfield Hills Academy. You were new to the school, and I chose you as my target. Not only did I torment you, but I turned the other girls against you, too. And once, I almost got you suspended. I told Mrs. Maples I saw you take the history exam answer key from her desk, when in fact, I'd taken it.

To say I am ashamed does not begin to convey my guilt. As an adult, I've tried to rationalize my childish cruelty — jealousy being the top contender, insecurity the second. But the truth is, I was a bully. I make no excuse. I am truly and desperately sorry.

I am so pleased to discover that you're a huge success now, that you have your own talk show in New Orleans. Perhaps you've long forgotten about Bloomfield Hills Academy and the rotten person I was. But my actions haunt me every day.

I am an attorney by day, a poet by night. Every now and then I'm even lucky enough to have a piece published.

I am not married, and I have no children. Sometimes I think loneliness is my penance.

I'm asking that you send one stone back to me, if and when you accept my apology, lifting both the burden of your anger and the burden of my shame. Please offer the other pebble and an additional stone to someone you have hurt, along with a heartfelt apology. When that stone comes back to you, as I hope mine will come back to me, you will have completed the Circle of Forgiveness. Throw your stone into a lake or a stream, bury it in your garden, or settle it into your flower bed — anything that symbolizes that you are finally free from your shame.

Sincerely yours,
Fiona Knowles

I set the letter down. Even now, two years after it first landed in my mailbox, my breath comes in short bursts. So much collateral damage came from that girl's actions. Because of Fiona Knowles, my family disintegrated. Yes, if it hadn't been for Fiona, my parents may never have divorced.

I rub my temples. I need to be practical, not emotional. Fiona Knowles is all the buzz now, and I'm one of her original recipients. What a story I have, right here in front of me. Exactly the kind of idea that would impress Mr. Peters and the others at WCHI. I could propose we bring Fiona on the air, and the two of us could tell our story of guilt and shame and forgiveness.

Only problem is, I haven't forgiven her. And I wasn't intending to. I bite my lip. Do I need to now? Or, is it possible I can finesse this? After all, WCHI is only asking for the idea. The show would never be filmed. But no, I'd better be thorough, just in case.

I pull a sheet of stationery from my desk, then hear a tap on the door.

"Ten minutes till showtime," Stuart says.

"Be right there."

I grab my lucky fountain pen, a gift from Michael when my show took second place in the Louisiana Broadcast Awards, and scribble my reply.

Dear Fiona,
    Enclosed you'll find your stone, signifying the lifted weight of your shame and the loss of my anger.

Sincerely,
Hannah Farr

Yes, it's halfhearted. But it's the best I can

do. I slip the letter and one of the stones into an envelope and seal it. I'll drop it in the mailbox on my way home. Now I can honestly say I returned the stone.

CHAPTER 3

I change from my dress and heels into a pair of leggings and flats. With my tote stuffed with fresh-baked bread and a bouquet of puffy white magnolia blossoms, I walk toward the Garden District to visit my friend Dorothy Rousseau. Dorothy lived next door to me at the Evangeline, a six-story condominium building on St. Charles Avenue, before she moved to the Garden Home four months ago.

I dash across Jefferson Street, passing gardens brimming with white foxglove, orange hibiscus, and ruby-red canna flowers. But even amid the beauty of springtime, my mind flits from Michael and his complete nonchalance, to the job prospect that now seems mandatory, to Fiona Knowles and the stone of forgiveness I just sent.

It's after three o'clock when I arrive at the old brick mansion. I walk up the metal ramp and greet Martha and Joan sitting on the front porch.

"Hey, ladies," I say, and offer them each a magnolia stem.

Dorothy moved into the Garden Home when macular degeneration finally robbed her of her independence. With her only son nine hundred miles away, I was the one who helped her find her new place, a place where meals were served three times a day and help could be summoned with the touch of a buzzer. At seventy-six, Dorothy weathered the move like a freshman arriving on campus.

I step into the grand foyer and bypass the guest book. I'm a regular here, so everybody knows me now. I make my way to the back of the house and find Dorothy alone in the courtyard. She's slumped in a wicker chair, a pair of old-fashioned headphones covering her ears. Her chin rests on her chest, and her eyes are closed. I tap her shoulder and she starts.

"Hi, Dorothy, it's me."

She removes the headphones, clicks off her CD player, and rises. She's tall and slim, with a sleek white bob that contrasts with her pretty olive skin. Despite her inability to see, she applies makeup every day — to spare those with vision, she jokes. But with or without makeup, Dorothy is one of the most beautiful women I know.

"Hannah, dear!" Her southern drawl is smooth and lingering, like the taste of caramel. She gropes for my arm, and when she finds it, she pulls me into a hug. The familiar pang lodges in my chest. I breathe in the scent of her Chanel perfume and feel her hand rub circles on my back. It's the touch, one I never tire of, of a daughterless mother, to a motherless daughter.

She sniffs the air. "Do I smell magnolias?"

"What a nose," I say, and remove the bouquet from my tote. "I've also brought a loaf of my cinnamon maple bread."

She claps her hands. "My favorite! You spoil me, Hannah Marie."

I smile. Hannah Marie — a phrase a mother would use, I imagine.

She cocks her head. "What brings you here on a Wednesday? Don't you have to get gussied up for your date?"

"Michael's busy tonight."

"Is he? Sit down and tell me your story."

I smile at her signature invitation to settle in for a visit and plop down on the ottoman so that I'm facing her. She reaches out and places a hand on my arm. "Talk to me."

What a gift, having a friend who knows when I need to vent. I tell her about the e-mail from James Peters at WCHI, and Michael's enthusiastic response.

" 'Never make someone a priority when all you are to them is an option.' Maya Angelou said that." She lifts her shoulders. "Of course, you just tell me to mind my own beeswax."

"No, I hear you. I feel like a fool. I've wasted two years thinking he was the one I'd marry. But I'm not the least bit convinced it's even on his radar."

"You know," Dorothy says, "I learned a long time ago to ask for what I want. It's not very romantic, but honestly, men can be such blockheads when you attempt innuendo. Have you told him you were disappointed in his reaction?"

I shake my head. "No. I was trapped, so I fired off an e-mail to Mr. Peters, letting him know I was interested. What choice did I have?"

"You have complete choice, Hannah. Don't ever forget that. Having options is our greatest power."

"Right. I could tell Michael I'm ditching the job of a lifetime because I am holding on to the hope that someday we'll be a family. Yup. That option would give me some power, all right. The power to send Michael running for the hills."

As if she's trying to lighten the mood, Dorothy leans in. "Are you proud of me? I haven't even mentioned my dear son."

I laugh. "Until now."

"All the more reason Michael is playing it cool. He must be terribly distraught about the idea of you moving to the same city as your ex-fiancé."

I shrug. "Well, if he is, I wouldn't know it. He never even mentioned Jack."

"Will you see him?"

"Jack? No. No, of course not." I grab the pouch of stones, suddenly anxious for a change of subject. It's too awkward to talk about my cheating ex-fiancé with his mother.

"I've brought you something else, too." I place the velvet pouch in her hands. "These are called the Forgiveness Stones. Have you heard of them?"

She brightens. "Of course. Fiona Knowles began this phenomenon. She was on NPR last week. Did you know she's written a book? She's going to be here in New Orleans sometime in April."

"Yes, I heard. I actually went to middle school with Fiona Knowles."

"You don't say!"

I tell Dorothy about the stones I received and Fiona's apology.

"My goodness! You were one of her original thirty-five. You never told me."

I gaze across the grounds. Mr. Wiltshire sits in his wheelchair under the shade of a live oak tree, while Lizzy, Dorothy's favorite aide, reads him poetry. "I didn't plan to reply. I mean, does a Forgiveness Stone really make up for two years of bullying?"

Dorothy sits quietly, and I'm guessing she thinks it does.

"Anyway, I have to write a proposal for WCHI. I'm choosing Fiona's story. She's a hot topic right now, and the fact that I was one of the original recipients gives it a personal angle. It's the perfect human-interest story."

Dorothy nods. "Which is why you returned her stone."

I look down at my hands. "Yes. I admit it. I had ulterior motives."

"This proposal," Dorothy says. "Will they actually produce the show?"

"No, I don't think so. It's more of a test of my creativity. Still, I want to impress them. And if I don't get the job, I might be able to use the idea for my show here, if Stuart would let me.

"So, according to Fiona's rules, I'm supposed to continue the circle by adding a second stone to the pouch and sending it on to someone I've hurt." I remove the ivory stone I received from Fiona and leave the second pebble in the velvet pouch. "And that's what I'm doing now, with this stone and my sincere apology to you."

"Me? Whatever for?"

"Yes, you." I tuck the stone into her hand. "I know how much you loved living at the Evangeline. I'm sorry I couldn't have cared for you better, allowed you to stay. Maybe we could have hired an aide for you . . ."

"Don't be ridiculous, dear. That condo was much too small to have another person underfoot. This place suits me fine. I'm happy here. You know that."

"Still, I want you to have this Forgiveness Stone."

She lifts her chin, and her unseeing gaze falls on me like a spotlight. "That's a copout. You're looking for a quick way to continue this circle so you can outline your episode for WCHI. What are you proposing? Fiona Knowles and I come on the set, creating the perfect Circle of Forgiveness?"

I turn to her, stung. "Is that so bad?"

"It is when you've chosen the wrong person." She gropes for my hand and plunks the stone back onto my palm. "I cannot accept this stone. There's someone much more deserving of your apology."

40

Jack's confession crashes down on me, splintering into a million jagged pieces. *I'm sorry, Hannah. I slept with Amy. Just once. It'll never happen again. I swear to you.*

I close my eyes. "Please, Dorothy. I know you think I ruined your son's life when I broke off our engagement. But we can't keep rehashing the past."

"I'm not talking about Jackson," she says, each word deliberate. "I am talking about your mother."

Chapter 4

I fling the stone onto her lap as if its mere touch burned. "No. It's too late for forgiveness. Some things are better left alone."

And if my father were alive, he'd agree. " 'You can't mow a field once it's been plowed,' " he used to say. " 'Unless you want to get stuck in the mud.' "

She takes a deep breath. "I've known you since you first moved here, Hannah, a girl with big dreams and a big heart. I learned all about your wonderful father, how he raised you single-handedly, since you were a teen. But you've shared very little about your mother, except to say she chose her boyfriend over you."

"And I want nothing to do with her." My heart speeds. It angers me that the woman I haven't seen or spoken to in over a decade still wields such power over me. *The weight of anger,* I imagine Fiona would say. "My mother made her choice clear."

"Perhaps. But I've always thought there was more to the story." She looks away and shakes her head. "I'm sorry. I should have shared my thoughts years ago. It has always bothered me. I wonder if I wasn't trying to keep you all to myself." She casts about for my hand and places the stone in my palm again. "You need to make peace with your mother, Hannah. It's time."

"You've got it backwards. I've forgiven Fiona Knowles. This second stone is meant to seek forgiveness, not grant it."

Dorothy raises her shoulders. "Grant forgiveness or seek it. I don't think there's a hard-and-fast rule for these Forgiveness Stones. The object is to restore harmony, yes?"

"Look, I'm sorry, Dorothy, but you don't know the whole story."

"I wonder whether you do, either," she says.

I stare at her. "Why would you say that?"

"Remember the last time your father was here? I was still living in the Evangeline, and y'all came for dinner?"

It was my dad's final visit, though we'd never have guessed it then. He was tan and happy and the center of attention, as always. We sat on Dorothy's balcony, swapping stories and getting tipsy.

43

"Yes, I remember."

"I believe he knew he'd be leaving this world."

Her tone, along with the almost mystical look in her clouded eyes, makes the hairs on my arms rise.

"Your father and I had a private moment. He shared something with me while you and Michael ran out for another bottle of wine. He'd had a bit too much to drink, I'll grant him that. But I believe he wanted to get this off his chest."

My heart pounds. "What did he say?"

"He told me that your mother still sent you letters."

I work to breathe. Letters? From my mother? "No. It was definitely the alcohol talking. She hasn't sent a letter in almost twenty years."

"Can you be sure? I got the distinct impression your mother has been trying to reach you for years."

"He would have told me. No. My mom wants nothing to do with me."

"But you've said it yourself, you were the one who severed contact."

A snapshot of my sixteenth birthday comes into view. My father sat across from me at Mary Mac's Restaurant. I can see his grin, wide and guileless, and picture his elbows on the white tablecloth when he leaned in to watch me unwrap my gift — a diamond-and-sapphire pendant much too extravagant for a teen. "Those stones are from Suzanne's ring," he said. "I had it reset for you."

I stared at the gigantic gems, remembering his big paws rifling through my mom's jewelry box the day he left, his claim that the ring was rightfully his — and mine.

"Thank you, Daddy."

"And there's one more present." He grabbed my hand and winked at me. "You don't have to see her anymore, sweetie."

It took a moment before I realized *her* meant my mother.

"You're old enough now to decide for yourself. The judge made that clear in the custody agreement." His face was utterly gleeful, as if this second "present" were the real prize. I stared at him, my mouth agape.

"Like, no more contact? Ever?"

"It's your call. Your mother agreed to it. Hell, she's probably just as happy as you are to be rid of the obligation."

I pasted a shaky smile on my face. "Um, okay. I guess so. If that's what you . . . she wants."

I turn away from Dorothy, feeling my lips tugging downward. "I was only sixteen. She should have insisted I see her. She should have fought for me! She was my mother." My voice breaks, and I have to wait a moment before I'm able to continue. "My dad called to tell her. It was as if she'd been waiting for me to suggest it. When he stepped out of his office, he simply said, 'It's over, sweetie. You're off the hook.' "

I cover my mouth and try to swallow, glad for once that Dorothy can't see me. "Two years later, she came for my high school graduation, claiming to be so proud of me. I was eighteen then, and so hurt I could barely speak to her. What did she expect after two years of silence? I haven't seen her since."

"Hannah, I know your father meant the world to you, but . . ." She pauses, as if searching for the right words. "Is it possible he kept you from your mother?"

"Of course he did. He wanted to protect me. She hurt me over and over again."

"That's your story — *your* truth. You believe it; I understand that. But that doesn't mean it's *the* truth."

Even though she's blind, I swear Mrs. Rousseau can see right into my soul. I swipe my eyes. "I don't want to talk about this." The ottoman scrapes on the concrete as I stand to leave.

"Sit down," she tells me. Her voice is stern, and I obey her.

"Agatha Christie once said that inside each of us is a trapdoor." She finds my arm and squeezes it, her brittle nails biting my skin. "Beneath that door lie our darkest secrets. We keep that trapdoor firmly latched, desperately trying to fool ourselves, making believe those secrets don't exist. The lucky ones might even come to believe it. But I fear you, my dear, are not one of the lucky ones."

She feels for my hands and takes the stone from me. She places it into the velvet pouch along with the other stone, and pulls tight the drawstring. With her outstretched hands, she searches the air until she finds my tote. Finally settling on it, she tucks the pouch inside.

"You'll never find your future until you reconcile your past. Go. Make your peace with your mama."

I stand barefoot in my kitchen, where copper pots hang from hooks above my granite island. It is nearly three o'clock Saturday, and Michael will be here at six. I like to time my baking so that when Michael arrives, my condo is filled with the homey scent of fresh-baked bread. My

47

blatant attempt at domestic seduction. And tonight I need all the reinforcement I can gather. I've decided to take Dorothy's advice and tell Michael straight up that I don't want to leave New Orleans — i.e., him. My heart speeds at the very thought of it.

With greased hands, I lift the sticky ball from the mixing bowl and turn it onto a floured breadboard. I work the dough with the heels of my palms, pushing it away, watching it fold over itself. In the cupboard beneath the island, less than a foot from where I stand, sits a shiny Bosch bread mixer. It was a Christmas gift from my father three years ago. I didn't have the heart to tell him that I am a sensualist, that I prefer to knead my dough by hand, a ritual that dates back over four thousand years, when the ancient Egyptians first discovered yeast. I wonder whether it was just another tedious task for the Egyptian ladies, or if they found it relaxing, as I do. For me, it is soothing, the monotonous push and pull of the dough, the chemical transformation, barely visible, as the flour, water, and leavening become silky and glutinous.

It was my mother who taught me that the word *lady* evolved from the medieval English phrase *dough kneader.* Like me, my mother had a passion for baking. But where did she learn this piece of trivia? I never saw her read, and her mother didn't even have a high school education.

I push a strand of hair from my forehead with the back of my hand. Ever since Dorothy ordered me to make peace with my mother three days ago, I can't stop thinking of her. Is it possible she really did try to contact me?

There's only one person who might know. Without waiting another minute, I rinse my hands and pick up my phone.

It's one o'clock Pacific Time. I listen as the phone rings, picturing Julia out on her lanai, reading a romance novel, or maybe doing her nails.

"Hannah Banana! How are you?"

The joy in her voice makes me feel guilty. For the first month after my dad died, I called Julia daily. But quickly the calls dwindled to once a week, then once a month. It's been since Christmas that I last spoke to her.

I gloss over details about Michael and my job. "Everything's great," I say. "How about you?"

"The salon is sending me to a class in Vegas. It's all about hairpieces and extensions these days. You might want to try one.

They're really convenient."

"I just might," I say, before getting to the point. "Julia, there's something I need to ask you."

"The condo. I know. I need to get it on the market."

"No. I want you to have it, I told you that. I'll call Ms. Seibold this week and see what's taking so long with the title transfer."

I hear her sigh. "You're a doll, Hannah."

My dad began dating Julia the year I left for college. He retired early and decided, since I was going to USC, he may as well move to L.A., too. He met Julia at the gym. She was in her mid-thirties then, a decade younger than my father. I liked her instantly, a kindhearted beauty with a penchant for red lipstick and Elvis memorabilia. She once confided that she'd wanted children, but she chose my father instead, who was, in her words, a big kid himself. It makes me sad that, seventeen years later, her dream of children has vanished, along with her "big kid." Giving her my dad's condo seems a sorry substitute for all she sacrificed.

"Julia, my friend told me something I can't seem to shake."

"What is it?"

"She . . ." I tug on a lock of my hair. "She thinks my mom tried to contact me, that

50

she sent me a letter — or letters. I'm not sure when." I pause, worried that what I say might sound like an accusation. "She thinks my dad knew about it."

"I don't know. I've already taken a dozen garbage bags to Goodwill. The man saved everything." She laughs softly, and my heart breaks for her. I should have been the one cleaning out his closets. Instead, just like my dad, I let her do the tough stuff.

"You never found a letter, or letters, or anything at all from my mother?"

"I know she had our address here in L.A. From time to time she'd send him tax documents or whatnot. But I'm sorry, Hannah. Nothing for you."

I nod, unable to speak. I didn't realize until now how badly I was hoping for a different answer.

"Your dad loved you, Hannah. For all of his flaws, he truly loved you."

I know my father loved me. So why isn't that enough?

I take extra care getting ready that night. After soaking in my favorite Jo Malone bath oil, I stand in front of the mirror in a lacy, peach-colored bra and matching panties, pulling the last section of my hair through a flatiron. Though my shoulder-length locks

51

have a natural wave, Michael prefers my hair smooth. I curl my lashes and apply mascara, then toss my makeup into my bag. Careful not to wrinkle it, I slip into a short, copper-colored sheath I chose just for Michael. At the last minute, I dig out my sixteenth-birthday present, the diamond-and-sapphire pendant. The very jewels that had been plucked from my mother's engagement ring blink up at me, as if they, too, can't get used to their remounted contemporary configuration. All these years, I've kept the necklace in the box, never having had the desire or the heart to wear it. A wave of sadness comes over me as I fasten the platinum chain behind my neck. Bless my father's soul. He was clueless. He had no idea his gift symbolized destruction and loss rather than its intended welcome into woman-hood.

At 6:37, Michael steps into my apartment. It's been a week since I've seen him, and he's in need of a haircut. But unlike my hair when it's shaggy, his sandy-blond locks fall in perfectly imperfect waves, lending him a youthful, beach-boy look. I like to tease Michael that he looks more like a Ralph Lauren model than a mayor. His cornflower-blue eyes and fair complexion make him the picture of success, one you might find skimming across Cape Cod at the helm of a Hinckley.

"Hey, beautiful," he says.

Without bothering to take off his coat, he lifts me into his arms, hiking my dress as he carries me to my bedroom. Wrinkles be damned.

We lie next to each other, staring up at the ceiling. "Jesus," he says, breaking the silence. "I needed that."

I roll onto my side and run a finger down his square jawline. "I missed you."

"I missed you, too." He turns his head and pulls the tip of my finger into his mouth. "You're incredible, you know that?"

I lie still in the crook of his arm, waiting until he catches his breath and we begin round two. I love these interim moments tucked in Michael's embrace, where the world is far away and our slow mingled breathing is the only sound I hear.

"Can I get you a drink?" I whisper.

When he doesn't answer, I raise my head. His eyes are closed and his mouth is slack. Softly, he begins to wheeze.

I glance at the clock. It's 6:55, eighteen minutes from door to snore.

He wakes with a start, his eyes wide and his

hair mussed. "What time is it?" he asks, squinting at his watch.

"Seven forty," I say, running a hand over his smooth chest. "You were sleepy."

He bolts from the bed, rummaging for his phone. "Jesus, I told Abby we'd pick her up at eight. We better move."

"Abby's joining us?" I ask, hoping I don't betray my disappointment.

"Yup." He grabs his shirt off the floor. "She broke a date to be with us."

I climb from the bed. I know I'm being selfish, but I want to talk about Chicago tonight. And this time I won't be coy.

I fasten my bra, reminding myself that Michael is a single father — and a very good one. He's spread too thin with his demanding job as mayor. I shouldn't force him to choose between time with me and time with his daughter. He's trying to satisfy us both.

"I've got an idea," I say, watching as he types a message to Abby. "Go out with Abby tonight, just the two of you. Maybe I can see you tomorrow."

He looks stricken. "No. Please. I want you to come."

"But Abby," I say. "I bet she'd like some one-on-one time with you. And there's that job in Chicago I mentioned. I really need some time to talk to you alone. We could do that tomorrow."

"I want to spend this evening with the two women in my life." He comes over to me and grazes his lips on my neck. "I love you, Hannah. And the more Abby's around you, the more she'll love you, too. She needs to see us as a threesome, a family. Don't you agree?"

I soften. He's thinking of our future, exactly what I'd hoped for.

We head east on St. Charles, arriving at his home in Carrollton ten minutes late. Michael trots to the door to retrieve Abby, and I sit in his SUV, staring up at the massive, cream-colored stucco home where a family of three once lived.

The same day I met him, at a silent auction for Into the Light, I discovered Michael had a daughter. I was drawn to the fact that he was a single father, like my own dad. As we began dating, I never once thought of Abby as anything but a positive. I loved kids. She'd be a bonus. I swear those were my thoughts . . . *before* I met her.

The iron gate swings open and Abby and Michael step from the house. She's nearly as tall as her father, and her long blond hair is pulled back in a clip tonight, showcasing her beautiful green eyes. She climbs into the backseat.

"Hey, Abby!" I say. "You look so pretty."

"Hey," she says, and digs into her bright pink Kate Spade bag to retrieve her phone.

Michael drives toward Tchoupitoulas Street, and I try to engage Abby in conversation. But as usual, she offers only one-word replies, never meeting my eyes. When she does have something to share, she looks directly at her father, prefacing each statement with "Dad," as if her nonverbal cues weren't enough to let me know I was null and void. *Dad, I got my SAT scores. Dad, I saw this movie that you'd love.*

We arrive at Broussard's Restaurant in the French Quarter — Abby's choice — where a willowy brunette escorts us to our table. Gaslights flicker as we pass through the courtyard into the candlelit dining room. I notice a well-dressed elderly couple staring at me as I pass their table, and I smile at them.

"I'm a huge fan, Hannah," the woman says, gripping my arm. "Every morning you make me smile."

"Oh, thank you," I say, patting her hand. "I can't tell you how much I appreciate that."

We three settle in at our table, and Abby

turns to Michael, seated beside her. "That must suck," she says to him. "You're out saving the city, and she's the one who gets the attention. People are so stupid."

I feel like I'm back at Bloomfield Hills Academy, being bullied by Fiona Knowles. I wait for Michael to defend me, but he just chuckles. "That's the price I pay for dating New Orleans' sweetheart."

He squeezes my knee under the table. *Shake it off,* I tell myself. *She's just a kid. No different than you once were.*

A thought invades my consciousness. I'm in Harbour Cove. Bob pulls into the Tastee Freeze, my mother in the passenger side. I'm slumped in the backseat, gnawing on my thumbnail. He looks over his shoulder at me, that dumb smile on his face. "How about a hot fudge sundae, Sister? Or maybe a banana split?" I cross my arms over my belly, hoping to muffle the growling of my stomach. "I'm not hungry."

I close my eyes and try to shake the memory. Dorothy and her damn stones!

I turn my attention to the menu, scanning the entrées for something that doesn't cost more than the dress I'm wearing. Being a southern gentleman, Michael always insists on paying. Being a descendant of

Pennsylvania coal miners, I'm mindful of money.

A few minutes later, the waiter returns with the bottle of wine Michael ordered, and pours Abby a glass of sparkling water.

"Would you care to start with an appetizer?" he asks.

"Uh, let's see . . ." Michael says, perusing the menu.

Abby takes control. "We'll have the Hudson Valley foie gras, the black Angus carpaccio, and the Georges Bank sea scallops. Bring a terrine of chanterelle mushrooms, *aussi, s'il vous plaît.*" She looks up at her father. "You're going to love their mushrooms, Dad."

The waiter disappears and I set my menu aside. "So, Abby, now that you've taken your SATs, have you thought more about where you want to go to college?"

She reaches for her cell phone and checks for messages. "Not really."

Michael smiles. "She's narrowed it down to Auburn, Tulane, and USC."

Finally, common ground! I turn to Abby. "USC? That's where I went! I think you'd love California, Abby. Listen, if you have any questions, just let me know. I'd be happy to write you a letter of recommendation, or anything at all you need."

Michael raises his eyebrows. "You might want to take advantage of that offer, Abs. Hannah's one of their star alums."

"Oh, Michael, that's ridiculous." It is ridiculous, but I'm flattered that Michael would say such a thing.

Abby shakes her head, her eyes still on her phone. "I've crossed USC off my list. I need somewhere more challenging."

"Oh," I say. "Of course." I grab the menu and bury my face in it, wishing I were anywhere but here.

Michael and I had been dating eight months before he introduced me to Abby. I couldn't wait to meet her. She'd just turned sixteen, and I was sure we'd be fast friends. We were both runners. Abby was on the staff at her school newspaper. We'd both grown up without our mothers.

Our first meeting was casual — coffee and beignets at Café du Monde. Michael and I laughed at the powdered sugar mess on our plates and ate a full basket of the delicious treats. But Abby decided Americans were gluttonous and leaned back and sipped her black coffee, tapping on her iPhone the entire date.

"Give her time," Michael said. "She's not used to sharing me."

I look up, aware of a stillness that's come

over the restaurant. Michael and Abby stare across the dining room, and my eyes follow. Beside a corner table about twenty feet away, a man descends to one knee. A brunette gazes down at him, her hand covering her mouth. He extends a small box, and I can see his hands shake. "Please marry me, Katherine Bennett."

His voice is so thick with emotion that I feel my nose burn. *Don't be a sap,* I tell myself.

The woman lets out a whoop and leaps into his arms. The restaurant erupts in applause.

I clap and laugh and brush back tears. Across the table, I feel Abby staring at me. I turn and our eyes lock. Her lips curl upward, but it's not a smile or a grin she's wearing. It's a smirk. No doubt about it, this seventeen-year-old is mocking me. I look away, shaken by her inside knowledge. She thinks I'm a fool to believe in love . . . and, quite possibly, her father.

"There's something we need to discuss, Michael."

Michael has mixed us each a Sazerac cocktail, and we sit on opposite sides of my white sofa. The flickering fireplace casts an amber glow over the room, and I wonder if the peaceful ambiance feels as false to Michael as it does to me.

He swirls his glass and shakes his head. "She's just a girl, Hannah. Put yourself in her shoes. It's hard for her to share her father with another woman. Please try to understand that."

I scowl. Wasn't I the one who suggested he see Abby alone tonight? I'd bring it to his attention, but I don't want to get sidetracked.

"This isn't about Abby," I say. "It's about us. I e-mailed my proposal to WCHI. I told James Peters I was interested in the position."

I watch his face, hoping to see a quiver of dread, a dash of disappointment. Instead, he comes to life. "Hey, that's great." He drapes his arm across the back of the sofa and squeezes my shoulder. "You have my complete support on this."

My stomach knots, and I fiddle with my necklace. "You see, that's just the thing. I don't want your support. I'd be moving nine hundred miles away, Michael. I want you to . . ."

I summon Dorothy's words, *I learned a long time ago to ask for what I want.*

I turn to him. "I want you to ask me to stay."

CHAPTER 5

Michael sets his glass on the coffee table and moves to my end of the sofa. "Stay," he says. He grips my forearms and his blue eyes bore into mine. "Please. Don't leave."

He takes me into his arms and kisses me, long and deep and promising. When he pulls away, he tucks a lock of hair behind my ear. "Sweetheart, I just thought you owed it to yourself to interview, regardless. It'd give you a bargaining chip when you're negotiating your next contract with WNO."

I nod. Of course, he's right. Especially now that Claudia Campbell is on the scene.

He cups my face in his hands. "I love you so much, Hannah."

I smile. "I love you, too."

"And leaving New Orleans doesn't mean you'd leave me." He leans back. "You know, Abby's old enough now to stay alone. Hell, she's busy most weekends, anyway. I could come see you once, maybe even twice a month."

"You could?" It's hard to imagine an entire weekend alone with Michael, where we'd fall asleep in each other's arms and wake the next morning with the whole day splayed before us . . . and then another day.

Michael's right. If I moved to Chicago, we might actually have more time together.

"And I could come back here to visit on the opposite weekends," I say, my enthusiasm growing.

"Exactly. Let's say you take the job for a year. You'll gain some national exposure. You'd be extremely competitive for a job in DC."

"DC?" I shake my head. "But don't you see? I want us to be together someday."

He grins. "I'll let you in on a little secret. I've been thinking about a run for the Senate. It's a little premature to talk about it, since Senator Hanses hasn't announced whether she's seeking reelection . . ."

I smile. Michael *is* thinking of the future. In a couple of years, he may be in Washington. And he's making sure my path leads me there, too.

Sunday night, when the weekend is over and I'm in my bed staring at the ceiling, I wonder why it is that I still feel empty. For once, I've asked Michael for what I wanted. And he gave me the right answer. So why do I feel lonelier than ever?

The answer comes to me at 1:57 a.m. I've asked the wrong question. I know that Michael wants me with him. And that's good. But the real question is: Does he ever intend to make me his wife?

Jade and I are power-walking in Audubon Park Monday afternoon. "So Marcus says to me, 'Please, baby, just one more chance. It'll never happen again, I swear.' "

I unclench my jaw and try to keep my tone neutral. "I thought he was seeing someone."

"Not anymore. He claims she was a sorry substitute for me."

"What'd you say?"

"I said, 'Oh, hell, no. I'm pretty sure I'm allowed to stop after one broken jaw.' "

I laugh and slap her a high five. "Good for you! You stay strong."

She slows her stride. "So why do I feel so damn guilty? Marcus was — is — a great father. Devon adores him."

"Look, nothing's preventing him from having a relationship with his son. He should be grateful you never told Devon, or pressed charges. If you had, he'd be out of Devon's life and off the force."

"I know. But Devon doesn't understand. He thinks I'm being mean to his daddy. It's like I'm being tag-teamed with Devon's pissy attitude and Marcus's begging. He keeps reminding me of the fifteen good years we had. That I'd been riding his ass for not getting the brakes on the car fixed. He'd been in the middle of a tough case, working nights and weekends. He was sleep-deprived and . . ."

I tune her out. I've heard Marcus's tale of woe at least thirty times, and I can't bear to hear it again. With the full support of her parents, she left Marcus last October, the very day he backhanded her, and filed for divorce the following week. Thank God she hasn't wavered. So far.

"I liked him, too, I really did. But what he did is inexcusable. You are not to blame, Jade. No man is allowed to hit a woman. Ever. End of story."

"I know. I know you're right. I just . . . please don't hate me for this, Hannabelle, but I miss him sometimes."

"If only we could copy and paste the good parts." I link arms with her. "I confess, I miss the good times with Jack sometimes, too. But I would never be able to trust him again. It's the same with you and Marcus."

She turns to me. "How was your date with

Michael? Did you tell him to get his ass in gear and buy you a diamond?"

I give her the rundown of our conversation Saturday night. "So, if I were to move to Chicago, we'd actually spend more alone time together, not less."

She looks skeptical. "Really? He'd leave his precious city every month? You wouldn't have to deal with Crabby?"

I can't help but smile at Jade's nickname for Abby. "That's what he says. Of course, now I really want this job."

"No! You can't leave," she says. "I won't let you."

The very reaction I'd hoped to hear from Michael.

"Don't worry. I'm sure they've got a huge pool of more qualified candidates. But I did send a pretty sweet proposal, if I do say so myself." I tell her about the Forgiveness Stones craze and the proposal to host Fiona and my estranged mother.

"Wait — your mother? You told me you lost her."

I close my eyes and cringe. Did I really tell her that? "Not literally. Figuratively. We had a huge falling-out years ago."

"I never knew that."

"I'm sorry. I don't like to talk about it. It's complicated."

66

"Well, I'm impressed, Hannabelle. You've made peace, and you're actually hosting your mother on television."

"Oh, hell no!"

"I should have known," she says, and shakes her head. "Boundaries."

"That's right," I say, ignoring the sarcasm in her voice. "It's just a proposal. I made it up. My mother and I haven't actually made peace."

"Gotcha. So tell me more about these Forgiveness Stones. They're kind of like a *get-out-of-jail-free* card?" Jade asks. "You confess some deep shameful secret, give the person a rock, and call it good?"

"I know. Pretty hokey, right?"

She shrugs. "I don't know. It's actually pretty brilliant. I can see why the idea has legs. Who doesn't need to be forgiven?"

"Right, Jade. Your biggest sin is probably the time you accidentally stole the sample cream at the Clinique counter."

I turn to her, smiling. But her face is clouded. "Hey, I'm kidding. I'm just saying, you're about the most straightforward, honest person I know."

She bends over and grabs her knees. "Hannabelle, you have no idea."

I move over to the grass, letting a runner pass by. "What is it?"

"For over twenty-five years I've had this huge lie trailing me like a block of stinky cheese. Ever since my dad's diagnosis it's been eating at me."

She straightens and stares off into the distance, as if she's trying to escape from the memory. What is it with these stones? Instead of granting peace, they're causing grief.

"It was my sixteenth birthday. My parents threw me a party. I think Daddy was more excited than any of us. He wanted it to be perfect. He decided to spiff up the basement rec room before the party. Paint, new furniture, the works. When I told him I wanted white carpet, he didn't bat an eye." She looks over at me and smiles. "Can you imagine? White carpet in a basement?

"About fifteen girls spent the night. Oh, and were we boy-crazy! So when a half dozen guys came knocking at the downstairs patio door bearing cherry vodka and some god-awful red wine, of course we let them in.

"I was terrified. I'd be grounded for life if my parents happened to come back downstairs, and skinned alive if they ever found out we were drinking. But they'd already checked in for the night. They were upstairs watching *48 Hours*. They trusted me.

"By midnight, my friend Erica Williams was as buzzed as a bee. She got sick. All over. So long, white carpet."

"Oh no," I say. "What did you do?"

"I tried my best to scrub it out, but the stain wouldn't budge. The next morning, Daddy came downstairs and saw it. I told him the truth: Erica had gotten sick. 'Was she drinking?' he asked. I looked him straight in the eyes. 'No, Daddy.' "

Her voice quakes, and I sling an arm around her shoulder. "Jade, that's nothing. Forget about it. You were just a kid."

"For years, he's come back to that tale, Hannah. Even on my thirtieth birthday he asked, 'Jade, was Erica drinking the night of your sixteenth birthday party?' And as always, I answered, 'No, Daddy.' "

"Maybe it's time to tell him, then. Give him a Forgiveness Stone. Because I'm pretty sure the lie is hurting you far more than the truth will hurt him."

She shakes her head. "It's too late. The cancer's spread to his bones now. The truth would kill him."

Jade and I are finishing our last lap when Dorothy calls, sounding more chipper than

69

she has in months. "Could you drop by this afternoon, dear?"

It's unusual for Dorothy to request a visit. More often than not she tells me it's silly for me to come by so often.

"I'm happy to," I say. "Everything okay?"

"Splendid. And bring a half dozen of those little pouches, could you, please? I think they sell them at Michaels."

Oh, great. The Forgiveness Stones again. "Dorothy, you didn't accept my stone. You're off the hook. You don't have to continue that silly Circle of Forgiveness."

"A half dozen," she insists, "for starters."

I should have known. Dorothy loves to partake in chain letters and e-mail pass-alongs. She's certainly not going to miss the chance to join a popular new fad like the Forgiveness Stones. She's been tagged and, regardless of whether or not she felt justified in receiving them, she will continue the Circle of Forgiveness, and then some.

"Okay, but the instructions say to send one letter of apology, not a half dozen."

"You think I've only hurt one person in these seventy-six years? Don't you know, deep inside, we're all just bundles of shame? I suppose that's the beauty of these silly stones. They give one permission — or perhaps an obligation — to be vulnerable."

70

■ ■ ■ ■

When I arrive late that afternoon, Dorothy's face has transformed. Her frown lines have softened, and she looks positively serene. She sits in the courtyard, under the umbrella table, with Fiona Knowles's audiobook in front of her. I scowl. The girl who treated me so badly is now an icon for forgiveness, and no doubt cashing in, big-time.

"People carry secrets for two reasons," Dorothy tells me. "To protect themselves or to protect others. That's what Ms. Knowles says."

"What a revelation. The woman is brilliant."

"She is," Dorothy says, obviously not catching my sarcasm — or perhaps choosing not to. "Did you bring my pouches, dear?"

"Uh-huh. White tulle," I say, placing them in her hand. "With tiny lime-green polka dots."

She fingers the fabric, and draws open the strings. "Beautiful. Now, there's a cup of stones on my nightstand. Fetch it for me, would you, please?"

I return with a plastic cup filled with pebbles. Dorothy pours them onto the table.

71

"Marilyn gathered these from the courtyard yesterday." With care, she separates the stones into groups of two. "This first set will be for Mari," she says. "Though she doesn't know it yet."

"Marilyn?" I'm surprised when she cites her closest and lifelong friend. But on reflection, it makes perfect sense. "Well, I guess when you've known a person your entire life, you're bound to have hurt her feelings at one time or another, right?"

"Yes," she says. "And it was a doozy." She closes her eyes and shakes her head, as if the very memory sends a shiver through her.

"I've always imagined that life is a cavernous room filled with candles," Dorothy says. "When we're born, half the candles are lit. With each good deed we do, another flickers to life, creating a bit more light."

"Nice," I say.

"But along the way, some flames are extinguished by selfishness and cruelty. So you see, we light some candles, we blow some out. In the end, we can only hope that we've created more light in this world than darkness."

I pause a moment, imagining my own room of candles. I wonder, have I created more light than darkness? "That's a beautiful analogy, Dorothy. And you, my friend, cast a very strong light."

"Oh, but I've extinguished my fair share along the way." She searches until her hand finds another set of stones. "These will go to Steven."

"How charitable," I say. "I thought you despised him."

I met Stephen Rousseau twice, when I was dating Jackson. He seemed like a decent man. But Dorothy rarely speaks of her ex-husband, except to say that she has no use for the lout who divorced her nine months after she'd had a mastectomy. Though three decades have passed, I suspect neither of Dorothy's scars has fully healed.

"I'm talking about Steven Willis, my former student. He was a bright boy, but his family life was atrocious. I let him slip through the cracks, Hannah, and I've never forgiven myself. I think his brothers still live in town. I'm going to track him down."

Such bravery. Or is it? Maybe an apology will soothe Dorothy's guilty conscience, but might it be an unwelcome reminder to Steven of a childhood he'd rather forget?

She moves her hand to the next set. "These are for Jackson," she tells me. "I never apologized for meddling."

This stops me cold.

"Had it not been for me, y'all would be

married now. I'm the one who advised him to fess up to you, Hannah. The shame he carried was too big a burden. A mother knows these things. His secret would have destroyed your relationship, and later your marriage. I was certain you'd forgive him if he confessed. I was wrong."

"I forgave him," I say, and squeeze her hand. "But you bring up a good point. Perhaps Jack would have been better off never telling me the truth. Some secrets are better left unshared."

She lifts her chin. "Like the secret you're carrying with your mother?"

I stiffen. "I never said anything about a secret."

"You didn't have to. A mother does not desert her child, Hannah. Have you sent her your stone yet?"

A mixture of sadness and defeat comes over me. "There were no letters. I checked with Julia."

She gives a little harrumph. "And that gives you a pass, the fact that your father may not have told his girlfriend?"

"I need time to think about this, Dorothy."

" 'Until you pour light onto whatever it is that cloaks you in darkness, you'll forever be lost.' That's what Fiona Knowles says."

CHAPTER 6

I stop by Guy's on Magazine Street and get takeout. It's dusk now, and I stand at my kitchen counter, staring blankly at the glow of my open laptop as I chow down on a fried oyster po'boy and a bag of Zapp's potato chips.

Until you pour light onto whatever it is that cloaks you in darkness, you'll forever be lost. Dorothy's words — or Fiona's — rattle me. What would it feel like to have a clear conscience, to feel whole and worthy and clean?

Damn it! I don't need this right now. As if my job and my relationship aren't enough to keep Guy's in business.

I move to the other side of the kitchen and throw open the freezer door. I peer into the frosty abyss until I spot it: a brand-new quart of sea-salt caramel ice cream. I reach for it, but then, at the last minute, I stop myself. I slam shut the freezer door, wishing I had a padlock. In the television business, calories are career killers. Though Stuart has stopped short of placing a scale in my dressing room, he has made it clear that horizontal stripes are no longer an option.

Get a grip!

I toss my wrappers into the trash basket and walk to the living room. From beyond the French doors, the day fades into evening. Families are eating dinner, mothers are bathing their children.

Without permission, my mind veers to Jack. Do I believe what I said to Dorothy today? Had Jack not confessed, I'd be oblivious to his affair and we would have been married three years now. He'd be consulting for restaurants here in New Orleans rather than in Chicago. Child number one would be a year old now, and we'd be working on our second.

Why did he have to screw it all up, literally? Amy was his goddamn intern! Twenty years old, for God's sake!

I push back sentimentality. Would I have wanted him to keep his secret from me? It's impossible to know. Besides, it was all for the best. I know that now. I wouldn't have met Michael. And Michael is a far better match for me than Jack ever was. Sure, Jack was sweet. And yes, he made me laugh. But

Michael is my rock. He's warm and wise, and what he lacks in the way of time, he makes up for in loyalty.

From across the room I spy my tote, splayed on a chair where I'd dropped it earlier. I cross the room and remove the little pouch. The stones tumble onto my palm. I move to my desk, rubbing them in my palm like worry beads, and pull out a sheet of stationery.

My heart speeds when I write the first word.

Mom,

I take a deep breath and continue.

Perhaps it's time we made peace.

My hand shakes so badly I can barely write. I toss the pen aside and rise from my chair. I can't do this.

The open French doors beckon me. I step onto my balcony, six floors above street level, and lean against the iron railing, admiring the haze of purples and oranges in the western sky. Below, the St. Charles Streetcar shuffles into view, stopping in the grassy strip that slices through the wide avenue.

Why is Dorothy so insistent? I shared my background with her the very day we met, in the lobby of the Evangeline. We'd been chatting for ten minutes when she suggested we continue our conversation upstairs. "I'm in apartment six-seventeen. Join me for a cocktail, won't you? I'll make us a batch of Ramos Fizzes — you do drink, don't you?"

I liked Dorothy from the start. Her personality was two parts honey, one part bourbon — and she had a way of looking directly into my eyes that made me feel like we'd known each other all our lives.

We sat in mismatched armchairs, sipping the delicious old New Orleans cocktail made with gin and cream and citrus juices. Between sips, she told me that she'd been divorced for thirty-four years, twenty years longer than her marriage. "Apparently Stephen was a breast man, and back then mastectomies weren't performed quite so delicately. It was a low point, but I rallied. The expectation for a southern gal with a three-year-old son was to hit the social scene until I found a new husband and a father for Jackson. Mother was appalled that I chose the single life, teaching English at Walter Cohen High School. Next thing I knew, twenty beautiful years had disappeared like raindrops on a summer sidewalk."

She spoke wistfully of growing up in New Orleans, the daughter of a popular obstetrician.

"Daddy was a dear man," she said. "But the wife of an obstetrician wasn't prestigious enough for Mother. She was raised in one of the grand mansions on Audubon Drive. Her expectations always exceeded Daddy's ambition."

The Ramos Fizz must have gone to my head, because before I knew it, I was telling her about my own family, something I rarely did.

I was eleven years old when my father was traded from the Atlanta Braves to the Detroit Tigers. In the span of six weeks, my parents bought a house in in the wealthy suburb of Bloomfield Hills and enrolled me in some la-di-da private girls' school. But I knew on the very first day I'd never fit in with the close-knit circle of sixth-graders. The descendants of auto tycoons like Henry Ford and Charles Fisher had no interest in a skinny newcomer whose father was an unsophisticated baseball player from Schuylkill County, Pennsylvania. At least that's what the ring-leader, Fiona Knowles, decided. And the other fifteen girls followed Fiona like lemmings off a cliff.

My mother, the pretty daughter of a coal miner and only thirty-one at the time, was my only friend. She was as much an outcast in our affluent neighborhood as I was. I could tell by the way she smoked her cigarettes down to a nub, staring out the window with a faraway look in her eyes. But what choice did we have? My dad loved the game of baseball. And my mother, who had no education or skills of her own, loved my dad — or so I thought.

My world upended on a chilly night in November, thirteen months after we'd arrived. I was setting the table, watching the snow fall from the window of our breakfast nook, complaining to my mother about the endless parade of gray days, the approaching winter. We both missed our Georgia home and loved to reminisce about the blue skies and warm breezes. But for the first time since we'd arrived, she didn't take my side.

"It's a trade-off," she said tersely. "Sure, the weather's nice down South, but that only accounts for so much. You need to change your attitude."

I was stung to think I'd lost my ally, but I never had a chance to rebut, because at that moment my dad stepped through the back door, grinning. At forty-one years old, he was one of the oldest players in Major League Baseball. His first season in Detroit had been a disappointment, souring his temper. But that night he tossed his jacket on a hook and grabbed my mother into a hug.

"We're going home!" he announced. "You're looking at the Panthers' new head coach!"

I had no idea who the Panthers were, but I knew where home was. Atlanta! Even though we'd only lived in Georgia for two years, we claimed it as our own. Our lives were happy then. We had neighborhood parties and barbecues and took weekend trips to Tybee Island.

My mother shooed him away. "You smell like a distillery." But he didn't seem to care. And neither did I. I let out a whoop, and he swept me into his arms. I breathed deeply, his familiar scent of Jack Daniel's whiskey and Camel cigarettes filling my nostrils. It felt foreign and embarrassingly wonderful to be held by this big, handsome man. I looked over at my mom, expecting to see her dancing with joy. But her head was turned to the window. She stared out at the gloomy night with her hands braced on the edge of the sink.

"Mom," I said, wriggling from my dad's clutches. "We're leaving. Why aren't you happy?"

She turned around then, her pretty face marred with red splotches. "Go up to your room, Hannah. Me and your dad need to talk."

Her voice was thick, the way mine sounded when I felt like crying. I scowled. What was her problem? This was our ticket out of Michigan. We'd be going back to Georgia, to warm weather and sunny skies and girls who liked me.

I let out a huff and skulked from the kitchen. But instead of climbing the stairs to my bedroom, I crouched behind the sofa and listened to my parents from the darkness of the living room.

"A college coaching job?" I heard my mother ask. "What's this about, John?"

"You haven't been happy here, Suzanne. You've made no bones about it. And frankly, I'm too old for this game. This college job is a tactic. In a few years I'll be able to compete for Major League assignments. And let's be honest, we've got more money than we'd ever imagined, even if I never worked another day in my life."

"Is it the drinking again?"

His voice grew loud. "No! Damn it, I thought you'd be happy."

"Why do I suspect there's more to this story?

"Suspect all you want. I've been offered this position, and I'm taking it. I've already told them so."

"Without asking me? How could you?"

I shook my head. Why was my mother upset? She hated it here — didn't she? And my dad was doing this for her, for us. She should be thrilled.

"Why can I never please you? What is it you want, Suzanne?"

My mom's tears practically seeped through the walls. I wanted to run to her and comfort her. But I covered my mouth and waited.

"I . . . I can't leave."

I had to strain to hear my dad, his voice soft and flat. "Je-sus Christ. It's that serious?"

And then I heard it, a sound as haunting as an animal's wail. My dad's desperate sobs, his choked voice, begging my mother to come with him. He needed her. He loved her.

At once, panic and terror and embarrassment filled me. I'd never heard my dad cry. He was strong and solid. My life's foundation was crumbling. From my hiding place, I watched my mom climb the staircase and then heard the bedroom door close.

In the kitchen, a chair scraped against the floor. I imagined my dad slipping into it, burying his face in his hands. Then it began again, the muffled howl of a man who'd just lost his love.

A week later the mystery was solved. Once again, my father had been traded, this time by his wife. His replacement was a man named Bob, a wood-shop teacher by day, carpenter during the off-season. My guidance counselor had given my mother his name. My dad had hired him the previous summer to remodel our kitchen.

I ended up getting what I'd hoped for, though it would be another nine months before I finally left Michigan and joined my father in Atlanta. My mother stayed behind with the man she loved more than my father. And more than me.

And now I'm supposed to make nice? I sigh. Dorothy doesn't know the half of it. Only four people know the rest of the story, and one of them is dead.

I actually tried to tell Michael my saga, but he spared me. It was our third date, and we'd had a wonderful dinner at Arnaud's. Afterward, we sat on my sofa drinking Pimm's Cups. He'd just confided in me the details of his wife's tragic accident, and we were both in tears. Though I'd never before shared my story, it felt safe and right that night, snug in the crook of his arm. I started at the beginning of my story, but of course I ended where I always did, just shy of telling him about the late-night encounter with Bob.

"So I moved to Atlanta with my dad. For the first two years, I saw my mother about once a month, always in a neutral location — usually Chicago. My dad wouldn't let me visit her home — not that I wanted to. He was protective of me, which I have to admit was a heady feeling. I'd never had much of a relationship with my dad when my mother was around. She and I were the twosome, and my dad was somewhere out in left field, literally and figuratively. He was always on the road, or at practice, or, more often than not, at the bar."

Michael raised his eyebrows.

"Yes," I said. "He was a party boy. Loved his whiskey." I looked down then, ashamed that I was still covering for the man who would be more aptly described as a hard-core alcoholic.

My voice broke, and I had to wait a moment before I was able to continue.

"So there you have it. I haven't seen or heard from her since my high school graduation. And I'm fine, I'm really fine. I have no idea what these tears are about."

"That's heavy stuff." Michael slung an

arm around my shoulder and pulled me close to him. "Shake it off, sweetheart. Your mom was really messed up. If only she knew what a gem she missed out on."

He kissed the top of my head then, and something about that protective, almost paternal gesture pried a corner of my heart loose. But it was Jackson's parting shot, spoken nearly a year earlier yet still reverberating in my head, that peeled my heart open: *No wonder it's so easy to let me go, Hannah. Fact is, you never really let me in.* For the first time ever, someone was threatening to break through the emotional barricade I'd worked so hard to build. I spat out my words before I had time to rethink them.

"He . . . her boyfriend . . . Bob . . . he touched me. My mother didn't believe me. That's when I left Michigan. But she stayed behind with . . ."

The horror in Michael's face stopped me from elaborating. "I'm going to give you a piece of advice, Hannah. There are some secrets you'll want to keep hidden. As public figures, our image is everything."

I looked at him, confused. "My image?"

"I'm just saying, you present yourself as the wholesome girl-next-door. You know, someone with a nice, normal background.

That's your brand. Don't give anyone reason to think that brand is inauthentic."

Hannah,
We're delighted to hear that you're interested in the position. The entire team was impressed by your proposal. A show with Fiona Knowles is exactly the type of programming we're aiming for, and your personal story gives it a unique angle.

My assistant, Brenda Stark, will be contacting you. She's scheduling interviews the week of April 7. Look forward to seeing you then.

James

"Shit," I say, staring at my computer screen. "I'm going to be sick."

Jade taps her finger against a brush of loose powder, sending ivory flecks cascading onto my plastic smock. "What is it?"

I open a Word document on my computer. "Check this out, Jade. Remember that proposal I had to write for WCHI? It sounds like they love it. But I told you, I made most of it up. I didn't tell them it took me two years to send my stone back to Fiona. And my mother . . . in my proposal I say that my mother would appear on the show. That's a lie. I never sent her a stone. I made that part up, too."

Jade touches my shoulder. "Hey, calm down. It's just a proposal, right? They're not going to film it."

I lift my hands. "I don't know for sure. But either way, it feels wrong. What if they ask me about it? I'm a horrible liar."

"Send her the stone, then."

"My mom? No. No, I can't just send her a stone out of the blue. I haven't seen her in years."

Jade scowls at me in the mirror. "Sure you can. If you wanted." She grabs a can of hair spray and shakes it. "But it makes no difference to me. I can't lie, I'm hoping you don't get the job."

"Don't get what job?" Claudia steps through the open door, wearing a plum-colored wrap dress. Her hair falls in loose spiral curls, reminding me of a Barbie doll I once had.

"Oh, hi," I say. "It's this job in —"

"Nothing," Jade says, interrupting me. "What do you need, Claudia?"

She steps over to the makeup chair. "I'm doing a silly segment on the morning news. The best-smelling mosquito repellant." She holds up two bottles of bug spray. "Can I get your opinions, ladies?"

She puts an open bottle next to Jade's

88

nose, then switches it to the second bottle, with a spray nozzle.

"The first one," Jade says, and turns away. I have a sneaking suspicion Jade never even inhaled. She just wants to be rid of Claudia.

"How about you, Hannah?"

I set my laptop on the counter and inhale the first one. "Not bad."

Next she puts the spray bottle to my nose. I sniff. "Hmm. I can't really smell this one."

"Oh, here," Claudia says.

The last image I see is Claudia's finger, pushing down the nozzle. Then a thousand needles pierce my eyes.

"Ow!" I holler. "Oh, shit!" I put my hands to my eyes, which are now clamped shut.

"Oh no! I'm so sorry, Hannah."

"Oh, damn! Ouch! Ouch! Ouch! My eyes are on fire!"

"Come here," Jade says. "We need to rinse your eyes."

I hear the urgency in her voice but I can't open my lids. With a hand on my arm, Jade pulls me to the sink and splashes water in my face. But my eyes refuse to open, even a crack. An involuntary stream of tears seeps past my closed lids.

"I am so sorry," Claudia repeats, again and again.

"It's okay," I say, doubled over the sink,

panting like I'm in labor. "No worries."

From across the room, I hear another set of footsteps approach. Judging by the quick gait, it's Stuart.

"What the hell's going on? Oh, Jesus! What the hell happened to you, Farr?"

"Claudia sprayed —" Jade begins, before I interrupt.

"I got mosquito repellant in my eyes."

"Oh, nice going. You're on in ten minutes." I feel him beside me now, and I imagine his head lowered to the sink, gawking down at me. "Oh, Jesus! Look at your face! You're a freak!"

"Thanks, Stuart." I can only guess how lovely I look, with my red, puffy eyes and wet cheeks smeared with makeup. But did I really need confirmation?

"Okay, I'm calling an audible here," Stuart says. "Claudia, I need you to pitch in. Can you start the show today, at least until this one looks remotely human?"

I pull my face from the sink bowl and look around blindly. "Wait. No. I . . ."

"Of course," I hear Claudia say. "I'm happy to help."

"Please, just give me a minute," I say, trying to pry my lids open with my fingers.

"You're a team player, Claudia," Stuart says. I hear his loafers clipping toward the door. "Farr, you're off today. And next time, don't be so careless."

"Oh, no worries there," Jade says, her voice oozing sarcasm. "And Stuart, don't you dare leave without taking this nasty piece of garbage with you."

I hear Claudia gasp.

"Jade!" I say, shocked that she could be so rude.

The room sizzles with tension, until finally Jade breaks the silence.

"Your mosquito spray," she says, and I hear her fling the can to Stuart.

The door closes, leaving me and Jade alone.

"That conniving bitch!" Jade says.

"Oh, come on," I say, holding a tissue to my eyes. "You don't think she did that on purpose."

"Sunshine, which syllable in *ma-nip-u-la-tion* don't you hear?"

CHAPTER 7

Two weeks later, I arrive at O'Hare Airport. It's a Wednesday morning and I'm dressed in a navy suit and heels, my carry-on bag slung over my shoulder. A burly man in his twenties greets me, holding a sign that reads HANNAH FARR/WCHI.

We step out of the terminal, and I'm smacked by a frigid headwind that knocks the breath from me.

"I thought it was springtime," I say, lifting the collar of my coat.

"Welcome to Chicago." He tosses my bag into the back of an Escalade. "Last week it was sixty degrees, last night it was sixteen."

We travel east on I-90, toward WCHI's headquarters in Logan Square. I wedge my hands beneath my legs hoping to warm them, and try to ease my anxiety about this job interview. Whatever possessed me to make up that forgiveness story?

From the backseat I gaze out the frosty

window, watching clouds spit a rain-snow mixture onto the glistening pavement. We pass suburbs of brick ranches with detached garages. And without warning, I think of Jack.

It's silly. Jack lives in the city, not the suburbs. But being here in Chicago makes me wonder what our life would have been like, had he not cheated on me. Would we be living in one of these cute houses, had I joined him like he'd begged me to? And would I be happier now, if I were oblivious to the fact that he'd screwed his intern? No. A relationship built on dishonesty could never work.

Looking for a distraction, I pull my phone from my tote and call the one person I think might actually miss me.

"Dorothy, hi, it's me."

"Oh, Hannah, I'm so happy to hear from you. Would you believe I received another pouch of Forgiveness Stones this morning? Patrick Sullivan — you know him, the gentleman with the deep voice? He always smells like he just left the barber."

I smile at Dorothy's description, based on smell and sound, rather than sight. "Yes, I know Patrick. He gave you a stone?"

"He did. He apologized for years of what he calls 'neglect.' You see, he and I go way

93

back. He's old N'awlins, like me. We were an item back at Tulane, until he earned a summer scholarship to study at Trinity College in Dublin. We parted amicably, but I never understood why he severed contact so abruptly. I thought we were in love."

"He finally apologized?"

"Yes. The poor man has carried a horrible burden all these years. You see, he and I were both applying for the prestigious Trinity Scholarship. We had plans of going off to Ireland together, spending the summer studying poetry and visiting the romantic countryside before returning home. The two of us spent hours perfecting our application essays. My goodness, the wastebasket in the commons was littered with pieces we'd written and scrapped.

"The night before the postmark deadline, Paddy and I sat in the commons, reading our final essays aloud to each other. I nearly cried when he read his."

"It was that touching?"

"No. It was that abominable. I knew he'd never get accepted.

"That night I didn't sleep a wink. I was quite confident that I'd receive the scholarship. I had the grades and a fine essay, if I can be so bold. But I didn't want to go without Paddy. And it would break his heart if I got the scholarship and he didn't.

"I made a decision the next morning. I wouldn't apply."

"He was okay with that?"

"I never told him. Together we went to the mailbox, but unbeknownst to him, the envelope I slid into the slot was empty.

"Three weeks later, Paddy got the news. He'd been accepted."

"Accepted? Oh no! You really could've gone together."

"His parents were so pleased. He'd be studying in their home country. I tried to hide my surprise . . . and my regret. He was over the moon and convinced that I'd hear my own good news soon. I certainly couldn't tell him I had so little faith in him that I'd disqualified myself.

"I waited two days before telling him I'd been rejected. He was sick about it. He swore he wouldn't go without me."

"So you both lost out."

"No. I told him he'd be a fool to stay back, that I'd be waiting to hear all about it come September. I absolutely insisted that he go."

"And he did?"

"He left in June. I never heard from him again. He ended up staying in Dublin for twenty-five years. Became an architect. Married an Irish lass and had three sons."

"And today he finally apologized for leaving you?"

"Like me, Paddy knew he wasn't competitive for the coveted award. And he, too, hated the idea of our separation. He needed something to boost his odds of getting the scholarship. That night in the commons, he took one of my discarded essays from the trash. Later, he retyped it. Apparently it was a lovely essay about the importance of family and finding our roots." She lifts her hands. "I haven't the foggiest recollection of it.

"He claims that's how he got accepted. My essay. Imagine that. He's been wallowing in guilt all these years."

"What did you tell him?"

"Well, I forgave him, of course. I would have forgiven him years ago, had he asked for it."

"Of course you would have," I say, wondering what might have been, had Patrick Sullivan trusted Dorothy's love. "What a story."

"These stones, Hannah, they're more popular here than a new male resident." She laughs. "At our age, the stones give us the opportunity to clear the air, to make amends before the final curtain, so to speak. It's a wonderful gift Ms. Knowles has given us. A

96

group of us residents are going to see Fiona when she's at Octavia Books on the twenty-fourth. Marilyn's coming, too. Perhaps you'll join us."

"Maybe," I say. "But I'm still not convinced. A stone seems hardly sufficient for stealing someone's essay. Or bullying someone, for that matter. Seems like people are being let off the hook a little too easily."

"You know, I've been thinking the same thing. Some grievances are just too big for a stone, or even a boulder. There are times when a simple apology isn't enough. Times when we deserve a little comeuppance."

I think of my mother and feel my pulse quicken. "I agree."

"That's why I've yet to send my stone to Mari. I need to come up with a way to truly atone." Dorothy's voice becomes soft, as if we're coconspirators. "How about you? Have you reached out to your mother yet?"

"Dorothy, please, you don't know the whole story."

"And you do?" Her voice is challenging, as if she's the teacher and I'm her pupil. " 'Doubt is not a pleasant condition, but certainty is absurd.' Voltaire said that. Please, don't be so sure of yourself, Hannah, dear. Hear your mother's side of the tale."

■ ■ ■ ■

Forty minutes later, the Escalade pulls to a stop in front of a sprawling two-story brick building. My little station in New Orleans would fit in just one wing of this monstrosity. A sign beside the entrance, nestled among a gang of fir trees, reads WCHI. I step onto the slushy pavement and take a deep breath. Showtime.

I meet James Peters, who leads me into a conference room, where five of the top executives at the station are gathered at an oval table. Three are men, two women. I'm prepared to be grilled, but instead it's more like a congenial chat among colleagues. They want to hear about New Orleans, my interests, what I envision for *Good Morning, Chicago,* who my dream guests might be.

"We're especially excited about your proposal," Helen Camps says, from the far end of the table. "Fiona Knowles and her Forgiveness Stones have become quite a craze here in the Midwest. The fact that you know her, that you were one of her original recipients, is indeed quite a story, one we'd be very interested in producing, should you be selected."

My stomach cramps. "Great."

"Tell us what happened once you received the stones," a gray-haired man whose name I can't remember asks.

I feel my face heat. Damn. This is exactly what I was afraid of. "Um, well, I received the stones in the mail, and I remembered Fiona, the girl who bullied me back in sixth grade."

Jan Harding, vice president of marketing chimes in. "Just curious — did you send the stone back right away, or wait a few days?"

"Or weeks," Mr. Peters says, as if weeks were the maximum time allowed.

I laugh nervously. "Oh, I waited weeks." Like, one hundred twelve weeks.

"And you sent the second stone on to your mother," Helen Camp says. "How difficult was that?"

Jesus, can we please wrap this up? I touch the diamond-and-sapphire necklace as if it's my talisman. "Fiona Knowles has a line in her book that really resonated with me." I think of Dorothy's favorite quote and repeat it like a damned hypocrite. 'Until you pour light onto whatever it is that cloaks you in darkness, you'll forever be lost.' "

My nose burns and tears spring to my eyes. For the first time, I realize the truth in these words. I am lost. So very lost. Here I am, making up a story of forgiveness, lying

99

to all of these people sitting in front of me.

"Well, we're happy you've been found," Jan says. She leans in. "And lucky for us, we've found you!"

James Peters and I sit in the backseat of a taxi as the driver speeds down Fullerton Avenue toward Kinzie Chophouse for our lunch meeting with two of the anchors. "Well done this morning, Hannah," he says to me. "As you can tell, it's a terrific group here at WCHI. I think you'd be a great fit."

Sure, a great fit who's misrepresented herself. Why the heck did I choose the Forgiveness Stones for my proposal? There's no way in hell I'd have my mother on the show. I smile at him. "Thanks. It's an impressive team."

"I'll tell it to you straight. You've got a terrific proposal and some of the best demo tapes we've seen. I've been aware of you for a decade. My sister lives in New Orleans and says you're the real deal. But your ratings have been on a downward trajectory for the past three months."

I groan. I'd love to explain my frustration with Stuart and the inane topics he selects, but that just sounds defensive. It is, after all, *The Hannah Farr Show.* "It's true.

100

They've been better. I take full responsibility."

"I know Stuart Booker. Worked with him in Miami, before I came here. Your talents are being wasted at WNO. You'll have a voice here, your ideas will be valued." He points a finger at me. "You come on board and we'll make the Fiona Knowles proposal happen, day one. That's a promise."

My heart does a double take. "That's good to know," I say, feeling simultaneously proud and panic-stricken and utterly despicable.

I'm still rattled at 9:00 p.m., when I enter the small boutique hotel on Oak Street. I scurry to the registration desk, as if to hasten my departure. I'm ready to leave this city, and the memory of my deceitful interview, behind me. As soon as I get up to my room, I'll call Michael and tell him I'm coming home early, in time for our Saturday-night date.

The thought cheers me. I'd purposely booked the return flight for Sunday, back when I thought Michael and Abby were joining me for a weekend in Chicago. But as I was packing to leave, Michael called saying Abby was "a bit under the weather." They had to cancel.

101

For a split second I thought about telling him to come anyway, alone, like he'd promised he'd do if I moved here. But Abby's sick — or at least claims to be. What kind of insensitive girlfriend expects a father to leave his sick daughter? I shake my head. And what kind of coldhearted monster doubts a sick child's motives?

I'm halfway across the marble lobby when I spot him. I stop in my tracks. He's sitting in an upholstered wingback chair scrolling his cell phone. He rises when he sees me.

"Hey," he says, stuffing his phone into his pocket and moving toward me in that lazy swagger of his. Time slows. His grin is crooked, just as I remember, and his hair is as shaggy as ever. But that southern charm I fell in love with is nearly palpable.

"Jack," I say, feeling light-headed. "What are you doing here?"

"My mother told me you were in town."

"Of course she did." It breaks my heart that Dorothy is still clinging to the hope that somehow, some way, Jack and I will get back together.

"Can we go somewhere and talk?" He jabs a thumb toward the elevator. "There's a bar here, right downstairs." He says it as if the proximity makes up for the fact that I'd be sitting down with my ex, alone, in a strange city.

We settle into a horseshoe-shaped booth, and Jack orders two gin martinis. "One up, one on the rocks."

I'm touched that he remembers. But I've changed since we were together. Martinis are no longer my drink of choice. These days I prefer something lighter, like a vodka tonic. But how would he know? We haven't shared drinks in over two years.

He talks about his job and his life in Chicago. "It's crazy cold," he tells me, and offers his familiar deep chuckle. But his eyes hold a trace of sadness since we parted, something I still haven't gotten used to. When we were together — especially in the early days when everything was new and full of promise — his eyes held only mirth. I wonder if I'm solely responsible for taking away his joy.

The waitress sets our drinks on the table, then disappears. Jack smiles up at me and holds his glass aloft. "To old friends," he says.

I study the man in front of me, the man I almost married. I take in his rosy cheeks and lopsided grin, his freckled arms and the fingernails he still bites to the quick. He's so real. And despite his infidelity, I like this man. I truly and genuinely like him. Some friends are like our favorite sweaters. Most days we opt for the T-shirts and blouses. But the sweater's always there, in the back of our closet, comfortable, familiar, and ready to keep us warm on those blustery days. Jack Rousseau is my sweater.

"To old friends," I say, feeling the shadow of nostalgia creeping in. I push it away as quickly as it came. I've got Michael now.

"It's good to see you," he says. "You look terrific, Hans. A little thin, but happy. You are happy, right? And you are eating?"

"Yes, to both," I say, laughing.

"Good. Great. Obviously, Mr. Right-Wing makes you happy."

I shake my head at his little jab. "You'd like him, Jack. He really cares about the people." And me, I think. But it'd be cruel to tell him this. "I've moved on, and so should you."

He twirls his toothpick of olives, and I can tell he's got something on his mind. *Please don't dredge up the past again!*

"Your mother's doing well," I say, trying to steer the conversation in another direction. "She's got a new obsession — the Forgiveness Stones."

He laughs. "I know all about it. She sent

me a pouch of stones the other day, and a three-page letter of apology. The sweetest woman on earth, and she's apologizing to me."

I smile. "I'm beginning to regret ever introducing her to the stones. She's handing them out like those Dove chocolates she always kept next to her TV."

He nods. "It's cool. I sent the second stone to my dad. Did you know that when he got remarried, back in 1990, I refused to go to the wedding?"

"You were protective of your mom. I'm sure he understood."

"Yeah, but it hurt him. He and Sharon are really happy. I see that now. It actually felt good, writing that apology. I wish my mom could find it in her to forgive him."

"Maybe he's never asked her to."

Jack shrugs. "Maybe. And sounds like she's got a love interest now."

"Love interest? Your mother?"

"Another resident. Mr. Sullivan."

"You think she's interested in Patrick Sullivan again?"

"Yeah, I'm picking up that vibe. She never dated after she and my dad split. Maybe all this time she's been waiting for ol' man Sullivan. Maybe he's the one who really shook her tree."

"Shook her tree?" I laugh and flip his arm with the back of my hand. "You're such a romantic!"

"What?" he says, laugh lines spreading across his cheekbones. "I shook your tree."

"Oh, get over yourself, Rousseau." I roll my eyes, but it feels nice to be joking with him.

"I'm just saying, my mom deserves a little romance, and maybe this Sullivan dude can deliver." He levels his eyes at me. "You know how I feel. You never give up on the people you love."

The accusation hits its mark. I look away, feeling his gaze burning through me.

"I should probably get going," I say, and push aside my drink.

He seizes my hand. "No. I wanted . . . I — I needed to talk to you."

I feel the warmth of his hand where it rests on mine, and watch as softness overtakes his gaze. My heart speeds. Jesus, I need to keep this light.

"Your mom tells me the restaurant consulting business is going well. Have you found Tony's Place yet?" Jack's ambition was to travel the world in search of the perfect restaurant — a dimly lit Tony Soprano–type place with killer martinis and red leather booths. He used to tease that when he found it, he'd buy it and call it Tony's Place.

He holds tight to my hand and doesn't crack a smile.

"I'm getting married, Hannah."

I stare at him.

"What?"

I see the muscle in his jaw clench. He nods his head ever so slightly.

I pull my hand from his and rub my arms, feeling suddenly cold. My favorite sweater is unraveling.

"Congratulations," I say, but my tongue feels thick. I lift my martini. My hand trembles and the liquid sloshes over the edge of the glass. I set it down with two hands and grab a napkin, busying myself while I try to find my voice, and my bearings.

"Hey, I wanted you to know. It's not like I didn't give you a million and six chances to change your mind." He sighs. "God, that sounded awful. Holly is great. You'd love her." He smiles. "And what really matters is that I love her."

I can't breathe. *Holly. Love her.*

"Your mom," I ask, my voice shaky, "did she know?"

"She knew I was dating Holly, but she didn't realize it was so serious. We agreed I

107

should be the one to tell you. She's pregnant. Holly that is, not my mother."

He offers his lopsided grin, and without warning, I burst into tears.

"Oh, God," I say, shifting away and swiping my eyes. "I'm so sorry. This is great news. I don't know what's wrong with me."

He hands me his napkin, and I blot my eyes. "A baby. That's wonderful."

But it's not wonderful. I've made a huge mistake.

"I wish things could have been different for us, Hans. You were just so . . . so certain. So black-and-white. So judgmental."

I cut him a look. "Judgmental? You were sleeping with your intern."

He lifts a finger. "One time, which I will forever regret. But the truth is, I was never the one for you, Hannah."

He's being kind, letting me save face. I love him more than ever.

"Of course you weren't," I say. My smile competes with the downward tug at the corners of my mouth. "These tears are just to make you feel good." My laughter gets tangled in a sob. I cover my face. "How do you know you weren't the one? How can you be so damn sure?"

He rubs my arm. "Because you never would have let me go. Like I say, we don't give up on the people we love."

I stare back at him, wondering whether he's right, or whether I have a character flaw, some innate inability to forgive, or maybe even to love. I think of my mother and the hard stance I've taken with her.

"You're like a steel rod, Hans. You refused to bend, even an inch. Most of the time it probably serves you well."

I fumble for my purse. "I have to go."

"Wait." He pulls some bills from his wallet and tosses them on the table. I hear him behind me, trotting to keep pace with me. I rush past the elevator doors, too rattled to share the tiny space with this soon-to-be-married man. I throw open the utility door and run up the cement stairs.

I hear his footsteps charging after me. Halfway up the staircase he grabs hold of my elbow.

"Hannah, stop." He spins me around. His eyes become tender. "He's out there, Hans, your fire, the man who'll melt your steel. But it's not me. It never was."

CHAPTER 8

I wait forty minutes before calling Michael. I'm too raw, and my voice still sounds thick. I don't want him to misconstrue my emotions. My tears over Jack take nothing away from my feelings for him.

Luckily, he's groggy when I call and doesn't pick up on my mood.

"How's Abby feeling?" I ask.

"Great." He says it so matter-of-factly that I wonder again if she was ever sick at all. Jack's right. I really am judgmental.

I give Michael a quick snapshot of my day at WCHI.

"I'm one of three final candidates. They seemed to like me, but I won't know anything for a few weeks. You know how slowly these things move."

"Congratulations. Sounds like you sealed the deal." He yawns, and I imagine him checking his bedside clock. "Anything else to report?"

I feel like an officer reading the minutes at one of his city council meetings. "No, that's about the gist of it."

I don't tell him about Jack. There's nothing to tell. But on impulse, I shoot him a question.

"Am I hard, Michael? Too judgmental?"

"Hmm?"

"Because I can change. I can become softer, more forgiving. I can open up more, share more. I really can."

"No. Absolutely not. You're perfect."

The king-sized hotel bed feels cramped. Thoughts of Jack and his future wife, of Michael and Abby, steal my sleep. I roll onto my side, trying to block out the interview and my fictitious claim of having made peace with my mother.

At the first hint of dawn, I exchange my PJs for my walking tights.

I stroll down Chicago's Lakefront Trail with my hands in my pockets, pondering my future. What if I actually get the job offer? Could I live here, alone in this city? I wouldn't have a single friend, not even Jack now.

I see a couple walking toward me, a pretty woman with auburn hair and a man in a Burberry coat. An adorable toddler sits balanced on his shoulders. What I wouldn't give to trade places with them.

My mind travels to my mother. It seems like the universe is conspiring against me. First Dorothy urges me to make peace. Then it's this damn proposal that's making me feel like I have an assignment. And last night, Jack's comment about not giving up on those we love. Is it possible I've judged my mother too harshly? The thought is out of my head before I have time to censor it.

My mind trips over itself, faster and more frenetic. I see glimpses of my mother's smile, finally genuine, when she looked at Bob. I see her standing at the picture window in our living room, waiting for his truck to arrive each morning during the remodel, and then dashing out to the driveway to meet him with a cup of coffee. I hear her laughter coming from the patio, where they'd sit sipping iced tea after Bob's long day of work. I watch her lean in, as if every word he spoke were poetry.

She loved the man. For whatever flaws she had, for whatever shortcomings of being a mother or a friend, my mother loved Bob with her entire heart and soul.

I realize now that my cloak of anger is actually a patchwork, and one of the emotions woven into the fabric is fear. How terrifying it was to witness my mother's love for someone else. Because in my young mind, her love for Bob meant she'd have less love for me.

I stop at a concrete landing and gaze out at the vast expanse of cold gray water separating me from my mother. The wind slaps my face, and my nose runs. Somewhere beyond the enormous cavity of Lake Michigan, in the suburbs of Detroit, my mother lives and breathes.

I crouch down, holding my head in my hands. What if she really has been trying to contact me? Could I possibly forgive her?

Jack's accusations come back to me. *Steel rod. Black-and-white. Judgmental.* I pull myself up, struck with a desire so intense my head swims.

I turn back in the direction I'd come, and then I break into a run.

I'm nearly manic when I reach my hotel room. I throw open my laptop, and within five minutes I've located her address and phone number. She's listed as Suzanne Davidson. Has she kept her maiden name all these years, hoping I might one day try to find her? She's no longer in Bloomfield Hills. She lives in Harbour Cove. A shiver goes through me. Dorchester Lane? I punch the address into Google Maps and time freezes. They're living in Bob's old cabin, the place where I spent my fourteenth summer. The hairs on my arms rise. The place my father swore I'd never set foot in again.

With shaking hands, I punch the numbers into the hotel's cream-colored phone rather than my cell. She'll never know it's me. I slide into the chair behind the desk. My heart thunders as I listen to the phone ring once . . . twice . . .

I think of all the phone conversations we had after I left, during the three years leading up to my sixteenth birthday. I remember her endless barrage of questions and my snappy one-word answers. I accused her of being nosy for wanting to hear all about my life in Atlanta. I'd be damned if I'd let her in. If she wanted to be part of my life, then she'd better get her ass home where she belonged.

She picks up on the third ring. "Hello."

I suck in a breath and clap a hand over my mouth.

"Hello?" she repeats. "Anybody there?"

She speaks softly, revealing just a hint of her Pennsylvania roots. I'm desperate to hear more of the voice I haven't heard in sixteen years.

"Hello," I say, my voice weak.

114

She waits for me to continue, then finally speaks. "I'm sorry. Who is this?"

My heart shatters. She doesn't recognize her own daughter. But why would she? I wasn't expecting her to . . . or was I?

But for some completely irrational reason, it hurts. *I'm your daughter,* I want to scream. *The one you left behind.* I put my fingers to my lips and swallow hard.

"Wrong number," I say, and hang up the phone

I bury my head on the desk. Softly at first, my sadness grows. That was my mother. The only person I ever truly loved.

I leap from the desk chair and rummage through my purse for my cell phone. This time I punch in Dorothy's number.

"Are you busy?" I ask, my heart pounding.

"Never too busy for my girl. What's on your mind, dear?"

"Do you think he — my dad — was telling you the truth about the letters — or a letter — from my mom? Did you believe him, Dorothy?"

I grip the phone, waiting for her response, knowing so much rests on this one answer.

"Sweetheart," she says softly, "it was one of the few times I did believe him."

CHAPTER 9

It's ten o'clock when I arrive at O'Hare. Instead of switching to an earlier flight back home, I purchase a new ticket, this one to Grand Rapids, Michigan.

"There's a flight leaving at eleven oh-four," the woman at the Delta counter tells me. "With the time difference, you'll arrive at twelve fifty-seven. I've got you returning to New Orleans tomorrow evening, ten fifty-one."

I hand her my credit card.

I arrive at the gate with ten minutes to spare before boarding. I sink into a pleather sling-back chair and dig into my tote for my cell phone. Instead, my fingers land on my velvet pouch.

I pull a stone from the pouch and settle it onto my palm. I study the speckles of beige on its smooth ivory skin and think of Fiona Knowles. Two years ago she selected this very stone for me. She set this plan in motion. Without the Forgiveness Stones, I wouldn't have considered making this trip. All the memories of my mother would still be stuffed away, safely.

I grip the stone tightly, hoping I'm doing the right thing. *Please let this stone build a bridge, not a wall.*

Across from me, I watch a young mother braid her daughter's hair. She smiles as the daughter rattles on about something. I tamp down any foolish expectations for this trip. This isn't likely to be a happy reunion.

I tuck the stone back into my purse and this time remove my cell phone. My pulse quickens. How will Michael respond when I tell him I'm going to Michigan? Does he remember what I told him about my mother and her boyfriend?

I tap the call button, happy for once that he's a busy man. It'll be much easier to leave a message.

"Hannah," he says. "Good morning, hon."

Shit. Of all days . . .

"Good morning," I say, trying to sound upbeat. "I can't believe I caught you."

"Just about to step into a meeting. What's up?"

"Hey, you'll never guess what I'm about to do. I'm going to Michigan for an overnight. I figured since I was here, I may as well pay my mother a visit."

I blurt it all out in one swift breath. And I wait . . .

Finally he speaks. "You think that's necessary?"

"I do. I'm going to try to forgive her. I think I need to make peace with my past before I can move on to the future."

The words — Dorothy's words — make me feel wise.

"If you say so," Michael says. "Just one piece of advice. Keep this stuff to yourself. Nobody needs to know your business."

"Of course," I say. Suddenly it seems clear. Michael doesn't want my reputation to tarnish his.

It's one thirty by the time the plane lands and I sign the agreement for the rental car.

"Just until tomorrow, then?" the young man at the rental agency asks.

"Yes. I'll have it back by six."

"Give yourself plenty of time. There's a storm coming in this afternoon."

When I hear the word *storm,* I think hurricane. But when he hands me a plastic scraper, I realize he's talking about snow and ice, not rain.

"Thanks," I say, and climb into the Ford Taurus, still wearing my suit and heels. I toss the windshield scraper into the back.

I drive north on I-31, singing along with Adele, reeling with thoughts of my mother. An hour passes and I notice the landscape change. It's hilly now, with giant spruce and birch trees lining the interstate. DEER X-ING signs crop up every few miles.

I pass a marker telling me I'm at the Forty-fifth Parallel, and I can hear Bob's voice as if I'm still in the backseat of his Oldsmobile Cutlass.

See that, Sister? You're exactly halfway between the North Pole and the equator.

Like I'm supposed to be excited about that? He's got that big dolphin grin on his face, and he's trying to catch my eye in the rearview mirror. But I won't look.

I push aside the image and try to concentrate on the scenery, so different from the south. It's prettier up here than I remember. It always made me feel claustrophobic, this northern isolation, but today, with the white snow and green spruce trees, it feels more serene than secluded. I crack my window, replacing the stale heat with a blast of fresh, crisp wind.

My GPS tells me I'm thirty miles from Harbour Cove. My stomach pitches. Am I ready for this? No, I'm not sure I am, or

119

ever will be.

I rehearse my plan for the umpteenth time. I'll find a motel for the night, and wake early. I'll get to the house before nine. Bob should be at work, and my mother should already be up and showered. I'm trusting that she is, above all her other flaws and foibles, kind. I want to believe that once she sees me, she'll welcome me. I'll tell her she's forgiven, and we'll both be free of our past. At least as much as we can be free of it.

I was fifteen the last time we spent a weekend together. Coincidentally, we'd met in Chicago, the very city I just came from. I'd flown in from Atlanta; she'd taken a train from Michigan. We stayed at a shabby airport motel rather than downtown. We ate our meals at a nearby Denny's and only went into the city for an afternoon. I saw a shirt I wanted at Abercrombie, and my mother insisted on buying it for me. When she opened her purse, I saw that the lining was torn. She searched her weathered billfold and counted her money, then recounted. Finally she wedged a folded twenty-dollar bill from a slot intended for photos.

"My hidden twenty," she told me. "You should always keep a hidden twenty in your wallet, in case of emergencies."

The advice wasn't what struck me. It was the realization that my mother was poor. I'd never thought about it. When I shopped with my father, he'd hand the clerk his plastic and we'd be off. Did my mother even have a credit card? Surely she got half my father's assets in the divorce. What did she do with all the money? Spend it on Bob, probably.

I should have been grateful that she'd splurged on the ratty motel room, that she'd spent her hidden twenty on me. I should have been furious with my father, for not giving her a better settlement. But instead, I felt a growing disconnect bordering on disgust.

When I got home, I asked my father why Mom had no money. "Bad choices," he said, shaking his head. "That shouldn't surprise you."

The insinuation was another dose of poison on an already ailing relationship. *Another bad decision, just like when she chose her boyfriend over you.*

All of the shame and gratitude and pity I should have felt for my mother then come crashing down on me now. With every passing mile, I'm more and more certain that I'm making the right decision. I need to see my mother. She needs to hear I've forgiven her. As nervous as I am, I can hardly wait for morning to come.

Who in the world would drink wine made in Northern Michigan? But every few miles I see a sign for another vineyard. I'd read somewhere about how the climate on Old Mission peninsula made for perfect grape-growing conditions. But I had no idea the notion had caught fire. But then again, what else do these people have to do?

When I reach the top of a hill, I see it. Lake Michigan. It's so vast you'd swear it's the ocean. I slow the car, taking in the brilliant blue water. But the sandy beaches I remember are snow-covered today, and huge boulders of ice barricade the shoreline. Memories flood my mind, my mother and Bob in the front seat of his Cutlass, cheering when first they spotted the lake. Me, alone in the backseat, refusing to look. "There it is, Sister," Bob would say, using the nickname I'd grown to hate and pointing ahead. "Isn't she magnificent?"

Even though I longed to take a peek, I refused. I wouldn't give him the satisfaction. I needed to hate this place. If I liked it, my resolve might weaken. I might like

Bob, too, and my dad would never forgive me.

"Will you come fishing with me in the morning, Sister? I'll bet you catch a bass or two. Or maybe the whitefish will be biting. You'll fry it up for us tomorrow night, won't you, Suzanne? Nothing better than Lake Michigan whitefish."

I ignored him, my usual MO. Did he seriously think I'd wake at 5:00 a.m. so I could fish with him? Get real, asshole.

I wonder now, what might have happened way out on those waters, with nobody in sight? The thought makes me shudder.

Just when it was, or what provoked it, I'm no longer sure. All I know is that at some point before my thirteenth birthday, Bob became creepy. The summer we first met, I actually liked him. I stood watching as he stripped the cupboards from our kitchen with a crowbar. His arms were tan and knotted with muscles. One morning he tossed me a pair of safety glasses and a hard hat, and dubbed me his assistant. I'd clean up the worksite and fetch him glasses of iced tea, and at the end of each day he'd give me a crisp five-dollar bill. He called me Hannah then. It wasn't until he started dating my mother that he took to calling me "Sister." And by then, no nickname, no amount of cajoling, could have softened my resolve. I had made a decision. He was the enemy. Every nice gesture, every compliment, were suspect.

I'm stunned when I enter the shopping district of Harbour Cove. The once-sleepy fishing village is now a bustling little town. Well-dressed women in trendy black parkas stroll the sidewalks, carrying designer purses and shopping bags. I pass quaint storefronts with awnings, an Apple store, art galleries, restaurants with chalkboards out front telling of their daily specials.

The town is nearly a picture book. A white Bentley turns left in front of me. When did Harbour Cove become so posh? Can my mother afford to live here?

My hands grip the steering wheel and a sick feeling comes over me. What if she's no longer here? What if the address on White pages.com is out of date? After all this time, what if I can't find her?

It dawns on me. In the span of three weeks, I've gone from not thinking of my mother at all, to dreading the thought of making contact, to a desperate longing to find and forgive her. But desperate or not, I need to wait until morning. I cannot risk running into Bob.

CHAPTER 10

I drive through Harbour Cove feeling antsy and anxious, and head north on Peninsula Drive. I pass a dozen signs for vineyards, and smile when I see MERLOT DE LA MIT-AINE. Cute. Merlot of the Mitten — Michigan's nickname. At least this vineyard doesn't take itself seriously. What the hell? It's 3:20 and a glass of wine and a clean ladies' room sound heavenly. I follow a patch of arrows up a steep dirt drive and wind my way back to a gigantic old barn and a parking area.

I stretch when I get out of the car and gasp when I take in the view. Perched atop a hillside on this pencil-thin peninsula, twisted grapevines covered in snow intertwine wooden fences and trellises. Barren cherry trees — still months from bearing fruit — form perfectly straight rows, like children lined up for recess. In the distance, I spy the waters of Lake Michigan.

My stomach growls, forcing me to turn away from the dazzling vista. I cross the empty parking lot, wondering if this place is even open. The only thing I've eaten today was a tiny bag of pretzels on the airplane. I quicken my pace, yearning for a glass of wine and a sandwich.

The wooden door creaks when I open it. It takes a minute for my eyes to adjust to the dimly lit room. Huge oak rafters suspended from the vast ceiling suggest that this place was an authentic barn at one time. Shelves of wine line the perimeter, and scattered tables display gourmet crackers and cheese spreaders, fancy corkscrews and wine aerators. Behind a cabinet I see an old-fashioned cash register, but nobody is in sight. Whoever owns this place must not care if they're robbed.

"Hello?" I call, and step through an archway into the next room. A huge fieldstone fireplace is ablaze, giving warmth to the big, deserted space. Round tables fill the wood-planked floor, but it's a U-shaped bar, made of old wooden wine kegs, that grabs my attention. Obviously, I've landed in the wine-tasting room. Great, now if I could just get some vino I'd be all set.

"Hey!" A man steps out from behind a wall, wiping his hands on an apron covered with pink stains.

"Hi," I say. "Are you open for lunch?"

"Absolutely."

He's a tall, fortysomething with a mop of unruly dark hair and a smile that makes me feel like he's actually happy to see me. I'm guessing he's the winemaker.

"Have a seat." He gestures to the empty room. "I think we can squeeze you in somewhere." He smiles, and I can't help but laugh. The poor guy has no business, but at least he has a sense of humor about it.

"Good thing I arrived before the rush," I say. I bypass the round tables and chairs and opt for a leather barstool.

He hands me a menu. "We're still keeping off-season hours. From the first of the year until May, we're only open weekends and by appointment."

"Oh, I'm sorry. I didn't realize —" I push back my stool, but he places a hand on my shoulder.

"No worries. I've been in the back experimenting with some soups. I was hoping for a guinea pig. You game?"

"Uh, if you're sure, then absolutely," I say. "Mind if I use the powder room first?"

He points to the back of the room. "First door."

The spotless bathroom smells of a lemon disinfectant. On a table behind the sink, I spy mouthwash and paper cups, hair spray, and a bowl of wrapped chocolate mints. I pop one in my mouth. Oh, that's good. I grab a handful and stash them in my purse, something to nibble on during tomorrow's flight.

After splashing water on my face, I look into the mirror, horrified at what I see. I have no makeup on, and I didn't bother straightening my hair this morning. I pull a clip from my purse and gather my wavy locks at the back of my neck. Next, I grab a tube of lip gloss. But just as I go to apply it, I stop. I'm up here in the middle of the boonies, where nobody knows or cares who I am. Do I have the guts to go au naturel? I tuck the tube back into my purse and grab another handful of mints on my way out the door.

When I return to the bar, I find a basket of breadsticks alongside a glass of red wine.

"Merlot," he says. "Two thousand ten. My personal favorite."

I lift the glass by the stem and put it to my nose. It's heady and pungent. Next I swirl it, trying to remember why I'm supposed to do this. The man watches me with a whiff of a smile on his face. Is he mocking me?

I narrow my eyes at him. "Are you laughing at me?"

He sobers. "No. I'm sorry. It's just . . ."

I crack a grin. "Of course. I'm doing exactly what every amateur wine connoisseur does when offered a glass of wine. The swirl."

"No, it isn't the obligatory swirl, though you're spot-on. Everybody swirls. I'm laughing because . . . you . . ." He points to my purse. It's open, and looks as if it's my trick-or-treat bag, so full it is with chocolate mints.

I feel my face heat. "Oh, geez! I'm sorry. I —"

His laughter is hearty. "No worries. Take all you like. I can't keep my hands off them, either."

I laugh, too. I like this guy's casual manner, treating me as if we're old friends. I kind of admire this regular Joe, trying to make a go in this northern town, with a business that operates only eight months a year. It can't be easy.

I skip the rituals and take a sip of the wine.

"Oh, wow, that's good. Really good." I take another sip. "And this is where I'm supposed to insert words like *oaky* and *buttery*."

"Or *musky* or *smoky*. Or my personal favorite, *This shit tastes like wet asphalt.*"

"No! Someone actually said that?" The sound of my laughter sounds foreign to me. How long has it been since I've truly laughed?

"Sadly, they did. Gotta have a thick skin in this biz."

"Well, if this is wet asphalt, you're welcome to pave my driveway." *Pave my driveway?* Did I actually say that? Shut me up now! I hide my face in my glass.

"Glad you like it." He stretches an arm across the bar, offering a large paw. "I'm RJ."

I fit my hand into his. "Nice to meet you. I'm Hannah."

He goes into the back room and returns with a steaming bowl of soup.

"Tomato basil," he tells me, and places it on the place mat before me. "Careful, it's hot."

"Thanks."

He hoists himself on the edge of the back counter facing me, as if he's settling in for a long conversation. The personal attention makes me feel special. I remind myself that I am his only patron, after all.

We cover the basics while I sip my wine and wait for my soup to cool. Where I'm from, what brings me to this neck of the woods.

"I'm a journalist. I grew up down South," I tell him. "I'm here visiting my mother." It might be a lie of omission, technically, but I'm not about to tell this stranger my childhood saga.

"She lives here?"

"Just west, in Harbour Cove."

He raises his eyebrows, and I can guess what he's thinking: that I grew up summering in one of the mansions on the lake. When people make assumptions about my background, I normally don't correct them. As Michael says, my image is important. Perhaps it's because I'm a thousand miles from my fan base, or perhaps it's because I sense this guy is real, I'm not sure. But for whatever reason, this time I correct him.

"It's a long-overdue visit. I don't have the best memories of this place."

"And your father?" he asks.

I stir my soup. "He died last year."

"I'm sorry."

"He would have loved your vineyard. His motto was *Why eat fruit when you can drink it?* And he wasn't talking about juice." I don't laugh when I say this. I don't even smile.

RJ nods, as if he gets it. "My dad would've agreed. Though he'd have extended that phrase to include rye and most grains as well."

So we have that in common — two fatherless children of alcoholics. I take a spoonful of soup. It's creamy and tangy, with a hint of basil.

"This is delicious," I say.

"Too much basil?"

"It's perfect."

Our eyes hold for a split second too long. I look away, feeling heat rise to my cheeks, the result of the hot soup or hot guy, I'm not certain.

He pours me a sample from a different wine bottle, then pulls a second glass from the rack. "What the hell," he says, and pours a dollop into his glass, too. "It's not every day I get to fraternize with my customers. Another six weeks and I'll be knee-deep in chaos."

I smile, but I can't help but wonder if he's just an optimist. "Have you worked here long?"

"Bought it four years ago. I spent my summers up here as a kid. It was my favorite place in the world. Went off to school and majored in plant science. After graduation, I got a job with E&J — Ernest and Julio Gallo Winery. Moved to Modesto and before I knew it, a dozen years disappeared." He stares at the red liquid in his glass. "But California, for as great as it is, just wasn't my style. One day I was dinking around on some real estate website and found this place. Bought it at auction for a pittance."

"Sounds like a dream," I say. I wonder whether he has a family, but I don't ask.

"It is, for me." He picks up an empty glass and wipes it with his towel. "I'd just been through an unpleasant divorce. I needed a fresh start and some distance."

"Two thousand miles will get you that."

He looks over at me and smiles, but his eyes are heavy. He busies himself wiping imaginary spots from the glass. "How about you? Married? Kids? A dog and a Subaru?"

I smile. "None of the above." Now is the time to tell him about Michael. And I should. I know I should. But I don't. It seems alarmist, as if I'd be sending a presumptuous message saying, *Warning! Keep away!* I don't sense that RJ is coming on to me. I'm enjoying the light and friendly banter. It's been a long time since I was just hanging out with a regular person, not a businessman or politician. It's also refreshing to be with someone who doesn't know me as Hannah Farr, talk show host.

I pull another breadstick from the basket. "Did you make these?"

"Naturally you'd ask. They're the only item on the menu that isn't made on site. I get them from *la boulangerie* Costco."

He exaggerates his French accent, and I laugh. "Costco? Really? They're not bad," I say, examining one of them. "Not as good as mine, but not bad."

He grins. "Oh, yeah? You think you can do better, eh?"

"I do. These are a bit dry."

"That's the whole idea, Hannah. Gets people drinking."

"Oh, subliminal seduction. Isn't there a law against that?"

"Nah. I tell Joyce at the bakery counter I want them dry as dust and doused with salt. These here breadsticks are the only thing keeping me in business."

I laugh again. "I'll send you some of mine. Rosemary asiago are my favorite. You'll see. Your customers will sit for hours just eating bread and sipping wine."

"Oh, now, that's a business plan. Fill up on the free bread and skip the thirty-dollar entrée. I can see why you're a journalist, not an entrepreneur."

"And for dessert, free mints," I add, patting my purse.

He throws his head back and laughs. My head swells, and I think I'm Ellen DeGeneres.

Our conversation continues at a leisurely pace. He teaches me about the elements that affect wine's taste and aroma.

"All these factors are generally lumped together and called the wine's 'terroir.' The terroir is thought to be the result of where and how the wine was produced. The type of soil, the amount of sunlight, the type of barrel."

I think of my own "terroir," and how each of us is the result of where and how we were raised. I wonder if I give off notes of judgment and rigidity. Of insecurity and loneliness.

I'm as relaxed as a dog in the shade when RJ jumps down from his perch. I hear it now. The sound of the door opening, and then stomping feet. Damn, another customer.

I glance at my watch — it's four thirty. I've just frittered away a good portion of the afternoon talking to a stranger. I should scoot. I still need to find a motel, and I'd like to do it while there's still daylight.

The footsteps grow louder. I turn around

and see two kids, their jackets covered with snow. The boy looks to be about twelve, lanky and tall, wearing a pair of jeans that barely reaches his ankles. The girl, a tiny, freckled redhead with a missing tooth, stares at me with wide eyes. "Who are you?" she asks.

The boy slings his backpack onto a table. "That's rude, Izzy," he says, his voice deeper than I'd expected.

"Izzy's just curious, Zach," RJ says. He walks over to the kids, gives Izzy a hug and Zach a fist pump. He takes their coats, shaking the wet snow from them. The floor becomes a puddle, but he doesn't seem to mind. As if reading my mind, he looks over at me. "It'll give me something to do later."

I grin.

"Kids, this is Ms. . . ."

"Hannah," I say. "Nice to meet you."

I shake their hands. They're adorable, but I can't help noticing the stains on the girl's dress, her hem that's come loose. They don't look as if they belong to the handsome vigneron dressed in Levi's and an oxford-cloth shirt.

"Tell me about your day," he says, tousling Izzy's hair, then turning to Zach.

They talk over each other, telling him about a reading test and the boy who got in a fight and tomorrow's field trip to the Native American Museum.

"Get started on your homework. I'll fix your snack."

"What time is Mommy coming?" Izzy asks.

"Her last appointment's at five."

He disappears into the kitchen while I try to figure out just who these ragamuffins are. I watch as they take their place at a table and pull out their schoolwork. His girlfriend's children, no doubt.

RJ appears five minutes later with a platter loaded with cheese and grapes and slices of fresh pear. He makes a show of serving them, placing a black napkin over one arm and bowing. They seem familiar with this ritual, and I don't get the impression he's doing it to impress me.

"Something to drink, my lady?"

Izzy giggles. "Chocolate milk, Your Majesty."

RJ laughs. "Ah, my status has been elevated. I'm royalty today?"

"You're the king," she says, her beaming face telling me that she, at least, considers him noble.

He delivers chocolate milk in two wineglasses, then becomes serious again.

"Finish your work before your mom gets here."

"What's the bonus today?" Izzy asks.

"Yeah," Zach says, opening his math book. "How about a ten-spot again? That was sa-weet."

"You never know," RJ says. "Maybe a ten-spot, maybe a turnip. I'll never tell."

The kids quickly turn to their work, and RJ returns to the bar. Instead of sitting on the ledge behind the bar, he pulls out a stool beside mine. I look at my watch.

"I should get going. You've got your hands full."

He throws up his empty hands. "You're not keeping me. Stay. Unless, of course, I'm keeping you."

"No."

He pours me a club soda and adds a lemon and a lime.

"Thanks. Just the way I like it."

He smiles, and whether it's the wine or the long, lazy afternoon, I feel like I'm with a friend rather than a stranger I met less than two hours ago. He wants to know what it's like to live in New Orleans, and he tells me he grew up downstate, his mother still lives there.

"She remarried and has a whole slew of step-grandkids. It's good for her, but I think my sister's a little jealous. My mom sees her step-grandkids more than she sees my niece."

"Does your mom get up here often?"

"Nah. She's like you. The place doesn't hold great memories for her." He peeks over at the kids. Zach is punching numbers into his calculator, and Izzy is coloring.

"Have you ever been to a vineyard?" he asks.

"Just as far as the tasting room."

"C'mon, I'll show you around."

I'm not prepared for the blanket of white when RJ opens the door. Huge chunks of cotton candy fall from the sky. I dash out the door forgetting that I'm wearing heels.

"It's gorgeous," I say, ignoring the wetness seeping into my shoes. I lift my face to the sky, stretch my arms, and spin. Flakes land on my nose, and I open my mouth to catch one.

RJ laughs. "Spoken like a true southerner. By this time of year, we're pretty sick of the stuff." He bends down and grabs a handful. "But like it or not, it's here, just as they predicted." He throws the snowball, aiming for a grapevine trellis. He misses, but he's got a good arm. *Good arm, good man,* my father would say.

"Come back inside," he says. "Before you freeze."

He's right. The short trench coat I'd packed was obviously the wrong choice. I'm disappointed, though. I feel like I'm inside a snow globe up here on this beautiful patch of earth.

RJ puts a hand on my back and guides me toward the door. "We'll save the tour for your next visit."

My next visit. I like the sound of that.

I'm almost to the entrance when my heel slips on the icy concrete. My right leg lurches forward, so that I'm nearly doing the splits. "Shit," I yelp, and hear the seam of my dress rip. RJ grabs hold of my arm just before I reach the ground.

"Oh, hey, steady . . . steady."

With his help, I pull my humiliated self to my feet. "Oh, now, that was graceful," I say, slapping snow from my legs.

He grips my arm tight. "You okay? I should have salted this area. Are you hurt?"

I shake my head, then nod. "Yes. I fractured my ego."

"The judges' scores are in. Nine-point-five. You gained an extra point for the split skirt."

His humor takes away the sting. I examine my new three-inch slit.

"Lovely."

"Looks like you've ruined your dress."

"Yup. And I just bought it last week."

"You know," he says, studying me, "sometimes you've just got to let yourself fall. It's when you resist, when you try to break the fall, that you get hurt."

I let the words wash over me, acutely aware of his protective hand still resting on my arm. I look up at him. His face is serious now. I notice the slight bump on the bridge of his nose, the shadow of a beard breaking through his olive skin, the gold flecks shooting through his brown irises. I have a sudden, almost overwhelming urge to reach out and touch the scar on the left side of his jaw.

The sound of an engine breaks the spell. We both look toward the driveway. A black SUV covered in road salt comes into view, pushing its way up the snowy drive. I tuck my hair behind my ear and wrap my coat tighter across my chest. God, I was seconds away from humiliating myself a second time. The wine has obviously gone to my head.

The vehicle rolls to a stop and a plump woman hops out, wearing a red jacket and bright pink lipstick.

RJ gives my arm a little squeeze before

stepping over to her. "Afternoon, Maddie," he says. He gives her a quick hug, then gestures to me. "Meet my friend Hannah."

I shake her hand. She's pretty, with flawless ivory skin and bright green eyes. And she's not the only one with green eyes right now. Every brain cell I possess is signaling that I'm being irrational. I have no reason to be jealous. I don't even know this man. And what's more, I'm in love with Michael.

"Come in," he says to Maddie. "Kids are doing their homework."

She answers by holding up a pack of Virginia Slims.

"Okay, then," RJ says. "Might be a minute. I have some bonuses to dole out."

"You spoil 'em, RJ. Keep it up and they'll get soft on me, think they're one of the Kardashians."

I don't know whether to follow him inside, so I stay outside with Maddie. I huddle under the eaves beside the door while she leans against her SUV and lights a cigarette, seemingly oblivious to the cascading snow. She's young — I'd guess around thirty. It's hard to believe she has a son as old as Zach.

"You a friend of RJ?" she asks, punctuating the question with a plume of smoke.

"We just met today."

She nods, as if finding a strange woman

142

here were typical.

"He's good people," she tells me.

I want to tell her that her endorsement wouldn't have mattered. I already knew he was good people. I could tell by the way he treated her children.

CHAPTER 11

It's nearly seven by the time the kids and their backpacks are loaded into the SUV and everyone has said their good-byes. Izzy and Zach wave to us as they pull away. RJ and I step back inside, and he closes the door. It's dusk now, but after being out in the frosty air, the rough-hewn room seems more cozy than gloomy.

"I really need to get going," I say, stopping just inside the door.

"Do you even know how to drive in this stuff?"

"I'll be fine."

"That's not a good idea. I'll drive you to your mom's. I'll swing back down tomorrow and bring you back for your car."

"Absolutely not," I say. "And besides, I'm not going to my mother's. I'll find a motel tonight."

He looks at me quizzically.

"It's complicated," I say.

"I get that." Something in his nonjudgmental tone makes me think he really does get it.

"Look," he tells me, "you'd be better off staying put for the night. I have no ulterior motive, I promise. I live upstairs. I'll sleep on the sofa . . ."

"I can't."

He nods. "Yup. You're right. Smart woman. But at least stay for a few more hours, give the road crews time to plow. I've got a couple of steaks, I can make a salad. Later, I'll drive you to town."

I'm tempted, but I shake my head. "It'll only get worse. I really need to go. And I can drive in this, I promise."

He looks at me and throws up his hands. "I can see I'm dealing with a hardhead. You win. I won't hold you here against your will."

"I appreciate your concern." And I do. I can't remember the last time someone's been so protective of me.

He stuffs his hands into his pockets. "Look, it was great meeting you. I really enjoyed just sitting here, talking to you."

"Me, too." I look around, as if it's the last time I'll see it. "And your place, it's beautiful. You should be really proud."

"Thanks. Next time you'll get the tour.

The vineyards are pretty spectacular when they're in bloom."

I blow air into my hands, teasing him. "And when might that be? August?"

He grins and shakes his head. "Southern girl."

His eyes are soft and locked on mine. Again I'm struck by a desire so strong that I cross my arms to resist reaching for him. I could take one step and I'd be in his arms. I'd lay my cheek against his chest. What would it feel like to have his arms close in on me, his hand stroke my hair . . . ?

Jesus, this is not a romance novel! We're just a couple of lonely adults. It's probably been months since RJ has seen a single woman in this northern no-man's-land.

He reaches into his wallet and hands me one of his business cards. "Here's my number." He flips it over and scribbles a number on the back. "This is my cell. Call me once you check into your motel. I need to know you made it safely."

I take the card, but it feels strange, as if I'm crossing a line. Why does it never seem the right time to tell him that I have a boyfriend? But that's ridiculous. I shouldn't have to tell him. He's just being a gentleman, after all. He wants to be sure that I make it home safely. I would sound insane if I blurted out that I have a boyfriend.

"Okay," I say. "I'd better hit the road."

"One more thing. Hang on." He hurries to the other side of the room and enters what looks to be a storage closet. A minute later he returns, holding up a pair of bright yellow Wellingtons.

"If you insist on leaving, I insist you take these."

"I can't take your boots."

"They came with the property. I've been waiting for someone like you to come along and claim them."

I lift my shoulders. "Just call me Cinderella." I immediately regret my attempt at humor. Cinderella got the slipper from the prince . . . and then she married him. Does RJ think that I think that he . . . Oh, God, I'm such an idiot!

I slide out of my heels and stuff my feet into the boots. They're at least a size too small, but he's right, they're better than my heels. "Thanks," I say. I spin around, modeling my new duds. I can only imagine what a sight I am, with my hair limp from the snow, my face barren of makeup, and now a pair of rubber boots beneath my torn dress. I wouldn't dream of letting Michael see me like this. "Where's the fashion police when you need them?"

But RJ doesn't laugh. He just studies me. "You look amazing," he finally says.

I gaze down at my feet. "You obviously have terrible vision."

"Twenty-twenty," he says, his eyes cutting into mine.

"I need to go."

He takes a breath and claps his hands. "Right. You stay put for a minute. Hand me your keys."

I watch from the window as he starts my car, then scrapes the snow and ice from the windows. This simple act touches me, perhaps even more than the food and wine.

"Okay," he says, stamping his feet outside the door. "Your chariot awaits. Call me as soon as you get settled."

I hold out my hand. "Thank you. You've provided food, shelter, clothing, and great company, all in one day. I really, really appreciate everything."

"It was my pleasure." He takes my hand in his. "I'll see you again."

He says it with such certainty I almost believe him.

I should have listened to RJ. I had no idea driving in this weather would be so stressful. Snow accumulates on my windshield faster than my wipers can shuck it away. A layer of frost builds where the blades don't reach, and I have to crane my neck to see out the window. A half hour into the drive, I'm tempted to turn back. But I plow on. The white snow reflects the moonlight, creating a shadowy landscape of blues and grays. I creep down the winding lane at the pace of a tortoise, and head south when I reach Peninsula Drive. Keeping my eyes peeled on the set of car tracks in front of my headlights, I follow the curve of the peninsula. In some places the wind has formed drifts, and there's nothing but a blur of white in front of me. I drive blindly, half the time I'm not sure I'm even on the road. My knuckles ache. My neck is in knots. My eyeballs sting. And I can't stop smiling.

It takes me almost two hours to make the trek back to town. I pull into the first motel I find and let out a huge sigh of relief when I shut off my engine.

The motel room is sparse but clean, and so inexpensive I thought I'd misheard the manager. "Prices quadruple in another month or so. For now, we're just happy to have business."

I don't know why I chose to call Michael first. Or why I washed my face and got into my pajamas before calling him. All I know is that when I finally decide to call RJ, I'm snuggled into bed with all the time in the world to talk.

I open my purse to retrieve his card. I check the front pocket, then the inside pocket.

"Where the heck . . . ?" I dump the contents of my purse onto the bed, becoming more frantic. It's not there.

I jump out of bed and dig through the pockets of my coat. "Damn it!" I push into my too-small Wellingtons and button my coat over my pajamas.

For fifteen minutes I search the rental car like a madwoman, before I'm finally convinced that I do not have RJ's business card. I must have dropped it somewhere between the front entrance and the rental car.

I rush back to the room and open my laptop. I search the vineyard's website, impressed when I see RJ's credentials: a PhD in plant science, numerous awards and patents pending. I find the phone number to the vineyard, but of course he doesn't list his cell phone number.

My hands shake as I punch the numbers into the phone. *Please answer. Please answer.*

"You've reached Merlot de la Mitaine."

Damn! The vineyard's automated message.

"For hours, press one. For directions, press two . . ."

I listen to RJ's deep voice until the last prompt is given. "To leave a message, press five."

"Uh, hi . . . this is Hannah. I lost the card you gave me. Just following your order. Letting you know I made it back to town. Because you wanted me to call, remember? Okay. Um . . . thanks. Thanks again."

Ack! I sound like a fool. I hang up without leaving my phone number. It wouldn't be right. I have a boyfriend.

I climb into bed and turn off the lamp, feeling like a kid who just realized that today wasn't Christmas after all.

CHAPTER 12

I wake the next morning, torn between heading back up the peninsula to let RJ know I didn't purposely blow him off, or going straight to my mother's. I opt for my mom's house, and maybe, just maybe, if I have time after I've met with her, I'll make a quick drive back up the peninsula.

Last night's storm has vanished, leaving behind a pristine, whitewashed day. But the weather forecast calls for another snowstorm beginning early afternoon. It's got to be tough living up here, and I feel a little surge of pride for my mother.

I try not to think about RJ as I drive, or my disappointment that I didn't get to talk to him last night. I need to forget about that nice vineyard owner. The harmless flirting was fun, but I have no business perpetuating it.

Birch Lake sits ten miles west of town, and I thank my GPS at every hairpin turn and snaking curve. It leads me straight to Dorchester Lane, a misleading name that sounds like it should be a cobblestone street in London rather than a narrow dirt road circling a small fishing lake.

Oak trees, still bare from winter, line both sides of the road like a crowd of cheering fans at the end of a marathon. The road hasn't been plowed, and I follow the tire tracks earlier vehicles have created. I cruise slowly, taking in the homes, and every now and then catching a glimpse of the frozen lake to my left. The houses create a checkerboard of old and new. Huge rebuilds belittle the quaint, sometimes tacky summer cottages I remember.

I'm confused when I pass what was once a home so tiny that I used to imagine seven dwarfs living there, but where now stands an impressive contemporary. I get my bearings a bit farther down the road when I spot a prefabricated double-wide trailer, exactly as I remember. I cruise slowly past an empty lot, then a patch of woods. Sweat gathers behind my neck. I'm close. I can feel it.

The car skids on the icy trail when I brake, and lurches to a halt. There it is. Bob's cabin. My heart thunders in my rib cage. I can't do this. This is a mistake dredging up the past.

But I must. If Dorothy's right, it's the only way I'll find peace.

My hands are clammy and I wipe them on my jeans, then check the rearview mirror. Nobody's on the road this morning. I rest my arms atop the steering wheel and gaze to my left. The wooden cabin looks miniature now, set in a pretty yard bejeweled with green fir trees and blue spruce. It's desperate for a coat of paint, and someone's covered the windows with clear plastic, for wind protection, I'm guessing. My stomach churns with anticipation and dread.

I sit for ten minutes, rehearsing what I'll say. *Hello, Mom. I've come to offer forgiveness.* Or maybe, *Hi, Mom. I'm willing to try to forget the past.* Or, *Mom, I've come to make peace, I forgive you.* None of the choices sounds quite right. I pray the right words will come when I'm face-to-face with her.

I'm staring at the house, trying to gather my courage for the reunion when the front door swings open. I crane my neck, staring, my heart picking up pace. Before my very eyes, a woman steps from the house. For the first time in sixteen years, I see my mother.

"Mom," I say aloud. My chest squeezes. I

crouch down in my seat, even though I'm sure my car is out of sight. She looks so different now. Somehow I expected to see the thirty-eight-year-old woman I last saw at my high school graduation, the one who was just starting to weather but still passed for pretty, even borderline beautiful.

But she'd be fifty-four now. Gone is the flashy woman with lips the color of raspberry sorbet. Her face is plain and her hair dark now, rolled into a lackluster bun. Even from here I can see she's still rail-thin. Please don't tell me she still smokes. She's wearing a green wool coat, unbuttoned to reveal a pair of black slacks and a pale blue blouse. A uniform, I'm guessing.

I stuff a knuckle into my mouth and bite down. *You're here, Mom. You're right here. And so am I.*

I put my car into gear and crawl forward, tears blurring my vision. My mother walks toward a brown Chevrolet parked in the driveway. She stops and brushes the snow from the windshield with her bare hand. As I pass, she looks over and waves, just another passerby to her. Her smile wrenches my heart. I lift my hand and keep driving.

I travel another mile down the lane before I stop the car. I lean my head back and let the tears roll past my temples. She's not a monster. I know this. With all my heart and soul, I know this.

I lower the window and breathe in the cold, biting air, fighting the impulse to race back to her now, throw open my car door, and wrap my arms around her too-thin body. Jesus, my mother is right here, almost within touching distance. The urgency to see her is sudden and fierce. What if she were to die, right now, today, without ever knowing I was here? The thought makes me dizzy, and I put a hand to my forehead. And then, before I have time to reconsider, I whip around in the nearest driveway and speed back toward the house. I need to tell her she's forgiven. I'll find the words, I'm certain now.

I slow the car when the property comes into view. My heart races and I take a deep breath. I can do this. The driveway is just up ahead. The brown Chevrolet is gone now and the house is dark. "No!" I cry. An overwhelming sense of despair comes over me. "I'm here now, Mom. Where are you?" I've let her down once again. But that's crazy. I didn't let her down. She let me down.

I peer down the lane, hoping to catch a glimpse of taillights or exhaust fumes, something that I could follow. But the bleak road looks as lonely and deserted as I feel.

I park on the opposite side of the road and step from the car.

My knees feel unsteady as I cross the road and enter the woods. I say a silent thank-you to RJ for insisting I take the Wellingtons. Brambles and branches poke at me as I push my way through the thicket. When I emerge a few minutes later, I'm standing in the snowy backyard of the cabin I detested.

The clouds have thickened now, and tiny snowflakes dance in the air. I gaze up at the old house, resting on a slight incline. The dark windows show no sign of life. Bob's not here. For some reason, I'm certain of it.

I wander down toward the lake and find myself at end of the dock. A pair of geese swoop down, creating a burst of spray on a patch of the lake's thawed surface before the water returns to its typical state of lull. I take a deep breath, then another. The tranquil setting seems to be an antidote for my unsettled state, and I find the sorrow, the old bitterness easing their grip on me. I study the frozen tundra, the wide-open plane of white ice. To my right, I watch a bird land on a barren, white-tipped tree branch. For the first time, I can almost see why my mother loved it here.

157

"Can I help you?"

I whip around, my heart tripping. A young woman stands at the other end of the dock. Her face is plain but pleasant, and her bright eyes take me in, curious. She's wearing a wool cap and a black down-filled parka. An infant bundled in a snowsuit is asleep in her front pack. She keeps one hand on the child in a protective way that both pleases me and disturbs me. Does she think I'm dangerous?

"I'm so sorry," I say, and make my way down the dock. "I'm probably trespassing. I'm just leaving."

I step from the dock and look away, uncomfortable, as I pass in front of her. I have no business being here, sneaking around when my mother's away. I hustle toward the woods, preparing to leave the same way I'd come. I'm almost to the opening in the hedge when I hear her call behind me.

"Hannah? Is that you?"

CHAPTER 13

I spin around. Our eyes meet. I stare at her blankly. Should I know this young woman?

"It's me, Tracy, from next door. Tracy Reynolds."

"Tracy. Yes, of course. Hi." I hold out my hand and she shakes it.

Tracy was ten that summer of '93, a three-year chasm that seemed vast and untenable back then. Almost every day she'd come to the door, inviting me to ride bikes or go swimming. The fact that I'd play with a ten-year-old illustrates how bored I was. My mother used to refer to Tracy as my friend, but I'd correct her each time. "She's not my friend. She's a little kid." Because having a friend might make this place bearable. And I was not about to let that happen.

"Of course I remember you, Tracy. You still live here?"

"Todd — that's my husband — well, he and I bought my parents' place seven years ago." She looks down at the baby. "This is Keagan, my youngest. Jake is a first-grader, and Tay Anne is in preschool."

"Wow. How nice. Keagan is darling."

"What are you doing here, Hannah? Does your mom know you're here?" I'm reminded of RJ, and our banter yesterday. If this woman were a glass of wine, I'd say she carries notes of curiosity and protectiveness, with a dash of resentment.

"No, I — I was nearby and . . . well . . . I just wanted a peek at the old place." I gaze up at the house, and watch a squirrel balance along a telephone line. "How is she, my mother?"

"She's fine. She works for Merry Maids, cleans houses. She's meticulous, as you know." Tracy laughs.

I smile, but inside I feel my chest squeeze. My mother is a cleaning lady. "Is —" I have a hard time spitting out the words. "Is she still with Bob?"

"Well, yes." She says it as if it's a given. "They moved up here full-time the year you left. You knew that, right?"

Did I know that? My mother would surely have told me. But did I listen? Or did I tune her out, not wanting to hear about her life with Bob?

"That's right," I say, irrationally miffed

160

that this woman knows more about my mother than I do. "They sold the place in Bloomfield Hills. He's still teaching." I say it with just a hint of a question, hoping I've guessed right.

"Goodness, no. Bob turned seventy-four last month. He never taught school up here. Honestly, I never even knew he was a teacher until a few years back. He's always worked construction."

A gust of wind comes from the north and I turn my face. "It's been a while since my mom and I spoke. She doesn't know I'm here."

"It's too bad about your falling-out." Tracy looks down at her baby and kisses his forehead. "She was never the same after you left, you know."

My throat tightens. "Neither was I."

Tracy tips her head toward a bench. "C'mon. Let's sit down."

This woman must think I'm a nut, showing up here out of the blue, tearing up like a two-year-old. But she doesn't seem to mind. Together we brush the snow from the concrete bench and sit facing the lake. The clouds roll by and I stare out at the water.

"Do you see her very often?"

"Every day. She's like a mother to me." Tracy lowers her gaze, and I realize she's embarrassed for the confession. After all, it's my mother she's talking about, not hers. "And Bob," she continues. "The kids adore him."

I feel my jaw clench. Does she let little Tay Anne near him? I wonder if she knows.

"He's still a joker. Remember how he'd tease us, call us boys?" She lowers her voice an octave in imitation. " 'What are you boys up to?' I had a huge crush on him when I was a kid. He was so handsome."

I turn to her, shocked. In my mind he's a monster. But yes, I suppose he was handsome, before he began to make my skin crawl.

"She never forgave herself for letting you leave."

I brace my hands on either side of the bench. "Yeah, well, that's kind of why I'm here. I'm trying to forgive her."

Tracy shoots me a look. "Bob never meant to touch you, Hannah. He loved you so much."

Jesus, my mother told her? And of course she gave her side of the story. I'm choked with fury, as raw as that summer night. "That's easy for you to say, Tracy. You weren't there."

"But your mother was."

Who the hell does she think she is? Suddenly I'm thirteen again, and I'll be damned if I'll let this little know-it-all make me feel bad. I stand to leave. "It was good seeing you," I say, and hold out my hand.

"I heard your father," Tracy says, ignoring my outstretched hand. "The following afternoon, when you were leaving."

My breath catches. As if in slow motion, I lower myself back on the bench. "What did you hear?"

She rubs circles on her sleeping baby's back. "I was standing in the driveway, and he was tossing your bags in the trunk. You were already in the car. You looked so sad. I knew you didn't want to go."

I try to re-create the memory. Yes, she's right. I was grieving that day, leaving my mother. My sadness hadn't yet hardened into bitterness and anger.

"I'll never forget it. Your dad said, 'When you've got someone by the balls, you squeeze.' That's exactly what he said, Hannah." She gives a little nervous giggle. "I remember because I'd never heard an adult talk like that. I was shocked. I didn't even know what he meant back then."

But she does now, and so do I. My dad was using the situation to his advantage, squeezing it for all it was worth. And in the end, the one being squeezed — and used —

was me.

Tracy gazes out at the lake and speaks into the silence. "I remember one time you and I were out there, on the dock, just like we were today. Except we had our bare feet dangling in the water. Anyway, Bob pulled up in his old fishing boat.

"He was so excited. He'd just caught a huge trout. *Check it out, Sister,* he said. He always called you Sister, remember?"

I give a slight nod, wishing she'd stop talking.

"He pulled this huge fish from a bucket of water in his boat and held it up for us. It was still alive, and the most gigantic fish I'd ever seen. He was so proud, like a schoolboy showing off the gold star on his paper. *We'll cook it up for dinner,* he said. Do you remember?"

The musky smell of the lake rises in my nostrils, and I can almost touch the cool spray from that old metal fishing boat as Bob pulled up to the dock. I feel the sun's heat on my already pink shoulders, and the warm breeze coming in from the east. And worst of all, I see the joy in Bob's face, the way his shoulders were set with pride as he hoisted the fish into the air, its silvery scales reflecting the summer sun.

I shrug. "Sort of."

"He ran up to the house to grab your mother and get his camera."

I look down at the sleeping baby, willing the images away. I can't bear to hear the rest. I want to tell her to stop, but my throat is too tight to speak.

"While he was up at the house, you jumped into his boat."

I turn away and close my eyes. "Please," I say, my voice thick. "Stop. I know the end of the story."

Bob came bursting down the hill five minutes later with his camera in one hand and my mother's elbow in the other. He chatted wildly as he walked, yammering to my mom about his big catch. But it was too late. The fish was gone. I'd tossed the bucket of water back into the lake.

I put a hand to my trembling lips, and feel a tiny fissure in my resolve. "I was such a bitch."

I say it more to myself than to Tracy. It's the first time I've ever acknowledged it, and it's almost a relief. Because it's true.

"Bob didn't miss a beat," Tracy says. "Told your mom he'd been careless, left the lid off and the darn fish had jumped back into the water." She smiles at me, and it's no longer a smirk of judgment. It's with humor now, and softness, as if she's trying to mend something in me. "He was protecting you, Hannah."

I put a hand over my face.

"The harder he tried to love you, the more you resisted."

I know that dance. It's the same one I have with Abby.

Tracy's baby starts to fuss and she rises. "Okay, little one, we'll be off." She puts a hand on my shoulder. "Feeding time. You're welcome to come over to my place to wait for your mom. She'll be home by three."

I swipe my nose with the back of my hand and offer a shaky smile. "No. Thanks. I'm good."

She shifts her feet, as if she's uncomfortable leaving me. "Well, okay, then. It was good to see you again, Hannah."

"You, too."

I watch her cross the snowy expanse toward the little house that was once her parents'. "Tracy?" I call.

She turns around.

"Please don't tell my mother I was here. Okay?"

She shields her eyes from a spear of sunlight slicing through the thick clouds. "Are you coming back?"

"I think so. Just not today."

She stares at me a moment, as if she's not

sure if she should say what's on her mind. Finally, she does.

"You know, Hannah, it's so hard to say 'I'm sorry.' Until you do. Then it's the easiest darn thing you ever did say."

I manage to wait until she's out of earshot before bursting into tears. She thinks I should be the one apologizing. And I'm not so sure she's wrong.

I linger in the backyard for another half hour, replaying Tracy's words, her stories, and my actions, all those years ago. What have I done?

You're thinking too much. I can hear my father's advice, just as he delivered it days after we'd left Michigan. I was struggling then, missing my mother. *There's a reason the rearview mirror is so small. You don't look back.*

Closer to the house, I catch sight of something jutting from a snowdrift. I trudge through the snowy yard, my eyes pinned to the site. It can't be. With each step, memories close in on me.

I reach the raised plank and brush it with my forearm. A shelf of snow falls to the ground. My God, I can't believe it's still here. My old balance beam.

The blue suede cloth Bob used to cover

the beam has disintegrated, revealing a graying piece of pine splintered down the center. Bob built it for me that very first week, when he saw me watching a gymnastics meet on television. He spent days gluing, sanding, and painting the boards. He anchored it with galvanized steel and two-by-four beams. "Give 'er a try, Sister," he said as he unveiled his gift. "And be careful. You don't want to break your neck."

But I'd be damned if I'd step on that stupid hunk of wood. "It's supposed to be four feet high," I said, "not two."

A gust of wind pushes in from the north and flakes of ice sting my cheeks. I run my boot over the frozen pine. Would it have killed me to walk across it, just once?

As if to atone, I hoist myself onto the weathered boards. Almost immediately my right boot slips. I land on my knees in the snow.

I fall back, and stare up at the sky. Overhead, the heavens twist and roil. I watch, wishing I could rewind my life, travel back in time. Because every belief I've held fast to for these past twenty-one years, I now question. And the very mission of this day — offering my mother forgiveness — suddenly feels all wrong.

Chapter 14

I head straight to the Garden Home Saturday morning. I need to see Dorothy. I need to tell her that I'm confused and no longer sure my mother needs forgiving. I'm surprised when I reach the porch and see Jade and her sister, Natalie, coming out the door.

"Hey!" I say. "What are y'all doing here?" The words leave my mouth before I have time to read their faces. It's their father.

"We're looking for a place for Dad," Natalie says, confirming my suspicions.

Jade shrugs. "We got the results of his PET scan yesterday. Chemo doesn't seem to be working."

"I'm so sorry." I lay a hand on her arm. "Is there anything you two need? Anything I can do for your mom?"

"Just your prayers." Jade shakes her head. "You'll never believe what Daddy said to me when we were driving home from his

169

appointment. He said, 'Jade, the night of your sixteenth birthday — was Erica Williams drinking?' "

I groan. "He's still talking about that party? Did you finally tell him?"

"I wanted to. I really did. But I just couldn't." Her voice is thick. "I looked him straight in the face and said, 'No, Daddy.' " She looks at me, then at Natalie. "He's so proud of his girls. I can't disappoint him now."

Natalie puts an arm around her sister, and I suspect they're both silently completing the sentence: *now that he's dying.*

Jade turns to me with a halfhearted smile. "How was Chicago?"

It actually takes me a second to think about Chicago. Right. The interview. I've been so consumed with thoughts of Michigan and my mother and Bob that Chicago seems incidental now. "I think it went okay. I'll tell you about it Monday."

"Did you tell Claudia you had an interview?"

"No. Just you. Everyone else thought I was taking a couple vacation days. Why?"

"The news was on while I was doing her makeup. They were talking about the blizzard in Chicago, and Claudia said, 'I hope Hannah's okay.' "

"That's weird," I say. "I'm sure I didn't tell her."

"Be careful. The girl doesn't miss a thing."

I find Dorothy in the parlor, seated at the piano playing "Danny Boy." I stand quietly and listen as she plays. I've heard her sing this song many times, but today the lyrics choke me up. It seems to be a song about a mother saying good-bye to her son, and wishing him a quick return.

It's I'll be here in sunshine or in shadow
Oh Danny boy, oh Danny boy, I love you
    so.

I clap. "Bravo."

Dorothy swivels on the piano bench, her face alight. "Hannah, dear!"

"Hello, Dorothy." My voice cracks and I wonder what's wrong with me. My emotions have been raw since my visit to Michigan. "Oriental poppies," I say. I bend down and kiss her cheek, placing the bouquet in her hands. As I do, I remember my mother's flower gardens, and the way she always compared her blossoms to the colors of fruit. "The color of Georgia peaches," I add.

She touches the velvet petals. "Beautiful.

Thank you. Now sit down and tell me your story."

Together we move to the sofa. We settle in beside each other and I smooth down a stray lock from atop her head. "First, tell me what's happening with Patrick Sullivan."

Her face blooms. "He's a real gentleman. Always was."

But he stole your essay, and your chance to study abroad, I want to remind her. I let it go. She's happy, I can tell. "Have the two of you rekindled the old flame?" I tease. "Is it better the second time around?"

She pulls her cardigan across her chest. "Don't be silly. He'd be sorely disappointed after all these years."

She's thinking of her mastectomy. We resist exposing ourselves for fear of disappointing. I squeeze her hand. "Not a chance."

"Now," she says, "tell me about your visit with your mother. Did you give her the stone?"

"I couldn't. It felt wrong." I tell her about seeing Tracy, and the stories of Bob, and the memories of that summer. "So now I can't give her the stone."

"And why is that?"

"Because I'm not sure she needs to be forgiven."

She looks me straight in the eyes, as if she can see right through me. "I never instructed you to grant forgiveness. I wanted you to make peace with your mother. It was you who decided to slap some halfhearted apology on the saga and call it good."

She's right. I never considered that the stone was intended for repentance. I bite my cheek. *Certain. Judgmental. Black-and-white.*

"There's more to the story, Dorothy. A piece I've never told anybody — not even Michael. But now I'm beginning to doubt myself. I'm no longer certain what happened that summer."

"Certainty is a fool's comfort. Learn to live with ambiguity, my dear."

I close my eyes. "I'm not sure I can. What if the story I've clung to for over twenty years is a lie?"

She raises her chin. "We humans have a wonderful trait — the ability to change our minds. And oh, what enormous power it gives us."

Change my mind, after all I've put my mother through? I lift a hand to my throat. My voice is choked when I speak. "But you'd all hate me if you knew what I've done — or what I might have done."

"Nonsense," Dorothy says and reaches for

my hand. "Fiona calls that owning our true selves, however ugly that may be. Relationships are all about being vulnerable, being real."

"I can't be real! I don't want to find my 'true self.' Because even if my mother could forgive me, I would never be able to forgive myself."

"Contact your mother, Hannah. Reveal yourself. Learn to love the ugly."

The Ritz-Carlton is packed with well-dressed donors Saturday night, all who've come to support the National Children's Alliance's Annual Spring Gala. Michael is impeccable in his black tuxedo, and he gushes over my red dress. But I'm not myself tonight. Instead of feeling proud, like I usually do when Michael and I are together, my smiles feel forced and artificial. It's as if I'm going through the motions, without any heart.

I tell myself it's because, for the first time in four years, I wasn't on the planning committee for this gala. I needed a break after chairing the Into the Light Christmas Ball. But I know that's not the real reason.

From across the ballroom I watch Michael do what he does best — schmooze. Even with people I know he dislikes. Every handshake and fist bump and pat on the back seems contrived tonight. I try to shake it off, but a cloud of melancholy trails me. I think of my mother's bare hand, brushing the snow from her windshield. Her sweet smile as I passed by. In my mind's eye I see the weathered balance beam and hear Tracy's words. I can't share any of this with Michael. He wants the smiling woman in the ball gown and strappy sandals, not the woman revisiting the tumbledown cabin wearing a pair of borrowed Wellingtons. And the truth is, so do I. How can I possibly put the lid back on this jar of snakes I've foolishly pried open?

Without warning, my thoughts travel to RJ and the easy banter we shared. Why is this stranger still creeping into my thoughts? Maybe it's because sitting in that tasting room on the leather barstool, sipping wine and talking to RJ, was fun. And I can't remember the last time I've had fun with Michael.

I finger my diamond-and-sapphire necklace and watch him chat with the new school superintendent, a single mom the city recruited last fall from Shreveport. She's tall and willowy, with a posture so upright you'd swear she was balancing the King James Bible on her head. She screams of self-assurance, someone without a ghost lingering in her closet.

I cross the room and make my way to them, chastising myself for daydreaming about RJ. I should be grateful for what I have. The man I'm dating is a catch.

"Hannah," Michael says, and places an arm on my back. "Meet Jennifer Lawson. Jennifer, my friend Hannah."

I take her outstretched hand, wishing that Michael had clarified that I was more than just his friend. But that's his way. He thinks the word *girlfriend* sounds juvenile. So do I, which is why I'd prefer the word *wife*.

"Welcome to New Orleans, Jennifer. I've heard so many wonderful things about you."

"Well, thank you. I've seen your show." She leaves it at that, without any editorial comment, and I naturally assume Jennifer Lawson's not a fan.

I smile and nod, listening to the two of them yak about the new magnet schools and the city's plan to invest in education. And all the while I cannot help thinking these two would be a far better match than Michael and me.

"Can I get you ladies a drink?" he asks.

And that's the moment it hits me. After all the wine-tasting and the soup and the breadsticks . . . I never paid RJ! I walked out of Merlot de la Mitaine without leaving so much as a tip. I'm horrified. I have never in my entire life left without paying a bill. RJ must think I'm either a complete mooch or a total ditz, and I can't decide which is worse. But I brighten when I realize what this means: I can contact him now. Yes! I have a valid, well-intentioned reason to look up the address of his vineyard and send him an apology and a check. In fact, it's the honorable thing to do. I begin composing the letter in my head when I hear Michael.

"Hannah, I take it that's a yes?" he asks, his brows raised.

"Yes," I say, putting a hand to my mouth in an attempt to tamp down my smile. "A 2010 Michigan merlot if they have it."

He looks at me quizzically, then saunters off to the bar in search of a wine I'm positive they don't have.

My apartment smells of bread Sunday afternoon. I've baked a loaf of cherry almond for work tomorrow, and two dozen rosemary asiago breadsticks for RJ.

After the last batch has cooled, I wrap the breadsticks in plastic, then slide them into a paper bag. I smile as I tuck them into a priority mailing box lined in bubble wrap and place the letter I've written on top. I'm practically giddy as I seal the package. Using my lucky fountain pen, I carefully address the label.

Merlot de la Mitaine
Bluff View Drive

Harbour Cove, Michigan

The bedside clock flips to 4:00 a.m., and I'm actually relieved to get out of bed Monday morning. It's my first day back since my "holiday," and Priscille, the station manager, has called a special department meeting to discuss a proposal. It doesn't take a genius to figure out what proposal she's referring to. She and Stuart have obviously gotten wind of my interview with WCHI and are calling me in to confront me.

I riffle through my closet in search of today's outfit. There's no way I can deny the Chicago interview, so I'll have to own it. I'll let them know Mr. Peters sought me out, rather than vice versa.

I choose a black Marc Jacobs suit, a white silk blouse, and a pair of three-inch heels that will have me towering over Stuart Booker. I need to appear confident today. I pull my hair into a tight clip and spray it flat, saving the sexy wisps for another day — or job. I don a pair of pearl earrings and spritz my neck with Must de Cartier, my least flirty scent. At the last minute, I decide to wear my glasses. Instantly, my girlish features become the face of a serious professional.

I'm the first to arrive at the station and head straight to the conference room, flipping on the overhead fluorescent lights. A rectangular table and twelve upholstered chairs on wheels take up the majority of the space. A whiteboard covers one wall, and a flat-screen television another. A black telephone sits on a corner desk, along with a cylinder of disinfectant wipes, a stack of Styrofoam cups, and the Keurig coffeemaker Priscille splurged on last fall. It is a space meant for decision making, not meal taking. But that doesn't stop me — especially when job security demands it.

I wipe down the table before placing a basket of my cherry almond bread in the center. Beside it, I position a bowl of wild cherry preserves and a stack of floral napkins. I fill the crystal pitcher I brought from home with fresh-squeezed grapefruit juice and stand back to assess. Nice, if I do say so myself. But will it convey to Priscille my competence and gratitude, or have I just set the stage for "The Last Breakfast"?

It's no surprise when Stuart arrives next, eleven minutes early. The man never misses an opportunity to impress Priscille. But I'm a fine one to talk.

My gut clenches when Claudia Campbell follows Stuart into the room. What is she doing here? And then it hits me. This meeting has nothing to do with the potential position at WCHI and everything to do with my precarious position here at WNO.

Since Claudia's arrival at WNO two months ago, Stuart has been gunning for her to cohost my show. He cites Kelly and Michael, Kathie Lee and Hoda . . . award-winning duos who bring great ratings. Priscille hasn't bought into the idea. So far.

Is that what they want to talk about today? Will Claudia be my new cohost? My hands shake as I set a vase of daisies on the table. I absolutely cannot let this happen. Being paired with a cohost is a thinly disguised demotion. It would be a huge red flag to WCHI.

Why am I worrying about WCHI? Who knows if I'll even get that job? I have far more pressing problems. I cannot . . . will not . . . lose *The Hannah Farr Show*!

Stuart's face is smug as he watches me watching Claudia. "Morning, Farr."

"Good morning, guys," I say, forcing a smile into my voice.

"Hey, Hannah. What a beautiful spread." Claudia looks over at Stuart. "You didn't tell me I was going to be fed."

"I'm full of surprises," he says.

And I'm doomed. Were the ratings higher last week when she substituted for me? Did the viewers love her? Tension knots in my neck. I'm busying myself by making coffee for Stuart and my future "foe-host" when Priscille arrives. Even in flats, she's six feet tall. She wears a black suit, much like my own. Her dark hair is knotted at the nape of her neck, mimicking mine. So why is it that she looks the picture of confidence, while I feel like a kid playing dress-up? I may as well have a giant nose attached to these black-framed glasses.

Stuart shifts into ass-kisser mode. "Good morning, Priscille. Can I get you some coffee?"

She lifts her WNO mug. "All set." She takes her place at the head of the table. Claudia and Stuart scamper, claiming chairs at her right and left. I slide in beside Stuart.

"I invited Claudia this morning to help us brainstorm," Stuart says. "She's full of great ideas, and let's face it, we need all the help we can get."

My mouth drops. "Stuart, I've been offering you story ideas for months. You shoot each one down."

"Your ideas are not commercial, Farr."

I lean past Stuart to catch Priscille's reaction, but she's preoccupied looking over a stack of papers.

"Hannah, your ratings were only slightly better last month," Priscille says. "I was hoping for a bigger bounce after your interview with Brittany Brees, but a bounce is a bounce. I'll take it. To sustain it, we'll need some killer shows." She folds her hands on the table and turns to Claudia. "So, Claudia, tell us about this fantastic idea of yours."

Stuart cuts to the chase. "Claudia scored an interview with Fiona Knowles."

Wait, hosting Fiona was my idea! Okay, so it was for another station, but still!

Priscille's face lights up like a Macy's parade. "This is big," she says. "Really big."

I need to say something, but what? I certainly can't tell Priscille and Stuart I proposed the idea for a job in Chicago I'm hoping to land. But if we host Fiona here and WCHI finds out, it won't be my original story any longer. They'll discover it was Claudia's story, and assume I stole *her* idea!

Claudia straightens. "Octavia Bookstore is

hosting Fiona Knowles on April twenty-fourth. I read about it in the *Times-Picayune*."

I clench my teeth. *Sure you did — in the article I'd clipped — you big snoop!*

"I knew we had to move quickly, so I connected with Fiona on Twitter. We've actually gotten to be pretty good buds."

Buds? Well, I happen to be an old classmate of Fiona's, and one of her original thirty-five, so take that! But I can't say this, either. The damn Chicago job has me in a stranglehold.

"Do you know that thousands of people are now sending virtual Forgiveness Stones on Facebook and Instagram?" Claudia says. "It's crazy!" She says *crazy* with three syllables — *ca-ray-zee* — and I cringe.

Priscille taps her pen against her coffee mug. "But a three-minute spot on the morning news is a goddamn waste. I see where you're going here, Claudia." She nods, her brain twelve steps ahead of everyone else's. "You're absolutely right. This interview is much better suited for Hannah's hour-long format." She points her pen at Claudia. "Good thinking."

"Uh, thanks." Claudia's smile twitches and she looks over at Stuart.

"Actually," Stuart says, "I'm suggesting Claudia guest-host this episode."

Guest-host? Alone? As in, hostile takeover? And I was worried about the two of us co-hosting! I turn to Claudia, but she looks straight at Priscille, refusing to meet my gaze.

"Just this one time, of course," she says.

"I — I'm not sure I like this idea," I say. Duh? Of course I don't like it. Who in their right mind would want the poised and polished Claudia Campbell dipping her French-manicured hand into their well? And she stole my idea! I look to Priscille for support, but she nearly glows with excitement. Oh, God, I need to stop this train wreck!

"I realize I went out on a limb when I approached Fiona," Claudia says. "I'm sorry if I overstepped my boundaries. It was completely spontaneous. She and I are both really excited about the interview."

In an instant I weigh my options. I need to preserve my job here in New Orleans at all costs. I cannot let Claudia weasel her way into my show.

A flash of genius comes to me. I'll contact Mr. Peters, tell him what's happened, and hope he believes me. I'll let him know I'm not sharing the tale of my mother's abandonment. That's their story, just as I'd promised. I've got another personal angle I can use here. Yes! I am holding the trump card in my hot little hands.

"My friend Dorothy Rousseau," I blurt out. "She received the stones a few days ago." I plow forward before I have time to think this through. I tell them about Patrick Sullivan and how he copied Dorothy's essay. "We could have an actual testimonial, you know, from someone who's been tagged to continue the circle. Both Patrick and Dorothy could be guests on the show."

"I like it," Priscille says. "These two could have a separate show, the day before Fiona's appearance. A warm-up act, so to speak. Patrick can talk about how it felt to live with his lie all these years, and Dorothy can tell us about the ability to forgive. People adore stories of redemption."

Stuart rubs his chin. "A two-part series, one a testimonial, prepping viewers for the second program, the big show, when Fiona appears."

"Exactly." Priscille is talking quickly, the way she does when she's excited. "We'll get the marketing team on it, have Kelsey create some buzz on social media. We don't have much time. The Dorothy/Patrick show will air a week from Wednesday."

"This might work," Stuart says, and turns to me. "You're sure these two will participate?"

"Absolutely," I say, completely unsure. "As long as I'm hosting."

CHAPTER 15

"Absolutely not," Dorothy tells me over the phone.

My stomach sinks. But I promised. And it would have solved everything. I stand behind my desk, the door to my office wide-open for all the station to hear. I was so confident she'd say yes, I didn't even close the damn door. I keep my voice low, hoping Stuart — aka Mr. Ears — isn't lurking in the hallway. "Just think about it, please. Run it by Patrick, see how he feels about coming on the show."

"How he feels about admitting he received a scholarship under false pretenses, live on air?" Dorothy says.

She's right. Who in their right mind would want to do that? Problem is, if I don't deliver, Claudia will host my show without me. And she'll be wildly successful. And I'll be . . . I massage my forehead, hoping to rub the image from my mind.

"Look, we'd be gentle on him. After all, he only copied yours so that the two of you could be together."

"Out of the question. I don't give a hog's hind end what Paddy did sixty years ago. And I won't allow his accomplishments to be marred. And that's exactly what would happen. Paddy would be vilified, and I'd come out looking like Saint Dorothy. It's an unfair setup."

"Okay." I let out a breath. "I can't argue with that. You're a good woman. I'll tell Priscille and Stuart it's a no-go."

"I'm sorry, Hannah Marie."

I hang up the phone. What a fiasco. And to top it off, I still have to e-mail Mr. Peters. My job here feels more precarious than ever, so I cannot blow it with WCHI. I stare into my computer screen, biting my lip. How will he respond when he hears we're hosting Fiona Knowles? I position my fingers on the keyboard.

Dear Mr. Peters,
As you are probably aware, Fiona Knowles is making the talk show circuit, appearing everywhere from *GMA* to *Today* to *Ellen*. She will also appear on *The Hannah Farr Show* on Thursday, April 24.

In no way does this compromise my commitment to WCHI, should we choose to film my proposal. Our show here at WNO will not include my personal story of receiving the stones and forgiving my mother. That's a WCHI exclusive.

My finger rests on the send button. What the hell am I doing? I'm doubling down, insisting again that I will host a show with Fiona and my mother, should I get the job. What happens if WCHI actually demands it?

"Hannah?"

I look up to see Priscille standing at my office door. Shit! I press send and quickly close my e-mail.

"Priscille. Hi."

"Just wanted to confirm the Patrick and Dorothy piece. Did you speak with her?"

My heart rushes. "Uh, I . . ." I shake my head. "I'm sorry. Dorothy isn't available."

Priscille's face falls. "You assured us you'd make it happen, Hannah."

"I know. I tried, but . . . look, I'm hoping to find a replacement. I *will* find a replacement."

My phone rings and I peek at the caller ID.

"It's Dorothy again," I say.

"Put her on speaker."

Something tells me I shouldn't, but I do as I'm told.

"Hi, Dorothy" I punch the speaker button and glance at Priscille. "You're on speaker."

"Marilyn and I would love to appear as your guests."

"Marilyn?" I remember the Forgiveness Stones Dorothy set aside for Marilyn. A doozy, she'd said about the secret she wanted to confess. But when I arrived the following day, Dorothy had only three sets of stones for me to mail, none of which was addressed to Marilyn.

"You sent Marilyn the stones?"

"No. I couldn't send them. This apology needs to be made in person. I've been waiting for the right time."

I feel Priscille's gaze on me. I hold my breath, half hoping Dorothy's about to tell me she'll make a live apology, and half hoping she won't.

"I think perhaps an apology on the air would be appropriate. On your show. What do you think?"

I think it would save my ass. I think it would be a great story. I think . . . it could backfire.

"Look, that's very generous of you, but a live apology is too risk—"

Priscille crosses the room. "I love it," she says into the speaker. "Dorothy? Priscille Norton here. Can you get your friend to agree to come on the show?"

"I believe I can."

"Perfect. Let's let her think she's coming on the show to talk about friendship. How does that sound? Then, once the two of you are onstage, you can make your apology."

Good Lord! She's turning the episode into a reality show, and setting up my dear friend for a horrible fall.

"I think that's fitting. Mari deserves a public apology."

"Terrific. I've got to run, Dorothy. We'll see you on the twenty-third. I'll leave you to Hannah now." Priscille gives me a thumbs-up before walking out the door. I lift the phone, taking it off speaker.

"Oh, Dorothy, this is a horrible idea. We're setting you up — and Marilyn, too. I cannot let you do this."

"Hannah, dear, I've been waiting nearly six decades for the right opportunity to apologize. You cannot begrudge me that."

I drop farther into my chair. "So what is it you want to apologize for?"

"You'll find out on the show, same time Mari hears it. And speaking of apologies, how are you coming along with your assignment?"

"My assignment?"

"Have you contacted your mother?"

Obviously, Dorothy has lost all sense of time. I just spoke to her about this Saturday. A pit forms in my stomach. Last night, as I lay in bed tossing and turning, I convinced myself once again that I'd been right all along. There is no need for an apology. I didn't do anything wicked. I was the victim once again, a role that's grown comfortable, where I know my lines and every nuanced gesture. But now, under these bright fluorescent lights with Dorothy hanging on the line, I'm questioning myself again. What, exactly, happened that night? And do I have the guts to find out?

"Um, yes, I'm . . . I'm working on it."

"So what's your plan? When will you see your mother?"

I rub my temples. This is complicated . . . way more complicated than Dorothy realizes.

"Soon," I say, hoping the vague response will suffice.

"I didn't intend to make this conditional, Hannah, but your reluctance concerns me. I assured your boss that Mari and I would appear on your show. Now I need your assurance that you'll contact your mother."

What? She's giving me an ultimatum. Why is this so important to her?

She waits silently on the other end of the line. Like we're two boxers in a ring, she has me cornered and the clock is ticking. The show is set to air in ten days, and even though I'm reluctant, Priscille is counting on her, and so is my career. I need to seal the deal. Now.

"Michael," I say, more to myself than to Dorothy. "It's time I tell him exactly what happened that night."

"Splendid, my dear girl! Telling Michael is a wonderful first step. And then you'll talk to your mother?"

I take a deep breath. "Yes."

When I make a promise, I do everything in my power to make it happen. Maybe it's because I let my father down all those years ago when I returned to Georgia without my mother. "Pull out all the stops," he'd told me. And I did. I truly did. And still, I fell short of getting my mother back home. So now, as an adult, I treat every promise as a contract, a way of making up for the huge pledge I defaulted on in my youth. Which is why I'm kicking myself for promising Dorothy I'd make peace with my mother.

It's Wednesday night, and Michael and I sit at a small table in the parlor of the Columns Hotel, listening to a local singer-songwriter. The musician strikes the last chord of his guitar.

"Thank you," he says. "I'm going to take a short break."

Waiters enter the parlor, and the room takes on the lively hum of table chatter. I sip my beer, mustering the courage to tell Michael about the Forgiveness Stones, and Dorothy's request, and the truth — or what I question is the truth — about that night.

I lean in and touch Michael's hand. "Dorothy thinks I need to make peace with my past." I tell him about the Forgiveness Stones and her insistence that I continue the Circle of Forgiveness.

"I'd say that's your call, not hers." Michael summons the bartender for another beer. "Let me guess. She thinks you need to forgive Jackson."

"No," I say, feeling a fresh sting at the mention of his name. "I've forgiven him."

"Then who?"

I slide a finger down my beer mug, creating a rivulet of water droplets from the condensation. "My mother." I look up and wait for the recognition in his eyes. Yes, he remembers the story, I can tell. He takes a deep breath and leans back in his chair.

"And what did you tell Dorothy?"

"I told her I would — reluctantly. I had no choice. She's doing me a huge favor by coming on my show. I owe her."

"Think it over, sweetheart," Michael tells me. "This isn't Dorothy's decision to make."

Michael is trying to protect me, just as my father did for half my life. To these two men, forgiving the woman who stepped out of my life without so much as a backward glance is out of the question.

"But ever since I visited Harbour Cove, I can't stop thinking about my mom. Which makes me feel like a traitor after all my dad did for me. He'd be so hurt if he knew I was questioning the past." I scoot my chair closer to his. "But Dorothy planted this seed, and I can't seem to stop it from growing. What if my father inadvertently forced my hand back then, you know, by making me choose between the two of them?"

"That seems childish."

He was childish, I almost say, before I'm smacked with shame. How can I be so ungrateful? "He needed me, Michael. Even though I was just a teenager, I was his caregiver. I made sure he got up every morning and got to work. I kept track of his practice schedule and games, I pretty much ran his life."

"His substitute wife," Michael says.

"Yes, which means he didn't want to lose me. It got easier when I started college and he met Julia. But what if he was wrong, or . . ." My voice trails off. I can't bring myself to say the word *manipulative.* "What if my mother was right and she really did love me? What if I'd jumped to the wrong conclusion that night and she knew it?"

"Wrong conclusion?"

I force myself not to look away. I need to witness his reaction. I watch as he lifts his head, then slowly nods. Good. It's coming back to him. I don't have to remind him of what happened that night.

"Your mother chose her boyfriend. Seems pretty cut-and-dried to me."

"I'm not so sure anymore. I'm beginning to doubt my story."

Michael's eyes dart around the room. "Let's step outside." He grabs my hand and leads me from the parlor, like a father with a naughty child.

The wide, wood-planked porch of the Columns is only slightly less populated than the parlor, yet somehow I feel safer out here beneath the dim glow of gaslights, less exposed. We stand at the porch's wooden railing. I gaze out at the pretty lawn and St. Charles Avenue beyond.

I swallow hard and turn to him. "That accusation I made against my mother's boyfriend, back when I was thirteen? I think I may have jumped to conclusions . . . the wrong conclusions."

"Whoa!" Michael holds up a hand. "Stop." His eyes dart around the porch, as if checking to make sure nobody heard. "Please. I don't need to know this."

"But you do."

"No, I don't." He steps closer to me, his voice just above a whisper. "And neither does anyone else. You can't seriously be thinking of exposing this tale, Hannah."

I turn away as if I've been slapped, grateful for the cover of evening sky. He thinks I'm a monster and that everyone, if they knew what I'd done, would think so, too. My gaze lingers on a young couple scampering up the sidewalk. The woman giggles into the ear of a stocky gentleman and has an air about her I can only describe as carefree. I feel a pang of envy. What must it feel like to be completely open and honest with someone, maybe even yourself? To live without that niggling doubt that you've made a grave mistake?

"I'm not sure what I did was wrong," I

say. "I'm not sure of anything, anymore. I want your opinion, or at least your support. Dorothy seems to think I must make peace."

I close my eyes and feel Michael's hand on my back. "You're being naïve, sweetheart." He wraps his arms around me, pulling me against him so that his chin rests on my head. "You might gain that relationship with your mother, but if word were to get out, you'd lose your entire viewing audience. People love nothing more than to see a celebrity fall from grace."

I turn to him, his gentle voice incongruent with his hardened face.

"This isn't just about you now, Hannah. Think about it."

My head snaps back. I don't have to think about it. I know what he's saying. We'd both be ruined if something scandalous leaked about me. I rub my arms, suddenly chilled.

"You need to stop second-guessing your decision. It's over and done with. This ugly family secret needs to remain buried, don't you agree?"

"Yes. No. I — I don't know!" I want to scream, defend myself, and make him listen. But the look in his eyes is a warning, not a question. And if I were to be totally honest, I'd admit that there's a small cowardly place in me that feels relief. I won't have to dredge up the past.

"Yes," I say, but shaking my head. "I agree."

CHAPTER 16

Some people hide their shame like a scar, terrified others will be horrified if it's exposed. Others, like Marilyn Armstrong, display their shame like a warning flag, announcing to people what they're in for, should they choose to proceed with the relationship. Like most southerners, Marilyn is a storyteller, and hers is a cautionary tale, a nonfiction exposé. It's a sliver of her life she calls her bump in the road. But I'm quite sure she's never gotten over the bump. I've heard her tell it many times, and she claims it's cathartic. But I have another theory.

I met Marilyn Armstrong a week after I met Dorothy. We three sat in the Little Room at Commander's Palace, eating turtle soup and drinking their signature twenty-five-cent martinis.

"I can't believe these are twenty-five cents," I said, fishing my olive from the glass. "I've lived in New Orleans for six months now. How could nobody have told me?"

"Used to be you could drink as many as you'd like. They've put a two-drink limit on them now. Probably because of us, Dottie!"

The two women laughed, the easy chuckle of childhood friends. Both New Orleans natives, the ladies shared more than a past. They shared a present, and a future. Dorothy stood bedside when Marilyn's husband died. Marilyn is godmother to Dorothy's only son, Jack.

Marilyn was a senior in high school back in 1957 when she met Gus Ryder, a twenty-year-old gas station attendant from Slidell. She was smitten by the older gentleman, so different from the boys she'd grown up with. Marilyn's father, a detective for the NOPD, sensed trouble. He forbade Marilyn from seeing Gus. But Marilyn was strong-willed. What her father didn't know wouldn't kill him. When she reaches this part of the story, she shakes her head at the irony.

Her dad was never around, except in the wee hours of the morning. He'd be none the wiser. And her mother, a fragile woman overwhelmed by five children, was a mere shadow in Marilyn's world.

And so it was that both parents were oblivious to Marilyn's daily rendezvous with her boyfriend, Gus. Each day she'd skip out at lunch and the two would spend the next forty minutes in the school parking lot, making out in the backseat of Gus's Chevy.

But lies leave bread crumbs of bad karma. Three months later, while sharing a Coke at K&B's soda fountain, Marilyn confided her worst fear to her best friend Dorothy. Gus had gone too far one day. She was six weeks late for her period.

"I'm a fool, I know. He didn't have a condom, and I didn't stop him."

Dorothy listened, horrified. Marilyn's world would change forever if she were to have a child now. Despite the low expectations for women in the 1950s, she and Mari had dreams. They were going to travel and go to college and become famous writers or scientists.

"Gus is furious. He wants me to . . ." She put a hand over her face. "He knows a doc who could help us —" Marilyn broke down, and Dorothy grabbed her in a hug.

"Slow down. You don't even know if you're pregnant. Let's take this one step at a time."

But the bad news was confirmed a few days later. Marilyn was pregnant, just as she suspected.

Telling her parents would be the hardest part. She was terrified that it might just be too much for her mother to handle. Lately, her mom had taken to long bouts of sleep in the afternoons, and sometimes she didn't come out of her room all day.

That afternoon, Marilyn's father picked her up after cheerleading practice. She sat in the passenger seat of his old green pickup truck, fidgeting with her class ring. She had to tell her daddy. He was the rock in her world. He'd know what to do.

"Daddy, I need your help."

"What is it?"

"I'm pregnant."

Her father turned to her, a sharp crease in his brow. "Come again?"

"I'm . . . Gus and I are having a baby."

What happened next was completely unexpected. Her father, the stern man who gave orders and offered solutions, shattered. His lip trembled, and he couldn't speak.

"It's okay, Daddy," Marilyn said, reaching a tentative hand to her father's arm. "Don't cry."

He pulled over to a curb and cut the ignition. He stared out the driver's-side window with his hand to his mouth. Every now and again he swabbed his eyes with his hankie.

She would have done anything — said anything — to give him peace.

"Gus and I have a plan. He's got a connection. We'll take care of it. Nobody needs to know."

That night, somewhere between two and four a.m., Marilyn's father suffered a massive heart attack. The ambulance was called, but Marilyn knew it was for naught. Her father was already dead. And it was all her fault.

It was an ugly, heartbreaking memory, but Marilyn never hesitated to tell it. She claimed that by sharing her story, she might prevent other young girls from making the same mistake. "I've got three daughters," she said. "If my story doesn't promote birth control, I don't know what will."

But I've often wondered if Marilyn's open secret might be a lesson to herself, as well, a self-inflicted penance. By reliving her shameful story enough times to enough people, she's hoping to be forgiven. The question is, will she ever be able to forgive herself?

I sit behind my desk eating an apple, skimming Fiona Knowles's book, *The Forgiveness Stones*. In one week from today, she'll appear on the show — which means we're only six days away from Dorothy and Marilyn's appearance. A dull throb kicks at my temples.

I know better than to ignore my instincts, and every instinct I possess is firing at the same time: *Do not allow Dorothy to apologize on live TV.* I should cancel. This scheme is too risky. But the devil perched on my shoulder is telling me that Dorothy and Marilyn will be terrific guests. They're both natural storytellers, and the women's lifelong friendship, Marilyn's story of shame, and Dorothy's hidden secret create a talk show trifecta.

So why do I feel so damn uneasy about this? Have I ramrodded Dorothy into being a guest? Or is my apprehension due to the fact that her appearance comes with a condition, a condition Michael has vetoed, just as swiftly as if it were an ill-advised plan from the city council?

Once again, I wonder if I'm using Michael's veto as an excuse. Regardless, I cannot allow Dorothy to humiliate herself in public. My stomach cramps, and I pitch the apple into the wastebasket.

I've begged Dorothy to reveal her secret before going on air. But each time, she refuses.

"Mari will be the first to hear it."

Is it possible Dorothy also had a pregnancy scare but never told her friend? Did she lose the baby, or worse, get rid of the child? What secret could be so shameful that she's never told Marilyn?

In the darkest recesses of my mind, I picture Dorothy revealing an affair she'd had years ago with Thomas, Marilyn's deceased husband. It's almost impossible to imagine, but what if she had? Dorothy has always spoken highly of Thomas Armstrong. She was even at his bedside when he died. And what about Jackson? Could he be the love child?

A shudder goes through me. For the umpteenth time, it's clear to me that Dorothy shouldn't be making her apology live on television.

And we're fooling Marilyn, too. Stuart agreed with Priscille, insisting we keep Marilyn in the dark. She thinks she's coming to talk about the importance of long-lasting friendships, which we will. But after a quick discussion, Dorothy will apologize for the burden she's been carrying. She'll offer Marilyn the Forgiveness Stone.

A nice, feel-good segment is what Stuart and Priscille expect. But what if Dorothy's apology isn't accepted, or what if the story isn't very compelling? I tell myself I'm too much of a control freak. It'll all be fine. But deep inside I know I'm fooling myself. I need to stop this episode.

"This is a bad idea," I tell Stuart when he comes to my dressing room with an expense receipt for me to sign. "I have no idea what Dorothy did to hurt Marilyn. Television is not the place to disclose secrets."

Stuart's props himself on the edge of my desk. "Are you nuts? It's the perfect place. People eat this stuff up."

I pull my lucky fountain pen from my drawer and take the receipt from Stuart. "I don't care how it's received by viewers, I want to know that it will be well received by Marilyn. I have less than one week to talk Dorothy out of this ridiculous stunt."

Stuart shakes his finger at me. "Don't even think about it, Farr. You may have had a slight bump in ratings, but the show is still on life support. This episode is about your only hope of resuscitation."

As soon as Stuart exits, I slump over my desk. I'm screwed! I can either lose my job or risk Dorothy losing her best friend. I sit up when I hear a knock on the open door.

"Hannah," Claudia says, her voice soft. "Mind if I come in?"

Damn. Since Monday's meeting, I've been avoiding her. "Sure," I say. "I'm just leaving." I place the fountain pen back in my drawer, and when I do, I spy the velvet pouch containing the pair of Forgiveness Stones. It feels as if the little pouch is in desk-drawer purgatory, begging to be sent on. I shove it to the far back corner and slam the drawer shut. I move past Claudia and grab my purse from my locker.

"I want you to do the Fiona Knowles show, Hannah. Solo."

I spin around. "What?"

"You do the show. Alone. I get the distinct impression I've stepped on your toes. I'm sorry. In New York it was so collaborative."

"Really? New York, the most cutthroat market in the world, was more collaborative? Your apology sounds more like an insult."

"No. I'm just saying, I'm not used to the way things work here. I moved too quickly, obviously."

"Did you steal my idea, Claudia? Did you open my file?"

"What?" She puts a hand to her throat. "No! Hannah, God, no! I would never do that."

"Because I'd already written a proposal to host Fiona."

She looks up at the ceiling and groans. "Oh, shit. I am so sorry, Hannah. No.

Honestly. I had no idea. You see, a few weeks ago the *Times-Picayune* ran an article about Fiona. I swear. I'll show it to you if you want." She gestures toward the hallway with her thumb, as if she's ready to lead me to her office.

I deflate. "No," I say, running a hand through my hair. "I believe you."

"That's how I found out about Fiona. I just wanted a fun little segment on the morning news. It was Stuart's idea to bring it to your show."

"With you as the guest host."

She looks down. "That was Stuart's idea, too. I can totally see why you're upset. You think I'm trying to steal your job."

I lift my shoulders. "It has crossed my mind, yes."

"I promise you, I'm not." She leans in and lowers her voice. "You can't tell a soul, but Brian just found out he's being traded next season. To Miami. Another three months . . . six max, and we're out of here."

She looks weary, and I think of my mother, and the forfeiture of roots, of control, that comes with loving a professional athlete.

"I'm sorry to hear that," I say. And I mean it. A gale of shame smacks me. Instead of welcoming Claudia the way I typically do with new colleagues, I've treated her as a

209

threat from day one. "We'll do the Fiona episode together, I insist."

"No, really. You take it. You're so much better at interviews than I am."

"I won't hear of it. We'll cohost, just as we'd planned."

She bites her lip. "Are you sure?"

"Positive." I take her by the arms. "And you know what else? I want you with me onstage when we film Dorothy and Marilyn."

"Really?"

"Really."

"Oh, thank you, Hannah." She throws her arms around me. "Just when I'm about to leave, I finally feel like I belong here."

I shake the rain from my umbrella Friday afternoon, before stepping into the Evangeline. Taking care not to slip, I creep across the marble lobby in my wet heels and stop in the mailroom, just as I do every day after work. I thumb through the envelopes on my way to the elevator. Bills, advertisements, bank statement . . . I stop midstep when I see it. A single white envelope with a double-M logo in the upper left corner. Merlot de la Mitaine. I opt for the stairs and dash up the six flights at record speed, forgetting all about my wet heels.

Without bothering to take off my coat, I slide a finger beneath the seal, vaguely aware of the gigantic smile that has taken over my face.

Dear Hannah,

Well, well, the woman can bake. Your rosemary asiago breadsticks were a huge hit. Customers devoured them and wanted more. As predicted, I didn't sell nearly as much wine as I did when serving those dried up strands of wheat I once called breadsticks, but what the hell? Life is a trade-off, don't you think?

Sadly, I had to tell those in need of a breadstick fix that the mysterious baker wouldn't let out her secret.

What I didn't tell them is that she also refused to let out her phone number, her e-mail address, or even her full name. Such are the frustrations of a single vintner in Northern Michigan.

But I like to think of myself as a glass-half-full guy. So, let me tell you how pleased I was to receive your letter. Actually, pleased doesn't quite capture it. More like stoked, juiced, thrilled, beside myself, manic, amped-up . . . all of the above. (And no, I did not consult a thesaurus for these adjectives.)

I laugh out loud and move to my favorite chair, never taking my eyes off the letter.

The morning after you left, I found my business card beneath the bench where you'd sat trying on the Wellingtons. If I'd realized it earlier, I would have hung out beside the office phone all night, hoping you'd do exactly what you did — leave a message at the vineyard. Instead, I sat up in my apartment, checking my cell phone every three minutes to make sure it was working, and beating myself up for being such an ass earlier. I shouldn't have asked you to stay. Please believe me when I tell you, once again, that my intentions were noble — well, mostly. More than anything, I wanted you to be safe. I hated the idea of you being on the roads in the storm.

And just so you know, I never once considered you a piker. I wouldn't have let you pay, even if you'd suggested it. That twenty-dollar bill you sent will be credited toward your next lunch at MM. Or, better yet, I'll take you to dinner. And just to up the ante and perhaps sway your decision, I'm even willing to splurge and throw in another $20.

The summer season officially opens Memorial Day weekend. We'll kick off the season with a jazz trio Friday and a terrific blues band Saturday night. It should be a good time, so please stop by if you happen to be in this neck of the woods. Or, please stop by any time, day or night, rain, sun, sleet, or snow. In case you couldn't tell, I wouldn't mind seeing you again.

Enclosed is another business card, with my cell number and e-mail address. Please don't lose it.

Until next time,

RJ

PS Did I tell you, I'm looking to hire an on-site baker? Think about it. The benefits are fantastic.

I reread the letter three times before placing it back in its envelope and putting it in my dresser drawer. Then I move to my calendar, calculating how long I need to wait before sending my reply.

CHAPTER 17

The coffee I drank earlier is percolating in my gut. I pause outside the stage entrance and say a quick prayer, as I always do. But today I make a special plea. *Please let this show go smoothly. Please grant Dorothy the right words to repent, and grant Marilyn the heart to accept it. Please help us set the stage for Fiona's big appearance tomorrow.*

I cross myself, wondering what else we might be setting the stage for. The end of their friendship? Will Dorothy let out a horrible truth that she'll forever regret, one that Marilyn won't forgive? *Dear Lord, forgive me,* I add preemptively.

I need to focus. Michael's probably right. Dorothy's "doozy" is little more than a silly harsh word spoken ages ago. Then how on earth will Claudia and I fill an entire hour? I need "killer shows," according to Priscille. I rub a kink from my shoulder, wondering once again why I ever agreed to this.

I peek out the entryway curtain. We have a full studio today. More than a hundred people have devoted their morning to *The Hannah Farr Show* — not including the television viewers. They've traveled miles to come here and be entertained. I straighten my stance and smooth down my skirt. I am going to deliver. Never mind my doubts. Never mind my instincts.

I step through the threshold onto the stage and plant a huge smile on my face. "Thank you," I say, gesturing for the crowd to sit down. "Thank you so much." The room calms and I launch into my typical preshow banter, my favorite part of the day. "I'm thrilled that you're here today. We're going to have a great time together." I take three steps down to the audience level, shaking hands and hugging those within reach. I wander up and down the aisles as I talk, my first chance to connect with my audience.

"What a great-looking bunch you are. Gosh, our audience is almost entirely women today. That's so unusual." I act shocked, though in truth women make up ninety-six percent of my demographic market. But today my little joke doesn't get the usual laugh. My anxiety has thrown me off-kilter. I shake it off and begin again.

"I see we've got one . . ." I look around at

the crowd of people. "Two . . . three men in the bunch. Welcome." This garners a smattering of applause. I sling an arm around a balding man wearing a plaid shirt and extend the microphone. "No doubt you've been dragged here by your wife, am I right?" He nods, red-faced, and the audience laughs. Good. They're warming up. Now if I could relax.

Stuart signals me to wrap it up. "Oh, darn. I guess I have to go to work now." The audience boos with good humor and I make my way back up onstage. Ben, the camera guy, begins counting down with his fingers.

"Are you ready for the show?" I ask the audience.

They clap.

I put a hand to my ear. "I can't hear you?"

The applause grows louder.

Ben's fingers show two . . . one . . . He points at me — showtime.

"Welcome to *The Hannah Farr Show*!" I smile at the thunderous applause. "I'm thrilled to have three special people here with us today. The first is our newest acquisition from New York City. You've probably seen her presenting the morning news, or perhaps featured in the *Times-Picayune*. She's the beautiful new addition to the WNO family and has graciously agreed to cohost today. Please help me welcome Claudia Campbell."

Claudia steps onto the set wearing a short pink dress and strappy sandals that make her legs look like perfectly shaped stilts. The crowd cheers, and I can almost see the ratings clicking upward. I smooth my navy jacket. Why the hell did I choose this frumpy suit? I glance down and spy a coffee stain on my silver blouse. Oh, lovely. I've dribbled.

Claudia thanks me, then explains the Forgiveness Stones phenomenon. "Tomorrow you'll meet the creator of the Forgiveness Stones, Ms. Fiona Knowles. But today, Hannah and I have two dear friends we'd like you to meet."

Hannah and I? Really? I didn't realize Dorothy and Marilyn were Claudia's friends. Jade's going to love this. But I tamp down my inner gossip girl. Claudia's the new kid and she's just trying to be part of the gang. I understand. She nods at me, and I take over.

"All I know about forgiveness," I say, "I've learned from my friend Dorothy Rousseau. Her compassion astounds me." I tell of how the Forgiveness Stones have become all the rage at the Garden Home. "It's all because of Dorothy. She could have opted out of the circle. She could have sent one pouch of stones to one person. Instead, she sent the stones far and wide, creating beautiful circles of love and forgiveness." I pause for effect. "Dorothy Rousseau is a woman of grace, and so is her lifelong friend, Marilyn Armstrong.

"Joining us today to talk about the power of friendship, please help me welcome New Orleans natives Dorothy Rousseau and Marilyn Armstrong."

The crowd claps as the two walk out, arm in arm. Marilyn smiles and waves at the audience, oblivious to what awaits her. I turn my attention to Dorothy, looking poised and dignified in her salmon-colored St. John suit. But her face is drawn and her lips pursed. Gone is the serenity I noticed in the last couple weeks. Again, my stomach clenches. Why didn't I put a stop to this?

The women take their places on the sofa, facing Claudia and me. We talk about their history and what their friendship means to them. I want to keep talking about good times and happy memories, but I see Stuart, from the control booth, twirling his index finger — his signal to move along.

I stare through Marilyn's wire-framed glasses, into her pale blue eyes. Has she always looked so trusting and innocent, or is it just today? My chest constricts. I don't want to do this. I should stop this, right now! Instead, I take a deep breath.

"Marilyn, Dorothy has something she'd like to share with you. I was reluctant to allow her to do this, but she insists on doing it live."

"It's an apology," Dorothy says. The tremor in her voice matches the thrum of my heart, our own two-woman band. *Don't do it. Don't do it,* I repeat silently. At this moment, I don't care that the entire show — and quite possibly my job — depend on her story.

She shakes her head and finally begins. "I did something that I am and will be forever sorry for." She gropes until she finds Marilyn's hand. "I have regretted my actions for over sixty years. But I've never had the courage to tell you."

Marilyn waves a hand at her. "Pssh. That's ridiculous. You're a wonderful friend — more like a sister, really."

"I hope that's true, Marilyn."

She uses Marilyn's full name, and I know what she's about to say is very serious. Marilyn senses it, too, I can tell. She laughs, but her foot bobs up and down. "What in the world, Dottie? We've been through hurricanes and miscarriages, births and deaths.

There's nothing you can say that will change that."

"This might." She stares blindly in the direction of Marilyn, her macular degeneration causing her gaze to be a little off-course. There's something in that faraway look that speaks of loneliness and heartbreak and regret, and my throat swells.

"You see," she continues. "I made a mistake — a disastrous mistake. You were a seventeen-year-old girl, terrified of being pregnant. I offered to help you." She looks out at the audience. "I thought maybe she was wrong, that she was worried for nothing. 'Slow down,' I said. 'You don't even know if you're pregnant. Let's take this one step at a time. Bring me a urine sample tomorrow. I'll give it to Daddy and he'll run a pregnancy test. Maybe it's a false alarm.' "

The hairs on my arms rise. I'd never heard this part of the story. "Dorothy," I say. "Shall we let you finish your story backstage?"

"No, thank you, Hannah."

"Dottie's father was an obstetrician," Marilyn tells the viewers. "The best in town."

Dorothy squeezes Marilyn's hand and continues. "The following day Marilyn brought me a Gerber baby food jar filled with her own urine. As promised, I took the sample to my daddy.

"Two days later, standing at Marilyn's locker, I delivered the bad news. 'You're going to have a baby.' "

Marilyn nods. "And I've always been grateful to the both of you." She looks at me. "I was a minor. I couldn't go to my family doctor without a parent. And back then, home pregnancy tests weren't reliable. It wasn't the news I wanted to hear, but facts are always better than hunches."

Dorothy stiffens. "But you see, I chose not to give you the facts. You were never pregnant, Mari."

I clutch my throat and hear Marilyn gasp. Murmurs rise from the audience.

"But I was," Marilyn insists. "Of course I was. I miscarried three days after the funeral."

"That was your period. My father suggested a simple vinegar-and-water flush. No need for a D and C. That's what I told you."

The audience chatters, and I see people shaking their heads, turning to their neighbors while cupping their mouths.

Marilyn's chin trembles, and she touches it with her fingers. "No. That can't be. I told my father I was pregnant. It killed him. You know that."

I hear a collective intake of breath from the crowd.

Dorothy sits upright, the picture of composure, except for the tears that pour down her wrinkled cheeks. I jump up and signal Ben to cut the camera, go to commercial break. He tips his head toward the control booth, where Stuart is spinning his finger, his signal to continue rolling. I glare at Stuart, but he ignores me.

"After my dad reported that you weren't pregnant, I took it upon myself to make you squirm for another day or two. I honestly felt it was for your own good. I believed that boy you were seeing was bad news. I wanted this to be a lesson for you. You weren't going to tell your folks until the weekend."

"My father died. He died! And you," Marilyn says, jamming a finger at Dorothy so forcefully that I'm sure Dorothy can sense it, "you let me live with that guilt for sixty-two years? I — I cannot believe —" She stops, shakes her head. When she continues, her voice is so quiet I can barely hear her. "How could you, of all people, be so cruel?"

People are shouting and booing now, like a bad *Jerry Springer* episode.

Dorothy covers her face. "I was wrong. I am so sorry. I had no idea it would turn out so badly."

"And you perpetuated the lie all these years?" Claudia asks softly.

Dorothy nods, and the heckling from the audience almost drowns out her words. "I planned to tell you, Mari. Honestly, I did. I decided it was best to wait until after your father's funeral."

Marilyn weeps now, and Claudia hands her a box of tissue.

"And then it . . . it just seemed too late. Time went on. I was too scared. I couldn't bear to lose your friendship."

"But it was a friendship built on lies," Marilyn says quietly. She stands up and looks around, as if she's dazed. "Get me out of here."

Someone claps, and soon the entire studio audience is clapping for Marilyn. Or, to put it another way, they've all turned on Dorothy.

"Mari, please," Dorothy says, her eyes darting around the room. "Don't go. Let's talk about this."

"I have nothing to say to you." Marilyn's heels click as she marches from the stage.

Dorothy claps a hand over her mouth and lets loose a guttural moan, fierce and primal. She pulls herself to her feet, blindly roaming the stage for the exit. She moves in the direction of her friend's voice, no doubt hoping that when she gets there she'll find forgiveness.

But Marilyn is gone. And so is their lifelong friendship. All thanks to a simple, heartfelt apology.

Michael's right. Some secrets are better left buried.

CHAPTER 18

I don't wait for the show to end. I don't wait for a commercial break. I rush to Dorothy, grab her hand, and lead her offstage. I hear Claudia's voice behind me, trying to control the chaos. She'll have to improvise the last ten minutes. Right now I don't give a damn about my show.

"It's okay," I say to Dorothy. "You are going to be okay." I usher her back to my dressing room and settle her on the sofa. "Sit here," I say. "I'll be right back. I need to find Marilyn."

I dash down the hall and reach the lobby just in time to see Marilyn pushing through the glass doors.

"Marilyn! Stop."

She ignores me and heads straight toward a waiting taxi. I dash after her.

"I am so sorry about what happened," I say, trotting behind her. "All of it. I didn't know."

Marilyn turns to me when she reaches the cab. Her thin lashes are spiked with tears, but her eyes are narrowed and hold a ferocity I've never seen.

"How could you?"

I take a step back, her very words, her accusation, knocking me off-balance.

The driver opens the back door, and Marilyn steps into the cab. I look on as the taxi speeds away, then double over with shame. In so many ways, for so many instances, I wonder just that: How could I?

I'm in tears when I return to my dressing room. I close the door and find Dorothy sitting on the sofa staring at the wall, just as I'd left her. Surprisingly, she's not crying. I take a seat beside her and reach for her hand.

"Are you okay?" I say, rubbing her soft skin. "I shouldn't have let you do that on air. I knew it was risky. I allowed you —"

"Nonsense," she says. Her voice is flat and calm. "It's called justice. I deserve Mari's wrath. And that drubbing from the crowd, and from all of our friends once word gets out? It's exactly what I need. Anything less would be unjust."

"How can you say that? You are a good person, Dorothy. The best. What you did when you were a teenager wasn't cruel. Sure it was a mistake — a big mistake — but you had good intentions. Marilyn will come to realize that."

She pats my hand, as if I were a naïve child. "Oh, sweetheart, don't you see? It's not the lie. It's never the lie. It's the cover-up that ruins us."

I feel the blood rush past my temples. She's right. She's absolutely right. If anyone should know about the consequences of covering up the truth, it's me.

Dorothy seems strangely at ease when we arrive back at the Garden Home. I settle her into the sunroom with her audiobook.

"Shall I get your phone? You probably want to call Marilyn."

She shakes her head. "Too soon."

What a lesson in wisdom and patience. If it were me, I wouldn't be able to resist hounding Marilyn, begging her forgiveness. But Dorothy seems to know that her friend needs time to heal. Or, perhaps, it's Dorothy who needs time to heal from her own self-inflicted wounds. If only I'd stopped her.

Just as I'm leaving, Patrick Sullivan shows up at Dorothy's side.

"I watched the show," he tells her.

Dorothy turns away. "Oh, Paddy. Now you know why I never searched you out, after you left me. I never felt worthy of you."

He perches on the edge of her chair and takes her hands. "No one is born an audacious person. One becomes audacious."

From where I stand, just outside the sunroom, I watch Mr. Sullivan lean over and kiss Dorothy's forehead. "You're an audacious lass, Dort. I love ya for it!"

She huffs. "How can you say that, knowing what I did? I never wanted you to see that part of me."

"An apology doesn't erase our blunders. It's more like a strikethrough. We always know the mistake is there, just beneath the black line. And if we search for it, we can still see it. But over time, our eyes begin to look past the error, and we only see the new message, clearer this time, and more thoughtfully penned."

An hour later, I scurry up the sidewalk toward the WNO entrance and catch sight of Stuart staring down at me from his second-floor window, no doubt wondering where I've been. What did he expect, that I'd let Dorothy fend for herself, that I'd point her to the east and expect her to find her way home after what we'd put her through? I seethe.

But my anger is misguided. It's not Stuart's fault that I made a mess of things today. I am the one responsible for ruining Dorothy and Marilyn's lifelong friendship. I should have insisted we cancel the show. Why didn't I trust my gut? I always get into trouble when I ignore my instincts.

Or do I? Was I right to trust my instincts back in the summer of '93?

I push back all thoughts of my mother and barrel down the hall to my dressing room. I don't have the luxury of wallowing in what-ifs today. Tomorrow we host Fiona Knowles.

I sit in my makeup chair while Jade peels a strand of long black lashes from my left eye. She started using the lash extensions a month ago, when she noticed my natural lashes thinning. Just another reminder that I'm not who I pretend to be. I'm a laminate, not a hardwood.

Across from me, Claudia sits with a notebook and pen, taking notes as I explain the format for tomorrow's show.

"I'll give a teaser for the Forgiveness Stones episode," I say, "then we'll go straight to break. When we come back, I'll introduce Fiona. You and I will sit facing her. That's when you'll take the lead with the interview. Sort of the opposite of what we did today."

In the mirror's reflection, Jade shoots me a look of warning.

"Are you sure?" Claudia asks. "I can just sit quietly and offer tidbits here and there."

"Now, that sounds like a plan," Jade says, dipping her finger into a jar of cream. She's still convinced Claudia is after my job. But I don't believe it. Ever since we had our heart-to-heart last week, Claudia's been sweeter than a pecan pie. She's perfectly willing to let me be the lead interviewer in the Forgiveness Stones episode, but truth is, I'm relieved I don't have to talk about the stones. Especially when I'm a recipient who has yet to complete her circle.

"No," I say, locking eyes with Jade in the mirror. "You're the one who knows Fiona. This will be your interview."

"Knock, knock," Stuart says, stepping into the room. He's carrying a clipboard. "Great show, Farr. The ladies knocked it out of the park."

I look at him, sure he's being sarcastic. I'm stunned when I realize he's serious. "Stuart, the show was a disaster. A lifelong friendship is in ruins."

He shrugs. "Not according to what matters. Kelsey says we're showing an uptick on social media. Tweets, mostly, and a couple hundred new Facebook likes." He hands me the clipboard. "I need some signatures here."

I yank the clipboard from his clutches. This man has no conscience. He doesn't give a damn about Dorothy or Marilyn or even me.

He pats his breast pocket. "Damn. Got a pen?"

"Top drawer," I tell him, and point to my desk. "The Caran d'Ache, please."

"You and your damn pen." He rifles through my desk. "Can't you just use a roller-ball?" He tosses a tube of ChapStick on the desktop. "Where is it, Farr?"

Thankfully, Claudia goes to help him. I close my eyes while Jade peels off the second lash. "Believe me, I'd never spend so much on a pen," I tell Stuart. "Michael surprised me with it when we took second place in the —"

"Ho-ly shit!"

I open my eyes. From the mirror's reflection, I see Claudia and Stuart stooped before my open desk drawer. In Claudia's hand, I spy the velvet pouch. The Forgiveness Stones.

"Oh, fuck," I say, and clap a hand over my mouth.

"Jesus, Farr, you've got the stones!"

I leap from my chair, but Stuart's already

231

snatched the little pouch from Claudia.

"And just in time for tomorrow's show!" he says, holding it aloft.

"Give me that, Stuart."

"What'd you do, Farr? What's the shameful secret you're afraid of exposing? Because anything short of murder will make for another spectacular episode."

"I didn't do a thing. Which is why I haven't continued the circle. I have nothing to atone for." As I say the words, I feel my face flush. I wouldn't dream of telling him my secret. And even if I wanted to, Michael has forbidden it.

"Get over yourself, Farr. Spill the beans."

"Just forget about it. They're not my stones."

"You cheated on Michael?"

"No! God, no!"

"You're the one who keyed Priscille's Beemer."

I shoot him a look. "Right."

"It's a family secret, isn't it?"

I open my mouth to protest, but the words won't come.

His eyes are victorious. "Bingo!"

I yank the pouch from his hands. "Look, I had a falling-out with my mother years ago. It's ugly and messy and I refuse to talk about it."

"Michael know about it?"

"Of course he does," I say, appalled at his nerve. "I won't do this, Stuart. I will not sacrifice my privacy for ratings. My past is not open for public consumption. End. Of. Story."

He snags the pouch from me. "We'll see about that."

CHAPTER 19

I nearly run to catch up with Stuart, pleading with him to give me the pouch. He ignores me and barges into Priscille's office.

She sits behind her walnut desk, simultaneously talking on the phone and typing an e-mail. My head feels light. Oh, damn. I'm going to pass out, right here in my boss's office.

"You're never going to believe this," Stuart says, waving the pouch in front of Priscille.

"I'm sorry, Thomas. Can I call you back?" She hangs up the phone and snaps at Stuart. "What is it?"

"Hannah received the stones. She's got some family drama or whatnot with her mother. Could the timing be more perfect?"

Priscille's face softens into a smile. "You don't say."

"This is it, the up-close-and-personal moment we've been hoping for!"

"Stop," I say. "You're not listening to me. I don't want to talk about this on air. It's private. Didn't you see what just happened to my friends?"

He ignores me. "This will be huge for our ratings. You've said it yourself, Priscille, one of Hannah's biggest flaws is that she doesn't let people in."

My mouth drops. Did she really say that? Sure, I'm a little reserved, but nobody would say I am distant.

"You're distant, Hannah," Priscille says. "Face it. You're a locked box, a bud that won't blossom."

"Clamped tighter than the knees of a nun," Stuart says.

I shoot him a dirty look, but Priscille doesn't seem to notice. She comes around to the other side of her desk and paces, tapping a pen in the palm of her hand. "Remember when Oprah walked out on-stage with a wagon full of fat? When Katie Couric had a colonoscopy live, on air? Open-book celebrities attract people. Why? Because they're courageous, they're vulnerable." She stops and turns to me. "And vulnerability, my dear, is that magic ingredient that separates those we like from those we love."

Stuart nods. "Exactly right. Talk about

your mother and your falling-out, whatever the hell it was. Tell your viewers how hurt you were. Shed a few tears. Let them know how freeing it felt when you finally forgave her."

But I haven't forgiven her. In fact, I'm no longer sure she needs forgiving. And I'm not going to dig up the past to find out, for my New Orleans audience, or WCHI, or any other station. Michael's right. My family secret will remain buried. Dorothy's revelation made that clearer than ever.

Priscille grabs a pad of paper. "They'll want to know what you did with the other stone. Do you have a good story?"

I feel like a piñata being poked, one that will soon come tumbling down. All my insides will spill from me. And instead of sweet treats, the world will see the rancid ugliness I've been hiding.

I put my hands to my head. "Please! I can't do this!" I look from Stuart to Priscille. "I won't do this. I *am* a private person. You're right. And there's no way I will air my laundry in front of thousands of viewers. It's not my style. And even if it was, I'm dating the mayor, people."

Stuart is three minutes into a riff about all the reasons I need to buck up and take one for the team when Priscille finally places a hand on his arm. "Let it go, Stuart. We can't force Hannah to be someone she's not." Her voice becomes soft and unsettlingly calm. She returns to her seat behind the desk and taps on her computer screen, signaling that the meeting is over.

I want to explain myself, tell her I am willing to do anything, *anything,* but talk about my past. But of course, she wouldn't understand unless I told her why.

Stuart tosses me the pouch of stones. As I turn to leave, Priscille delivers her knockout punch. "Claudia's cohosting tomorrow, right?"

I slam the dressing room door. "It was a threat!" I say. I step over to the sink, where Jade stands, rinsing out her makeup brushes. "Priscille and Stuart don't give a damn about my privacy. It's all about ratings."

Jade tips her head toward the back of the room, reminding me that we're not alone. I turn to see Claudia, still sitting on the sofa in the back corner, waiting to finish our discussion of tomorrow's show. Right now I'm so furious I don't care if she hears my rant.

"They say I'm distant. Can you believe that?"

Jade turns off the faucet and grabs a towel. "Hannabelle, when's the last time you answered a personal question from a viewer? Or let anyone besides me see you without makeup?"

My hand goes to my cheek. "Yeah? So I like to look presentable. What's wrong with that?"

"Makeup is your shield. For a public person, you're pretty damn private. Just sayin'." She pats my shoulder and reaches for her purse. "I'm off to lunch. Want anything?"

Yes! A fried oyster po'boy and a praline pecan pie. "No, thanks."

"Stay in trouble," she says, and closes the door behind her.

I grab two fistfuls of hair and groan. "What am I going to do? I need this job." I flinch when I feel someone touch my arm. Claudia.

"Oh, hi." I straighten and tuck my hair behind my ears.

"I'm so sorry, Hannah," she says. "I don't know what to say. I feel like this is my entire fault for suggesting we host Fiona in the first place. I'm so stupid! When I pulled the pouch from your desk drawer, it didn't even register. I had no idea it held the stones."

I study her face, her pink cheeks and her

blue eyes, wide and innocent. Beneath a thick layer of foundation, I spy a tiny scar on her chin. Did she have a childhood accident? Fall off a bike, maybe, or out of a tree? She touches it with her polished fingertips, and I look away, embarrassed that I'd been staring.

"It's gross, I know. Damage from my headgear. My orthodontist had me wear this wire-and-elastic contraption around my face. After a month, he discovered it was too tight. By then the damage was done. Permanently. My mother was livid. That's when she stopped entering me in pageants." She gives a tight little laugh. "Actually, it was a relief."

So Claudia was a child beauty pageant contestant — her mother's dream, not hers. "It's hardly noticeable," I say. "You're gorgeous."

But still her fingers hover over the scar. My heart swells with affection. Despite her perfectly ironed hair and flawless spray tan, Claudia seems real now. Someone with scars and insecurities. Someone I can relate to. Is this what Priscille was talking about when she spoke of vulnerability?

I take her arm and lead her to the sofa. "None of this is your fault, Claudia. It's these stupid stones. Maybe Jade's right." I blow out a stream of air. "I'm scared. I can't talk about the stones. Because if people knew the real me, they'd be horrified." I hurl the pouch into the metal wastebasket, and it lands with a thud. "Fiona's damn stones are supposed to help us embrace our ugliness. Instead, I'm more concealed than ever."

Claudia touches her scar again, and I wonder if she realizes I'm talking figuratively, not literally. "If forgiveness were easy," she says, "we'd all be sleeping like babies."

"Yeah, well, even if I wanted to seek forgiveness, I've been forbidden. My story is so appalling that my boyfriend is afraid it would ruin me — and him."

"That's cold," Claudia says. "Believe me, I get it. I really do. I did something really shitty to my best friend. To this day, I've never told anyone, including her. So don't feel bad. I couldn't tell my secrets on air, either."

I study her. "Thanks. Really. Sometimes I feel like I'm the most evil person alive, that nobody else has ever made such a horrid mistake."

"Nope," Claudia says. "I'm right there with you, my friend." She takes a deep breath and closes her eyes, as if the memory is still painful. "It was three years ago. Lacey — that's my best friend — was about to get married. Four of us girls took a final singles trip to Mexico.

"The first day we were there, Lacey met this guy at the pool, Henry from Delaware. That's what we called him — Henry from Delaware. He was adorable, he really was. To make a long story short, she fell for him."

"But she was already engaged."

"That's right." Claudia adjusts herself on the sofa so that she's facing me. "I thought it was one of those vacay-dates, you know, when you're away and everyone you meet is suddenly über-exciting. We were in Cancún for four days, and she and Henry spent two of them together. I was so angry. Lacey was finally getting married, like she'd always wanted. Mark, her fiancé, was a solid guy, and he adored her. And there she was, about to risk it all with this Henry from Delaware — some guy she barely knew.

"I like to think I was protecting Lacey, but who knows? Maybe I was jealous. The night before we were leaving, Lacey told me she was having second thoughts about Mark."

She leans in. "Hannah, I'm telling you, Lacey was the poster child for making bad decisions. I had to help her."

She pauses then, as if mustering the courage to finish her story. I hold my breath, hoping she will.

"It was a hot night, and we were crammed into this crowded bar called Yesterdays. Lacey and our other two friends were out on the dance floor. It was just Henry from Delaware and me, standing alone at the bar.

"He was charming. I could see why Lacey was tempted. He started asking me all kinds of questions about Lacey. He was really into her, I could tell. And of course I knew she liked him, too, so much that she was about to throw her life overboard for him. This was a disaster. I could not let her screw it up with Mark. I had to do something to stop this train wreck, right?"

"You did," I say, wondering if she can hear that my phrase is one part statement, two parts question.

"So I told him the truth. I told him all about her engagement, something Lacey made us swear we wouldn't tell. I told him what a great guy Mark was, how Lacey adored him, how they'd invited over four hundred guests to the wedding. I even pulled out my phone and showed him pictures of Lacey trying on wedding dresses.

"He was devastated, I could see it. I'd probably said enough, but just to be sure, I went one step further. I lied and told him that Lacey had come to Mexico with a mission. She'd bet us that she could make someone fall in love with her one last time. He was just an ego boost for her, a conquest, that's all."

I cover my mouth.

"I know, right? Henry's face . . . I'll never forget it. It was the purest look of heartbreak I'd ever seen."

"So what happened?"

"He wanted to confront Lacey, but I talked him out of it. She'd only deny it, I said. The best revenge was to walk away, without giving her a reason."

"And he did?"

"Yup. He plopped a twenty-dollar bill on the bar and left."

"They never said good-bye?"

"Nope. We were out of the country, so nobody was using cell phones. When she finally came off the dance floor, I told her I'd seen Henry chatting it up with some girl at the bar. She was crushed.

"I honestly thought I'd done the right thing. Sure, Lacey was bummed, but she'd get over it in a day or two. She had Mark, right? I assured her — and myself — that it was all for the best. I was saving her.

"But she cried all the way home. I think

she really loved this guy."

"So what did you do?"

"By then it was too late. Even if I wanted to, I had no way of contacting Henry. So I kept it a secret. I've never told a single person until now, with you." Her eyes are heavy, but she smiles at me. I squeeze her arm, my heart breaking for her.

"Did she marry Mark?"

"She did. It lasted sixteen months. To this day, I swear she pines for Henry."

Poor Claudia. What a burden. I pull her into a hug. "Hey, your intentions were pure. We all make mistakes."

She covers her face with her hands and shakes her head. "Not like mine. Not mistakes that ruin lives."

It's not the lie. It's never the lie. It's the cover-up that ruins us. I sit upright. "So find him, this Henry! I'll help you." I leap from the sofa and head to my desk. "We're journalists, after all. We'll do a search for twentysomething Henrys in Delaware." I grab a notepad and a pen. "We'll post about it on Facebook and Instagram. You've got pictures, right? We'll find him, and Lacey and Henry from Delaware will live happily ever . . ."

She's looking at her fingernails, whether bored or nervous or scared, I couldn't say.

But still I continue. "Don't worry, Claudia. It's not too late. And just think how great you'll feel when your secret is out in the open." As I say the words, I wonder if I'm talking to her or to myself.

Eventually she nods. "Sure. Just let me think about it for a bit, will you?"

And there it is. Claudia Campbell is just like me. She, too, has stuffed her inner demon behind the trapdoor. And like me, she's terrified of what might happen if that door should spring open.

Maybe it's Claudia's tears. Maybe it's her scar, or Priscille's voice telling me I am distant. Or maybe it is just a moment of weakness. I only know that for whatever reason, I choose this person, this moment, to pry open my trapdoor.

"Wait until you hear what I did."

CHAPTER 20

It happened in July, on a whim, something I did impulsively, without malice or premeditation. At least I can say that.

We'd gone up north, a phrase Michiganders use when talking about the fingertips of the mitten-shaped state. Bob owned a tiny cabin in Harbour Cove, a sleepy old fishing village on the shores of Lake Michigan. Miles from town, his rustic place sat on a murky lake meant for fishing, not swimming. Bob had to be out of his mind to think anyone — let alone a thirteen-year-old girl — would want to spend her summer in this no-man's-land. The only person remotely close to my age was a ten-year-old girl next door named Tracy.

For three days, the humidity had been stifling. We'd been hit with a record-breaking heat spell not even the air conditioner could tame. Bob and my mom had gone to the movie theater to see *Sleep-*

less in Seattle. Bob invited me to tag along, almost pleaded that I join them. "Come on, Sister, I'll buy you some popcorn. Heck, I'll even throw in some Junior Mints."

"I hate Junior Mints," I said, never looking up from my *YM* magazine.

He tried to act disappointed, but I knew he was relieved I wouldn't be tagging along. He was nothing but a phony. He probably wished I'd die . . . or at least be shipped off to Atlanta.

I called my dad that night. It was an hour earlier his time, and he had just gotten off the golf course.

"Hey, how's my girl?"

I pinched the bridge of my nose. "I miss you, Dad. When can we come to Atlanta?"

"Anytime you want, cupcake. The ball's in your mom's court. You know that, don't you? I want you here, and your mother, too. I love you both. You work on her, won't you, doll?"

I started to tell him about my awful summer, but he cut me off. "Hold on," he said. He covered the phone and spoke to someone in the background. He laughed, then came back to me. "Call me tomorrow, won't you, sweetie? We'll talk then."

I hung up the phone, feeling more alone than ever. I was losing my father, I could tell. He seemed more distant now, not nearly as desperate for my mom and me to move home. I had to do something before he forgot all about us.

I flopped down on the sofa and turned on the television. I stared at the ceiling, listening to *Married . . . with Children,* while tears pushed past my temples and drained into my ears.

At some point, I fell asleep. I startled when I heard the car pull in the driveway. I sat up and stretched, my skin damp and sticky from my nap and the night's relentless heat. The television was still on, tuned to *Saturday Night Live.* I spied my bra on the arm of the sofa, where I'd tossed it after taking it off earlier. I grabbed it and stuffed it under the sofa cushion.

I heard their laughter as they approached the screen door. I didn't have time to make a mad dash to my bedroom. So I lay back down and squeezed shut my eyes. I didn't want to hear about their stupid movie.

"I bet someone wants popcorn." It was Bob, the buffoon. Footsteps neared the sofa, but I pretended to be asleep. I could feel Bob and my mother hovering over me. I could smell the popcorn and his aftershave, and something else, something I used to smell on my father. Whiskey? But that couldn't be. Bob didn't drink.

I lay still, suddenly self-conscious of my half-naked state. I could feel my newly budded breasts pressed against my clingy tank top, my long bare legs draped across the sofa.

"Shall we leave her here?" Bob asked, his voice low. I pictured his dark eyes peering down at me. A prickle went up my spine. I longed to cover myself, or shoo him away.

"No," my mom whispered. "Let's take her to bed."

Without warning, one hot, calloused hand found its way under my bare legs. The other wedged itself beneath my shoulders. These weren't my mother's hands! My eyes flew open and Bob's shadowy face loomed large. My scream was as piercing a sound as I'd ever heard. And it felt fucking amazing! All my pent-up rage and disgust and frustration bellowed from my lungs. Every white-hot atom of hostility and jealousy and madness that had been simmering for the past eight months scorched my throat.

Bob's face was a portrait of confusion. He seemed ignorant of the situation, baffled as to why I was screaming. If only he'd have let loose his hold on me right then and there, everything would have been different. Instead, he pulled me tighter, swaddling me like an infant he'd awoken from a nightmare.

"Let me down!" I screamed, wriggling from his grasp like a feral animal. But he held firm. My skimpy shorts twisted in the transition. My rear, partially exposed now, wedged in the crook of his arm. My bare skin pressed against his bare skin. It sickened me.

"Get away from me!" I bellowed.

He startled. To this day I can see his eyes widen, as if he were terrified of me. He fumbled as he lowered my writhing body back onto the sofa.

And that's when it happened. His hand grazed my crotch as he pulled it out from beneath me.

What the hell? What the hell! At last, I had my moment of opportunity.

In one swift instant, I made my decision. I could finally keep my promise to my dad.

"Get your hands off me, you fucking pervert!" I looked away from Bob. I didn't want to see his face. I didn't want to have to decide whether his touch was intentional or innocent. I hurled myself from the sofa, tripping over my flip-flops and scraping my knee as I landed on the wood floor.

When I looked up, I saw the shock in his eyes, the hurt . . . and what I decided was guilt. I'd struck a chord, I could tell. And I yanked it for all it was worth. "You asshole! You sick bastard!"

I heard my mother gasp. I turned to her before I had time to think. "Get him out of here!" Tears sprang to my eyes. I jumped to my feet, yanking an afghan from the back of the sofa to cover me.

My mother's eyes, round and bewildered, traveled from daughter to lover. Her mouth hung open, and all I could think of was a trapped animal, terrified and uncertain of her next move. She was questioning herself now, I was sure of it. She was doubting her lover, everything she believed. She was questioning me, too. I could tell. Good. The moment of truth. Let her choose between us.

She seemed frozen, unable to move or even comprehend the situation. I felt myself soften for a second, before I shook it off. I couldn't lose my momentum. I had to make this an issue. I'd waited eight months for this opportunity, and I wasn't about to waste it. "Mother!" I screamed.

Still, she stood unmoving, as if strategizing her next move.

I became strangely calm and drew in a breath. "I'm calling the police." My voice was flat but strong, void of the earlier hysteria.

I started for the phone, struck by an almost out-of-body feeling, like I was playacting and the director had walked off the set. I was ad-libbing, with no idea of my next line or scene, or how the play would end.

My mother came alive and grabbed me by the arm. "No!" She turned to Bob. "What happened? What did you do?"

Ah, yes. At last I'd won. A billowing bubble of gratification filled me. We'd leave this godforsaken place. We'd go back to Georgia, to my dad. We'd be a family again. But as quickly as the bubble rose, it sank. Doubt crept in when I saw the pleading look in Bob's eyes.

"Nothing," he said. "You saw me, Suzanne. For goodness' sake, I didn't do a thing!" His voice was filled with desperation. He sought me out. "Sister, I'm sorry. You don't think —"

I couldn't let him finish. I would not allow him to break my resolve. "Shut up, you child molester!" I slipped from my mom's grasp and darted to the telephone.

I never called the police. Instead, I called my dad. He arrived the next day. After months of being a helpless bystander while my life was being dismantled, I was calling the shots now. My parents were in the same town, the same room! The power was intoxicating.

My father was strong again. He used words like *unfit* and *pedophile.* But my mother was strong now, too. She'd witnessed the event, after all. She knew what happened, he didn't. She countered with words like *manipulative* and *bully.*

Six hours later, I was on my way to Atlanta to start a new life with my father. They'd struck a deal. She'd allow me to go with him, and my dad wouldn't press charges. My mother had sold me out.

I can almost see that girl, watching out the airplane window as Michigan disappeared below the clouds, along with her mother . . . and her innocence.

"And there it is," I tell Claudia. "A tale was put into motion, and the thirteen-year-old staring out the window of that 757 saw no way to stop it. The tale was part fact, part fiction, but which was which, I wasn't entirely sure. I knew I'd drive myself crazy second-guessing. So instead I claimed the tale as fact and clung to it like a tree in a tsunami."

CHAPTER 21

Claudia and I enter stage right and the audience erupts. Together we smile and wave, like a pair of Miss America contestants who've chosen to share the crown. It no longer feels like I am auditioning for my job, or that Claudia is crouched on the sofa with her teeth bared, waiting to pounce. Her presence as my cohost is comforting today, rather than threatening. All because we shared our secrets.

We begin with the usual introductions, then welcome Fiona. I stand back and take in the older version of the girl who tormented me for two years. She's petite, with dark hair and sharp green eyes that used to cut right through me. But those eyes are soft now, and she smiles when she sees me.

She crosses the stage and takes my hand. She's wearing a navy wrap dress and a pair of wedge sandals. "I'm so sorry, Hannah," she whispers into my ear. Without intending to, I pull her into a hug, surprised to feel a lump rise in my throat.

When I called her hotel last night, Fiona graciously agreed with me. I sensed she was just as relieved as I was that we wouldn't be talking about our history on today's show. The conversation was short. We didn't reminisce about our days back at Bloomfield Hills Academy. Given her change of heart, I'm guessing those memories are just as painful for her as they are for me, maybe even more so.

Claudia and I take our places in the matching chairs facing Fiona. For twenty minutes, Claudia lobs brilliant questions, and Fiona returns them with witty and insightful answers. I look on, feeling oddly separated from my show, just the way I'd insisted.

"The stones have been such a blessing in my life," Fiona explains. "I feel as if I've given back to the universe a small piece of myself."

How did you come up with the idea for the Forgiveness Stones?

"The idea came to me after I'd attended a friend's wedding. I'd taped the wedding toast and forgot to turn off my camera. I left the table having no idea that the phone was still recording. The next day I replayed it. I was about to turn off the video when I heard the audio of my friends — and what they said wasn't pretty.

"I mean, who would've thought that when one friend leaves a group, the other women might talk about her?"

Chuckles rise from the crowd. I smile. She's a pro, no doubt about it.

"For the first two days, I was angry and defensive. Then I just felt sad. Deep down, bone-sad. The truth was painful. I was a snob, what some might call a mean girl. But more than anything, I was a fraud. And I'd been a fraud all my life. You see, at that wedding, I made everyone believe I was a successful attorney. I'd even rented a Mercedes, just to impress my old friends. Truth was, I drove a twelve-year-old Kia. I hated my job. I was nothing more than an ambulance chaser, with a salary that barely covered my law school loans. I lived in a shabby studio apartment, and spent most nights alone watching Bravo and eating Hot Pockets."

More chuckles from the audience.

"But I was too afraid to let people see that person. She wasn't good enough. It's ironic, don't you think? We try so hard to camouflage our weaknesses. We don't dare

256

let that soft part show. But it's that very place, that sweet spot of vulnerability, that allows love to grow."

Our eyes meet briefly then, and I have the strongest urge to move to the sofa and sling an arm around her. Instead, I turn away.

"I wanted to find a way to atone," she says. I think of Dorothy and her grace and bravery. I wish I were wired that way.

"Of course, I had no idea if people would forgive me. I kept — and still keep — a vase of flowers on my bookshelf, filled with pebbles. Somehow, the stones spoke to me. They served as an anchor. They also symbolize weight. It just happened magically.

"After I'd sent the stones to several of my friends at the wedding, I realized I had more apologies to make. So I just kept sending stones. About a week later, they started showing up in my mailbox, with letters telling me I was forgiven. The incredible weight of self-hatred I'd been carrying for years became lighter and lighter. It's a powerful thing, shedding shame. And the people who forgave felt better, too. I knew I had to share the gift with others."

"And you'll be hosting a reunion this summer," Claudia says.

"That's right." Fiona sighs, as if it's a

mighty task. "We've chosen Chicago's Millennium Park for our First Annual Forgiveness Stone Reunion. Recipients of the stones will gather on August ninth to celebrate their weight loss, so to speak." She winks, and the audience laughs. "But it's a huge undertaking. We're always looking for volunteers. You can sign up on my website." She looks at the audience. "Any takers?"

The crowd nods and claps. Fiona points to an elderly woman. "Great. You're hired."

Claudia puts her hands to her heart. "What a blessing you are to the universe. We'll have you back on the show after the reunion to tell us all about it. But now it's time for my favorite part of the hour. Let's open it up for questions."

I feel the back of my neck bristle. It's really not her show. But this was what I wanted. And so far it's working. I haven't had to endorse the stones or Fiona Knowles, and there's only fifteen minutes to go. Nothing we've discussed infringed upon the proposal I presented to WCHI. James Peters should have no problem with this.

As planned, I step down to the audience level with the microphone, while Claudia and Fiona remain onstage.

Today's crowd isn't shy. Hands fly up, ambushing Fiona with questions.

"Aren't some apologies better left unspoken?"

"Perhaps," she says. "An apology that's sure to hurt someone, and has no purpose other than to relieve one's guilt. That's when you have to learn to forgive yourself."

I think of Dorothy's apology, her misguided attempt to relieve her guilt. But that was never her purpose. She was hoping to relieve Marilyn's.

I hand the mike to a tall brunette.

"What's the best story of redemption you've heard?"

Fiona glances at Claudia. "Do you mind?"

Claudia closes her eyes and nods. "Go ahead."

Fiona launches into the same story Claudia had told me, about her trip to Cancún and the mess she'd made of Lacey and Henry's relationship. I look on, my mouth agape. I can't believe Fiona is outing her — on air! I sneak a peek at Claudia, expecting to see her slouched in her chair, red-faced with humiliation. Instead, she sits up straight, with her head held high. The woman is clearly made of stronger material than I am.

"Lacey's marriage to Mark ended after sixteen months," Fiona tells the guests. "Claudia just couldn't forgive herself for what she'd done to Lacey and Henry. So she did what any good journalist — and friend — would do. She tracked down Henry."

Wait . . . what?

A collective sigh of approval comes from the audience. Fiona nods to Claudia. "Please, you tell the rest."

Claudia smiles and stands. "I made it my life mission to find Henry." She puts air quotes around *Henry.* "Obviously, I've changed names here to protect their privacy." She closes her eyes and lifts a hand, pausing like a Broadway actress. The audience sits stock-still, waiting for the story's climax. "Seven months ago, I finally did it. Henry and Lacey are getting married in September!" Her voice has the same excited squeal as Oprah's when announcing that every member of the studio audience has just won a shiny convertible.

The crowd cheers like they'd been handed the keys. I stand with the microphone at my side, trying to clear my head. Did I miss part of the story? Because I'm pretty sure I'm the one who suggested Claudia find Henry, just yesterday. And she sure as hell didn't find him last night.

A middle-aged woman three seats from the aisle raises her hand. I lean over and pass her the mike.

"My question is for you, Hannah," she says. "What's your story of redemption?"

"I . . . my story?"

"Yes. Have you received a pouch of Forgiveness Stones?"

The breath is knocked from me. Across the studio, my eyes collide with Claudia's. Her mouth is slightly open, and her hand is on her chest. She's as stunned as I am.

I turn to Fiona. No, we agreed to keep our past a secret.

I look up to Stuart in the control booth. He's got a victorious grin on his face. How dare he!

"Um, well, yes. I did. It was quite a surprise." I try to laugh, but it rings hollow.

I scamper up the aisle to a young woman wearing a long black skirt. "Your question, miss?"

"So, did you send your stone on to someone else?"

Shit. Another question for me! Something about her is familiar. Yes . . . the station's new IT gal, Danielle. Damn Stuart! He's planted audience members to ambush me. Or was it Claudia?

Again, the crazy laughter spills from my throat. "Ha, uh, yes . . . er, no. Not yet. But I will."

261

The woman beside Danielle takes the mike without asking. "Who are you apologizing to?"

I glare at the control booth, aiming my ire directly at Stuart Booker. He shrugs, as if he were a helpless child.

"Well, um, my mother and I . . . we had a disagreement a while back . . ."

What's happening here? I'm being dragged down a deep abyss. Michael will be furious if I reveal my story — the story so horrible he wouldn't even allow me to tell *him.* And what's more, this story isn't mine to tell. It belongs to WCHI. My head feels light. I turn to see Claudia at my side. She places an arm around me and takes the microphone from my hand.

"Hannah is one of the bravest women I know." She gazes out at the sea of faces. "She and I spoke about this just yesterday."

"Please, Claudia. Don't," I say, but Claudia holds up a hand to silence me.

"Hannah and her mother have a very tenuous relationship, like most mothers and daughters." She smiles and I see heads in the audience nod.

"Hannah longs for a relationship with her mom, but it's complicated. Her mother abandoned Hannah as a child."

An audible moan of sympathy comes from

the crowd. I cringe, grateful that my mother will never see this show.

"It was extremely painful, as you can imagine. Hannah suffered severe emotional scars, scars that may never heal."

I can't believe it. She's turning this around, making me appear sympathetic. Or is she? I feel like monkey in the middle, being thrown back and forth. Is Claudia trying to save or sink me?

"It was a man — a pretty despicable man — whom her mother decided was more important than her daughter."

"Claudia, no," I say, but she plows forward, and Ben's camera is fixed solely on her.

"Which is why Hannah feels so passionately about her cause, Into the Light. Most of you know Hannah Farr is a staunch supporter of this organization supporting victims of child sexual abuse. She hosts their annual fund-raiser and Christmas ball; she's on their board of directors.

"I, for one, am amazed that Hannah has the grace to forgive her mother, after all she's been through. But bless her heart, she's ready to do just that."

I stare at Claudia, stunned. How could she? But the audience purrs and coos like a litter of contented cats. Claudia is telling them exactly what they want to hear. Hannah Farr is a good woman, someone with a huge heart, a victim so magnanimous that she's willing to turn the other cheek and forgive her evil mother.

Claudia hands the mike to a young Latino woman. "Hannah, when will you send the stone to your mother?" the woman asks.

I pull myself from the fog, my head thick. "Soon. Very soon." I rub the back of my neck, feeling the sweat that's gathered. "But it — it's tricky. I can't imagine sending her a stone out of the blue. And I haven't had the time. She lives in Michigan . . ."

"A trip to Michigan, then?" Claudia asks, her head cocked and her brows raised.

From over her shoulder, I see Stuart at stage left, raising his arms, rallying the audience to applaud. As instructed, the entire audience erupts in claps and whistles. Jesus, is everyone in cahoots on this?

"Okay, then," I say, feeling sick to my stomach. "I will. I'll deliver the stone to my mother."

CHAPTER 22

"You set me up," I say, pacing the floor in Stuart's office. I am clearly out of control, but I can't stop myself. "I told you to stay out of my business! How dare you invade my personal life!"

"Calm down, Farr. It's the best thing that's ever happened to your career, mark my words. We've already gotten over a thousand comments on our website. People are tweeting about Hannah Farr's sweet forgiveness as we speak."

But is it sweet forgiveness? Or is it rotten fabrication? And what will Michael say? And what will James Peters do if he catches wind of this? I cringe. Neither man is going to like this. Not at all.

"We'll give you a week off. Go track down your mom, tell her she's forgiven, kiss, and make up. The show will pay your expenses. Ben will accompany you."

"Absolutely not! *If* I see my mother, which

I haven't committed to, I'll do it alone. No cameras. Not even a still photo. This is my life, Stuart, not a reality show. Do you understand?"

He raises his eyebrows. "So you agree to go?"

My thoughts drift to my mom. It's time. I owe it to her and to Bob. Even though I'm furious that Stuart manipulated me, I finally have a reason to return to Harbour Cove. Not even Michael could argue. The story is out now. Hannah Farr is willing to forgive.

And to honor Michael's privacy, my mother's dignity, and my own reputation, nobody will know the details. I will be the only one who knows that it's not a trip granting forgiveness, it's a trip seeking it.

I let out a breath. "Yes. I'll go."

Stuart smiles. "Excellent. And when you return, we'll have your mother on the show. The two of you can tell your story on —"

"No way. Didn't you learn anything from Dorothy's appearance? I'll have a show about mother-daughter relationships. I'll talk about the reunion with my mother and share the good parts. But I won't have my mother sitting onstage being judged by the entire city of New Orleans. End of story."

"Fair enough."

I walk away, wondering who it is I am

protecting — my mother or myself.

I'm storming back to my dressing room when I meet Jade in the hallway, leaving for lunch. She shakes her head. "So you finally believe me?" she asks. "I warned you Claudia's nothing but a conniving little bitch. She's been after your job from day one."

"That was Stuart's stunt, not Claudia's." I pause a minute before revealing my secret. "You have to promise not to tell anybody, Jade." I pull her close and lower my voice. "Claudia's fiancé is being traded to Miami. She doesn't want my job. She never did."

Jade stares at me, her face incredulous. "Brian Jordan is going to the Dolphins?" She scowls. "Okay. So, she's simply a bitch. Not a *conniving* bitch."

"More like insecure. It's a job hazard in broadcast journalism. I should know."

I throw open my office door and nearly collide with Claudia.

"Oh, excuse me," she says. "I was just leaving you a note." She takes me by the arms. "You doing okay, sweetie?"

"No. You saw it. Stuart set me up."

She rubs my arms. "It'll be okay. You really do need to go see your mom, Hannah. You know that, right?"

I feel myself bristle. Who is she to tell me what I need to do? I stare into her oval face, her pure blue eyes and perfectly arched brows. But once again, I'm drawn to her tiny scar. The sight of it, expertly camouflaged with makeup, softens me. "Yeah, well, I had hoped to do it on my terms, not WNO's."

"When are you leaving?" she asks.

"I don't know. In a week or two. I need to make a plan first." I turn to her. "Hey, how are you feeling about the show? I couldn't believe Fiona outed you like that. Good thing you were able to think on your feet, right? But you realize, if Lacey happens to see the episode, it'll all be exposed."

She looks on with the slightest smirk on her face, as if she's amused by me. "Hannah, you don't actually believe there is a Lacey, do you?"

She winks at me, then strides from the office.

I stare at the open door, my mouth agape. What. The. Hell?

I stagger over to my desk and plop down on my chair. Jesus, did she make up that entire story, knowing I'd pour my heart out in return? But how would she have known I had a secret?

I stare blankly at my laptop . . . my laptop. Yes. Of course . . . it was open the morning she came in to test her mosquito repellants! I was showing Jade the proposal. Claudia must have seen it after she blinded me. I drop my head into my hands. How could I have been so careless?

From atop my desk I spy a note. I pick it up.

Hannah,
  Just wanted you to know I'm happy to sub for you while you're in Michigan. No worries, sweetie, the show will be in good hands!

Hugs and smiles,
Claudia

Sometimes no amount of makeup can cover our ugly flaws. I drop the note into the shredder and watch it turn to confetti.

CHAPTER 23

I'm still reeling from the show when I slam the door of my condo. I toss the mail on my kitchen island. One letter slides across the granite and lands on the tile floor. I squat down to pick it up and spy the vineyard's logo. I close my eyes and hold it to my heart, savoring this day's only token of joy for as long as I can before tearing open the envelope.

Dear Hannah,

At the risk of sounding like a schoolboy, I reluctantly admit that I run to the mailbox each day, in hopes of finding a letter — or perhaps a loaf of bread — from you. The sight of your handwriting on that pink stationery makes my heart soar.

Have you heard anything more about the position in Chicago? It sounds like a terrific opportunity, but I must say, my enthusiasm is partially selfish. You realize, don't you, that you and I would be but a mere five hours from one another?

I look forward to your next visit, whenever that may be. It's getting warmer every day now, and aside from the mountains created by snowplows, you'll be glad to know the white stuff has melted. Chances of slipping on a sheet of ice and tearing the seam of your dress are considerably lower now.

I laugh, and hoist myself onto a barstool.

At dawn, when the sun is crowning and a sleepy haze covers the vines, I have a ritual of walking the property. It's during these early hours, when I'm alone with my land, that I think of you most often. I imagine you giving me shit for something, like the *Duck Dynasty* ball cap from Zach and Izzy I sometimes wear, or the too-small flannel jacket that once belonged to my father that I grab on cold days. Or maybe you'd bust my chops for working so hard on a business that, in a good year, barely breaks even. Call me a fool, but I love it. I get to live life on my terms. No boss. No commute. No deadlines. Well, yes, maybe deadlines, but all in all, I'm living my dream. How many people can say that?

My only complaint, and it's a major one, is that I don't have a companion. Yes, I date occasionally. But with the exception of you, I've not met anyone who keeps me awake nights, trying to picture her smile, or imagining what she's doing at that very moment. Besides you, there's nobody whose laughter I try to re-create, or whose eyes I care to get lost in.

In case you think I work too hard, rest assured, I have complete flexibility four months of the year. Last year I spent a month in Italy; next winter I'm going to Spain — though Chicago could also be a contender. Just sayin'.

Please let me know when you're returning to this neck of the woods. There's a winemaker you could make very happy.

Yours,
RJ

PS Should you ever decide to give up journalism, that baker's position is still available.

It's dusk, and Jade and I stroll down

Jefferson Street, on our way to meet Dorothy and some of the other residents at Octavia Books to hear Fiona Knowles. I feel like a fraud, pretending to be an advocate of Fiona and her stones, but what choice do I have now? I've been tagged and outed.

"I got a letter from RJ today," I tell Jade.

She turns to me. "Yeah? The vineyard guy? What'd he say?"

"Nothing . . . everything. He's really great. Someone I'd like to know better, if I were a single woman living in Michigan."

"Michigan's just a pole vault across the lake from Chicago, right? Keep your options open in case the mayor doesn't step up."

"Nah. It's just a fun pen pal friendship. I won't even give him my e-mail address. Somehow that seems like it's crossing a line."

"Maybe it's a line worth crossing."

"Stop," I say. "You know how I feel about Michael."

We turn onto Laurel Street. "Will Marilyn be here tonight?" Jade asks.

"No. I called her this afternoon to remind her, but she wasn't interested. Not that I blame her. I apologized yet again for yesterday's fiasco, but she cut me off. She never even mentioned Dorothy."

"Poor Dorothy. At least you're finally making peace with your mom. Dorothy's happy about that, right?"

"Yes." I smile. "She'll finally be off my case."

"She just wants to make sure you hear your mom's side of things," Jade says, "before it's too late."

"Okay, Jade, are you talking to me now, or to yourself?"

She stuffs her hands into her pockets. "You're right. I need to tell my dad the truth about my birthday party. I know I do."

But does she? Even though I've been encouraging her to tell him, a pit forms in my stomach. A clean conscience just might be overrated, especially for something as trivial as her white-carpet lie.

"Maybe you should just leave it alone, Jade. What's so bad about letting him think his daughter is perfect?"

The bookstore is packed with mostly women. Is it my imagination, or are people pointing at me, smiling? One woman from across the room gives me a thumbs-up. And then it dawns on me. They watched the show. They think I'm the selfless, big-hearted daughter, willing to forgive her horrific mother.

Jade and I take a seat behind Dorothy and Patrick Sullivan. Patrick chats while Dorothy sits quietly with her hands in her lap. I touch her shoulder and lean in.

"It's sweet of you to come," I say to her. "I wouldn't blame you if you wanted nothing to do with Fiona and her Forgiveness Stones after what happened yesterday."

She turns her head so that she's in profile, and I see dark circles beneath her eyes. "Forgiveness is a lovely trend. I still believe that. And I'm pleased to hear that you're finally taking action and going to see your mother." She lowers her voice. "Does this compromise your proposal with WCHI?"

A net of dread falls over me. "I got an e-mail reply from Mr. Peters this afternoon."

"Was he upset that you'd used their Forgiveness Stones proposal?"

"He wasn't pleased, but he understood. The guy's a prince. He asked me to write another proposal, and I'm working on it, this one on the amount of freshwater that's being used for oil fracking. It could affect the Great Lakes."

"Oh, goodness. That sounds dreadful."

"It does," I say, unsure whether Dorothy's referring to the fracking business or the proposal itself. The fact is, they both sound dreadful. I worry that I've blown my chance at the Chicago job. Thank goodness things at WNO seem to be on an upswing. "Any word from Marilyn?" I ask.

"Not yet."

"Please, let's go see her this weekend or next week, sometime before I leave for Michigan. We'll explain again that you —" Dorothy's lips are set and she shakes her head. We've been over this a dozen times. She wants to give Marilyn time. But I'm frustrated that she's not trying harder. After all, you don't give up on those you love.

I hang my head. I'm a fine one to talk. If I hadn't been forced into it, it's possible I would have given up my mother altogether.

"Perhaps when you return from Michigan, I'll have heard from Mari."

"I hope so."

"Hope so?" She swivels in her chair and scowls. "I have no use for hope. Hope is wishing that Mari will return. Faith is knowing that she will."

I turn my attention to Fiona when she walks onto the floor. She bypasses the podium and stands exposed. For the next forty minutes, she delights us with her clever stories and keen insight.

"When we're ashamed of something, we can either remain mired in self-loathing, or we can atone. The choice is actually pretty simple — do we want to lead a clandestine life or an authentic one?"

I reach out to squeeze Dorothy's shoulder. She reaches back and pats my hand.

While Jade and I wait in line to have our books signed, at least a dozen women approach me, congratulating me and wishing me luck on my journey to Michigan.

"What an inspiration you are," a striking brunette says, clutching my hand. "I'm so proud of you, Hannah, forgiving your mother after so many years."

"Thank you," I say, feeling my cheeks burn.

Fiona says we keep secrets for two reasons: to protect ourselves or to protect others. It's clear I'm protecting myself.

It's almost midnight, and I sit at my desk, trying to compose a letter that sounds friendly but not flirtatious.

Dear RJ,

It was great to hear from you, my friend. Just wanted to let you know I'll be in Michigan for a few days, beginning Monday, May 11. I'm planning to stop by the vineyard, hoping to cash in on that tour you promised me.

Just in case you've forgotten me, I'll be the one bearing breadsticks.

Best,

I toss my fountain pen onto the desk and read what I've written. *My friend?* No, scratch that. But what tone, exactly, am I trying to convey? I lean back in my chair and stare up at the ceiling. God, what's wrong with me? Why am I playing with fire here? I've got Michael. I have no business returning to the vineyard. It's so wrong.

I sit up in my chair and revise the letter once more. When I read it this time, it's not so bad. Actually, it's quite innocent. It could just as easily be written to a woman friend I'd just met.

Before I have time for my good angel's rebuttal, I snatch the pen and sign my name. I stuff it into an addressed envelope, dash downstairs, and slip it into the mail slot.

Oh, God! Jesus God! What have I done? I wipe my hands on the front of my jeans, as if they're dirty. Lord, help me. I'm just as bad as my ex-fiancé Jackson Rousseau.

Well, not quite.

At least, not yet . . .

CHAPTER 24

I'm dressed in leggings and boots and a North Face fleece jacket when I step from the airport, wheeling my suitcase behind me. Instead of being hit with an arctic blast, like I was last month, today's Michigan weather feels almost tropical. I remove my fleece, fish my sunglasses from my tote, and stroll over to the rental-car booth.

I should be in Harbour Cove around three, with plenty of time to find my rental cottage during daylight. Like last time, I'll wait until morning to visit my mother. I need to see her alone.

In my fantasies, my mother will be understanding. She may even tell me she's as unsure about that night as I am, which would completely relieve my guilt. But even in my wildest family reunion fantasies, it's impossible to imagine receiving Bob's forgiveness.

I sit behind the wheel of my rented Ford

Taurus in the airport parking lot and call Michael.

"Hey," I say, always surprised when he answers. "Good morning."

"Morning." I can't decide if he's tired or still angry. I decide he's tired.

"I've just landed. It's actually nice today, sunny and warm." I fasten my seat belt and adjust my mirrors. "What's on your agenda today?"

"Endless meetings."

"Campaign meetings again?" Though Michael hasn't officially announced his candidacy for the Senate, he spends much of his time with political consultants and big donors, brainstorming strategies for winning the election.

"No," he says, as if the notion were absurd. "I do have a city to look out for. I do have obligations to my constituents."

"Of course," I say, trying to ignore the sting in his tone. "Anything important?"

"I'm having dinner with Mack DeForio tonight, along with the new superintendent."

The chief of police and the woman I'd met at the fund-raiser, the one with perfect posture. "Jennifer Lawson," I say, shocking myself. How did I remember her name? "Well, I hope it's productive."

A silence follows, and I'm not sure how to break it. He isn't asking what I'm doing today because he knows. And he's livid. When I broke the news of my trip to Michael, explaining the orchestrated on-air confession, it was as if he didn't believe me. And now, with this stilted conversation, I wonder if he'll ever trust me again.

"Michael, I know you're angry. I swear I'll make it right. Nobody's going to know the details."

"You mean nobody's going to find out that the mayor of New Orleans has a girlfriend who lied about being molested?" I hear him sigh, and I picture him shaking his head. "Jesus, Hannah, what were you thinking? You're the name and face of Into the Light. And by association, so am I. People don't forgive acts like this. You're risking every ounce of trust these victims — as well as your viewers — have in you."

I feel a chill, despite the seventy-degree temperature. They'll never trust *him,* is what he really means. And what saddens me most is that his trumped-up, overinflated ambition is what's most important to Michael. Not my relationship with my mother. Not the possibility that I might actually find peace with my past. But rather, his political career.

"I told you, they'll never know." And then, before I have time to stop myself, I add, "It's not as if you've never said something that wasn't true."

There's a deafening silence on the other end. I've gone too far.

"I need to scoot," he says. "Have a good day."

He hangs up without a good-bye.

My stomach does a little cartwheel when I see the sign for Merlot de la Mitaine. God, am I twelve years old, or what?

I read once that women should never stop having crushes. Even elderly women and married women should partake in good-natured flirtation from time to time. The article claimed that the playful dalliance provided a harmless way of honing our feminine wiles, of keeping abreast of the craft of seduction. Doing so would actually improve your current relationship, the writer stated.

So, if I were a master of manipulation, I could claim that I owed it to Michael, and our relationship, to visit the vineyard this afternoon.

But I'm not a master manipulator. And I don't want to be.

Dorothy has always been my touchstone.

And when I told her about RJ and our little correspondence, her response was the seventy-six-year-old's equivalent of Beyonce's *If you liked it, then you should have put a ring on it.*

"You've no reason not to see this fella. Until you're in a committed relationship, you're free to speak with whomever you choose."

But that's just the problem. I think I am in a committed relationship. I'm just not sure Michael agrees.

I lower my window and suck in the Michigan air, wondering if it's just my imagination or if it really does smell fresher up here.

An entrance arrow points left, and I turn onto the long winding drive, feeling a rush of anticipation I haven't felt in years. What will RJ's reaction be when he first sees me? I wonder if he got my letter yet, or if my visit will be a complete surprise. Will he recognize me immediately? That single look will tell me everything I need to know about his feelings — or lack of feelings — for me. I pick up speed.

A dozen cars fill the parking lot today. A young couple walk out of the gift shop, each carrying a paper bag with the vineyard's double-M logo.

I smooth down my hair before stepping inside. A middle-aged woman stands behind the cash register, but she's busy ringing up a purchase and doesn't see me.

From beyond the arched doorway, I hear the hum of conversation and laughter and soft background music. I peer into the adjoining tasting room. Unlike last time, a crowd of about fifteen is gathered around the U-shaped bar, talking and laughing and sipping wine.

I take a deep breath. Here goes nothing.

I step through the archway, a bag of breadsticks in one hand and a pair of yellow Wellies in the other. I see him before he sees me. He's behind the bar, talking to three young women as he pours wine into their glasses. I slow my pace. This was a mistake. A huge mistake. RJ is at work. I'm going to embarrass him — and myself — with my silly breadsticks and these boots. Why did I lug the Wellingtons all the way here?

I see him laugh at something one of the women said. I'm going to be sick. He's a player. I'm an idiot, thinking I might have been special. Yesterday it may have been me basking in his spotlight, but today he's flirting with these pretty young women. And tomorrow? It's anyone's guess.

I'm standing stock-still in the middle of

the room, halfway between the entrance and the bar, debating whether I should make a run for it or try to sneak out quietly, when he looks up. Our eyes collide.

Everything becomes a blur. I hear my name. I see him set down the bottle, nearly tipping over a glass. I catch sight of the three women at the bar, turning to look at me, their faces curious. Then RJ crosses the room. His eyes stay locked on mine, and even though he's shaking his head, I know he's not chastising me. His eyes are bright, and I see a pink blotch on his cheek.

And at once I'm in his arms. The boots fall to my side. I feel the softness of his shirt against my cheek and inhale the clean smell of linen, of him.

"Southern girl," he whispers in my ear.

I can't speak. All my life, I will never forget this welcome.

Merlot de la Mitaine is a perfect distraction from the task ahead of me. I try not to stress about tomorrow's meeting with my mother, and concentrate instead on the lively, lighthearted atmosphere of this place.

RJ's wine-tasting bar is a melting pot of sorts, where bikers sit alongside prepsters. Whether it's the wine or RJ's easygoing personality, the patrons seem to lower their guards and drop all pretenses. Two hours disappear as I sit sipping wine and gabbing with customers who come and go. RJ raves about my breadsticks and passes them out to the others at the bar, giving me full credit. I look on as he greets returning customers by name, asks the new arrivals where they're from and what brings them here. He's the one who should have a talk show. He's charming, yes, but not in a calculated way. It's more of a validating, *I-genuinely-like-you* kind of appeal. I watch as he slowly folds a surly-looking man into a conversation he's having with two nuns from Canada. By the time he's worked his magic, Mr. Grump is picking up the tab for the sisters, and the three are making plans to meet for dinner.

The only break RJ takes is at four-thirty, when Zach and Izzy arrive, lugging their backpacks just like last time. He waves to them when they enter the room, then signals to Don, one of the servers, who takes RJ's place behind the bar.

I catch myself smiling as RJ and the kids share hugs and fist bumps. Like before, he helps them settle into a table before disappearing to retrieve their snacks.

Is this guy for real? And what, exactly, is his connection to these children or their mother? Nobody is this nice. Or have I just become cynical?

By six o'clock the crowd wanes, and it's Don now who holds court with the remaining six customers behind the bar. I sit at the back table, helping Izzy with her math, when she lets out a squeal.

"Mommy!"

I turn around and see Maddie walking toward our table. She's dressed in black from head to toe. A dress code at her job, I'm guessing. She slows when she sees me. For a moment I think she's angry, that maybe she really does have a thing for RJ. But then her face softens and she grins.

"Hey! I remember you." She points a purple nail at me. "Glad you're back. I had a feeling about you two."

Of course, Maddie's "feeling" is nothing but a wild notion. Still, I feel like I'm a teenager and my friend just told me the boy I like, likes me, too.

RJ and I stand outside waving good-bye to the kids. The view is so different today than it was on that snowy day four weeks ago. The thin branches of the cherry trees are bursting with buds, and new grass the color of limes blankets the orchard.

"It's really beautiful up here," I say. And it

is. The green of the grass contrasts with the red branches of the cherry trees and the blue water beyond.

"Cherry Capital of the World," RJ says.

"Really?"

"The lake effects on this peninsula . . . and that one there" — he comes up beside me and points across the bay to another finger of land — "create a perfect microclimate for cherry growing. Same goes for *vinifera* grapes, the ones used in wine making."

I gesture to what looks like a chest of drawers in the orchard, each drawer painted in a pretty pastel shade. "What's that?"

"One of my bee houses," he tells me. "A single acre of cherries requires about a hundred and forty thousand bees. A few more weeks and they'll be dancing around the blossoms, working their magic." He points to the trees. "And all of those buds you see will soon turn into big white blossoms. From a distance they take on the hue of the red branches or the green of the leaves, so when you're driving down the peninsula, you'd swear you see orchards of pinks and greens. It's a pretty spectacular sight against the blue backdrop of the lake. You really need to see it."

"Maybe I will someday." I look at my

watch. "But for now, I better get going."

"Not on your life. I'm taking you to dinner. I've already made the reservation."

CHAPTER 25

A better woman would have said no. Even a mediocre woman would have felt guilty. But when RJ suggests we have dinner at his favorite restaurant, I hesitate just long enough to leave Michael a quick message.

"Hey, it's me," I say, standing in the powder room, popping a chocolate mint into my mouth. "You're probably at your meeting with Jennifer and DeForio. Just wanted to let you know I'm heading out to dinner. I stopped at a vineyard up here, and now I'm going to grab a bite with the owner. I'll call you later."

I know I'm making excuses, and I know I'll probably burn in hell, but I convince myself that I'm still within the boundaries of what's right. Okay, so maybe I'm straddling the line a bit, but I've got at least a toehold on the good side.

We sit at a window table overlooking Grand

Traverse Bay, eating steamed mussels and grilled rare tuna and scallops drenched in whiskey sauce. But it could have been a fast-food burger. It wouldn't have made a difference. It still would have been the best date of my life. That is, if it were actually a date, which it isn't.

He pours me a glass of wine. "White Burgundy is made from Chardonnay. It's the perfect complement to the butter-based sauce on these mussels." He shakes his head. "I'm sorry. I sound like a pompous ass. You're from New Orleans. You know more about food and wine than I do."

"Yeah, pretty much," I say.

He looks at me. "Really? You're a foodie, eh?"

"No," I say, trying to keep a straight face. "I was referring to the pompous-ass statement."

His face falls before he realizes I'm joking. I burst out laughing, and then he does, too. "Ah, you got me. I really did sound like a jackass. I am so sorry."

"Not at all. You have no idea how I've longed for a tutorial on white Burgundy."

He grins at me and lifts his glass. "To white Burgundy and red faces. And to unexpected visitors."

As we sip our wine, I ask him about Zach

and Izzy, the ragamuffins who visit him after school each day.

"I get as much out of having them over as they get out of coming. It's a win-win."

"Really?" I say. But I don't buy it. This guy has a soft heart, no doubt about it.

"In the summers they're a great help. Zach's a natural beekeeper. He claims he's charmed them, and I can't disagree. I'm fermenting the honey, experimenting with an ancient drink called mead. If it sells, the profits will go to Zach's college fund."

"And what does Izzy do?"

"Izzy helps with . . ." He pauses, as if he's trying to think of something. "She helps in the kitchen."

I chuckle. "Oh, yeah, a five-year-old is a lot of help in the kitchen. You don't fool me, RJ. She's more trouble than she's worth. You just adore them. Admit it."

He laughs and shakes his head. "They're pretty special. Maddie has her hands full trying to raise them on her own. She's not always the most responsible, but she's young and doing the best she can."

"I'm sure you're making a huge difference in their lives. Where's their father?"

A cloud crosses RJ's face. "Died. Almost two years ago now."

"Was he ill?"

RJ inhales. "Yeah. He was. Sad story."

I want to ask more, but the shadowed look in RJ's eyes tells me the subject's closed.

We spend the next hour talking about our passions — his wine making and cooking, my baking. We talk about our greatest achievements and biggest disappointments. Without going into detail, I tell him about my mother. "It's been a difficult relationship since I was a teen, and I'm finally realizing that a big part was my fault. I'm hoping we can come to some sort of peace treaty now."

"Good luck with that. From a selfish standpoint, I'm hoping the two of you become inseparable."

My heart speeds, and I twist the napkin in my lap. "Tell me about your biggest disappointment."

He tells me about his marriage, the good and the bad.

"Problem is, we didn't share the same dream. Staci was furious when I told her I wanted to leave E&J. And I was stunned she didn't know I'd always wanted my own vineyard. Frankly, I don't blame her for not wanting to uproot her life. And the truth is, I'd probably still be married, and still stuck in the corporate grind, if it hadn't been for her boss, Allen. They married last

November."

"Oh no. I'm so sorry."

"What do you do?" He throws up his hands. "She's happy, Allen's happy. We were never a great fit. I see that now."

"I get that." I'm shocked to hear myself tell the story of Jack, and our meeting in Chicago, and how I felt when I heard he was getting married.

"It was just the shock of it," I tell him. "He claimed he wasn't the one, but at that moment, when I realized he was getting married and having a baby, I just panicked. I mean, what if I'd made a mistake? What if I should have given him another chance? But it was too late. That door had been slammed shut and dead-bolted."

"So what do you think? Was he the one?"

"No. He wasn't. Jack was a great guy. But he said something to me that I'll never forget. He said, 'When you love somebody, you never give up on them.' "

RJ seems to mull it over. "I think he's right. If you'd wanted that relationship, you'd have figured it out. There's someone else out there, I suspect."

I feel my face heat. *Yes, I suspect there is. And I suspect his name is Michael Payne. And I suspect I shouldn't be enjoying your company quite so much.*

He folds his hands on the table and leans in. "Okay, how's this for a cliché first-date topic: tell me something that's on your life list."

I smile and dip a piece of French bread into the wine sauce. "That's easy. I want a tree house."

RJ laughs. "A tree house? C'mon. I thought that fantasy ended around age seven."

I like the way he teases me and how our conversation flits from serious to silly. "Not for me. I want my very own tree house, with a ladder and a rope. It'll have a view of water, and it'll be big enough for a chair and a bookshelf and a table to set my coffee, which is all I need to make me happy. The rest of the world can go away."

"Real nice. So, it's like a private tree house. Let me guess, you'll have a sign on the door that says NO BOYS ALLOWED."

"Maybe," I say, playing coy. "Unless they know the secret password."

I feel his eyes on me. It's so intense I have to look away. He lowers his voice and leans in some more, so that our faces are only inches from each other. "And what's the secret password?"

My heart races and I lift my wineglass. My hand trembles and I set it back down. I gaze across the table, into the eyes of someone I have no business liking as much as I do.

"I have a boyfriend, RJ."

CHAPTER 26

RJ raises his eyebrows, and I hear the sharp intake of his breath. But just as quickly, he recovers. "Interesting password. I was thinking more like, two knocks, then three quick taps. *I have a boyfriend, RJ.* I think that's one I'll remember."

I groan. "Look, I'm sorry. I kept telling myself that this was okay. That you were a nice guy, a friend, someone I'd enjoy having dinner with, whether you were a man or a woman." I stare down at my napkin. "But the truth is, I'm enjoying myself too much. And it's wrong." I force myself to look at him. "And it's scaring me."

He reaches across the table and touches my arm. "Hey, it's okay. You go home and tell the bloke that you've met someone else. You're dumping him for some guy you barely know, a real catch who lives in the hills of Michigan. You tell him that you're going to pursue a long-distance relationship, because, well, one thousand two-hundred eight-point-six miles is so easy to overcome." He tilts his head. "And yes, that is the correct distance from your doorstep to mine. Which means yes, I've given this some thought."

His eyes are so tender that I want to grab him into a hug. But I'm not sure I could offer comfort now. It feels like we're a couple of kids who've fallen in love at summer camp, and now, because of families and schools and different hometowns, we're about to be separated. And already I'm heartsick.

It's midnight by the time we get back to the vineyard. I haven't even checked into my rental cottage yet.

"You're okay to drive?" he asks.

"Yes." I drank only a half glass of wine with dinner, two hours ago. "Thanks for everything."

Our eyes lock, and before I know it, I'm in his arms. I lean into him and feel the heat of his chest and the gentle touch of his hand, stroking my hair. I try to etch this moment into my memory — the weight of his cheek resting against my head, the warmth of his breath on my ear. I close my eyes, willing the world to disappear.

He kisses my head, then steps back. We stand staring at one another until finally I force myself to turn away.

"I need to go," I say, my heart simultaneously fluttering and shattering. "I've got a busy day tomorrow."

"I'm sorry," he says, and jams his hands into his pockets. "I got a little carried away."

I want to tell him it's okay, that I got carried away, too. I want to return to that place against his chest and feel his arms around me all night. But that's wrong. I'd never forgive myself.

"Will I see you again?" he asks.

I lift my shoulders, the hopelessness of the situation bearing down on me. "I don't know."

"I suppose calling you is out of the question."

"Honestly? I'd love it. But I don't operate that way. I'm too invested in Michael." It's the first time I've said his name aloud, and RJ stiffens.

"I hope Michael knows what he's got in you."

I put a hand on my throat and nod. I hope so, too. But I'm no longer sure. Ever since I stumbled into RJ's little vineyard last month, I've had doubts about Michael.

He looks down at me and smiles, but his

eyes are heavy. "When you decide to kick him to the curb, I want to be at the top of your dance card, you hear?"

I try to smile. "Absolutely." But we're both dreaming. Even if I were single, there's no way we'd ever be anything more than an occasional fling. Our careers would kill any chance of permanence. And more than anything else, I want permanence.

I wake the following morning in my rental cottage, my gaze at once drawn to the floor-to-ceiling windows overlooking the bay. The sun is just crowning the horizon, mopping the sky with pinks and oranges. I stare out at the bay, covered with a blanket of mist, and say a silent prayer for the day ahead.

I move to the living room, taking in the stone fireplace and oak floors and built-in bookcases. Definitely my kind of house.

I'd love to show this place to RJ, maybe have him over for dinner. But of course I can't. Again I feel a pang of sadness. How is it possible to feel such a connection to someone I barely know? Is it because lately Michael seems so distant? I'd hate to think I'm one of those women who needs a backup man, but maybe that's what it is. Michael's distance is making me vulnerable.

I brew a cup of coffee and take it onto the

deck, along with my laptop. It's chillier than I realized, but the beauty is so captivating I refuse to leave. I wrap my robe tight across my chest and tuck my bare feet under my legs. I gaze out at the majestic view, thinking of RJ and how right it felt to be with him.

I groan. This is crazy! I throw open my laptop and connect with the Internet. James Peters appears in my in-box.

I hold my breath, waiting for his message to appear.

Hannah,
   Thank you for your proposal on fracking and the Great Lakes. Rest assured, you are still in contention for the position. We plan to have a decision in the next day or two.

Best,
James

I let out my breath. Good. I still have a chance. And if I happen to get the job, I won't have to worry about how to finesse the proposed show. I'd no sooner have my mother on the air in Chicago than I would New Orleans.

I'm reading an e-mail from Jade when my phone rings. I glance at it. Michael. Instead of smiling, I sigh, preparing myself for another stilted conversation. Just a couple more days and we'll be back to normal. At least that's what I tell myself.

"Good morning," I say, with more cheer than I feel.

"How goes it in Michigan?"

"Good. I'm sitting on the deck looking out at Grand Traverse Bay. It's like a postcard."

"Really?"

"I know. It's weird, I don't remember it like this."

"Have you seen her?" His voice is clipped. He doesn't want to hear about my memories. He only wants to hear that I've made peace with my mother and I'm on my way home.

"I'm going over there this morning. I'm hoping to time it so that she's still home but Bob is off to work."

"What'd you do last night? I tried calling."

My heart speeds. "I went to a great French restaurant," I say truthfully.

"Oh, right. I got your message. With the vineyard owner." He laughs. "Hell, I wouldn't even admit that."

He's making fun of RJ. I bite back my anger. "He makes a great wine. You'd be surprised. And the vineyard is gorgeous. This whole area is pretty spectacular."

"Well, don't fall in love with it," he tells me. "I want you back this weekend. We've got the City Park fund-raiser Friday night, remember?"

Another fund-raiser. More bullshitting and promise making. More hand shaking and shoulder slapping. For the life of me I can't muster any excitement for it.

"Yes," I say. "I'll be there. Of course I'll be there." I pause only a moment before adding, "I only wish that sometime you'd be there for me."

The words tumble out of my mouth before I have time to rein them in. I wait, hearing nothing but a good ten seconds of silence at the other end of the line.

"Am I supposed to know what that means?" he asks, his voice frostbitten.

My heart thumps wildly. "I'm doing something today that has my stomach in knots, Michael. You haven't so much as wished me good luck."

"I made it clear that I think it's a mistake, dredging up the past. I advised against it, but you won't listen. Instead, you plow forward, full steam ahead. So maybe your definition of 'being there for you' differs from mine."

I won't let him manipulate me. "Look, I know you don't approve of what I'm doing, but I need you to trust me. I'm not going to hurt us — if there even is an 'us.' " Whether it's because I'm a thousand miles away, or because I spent last evening with a man I found very interesting, I feel emboldened today, as if the balance of power has shifted. "Sometimes I wonder if we're ever going to get married. I'm thirty-four years old, Michael. I don't have all the time in the world."

My heart thunders in my chest, and I wait. Jesus, what have I done?

He clears his throat, the way he does before making an important political point. "You're on edge. I get that. But yes, to answer your question, there is an 'us.' At least *I* think so. I've made it clear from day one. I want to wait until Abby finishes school before I think about remarrying."

"She graduates next spring. It's not too early to make plans. Can we talk about this?"

"Jesus, Hannah. What's gotten into you? Yes, we can talk about this when you get back." He chuckles, but it's the same forced chuckle he uses with his opponents during debates. "Now I need to scoot. Be careful today." He pauses. "And, for the record, good luck."

CHAPTER 27

I can't make a decision this morning. Every choice — from jewelry to hair — seems crucial. A pair of leggings or a skirt? Hair curled or straight? Lipstick or ChapStick? Necklace or no necklace?

"Shit," I say aloud when I drop my blush compact. It ricochets off the tile, shattering the mirror and scattering pink shards of powder across the floor. My hands shake as I pick up the pieces.

What if I've waited too long? Maybe my mother no longer has those loving feelings that bond a mother to her daughter. Maybe she's forgotten about me, taken Bob's side. He may have brainwashed her.

Surely Bob hates me. A thick, sobering dread fills me, and I imagine a dozen possible scenarios, none of them good. Will he yell at me? Would he dare strike me? No, I don't remember him as a violent man. In fact, I remember him never raising his voice.

The most vivid memory of him is the one I witnessed after I'd called him a pervert. It's the haunting memory of a face crumpling in disbelief.

At half past eight, I drive by the house one more time, my reconnaissance mission. My hands are damp with perspiration, and I hold tight to the steering wheel. I'd hoped to see my mother outside again today. Alone. I could walk up to her and tell her I'm sorry, and be done with it. But the brown Chevy sits alone in the driveway. Nobody's outside this morning.

I slow. Beyond the picture window, I think I see movement. Is she inside? What if I ring the bell and Bob answers? Would he recognize me? Could I claim I had the wrong address and leave unnoticed? Maybe I should just wait until she comes home this afternoon.

No. I need to do this. It's already Tuesday. I don't have much time.

I park in the road again, but this time I trek up the driveway instead of sneaking through the woods. The drive is unpaved, like the road, and the loose gravel shifts beneath my flats. I wonder how my mother navigates this cobbled patch. At once, it comes back to me, that final scene, in my father's rental car in this very driveway. He shoved the gearshift into reverse and we backed away. My mother ran after the car, like a dog chasing after its owner. We'd reached the end of the driveway when I saw her slip on the loose gravel. She fell to her knees, sobbing. My father saw it, too, I know he did. When we got onto the road, he stepped on the gas. I swiveled in my seat and watched, horrified, as tiny stones flew at her from the car tires. I turned back around. I couldn't watch anymore. Instead, I added another layer of steel to my heart.

I put a hand to my head. *Stop these memories. Please!*

The concrete steps give way when I take my first step up to the porch. I grab hold of the iron rail. Up close, the wood-framed house looks worse than it did from the road. The gray paint is peeling, and the screen door is falling off its hinges. Why the hell doesn't Bob fix this? And why did I wear this old necklace? It's probably worth more money than this cabin. After all my years of anger, it's odd to feel protective of my mother.

Faint voices and laughter seep through the closed door. I recognize Al Roker's voice on *Today.* A vision of my mother comes to me. She's leaning into the bathroom mirror, the *Today* show blaring from the living

307

room so she could hear while she applied her makeup. I wonder now if her love of morning television influenced my career path. Did I hope that one day she'd hear me? Or was it as I suspect, I chose a career where I could ask the questions, not answer them?

I take one deep breath, and then another. I clear my throat, rearrange my scarf to hide the diamond-and-sapphire necklace, and ring the doorbell.

She's wearing a blue smock and a pair of black slacks. And she's tiny. So very tiny. Her hair, which was once her best feature, is dull brown and brittle-looking. Around her mouth is a nest of lines and wrinkles, and dark circles hover beneath her eyes. It's the broken face of a fifty-four-year-old woman who's had one hell of a life. I put a hand to my mouth.

"Hello," she says, and pushes open the screen door. I want to scold her, to tell her she's naïve, that she should never open the door to a stranger. She smiles at me, and I see stains on her once-pretty teeth. I search her face for familiar pieces of her and find them in her pale blue eyes. Kindness still lurks there, and something else. Sadness.

I open my mouth to speak, but my throat

closes. Instead, I simply stare at her, and watch as her eyes and mind register my identity.

A moan as primal as an animal's wail comes from her throat. She steps onto the porch and the door slams behind her. Her tiny frame nearly knocks me over when she bangs into me full-force. "My girl," she cries. "My beautiful girl."

It's as if twenty years dissolve on sight, and we're just a mother and a daughter, caught in the most fundamental, instinctual love.

She pulls me to her chest and rocks me. She smells of patchouli oil. "Hannah," she says, "Hannah, my dear Hannah!" Back and forth we sway like a wind sock. Finally she pulls back and kisses me on the cheek, the forehead, the tip of my nose, just as I remember her doing before I went off to school each morning. She sobs now and, every second or two, steps back to stare at me, as if she's afraid she's dreaming this moment. If I ever doubted her love for me, the thought has vanished.

"Mom," I say, my voice breaking.

She covers her mouth with her hand. "You're here. You're really here. I can't believe it. I just can't believe it."

She takes me by the hand and pulls me

toward the door. I don't move. From inside, I hear the blare of the television. My head swims. My legs are concrete posts, rooted to this spot. I turn to look back at my car. I can leave now. I can say I'm sorry and leave. I don't need to go back inside this place — the place I swore I'd never set foot in again. The place my father forbade me from visiting.

"I won't stay," I say. "You need to get to work. I can come back later."

"No. Please. I'll call for a substitute." She tugs on my hand, but I pull back.

"Is — is he here?" I ask, my voice shaky.

She bites her lip. "No. He don't get home till three. It's just us now."

Just us. Mother and daughter. No Bob. The way I wanted it to be — then and now.

With my hand in hers, I enter. The smell of wood smoke and lemon oil takes me back to the summer of '93. I breathe deeply, hoping to slow my frenetic heartbeat.

The living room is cramped but spotless. In one corner I spy the old wood-burning stove. I'm relieved that the old brown sofa is gone now. They've replaced it with an oversized beige velour sectional that seems to swallow the small room.

My mother chatters about all of the changes as we pass through the living room into the tiny kitchen. "Bob built these new cupboards about ten years ago."

I run a hand over the pretty oak. They've kept the same vinyl flooring — squares and rectangles that are supposed to look like ceramic tile — and the white Formica countertops.

She pulls a chair from the oak table, and I sit down. She sits facing me, holding both my hands in hers.

"I'll get you some tea," she says. "Or coffee. Maybe you like coffee better."

"Either is fine."

"Okay. But first I got to look at you." She stares at me, her eyes drinking me in. "What a beauty you are."

Her eyes shine, and she reaches out to smooth my hair. It strikes me now that I've robbed her of so much, so many mother-daughter moments. The woman who loved to do hair and nails and makeup would've loved teaching her daughter her tricks. Senior proms, homecomings, graduations. They'd all been stripped from her clutches, no different than if I'd died. Or possibly worse. Instead of leaving her through accident or illness, I'd left her by choice.

"I'm so sorry, Mom." The words tumble from my mouth. "I came all this way to tell you."

She hesitates, and when she speaks, each word is measured, as if she's afraid one wrong syllable could send the entire confession tumbling. "You . . . you're sorry for what you done to Bob?"

"I . . ." I've practiced the sentence for weeks now, but still it gets stuck in my throat. "I'm not sure . . ."

She nods, signaling me to continue, and her eyes never leave mine. There's a ferocity in those eyes, as if she's hoping against hope I'll deliver the message she's desperate to hear.

"I'm not sure what really happened that night."

I hear a gasp. She puts a hand to her mouth and nods. "Thank you," she says, her voice strangled. "Thank you."

We finish our tea, then take a stroll in the garden. It's the first time it's occurred to me. My love of flowers came from my mother's passion. She points out every plant and flower, each one with a special purpose, planted in memory of me.

"Here's the weeping willow I planted the year you left. Look how big it's grown." She looks up at the tree, its reeds bending toward the lake like Rapunzel's hair. I imagine my mother digging the hole, placing this spindly tree into the earth, trying to replace her daughter.

"These lilacs always remind me of your first ballet recital. I brought you a bouquet of lilac blossoms that day at Gloria Rose's Studio. You told me it smelled like cotton candy."

"I remember," I say, recalling that worried little girl peeking out from backstage, wondering why her parents weren't in the audience. "I panicked. I thought you weren't coming. You and Daddy had had a fight."

It's odd that the memory found me, after all these years. That recital was long before we'd moved to Detroit. I'd convinced myself they never fought until Bob came along.

"Yes, that's right."

"Why were you fighting, if you don't mind my asking?"

"It don't matter, sweetie."

For some reason it does. "Tell me, Mom. Please. I'm an adult now."

She laughs. "You are. Do you realize you're the very age I was when you left?"

You left. She doesn't say it in an accusatory way, but still the words sear my soul. She was so young when I left her. And the life I went on to have is so vastly different than hers, then and now.

"You and Daddy married so young. You

313

used to tell me you just couldn't wait."

"I was desperate to leave Schuylkill County." She plucks a frond of Spanish bluebell, rolls it between her fingers, and inhales the scent. "Your dad was being transferred to Saint Louis. He wanted someone to go with him."

I cock my head. "You make it sound like a marriage of convenience."

"He wasn't exactly a world traveler back then. Neither of us was. It was scary leaving Pittsburgh. He liked having me along, I guess."

"But you loved each other."

She lifts her shoulders. "Even then, when we were happy and passionate, I knew I'd never be enough for him."

I reach out and pull a loose strand of hair from her smock. "You? You were so pretty." I correct myself. "You *are* so pretty. Of course you were enough for him."

Her eyes dim a shade. "No, honey. And that's okay."

"Why would you say that? Daddy was crazy for you."

She looks out at the lake. "I was nothing special. School was always hard for me. I missed a lot."

My heart breaks for her. My dad used to correct her poor grammar, buy her books on the proper use of English. "You sound like a coal miner's daughter," he'd say, which, of course, she was. "Don't you pick up those bad habits," he'd tell me. "Smart people don't say . . ." He'd fill in the blank with "You done good," or "ain't," or "I got to go." She'd laugh and wave him off, but once I remember seeing her lip tremble just before she turned her face. I came up behind her and wrapped my little arms around her middle. I told her she was the smartest person in the world.

"Your granddad used to make me stay home and take care of the kids whenever Mama had a cleaning job." She looks down at her smock. "Can you believe it? I'm a cleaning woman now, too."

I see now that she's embarrassed. Here comes her daughter with her designer clothes and college degree, and she feels ashamed. I feel a gorge of love so deep that I can barely speak. I want to tell her that it's okay. That I'm just a girl who needs her mother. But it feels too awkward. Instead, I lighten the mood.

"I bet you're the best one in the whole crew. You were always such a clean freak."

She laughs, and I turn to her. "But in the end, you really were enough. You were the one who found someone else, not Daddy.

He was crushed."

She looks away.

"Isn't that right?" I ask, feeling my pulse quicken.

Her eyes meet mine, and she doesn't say a word. Already I know the answer, but still I have to ask.

"Daddy was faithful to you, right, Mom?"

"Oh, honey, it wasn't your dad's fault."

I put a hand to my head. "No! Why didn't you tell me?"

"It was the way things were with professional athletes — probably the way they still are. I knew it when I married him. I just thought . . ." She laughs, a sad little laugh. "I thought I could change him. I was young and stupid. I thought all it took to keep him was to be pretty. But there was always someone younger, someone prettier and, well, a whole lot more fun."

I think of Claudia, and my own insecurities. "You must have hated feeling like you had to be perfect."

She tucks a strand of hair behind her ear. "Them players could have any woman they wanted."

My anger rises. "How many?"

She points to a hedge of rosebushes, still a month from blooming. "You always loved the roses. Funny, they've never been my favorite. I prefer these." She points to a flock of daffodils.

"How many women, Mom?" I repeat.

She shakes her head. "Hannah, stop. Please. It ain't — isn't — important. You can't blame him. Most all the athletes did it. Them girls was theirs for the taking."

My heart goes out to that young woman with the tight jeans, desperate to stay young and pretty yet never feeling like she was good enough. With every passing year, she must have cursed time.

"No wonder you weren't happy. Why didn't you ever tell me this? I would have understood."

" 'Honor thy father,' " she says quietly, quoting the Bible. "I had no business telling you then, and I have no business telling you now."

I want to scream! But it would have explained so much. All those years I'd demonized her — and my father let me. If only I'd known what she'd had to endure, I would have been more sympathetic.

"I had a feeling someday you'd figure it out for yourself, when you got older and we were more like best friends than mother-daughter." She smiles at me, and I see all of her lost dreams in those pale blue eyes.

She squats down to pick a dandelion from

the flower bed. "Your father craved love. He needed it like water. He just couldn't give it."

I want to tell her she's wrong, that my father was a loving man. But just below the surface, I feel the truth bubbling. And I know she's right.

I watch her shake the soil from the weed, and I feel my own "soil" fall from me. Everything I'd held fast to, every truth I'd held, crumbles. Maybe my father really did manipulate me. Maybe he purposely poisoned my feelings, and kept me from my mother. Maybe *his truth,* as Dorothy called it, wasn't *the* truth.

She tosses the weed behind a bush. "You were the one exception. I do believe he loved you, Hannah Marie."

"As best he could," I say, knowing that it was a selfish love but all he was capable of giving. A thought occurs to me. "Did you send me letters, Mom?"

She turns to me, her eyes wide. "The first of each month," she says. "Without fail. I finally stopped when one was returned to me with a note saying John had died. She told me to stop writing."

She? I feel myself sway. "Who was it from?"

"A gal named Julia."

I lift my hands to my head. "No. Not Julia." But even as I try to deny it, I know it's true. Like me, Julia was another of my dad's enablers. She showed her love by protecting him. How can I be angry when I was no different?

"I wish you'd sent the letters directly to me."

She looks at me as if the thought were ridiculous. "You wouldn't give me your address. After you left Atlanta, I asked for it over and over. Finally, your dad told me I could send letters to him. He promised he'd give them to you."

And she listened to him. Just like I did.

"How could you let me go?" The words spill from my lips without forethought.

She steps back and looks down at her hands. "Your dad's lawyer convinced me it was best for everyone, including you. You'd have been forced to testify. Bob could've spent years in prison."

So there it is. Her own Sophie's choice. She probably gave up her half of the divorce settlement, too.

She grabs me by the arms. "You got to believe me, Hannah. I loved you. I thought I was doing the right thing. I really did." She turns away and kicks the ground with the toe of her sneaker. "I was so stupid. I

319

thought you'd come back when you turned sixteen and could decide for yourself. When your dad told me you never wanted to see me again, I nearly lost my mind."

A wave of dizziness comes over me and I fight to understand my father's selfish actions — and my own. Why did he keep my mother from me? Did he think he was being helpful? Or did his competitive spirit crave revenge? Was his need to punish my mother so profound that he ignored the fact that he was punishing me, too? I feel the cargo of anger I've carried for my mother spilling out, creating a whole new heap, this one for my father. And once again, I'm entrenched in bitterness and anger.

I look up at the sky. No! I've come so far to rid myself of the rage I've carried. I have two choices. I can let the anger bury me again, or let it go.

Fiona's words take shape in my head. *We keep secrets for two reasons. Either to protect ourselves or to protect others.*

My father was protecting me, at least he thought he was. Yes. I will choose to believe this. Because the alternative, that he was protecting himself, is too heavy a notion.

I lay a hand on her back. "Don't cry, Mom. It's okay now. You did what you thought was best. So did I." I swallow hard.

"And Daddy did, too."

My mother swipes her eyes, then turns toward the dirt road, looking north with her head cocked. I hear it, too. The distant rumble of an engine. "Bob's coming."

CHAPTER 28

A volt of electricity shimmies up my spine. The moment I've avoided my entire adult life has arrived. "I need to go."

"No. Stay."

"I'll sit in my car. You can explain why I'm here. If he wants me to leave, I will."

My mother smooths down her hair and pats her pockets, then fishes out a tube of Maybelline.

"No," she tells me, her lips now a tawny rose. She tucks the lipstick back into her pocket. "Bob won't remember you."

I'm struck by the comment. My mother doesn't try to sugarcoat it. He's forgotten all about me. To Bob, I am dead.

A county bus, not much larger than a van, pulls up to the house. So, my mother is a house cleaner and Bob is a bus driver. A bus driver who doesn't remember his wife's daughter.

The green-and-white vehicle comes to a

halt in the driveway. My mother stands alongside the bus, waiting for the doors to fold open. When they do, the driver appears — a wiry twentysomething with a tattoo sleeve.

I'm confused for a moment. Who is this guy? Certainly not Bob. I see someone on the other side of the driver. An elderly man, stooped and frail, gripping the tattooed man's elbow.

My mother steps forward and kisses the old man's cheek. "Hi, honey."

My hand flies to my throat and I gasp. Bob? No. It can't be.

My mother thanks the driver and offers her hand to Bob. He clutches it and smiles. Whether it's his stooped posture or osteoporosis, he seems to have shrunk six inches. I look for some resemblance, some sign of the beefy construction worker with broad shoulders and a hearty laugh. But all I see is a feeble man wearing a pale green shirt with a purple stain down the front, clutching my mother's hand like a five-year-old boy.

In seconds, my brain makes assumptions. He's had an accident. He has a disease.

"Aren't you the pretty one," he says to my mother, as if he's never seen her. He spots me and breaks into a grin. "Hello," he says in a singsong voice.

"Bob, you remember Hannah, my daughter?"

Bob chuckles. "Aren't you the pretty one."

Slowly, I move toward him. He looks elfin now, with a tiny, smooth face and enormous ears that look like they've been attached to the sides of his head like Mr. Potato. He wears white sneakers and a pair of chinos cinched with a brown leather belt, accenting a balloon-sized paunch.

All my fear has vanished, and in its place I feel pity and sadness and shame. My hands fall to my sides. "Hello, Bob."

He looks from my mother to me. "Hello," he says, and smiles.

My mother puts an arm around me. "Bob, this is my daughter." She speaks kindly but deliberately, as if she were speaking to a child. "This is Hannah. She's come to visit."

"Aren't you the pretty one."

In an instant, I know his diagnosis. Alzheimer's.

Bob sits at the kitchen table putting together a children's puzzle while my mother and I prepare dinner. I watch him examine a wooden fire truck, running his finger over its edges, contemplating in which of the five slots it belongs.

"You doing okay, honey?" my mom asks again. She pulls a Ziploc bag from the freezer. "Homemade garlic toast," she tells him. "You love it, don't you, hon?"

I'm in awe of her cheerfulness, the unapologetic dignity she gives her husband. I sense no bitterness, no impatience or anger. She seems almost giddy with joy that I'm here, and it both pleases and pains me. I should have come back twenty years ago.

She touches me every minute or two, as if by touch she's confirming that I'm really here. She fixes spaghetti, which she remembers as my favorite. She sautés ground beef and onions, and mixes in a jar of Prego spaghetti sauce. The Parmesan cheese is from a green container rather than freshly grated. The only culinary trait we share is our love for homemade bread.

Again, I'm struck by how very different my life is than hers. Who would I have been, had I stayed with my mother? Would I be living here in Northern Michigan, fixing Chef Boyardee for my family? And the bigger question, is my life better for having left, or worse?

Our dinner feels like an outing at Chuck E. Cheese's. While my mother and I try to talk, Bob interrupts, interjecting the same questions over and over again. *Who's she? Aren't you the pretty one. Going fishing in the morning.*

"He hasn't fished in years," she tells me. "Todd puts that old boat in the water for him every year, but it just sits there. I really got to sell it."

We talk about the years in between. My mother tells me they moved north after Bob lost his teaching job.

"It was another hurdle," she says. "Leaving teaching was hard enough, but wow, losing his coaching job nearly did him in."

I don't want to ask the question that's burning in me, but I must. "Did . . . my situation . . . have something to do with him losing his job?"

My mother wipes her mouth with a napkin, then feeds a forkful of spaghetti to Bob. "Mrs. Jacobs. Remember her? She lived in the ranch next door."

"Yes," I say, recalling the old biddy I once overheard calling my mother "flashy."

"She'd gotten wind of the fallout."

The fallout. She's talking about the incident. The accusation. *My* accusation.

"Who told her?" I ask. "The . . . incident . . . happened here, three hundred miles from Bloomfield Hills. How'd she find out?"

My mother wipes Bob's mouth, then

326

holds a glass of milk to his lips. She's not answering my question.

"Dad," I say aloud. My father must have told Mrs. Jacobs about my accusation. He knew her reputation as a gossip. He knew she wouldn't be able to keep it quiet. Which, of course, is exactly why he told her. Another shot of revenge.

"Oh no," I say, feeling the weight of my shame, sensing the ripples of damage from that one accusation. "And she reported him?"

My mother leans in and touches my arm. "In some ways, it freed us, honey. We left Detroit and come here. We got us a fresh start."

"Why didn't Bob teach here?"

"Construction was booming at the time. Still is."

"But he loved teaching, and coaching, too."

She turns away. "Life is a trade-off, honey. It was too risky. If anyone would've made a complaint against him, he'd be a sitting duck."

Aftershock. Collateral damage. Whatever you call it, it's wreckage, the result of my accusation. I push my plate away, unable to eat another bite.

■ ■ ■ ■

We sit on the back porch that evening. I take a seat in a molded plastic chair, and my mom leads Bob to the porch swing. The spring air is chilly, and my mother retrieves sweaters for all of us. She tucks a blanket around Bob's shoulders. "Are you warm enough, sweetheart?"

"Oh, yeah."

"This porch is your favorite spot, isn't it, hon?"

"Oh, yeah."

I watch, touched by the loving care my mother provides to this shadow of a person she calls her husband. And it's taking a toll on her, I see it. I think of my father at age fifty-four. He traveled the world, played golf five days a week. He had health and money and Julia. This isn't fair. My mother should be traveling and enjoying life. Instead, she's tethered to a man who sometimes recognizes her, sometimes doesn't.

"Who's she?" Bob asks for the umpteenth time, pointing to me.

My mother starts to explain, but I interrupt. "Let me, Mom." I rise and take a deep breath. "I've come a thousand miles to apologize. This isn't the way I intended it to be, but still, I need to do it."

"Honey, that's not necessary."

I ignore her and walk over to the porch swing. Bob scoots aside and pats the place next to him. I sit down.

I should take his hand. I should pat his back or rub his arm, something to let him know I'm his ally. I hate myself for it, but I can't. Even now, in his compromised state, the thought of touching him is too unsettling. Is my reaction instinctual? I close my eyes. No! I cannot keep second-guessing that night. Bob's touch, no matter how intentional it felt, was accidental. Period. End of story. My entire relationship with my mother depends on that truth. And I'll learn to believe it. I know I will.

"Who's she?"

I take a deep breath. "I'm Hannah, Bob. Suzanne's daughter. Do you remember me?"

He nods and smiles. "Oh, yeah." But he doesn't. I know he doesn't.

Finally, I muster the courage to take his hand. It's cool, with big earthworm veins meandering over bone and under age spots. But it's soft. He squeezes my hand, and my heart wrenches.

"I hurt you once," I say, and feel my nose burn with shame.

"Aren't you the pretty one."

"No," I say. "I'm not pretty. I accused you of something. Something very bad."

He's looking off into the woods, but his hand is still in mine.

"Listen to me," I say, through clenched teeth. For some reason, it comes out angry.

He turns to me, the face of a child who's been scolded. Tears flood my eyes and I try to blink them away. He stares at me, bewildered.

"I want to tell you I'm sorry." My voice is husky, trembling.

My mother comes to my side, patting my back. "Shhh. It's not necessary, honey."

"I accused you of touching me," I say. Tears stream down my cheeks now. I no longer try to be stoic. "I was wrong to do that. I had no proof. You didn't mean to . . ."

He lifts his free hand and touches my face. He trails a tear with his finger. I let him. "She's crying," he says, looking to my mother. "Who is she?"

I swallow hard and swipe my eyes. "Someone very small," I say softly. I start to rise, but he has a firm grip on my hand.

"Aren't you the pretty one."

I look over at this man, a picture of innocence. "Will you forgive me?" I ask. I know it's not fair. He isn't capable of granting forgiveness. But still, I have to ask. I want to hear it. I *need* to hear it. I turn to him. "Please, Bob, forgive me. Will you? Please?"

He smiles. "Oh, yeah."

I cover my mouth and nod, unable to speak. Slowly I open my arms and pull his frail body to mine. He clutches me, as if the human touch is instinctual, the last vestige of our humanity.

I feel my mother's hand on my back. "We forgive you, honey."

I close my eyes and let the words wash over me. So much healing in those four words.

CHAPTER 29

My mother invites me to spend the night, but I don't. Instead, I drive toward my beautiful rental cottage, feeling guilty. The privileged daughter gets to walk away from the shabby cabin and a man in the throes of dementia, but my mother cannot escape. Thoughts of the day ramble in my head. Did I make any progress? If so, why do I feel so damn horrible? The single accusation, made twenty years ago, created a domino effect. My mother's life and Bob's were forever altered by my actions. They can never reclaim his reputation.

My heart begins to race, and my breath comes in uneven bursts. I pull off to the side of the road. The diamond-and-sapphire necklace chokes me and I fumble to unhook it. I free it from my neck and slide it into my purse. I need to talk to Michael. I need someone to assure me that my actions were those of a thirteen-year-old. That I didn't mean for their lives to be ruined.

I quickly punch in his number. His voice mail picks up. I click my phone off without leaving a message. Who was I kidding? He doesn't want to hear my story. I close my eyes and work to breathe, until finally I can drive again.

Two miles down the road, I pass the sign for Merlot de la Mitaine. Without forethought, I turn down the gravel lane and make my way to the parking lot. The tension eases, and I rub my neck. A half dozen cars are in the lot, and the place is lit up. I have a sudden urgency to see RJ. I want to tell him about today. I want to feel his arms around me, comforting me, telling me it's okay. And barring that, I need a glass of wine.

I lock my car and scurry toward the entrance. Just before reaching the door, I stop. What am I doing? This isn't fair. I told RJ I have a boyfriend. Now suddenly I turn to him because I need sympathy? How pathetic. Am I just like my father, craving love but unable to give it? Using people for my own purposes?

I turn around and hurry back to my car. I speed away, before RJ even knows I was there.

■ ■ ■ ■

I return to the house the next morning. My mother has a breakfast of pancakes and sausage waiting for me — something I haven't eaten in years. Bob sits in the living room, thumbing through an old Sears catalog. From the other side of the kitchen counter, my mother watches me eat.

"More juice?" she asks.

"No, thanks. But these pancakes are delicious," I say, prompting her to add another stack to my plate.

By the time we finish the dishes it's after ten. My flight leaves at six, and I'd planned to get to the airport early, make a call to Michael and catch up on e-mails.

But it's a glorious day. A day for fishing.

I step into the living room and find Bob asleep on the recliner, the weathered catalog on his lap. I take it from him and place it on the end table. When I do, I see that it's turned to the girls' underwear section. A chill comes over me. Jesus, is he . . . ? I stare down at him, sleeping, with his mouth slack and his skin sagging. *He's just a child,* I tell myself. *He's no different than a young boy.* And I pray to God it's true.

■ ■ ■ ■

I take Bob's elbow, and he skips through
the grass toward the lake. In his hand he
lugs his old red tackle box, the same one I
remember when I was a girl. It's locked,
just as it always was.

"Going fishing," he says.

"No fishing today," I tell him. "But we're
going for a boat ride."

I settle Bob onto the boat's metal bench
seat, and my mother secures an orange life
vest to his chest. He keeps the tackle box
on his lap and places a hand on it like it's
his favorite toy. The hinges are rusty now,
and corrosion covers the old padlock.

I narrow my eyes, wondering why he has
a lock on a tackle box. The entire contents
can't be worth much more than fifty dollars. Two keys dangle from the boat's key
chain. I'm guessing the little one is to the
tackle box.

"What's in that box of yours, Bob?" I ask,
and knock on the metal case. "Fishing lures?
Bobbers?"

"Oh, yeah," he says, but he's gazing off in
the distance.

Big, billowy clouds hang overhead, playing hide-and-seek with the sun. The water

335

is a sheet of cellophane today, and I count at least a dozen other fishing boats.

"Looks like a good day for fishing," I say. "See all your old pals?"

"Oh, yeah."

I fill the tank with gas, then prime the pump. It's strange how it comes back to me. I was barely listening the day Bob showed me how to start the boat.

I pull the start cord and each time it spits and chokes, but never catches. My arm aches, but I won't give up. I owe Bob this boat ride. I prime the pump again, and finally the engine chugs to life.

We push off, and the engine coughs and blows smoke. The familiar diesel odor mingles with the pungent scent of the lake. I sit holding the engine's handle, pointing the small craft into the lake. My mother perches beside Bob, shouting over the engine for him to sit down. He wants to stand. He's like a child at the fair, dizzy with joy and excitement.

He laughs and smiles, raises his head to the sun and breathes in the fusty scent of the lake. My mother laughs, too, and I smile at their happiness. I slide the engine handle and we head west. A wave splashes up on the boat's bow, sending drops of cold water raining down on us. Bob lets out a whoop and claps his hands.

"Going fishing," he says again.

We flit about on the water for a good forty-five minutes before my mother notices a couple inches of water have collected in the boat's bottom. I turn toward shore and tie the boat at the dock. Bob holds my mother's hand, and the three of us traipse up the grassy hill toward the house.

We pass by the old balance beam, and on impulse I step up on it.

"You made me this beam, Bob. Thank you. I should have told you years ago. I love it." I flit across the narrow plank, laughing as I steady myself with my outstretched arms.

Bob holds out his hand to me. I perform a clumsy little leap, then look over my shoulder at him.

"Thank you, Bob."

He smiles at me and nods. "Sister's beam."

Our good-bye is bittersweet. This time, it's temporary. My mother and I both recognize how much we've lost, and how much making up we have ahead of us.

"Next month," she tells me. She pulls me into her arms, and I hear her whisper, "I love you."

I step back and look into her blue eyes, bright with tears. "I love you, Mom."

I drive out of Harbour Cove, my emotions raw. Yes, it's wonderful to have a mother again, but can I ever forgive myself for what I've put her through? And Bob, too. What would their lives be like, had I not jumped to the wrong conclusion?

A few miles out, I pull over at a rest stop and call Michael.

"Hello, sweetheart."

"Hey," Michael says. "Where are you?"

"Just leaving Harbour Cove, on my way to the airport."

"Doing okay?"

"Yes. Coming here was the right decision. I promised my mom I'd come back in a month or two. It's surreal, having a mother again."

"So everything's copacetic?"

What he wants to know is whether I'm going to reveal any secrets on the air. Despite Stuart's urging, I never mentioned the show to my mother. She'd come if she knew Stuart wanted her onstage during the segment. But I won't let my mother be a prop for my trumped-up story. My entire viewing audience, along with Stuart and Priscille, believe I traveled to Harbour Cove to grant forgiveness, not to seek it. And that's exactly what I must tell them.

"Yes," I say. "You have nothing to fear. I won't reveal any ugly secrets."

I hear the snark in my voice and imagine he hears it, too.

CHAPTER 30

It's nearly midnight when the plane touches down Thursday evening. I turn on my telephone when I get to baggage claim and see two missed calls, both with a three-one-two area code. Chicago. My hands fumble to retrieve my e-mail, and I warn myself not to get too excited.

Dear Hannah,
Congratulations. You are the final candidate for host of *Good Morning, Chicago.* The last step will be an interview with Joseph Winslow, the owner of the station.

Attached you'll find the details of the compensation package we've put together. Please let me know when it's convenient to talk.

Sincerely,
James Peters

I open the attachment and stare at the figure at the bottom of the page. And all of the zeros. No way! I'd be rich! And I'd be closer to my mother, and . . .

A quick flash of RJ comes to mind. I tuck it away. He's just a nice man, a man I barely know, who came along when I was feeling vulnerable.

I read the e-mail three more times before tucking my phone away. As I do, it hits me. The entire purpose of interviewing in Chicago was so I could spend weekends with Michael and be positioned for a job when he goes to DC. What a strange turn of events, that my only thoughts after receiving the offer were that I'd be closer to my mother and RJ.

Jade strides into the dressing room Friday morning, five minutes early. "Welcome back," she says, and hands me a scone from Community Coffee.

"Hey, thanks." I click off my e-mails and rise from my desk. "You're in a good mood today. Did you get lucky last night or something? And please tell me it wasn't Marcus."

She shoots me a look. "Officer Asshole isn't getting any piece of this booty. If I got laid, I'd be passing out champagne glasses, not blueberry scones. But I do have some things to tell you." She moves to the locker and stashes her purse inside. "First, tell me about your trip. How was your mother?"

I shake my head and smile. "Wonderful . . . and awful." I tell her about my mother, and Bob, and our two days together. "I'm so ashamed. I really screwed up her life."

She takes me by the arms. "Hey, you finished step one. You apologized. Now you need to complete step two. Forgive yourself, Hannabelle."

"I'll try. It just seems too easy, like I need to do something bigger, a penance or something to make up for what I've done."

"Oh, I think you've done your penance. You've been without a mama for years."

I nod but inside I know that's not enough.

Jade motions to the makeup chair. "Have a seat."

I scoot into the chair and describe the beautiful vineyards. She raises her eyebrows when I tell her about my evening with RJ.

"You like this guy."

"I do. But I love Michael." I turn away and snatch the mail from the counter. "Enough about me. What's happened since I've been gone? How's your dad?"

She unfurls a black apron and meets my

eyes in the mirror. "I finally told him."

I swivel so that I can see her directly. "What happened?"

"We were on the sofa, looking at an old photo album. He was talking about the past — it's always the past now, never the future. There was a picture of him and me in the driveway of our old house on LaSalle. Natalie had taken it. We'd been washing his old Buick Riviera, and we'd gotten into a water fight." She smiles. "I remember it as if it were this morning. My mother was furious at the mess we'd tracked into the house. We were soaked."

"Great memory," I say.

"It was. So he and I were reminiscing, and out of the blue he looked over at me and said, 'Jade, honey, you've been a wonderful daughter.'

"I finally knew for certain I was losing him. And he knew it, too." She puts her comb down. "I had to tell him the truth. I went straight to my purse and found my little pouch. Then I sat back down and placed a Forgiveness Stone on his palm. 'I lied to you, Daddy,' I said. 'All those years ago, I lied. Erica Williams was drinking that night of my birthday party.'

"He handed the stone back to me. My heart broke. I thought he was refusing it.

But then he laid his palm on my cheek and smiled. 'Sunshine, I know that. I've always known that.' "

I reach out and squeeze Jade's hand.

"All this time he's been waiting for me to trust him. Now I know, his love is strong enough to bear the weight of my weaknesses. It always was."

The following Wednesday, the studio is packed. As promised, it's time for *The Hannah Farr Show* part two, and I'm both the host and the featured guest. Though I share the stage with Claudia again, along with a panel of reunited mothers and daughters, I've been pitched as the main attraction. Stuart ran ads all last week promoting the highly anticipated episode where Hannah Farr reveals all about her mother-daughter reunion. Of course, I have no intention of revealing all, but I'm not about to tell that to Stuart.

We're twenty minutes into the show, and I feel like a fraud. I'm being heralded as the loving daughter, the all-forgiving child. We discuss the importance of mother-daughter relationships, and Claudia lobs questions to me and the other guests about our mother-daughter reunions. I talk of my mother's choice of Bob over me, trying to keep it vague, so that I'm not actually accusing my mom of leaving me. But it's clear that's what the audience assumes.

I breathe a sigh of relief when I open the show to questions. Only twenty more minutes. It's almost over now.

A middle-aged woman grabs my hand. "Hannah, I admire you so much. My mother abandoned my siblings and me. I've never been able to forgive her. How did you find it in your heart to forgive your mother?"

My pulse quickens. "Thank you. I'm not sure I deserve your admiration. My friend Dorothy seemed to know that I needed to make peace with my mother. And she was right."

"But Hannah, your mother abandoned you."

But she didn't, I want to say. *I abandoned her.* "Even though we hadn't spoken in sixteen years, I never felt like she'd actually abandoned me. I always knew she loved me."

"Loved you?" She shakes her head. "She has a strange way of demonstrating it. But bless your heart for believing it."

The woman takes her seat, and another guest raises her hand. "It's so hard for us mothers to understand your mom. I'm guessing if she had the courage to be here today, we would be very hard on her. Is that why she's not here?"

"No. Absolutely not. It was my idea to keep her out of this. I know my mother would have come today, had I asked her."

"Well, you're my hero, Hannah. Despite the lack of motherly guidance, you've become a lovely young woman. And a very successful one, I might add. I wonder if you've considered your mother's motives. Is it possible she's trying to patch things up now because you're a celebrity, a woman of means, so to speak?"

I force myself to keep the smile on my face. My mother is being painted as a selfish, coldhearted, opportunistic bitch. How dare they? My blood pressure soars, and I remind myself that I'm the reason these women are hostile toward my mother. I've presented her as the wrongdoer. And now, Jesus, I'm the loving, forgiving victim. After all I've learned in the past two months, I'm a bigger fraud than I've ever been.

The woman continues. "You hear tales of celebrity reunions where the parent who abandoned the child has ulterior motives . . ."

I cannot allow my mother to take the heat for this. I need to come clean. In my mind I hear Fiona's words. *The choice is actually pretty simple — do we want to lead a clandestine life, or an authentic one?*

I turn to the woman. Her forehead is creased and her lids are heavy, as if she can barely contain the pain she's feeling for me. I stare into her sympathetic eyes. "The truth is . . ."

Camera one zooms in for a close-up. I bite my lip. Should I do this? Can I do this?

"The truth is . . ." My heart hammers in my chest, and I hear that voice of doubt, once again, questioning that night and Bob's touch. I silence it. "The truth is, I'm the one who needed to be forgiven, not my mother."

I hear a rumble of murmurs from the crowd.

"Oh, honey, it's not your fault," the woman tells me.

"But it is."

I turn and make my way back to the stage. I sit down on the sofa, beside another mother-daughter team. Looking straight into the camera, I begin talking. And this time, I tell the truth . . . at least, I think it's the truth.

"I have a confession to make. I am not the victim in this scenario; my mother is. I made an accusation over twenty years ago and ruined a man's life. And by doing so, I

347

ruined my mother's life, too."

From my perch onstage, I watch the woman's face reshape before my eyes, rearranging itself into bewilderment, and then horror, as the details of my life flow from my lips for the next fifteen minutes.

"So you see, I was a girl who decided that my truth was the truth. I was selfish and judgmental, and in the end, that single decision led to consequences my young heart could never have imagined. And as a woman, even when I knew better, I continued to perpetuate my story. It was a whole lot easier to believe *my* truth than to examine it closely and discover *the* truth.

"Did Bob accept my stone? No. Not really. It was too late. He suffers from dementia. He will never understand my confession, or feel the grace of vindication." My eyes well and I blink back tears. I cannot invite sympathy. "But even so, I feel grateful for the Forgiveness Stones. They led me back to my mother, and just as important, to my true self."

I blot my eyes on my knuckle. The studio is deadly silent. From the corner of my eye I see Stuart lifting his arms frantically. He wants them to applaud? Jesus, Stuart. I don't deserve an ovation. I am not the hero in this scenario, I'm the villain.

"But you never paid for your lie."

I spin around to see Claudia. She's been so silent I almost forgot she's my cohost. The words *your lie* brand my soul. I never actually called my decision a lie, because to this day I'm not certain.

She tilts her head, awaiting my reply. I'm tempted to tell her yes, that I had, indeed paid, just as Jade insisted. I'd lost my mother and all those years with her. But that's just the old me, clinging to a thread of righteousness.

"You're right," I say. "I haven't paid."

CHAPTER 31

Stuart grabs my elbow as I exit the stage, but I shake him off. I don't want his high fives. I don't want to hear how wise I was to finally open up to my fans, that ratings will soar and this is the best thing I could do for my career. The idea of benefiting from this episode sickens me. I didn't plan the confession, and I certainly didn't do it to boost ratings.

I have to stop every few miles on the way home to dry my eyes. I can't quit crying. It's as if my on-air confession finally broke the dam. I'm naked, without pretense. I'm finally allowed to feel shame and guilt and grief and regret. I own my horrible mistake now, and the freedom of it is both excruciating and liberating.

I pull into a convenience store parking lot and dial Michael. His voice mail picks up and I remember he's in Baton Rouge until Friday.

"It's me. I told the truth, Michael. I didn't mean to, but I had to. Please understand."

That evening, I'm eating takeout on my balcony when Jade buzzes.

"Come on up," I tell her.

I grab another wineglass and make her a plate of red beans and rice.

"I thought maybe you'd be out with Michael tonight," she says. "Seeing how it's Wednesday."

"No. He's meeting with a couple major donors in Baton Rouge. You know, golf . . . martinis . . . boys' stuff. I'll see him this weekend."

"Where's Crabby?"

I fight back a smile. "Staying with her grandmother."

Jade raises her eyebrows. "Funny how he manages to find free time when he needs something."

My phone buzzes. Three-one-two area code. I let out a yelp. "Oh, my God! It's Chicago." I rise. "I need to take this call."

"Take a deep breath! And tell them you won't come without a six-figure deal for your favorite assistant."

"Hello," I say as I step through the French doors. I peek at Jade. She gives me a thumbs-up, and I cross my fingers.

"Hannah, Mr. Peters here."

"Hi, James — Mr. Peters."

"You can imagine, I was quite surprised to see your show today."

I smile. "You watched the show?"

"My sister alerted me to it. She sent me a YouTube clip."

"How nice of her. Obviously, my perception of things changed from when I pitched the idea several weeks ago. I really did think *I'd* be accepting *her* apology. But then I heard my mom's story. Of course, I had no intention of confessing today, but it just felt wrong to let her take the blame."

He hesitates. "But Hannah, you pitched this as your original idea."

"That's right."

"According to Stuart Booker, it was his idea — and your cohost's."

The air is sucked from the room. I collapse onto a chair. "No. That's not true. You see, this new anchor, Claudia, she's been gunning for my job since . . ."

I hear the drama in my rant, the pettiness and blame. Now is not the time to accuse. I must take the high ground.

"I'm sorry, Mr. Peters. It was a misunderstanding. I can explain."

"I'm sorry, too. Joseph Winslow has canceled your interview. You're no longer in contention for the position. Best of luck, Hannah. And don't worry, I didn't reveal a thing to Stuart."

I return to the balcony, feeling a strange sense of disorientation.

Jade lifts her wineglass. "Shall we toast to the new host of *Good Morning, Chicago?*"

I sink into my chair. "I lost the job. They don't want me. They saw today's show. They think I stole the idea from Claudia."

"Oh, shit." I feel Jade's hand on my back. "What'd you tell him?"

I shake my head. "It was no use defending myself. I feel like such a fraud. At least he didn't tell Stuart about the interview. I can't afford to lose this job, too."

Jade grimaces.

"What?"

"I hate to pile on, doll, but, there's more bad news."

I stare at her. "What?"

"The station's been flooded with e-mails, tweets, and phone calls all afternoon. People are accusing you of . . . well . . . of being a phony."

My head spins. Michael was right. People love to see a celebrity — even a minor one like me — fall from grace. I stare at her, my hand over my mouth.

"Stuart and Priscille want to meet with you first thing in the morning. I told Stuart I'd be seeing you tonight. I figured you'd rather hear the news from me."

"That's just great. Stuart and Priscille were the ones who started this campaign for self-disclosure in the first place!"

She pats my hand. "I know, Hannabelle. I know." She takes a deep breath. "And one more piece of news, while I'm at it. Claudia's fiancé, Brian Jordan?"

"Yes?"

"He just signed another two-year contract with the Saints. Heard it on ESPN this afternoon."

My mouth falls open. "But that can't be. He's being traded to Miami. Claudia told me."

"He's not going anywhere, doll. And neither is Claudia."

I arrive at Priscille's office the following morning, as ordered.

"Good morning," I say to the back of her head, and step into her office.

"Close the door," she says, continuing to type. Stuart sits facing Priscille's desk and gives me a terse nod. I slip into the chair beside him.

After another minute of keyboard tapping,

Priscille swivels in her chair to give us her undivided attention. "We've got a problem, Hannah." She tosses the *Times-Picayune* onto her desk. An article by Brian Moss takes up the front page. The headline reads THE HANNAH FARR-FETCHED SHOW.

I close my eyes. "Oh, God. I am so sorry. Listen, I'll explain to my viewers —"

"Absolutely not," Priscille says. "We move forward. No explanations, no apologies. In a week or two, this scandal will blow over."

"Don't speak to anyone about it," Stuart adds. "Not the press, not even your friends. We're in damage-control mode."

"Got it," I say.

My hands shake when I step from Priscille's office. I walk with my head down, checking my phone on the way back to my dressing room. Two text messages and three missed calls. All from Michael. *Call me. ASAP.*

Shit. He's seen the newspaper.

I close my office door and dial his number, certain he'll pick up this call.

I'm right.

"Oh, Michael," I say, my voice trembling. "You've probably heard. I'm getting skewered by my fans."

"What have you done, Hannah? All we've worked for could be destroyed now."

I bite my lip. "Look, it's not exactly Armageddon. Stuart and Priscille suggest I lie low for a bit. Things should die down in a week or two."

"That's easy for you to say," he says. "What about me? I can't lie low."

I'm stung by his snide tone, but what did I expect? I always knew this issue was more about him than about me.

"I'm so sorry, Michael. I didn't mean for this to —"

"You were warned, Hannah. I told you this would happen. You didn't listen to me."

And he's right. He did warn me. And despite the wrath of Michael, and my viewers, I made the right decision. There's no way I could sit there and be hailed as a generous and forgiving daughter when I'd created the whole mess.

"Will I see you this weekend?"

He pauses just a fraction of a second too long, and I know he's weighing his options. "Yes," he says. "I'll see you tomorrow."

"Okay. Friday it is."

I punch off the phone and drop my elbows onto my desk. I've finally come clean after twenty years. So why do I feel so dirty?

The studio audience is sparse today. Perhaps it's my imagination, but those who have come seem reserved and borderline hostile.

Today's guest is a plastic surgeon whose specialty is tattoo removal. He compares a tattoo to a self-inflicted branding. The term *brand* makes me think of Michael. Have I really tarnished his brand? No, not a chance. The people of New Orleans trust Michael. If he shows them he's able to forgive my teenage transgression, they'll love him more than ever.

When the show ends and I step down to the audience level for the after-show chitchat, the majority of the guests rise from their seats and file out of the studio, without so much as a quick wave or smile.

"What'd y'all think of Dr. Jones?" I ask, my voice unnaturally cheerful.

From the center aisle, a woman turns to me. Something about her is familiar. Yes, I've seen her before. But where?

She's nearly to the exit when she shouts down at me. "You've lost us, Hannah Farr. The only reason I came today is because I'd already purchased tickets. You are such a disappointment."

My hand flies to my throat and I struggle for air. I watch as she shakes her head, then turns around and walks out the door.

I remember her now. She was the same woman who took my hand that night at

Broussard's with Michael and Abby. *"I'm a huge fan, Hannah,"* the woman had said, gripping my arm. *"Every morning you make me smile."*

I missed my chance. I should have asked the surgeon how to get rid of my new tattoo — the one depicting a woman with two faces.

CHAPTER 32

For the rest of the day I try to convince myself that this Hannah Revolt will blow over. Against my better judgment, I listen to Priscille and Stuart and don't reply to any of the nasty posts or e-mails. At midnight Thursday, I stop checking the Twitter feed. The abuse is just too much.

I'm hightailing it to my dressing room after Friday's lackluster show when my phone chimes. A text from Priscille. *Meeting in conference room, now.*

My heart sinks. This cannot be good.

The stark room wakes when I turn on the overhead lights. This space that usually sizzles with shared energy and ideas feels ominous today, as if I'm stepping into an interrogation room, waiting for a burly officer to arrive and entrap me. I take a seat and scroll through my iPhone. Finally I hear Priscille's footsteps clipping down the hallway. I sit up. Where are the sounds of Stuart's steps? He's always included in our meetings. Another wave of dread slams into me.

"Thanks for coming, Hannah." Priscille gives me a terse smile, then closes the door and sits down beside me. She has no notebook, no laptop — not even her ubiquitous coffee mug.

I clutch my shaking hands and force a smile. "No problem. How are you? The show was terrific this morning, don't you thi—"

"I have bad news," she says, cutting me off.

My stomach drops. This scandal isn't going to blow over. I'm in trouble. Big trouble.

"I am so sorry, Priscille. I'll apologize to my audience. I can do a better job of explaining what happened. I was young at the time. If they —"

She holds her hand up and closes her eyes. I feel the prickle of tears and blink madly. "Please. Please just give me a break."

"We had an emergency board meeting at six a.m. I tried to make a case to keep you, but in the end, even I had to agree. You need to go."

I stare at her, my vision fuzzy and unfocused.

"I talked them into calling it an 'indefinite leave.' It'll make it easier when you apply for new positions. Being fired is tough to explain."

The knife twists. "No. Please!" I clutch her arms. "After all these years. One mistake . . ."

"That's not the way we see it. You were the face, the voice, of Louisiana women. Your reputation was impeccable. We all admired your affiliation with Into the Light. You did countless shows on sexual abuse, pedophilia, rape, incest. But this, quote, one mistake, as you call it, negates everything.

"And the worst part is, you set yourself up for this, Hannah. You made such a show of highlighting your goodness, calling out the despicable man, the mother who abandoned you. Had you not been so damn self-righteous, talking of your grace and willingness to forgive, I'm confident you'd be more popular today than ever."

"No, that was Claudia. She's the one who said I was abandoned. It was Claudia who talked of the despicable man and my grace and forgiveness. She set me up!" I rise and point to the television monitor. "Get the tape of the show with Fiona. See for yourself!"

If looks could talk, Priscille's would say,

361

Oh, dear girl, your pathetic tale rings of desperation.

I plop back down on the chair and hide my face. Claudia masterminded this entire event. How did she do this? If I didn't detest her, I'd revere her.

"Regardless," Priscille says, "your reversal smacks of hypocrisy. And hypocrisy, my dear, is something people cannot forgive. Claudia has agreed to take your spot until we find a replacement."

I struggle to breathe. Of course she has. Somewhere in the depths of my fog and despair, a thought rises to the surface. Maybe this is it. Maybe I'm finally getting the humiliation and smack-down that I deserve — my payback.

Priscille talks about severance pay and a COBRA for continuing medical insurance, but nothing registers. My mind is reeling. I've never been fired from a job — not even that summer job at Popeyes Chicken, when I mixed up the diet and regular sodas. But now, at age thirty-four, I've been canned, terminated, given the boot. I've gone from local celebrity to unemployed disgrace.

I double over in my chair and grab my head. I feel Priscille's hand on my back. "You'll be fine," she tells me. Then I hear her chair scoot back.

I suck in one jerky, spastic breath. Then another. "Wh-when is my last show?"

I hear the squeak of the door opening.

"It was today," Priscille says, and closes the door.

I slam shut my office door and throw myself on the sofa. I ignore the tap on my door and don't bother looking up when I hear someone's footsteps approach.

"Hey, you," Jade says, her soft voice butter on my burn. She rubs circles on my back.

I finally sit up. "I'm on leave. Indefinitely. Basically, I've been fired."

"You're going to be okay," she tells me. "You can finally spend some time with your mama. Become a connoisseur of Michigan merlot."

I can't even smile. "What am I going to tell Michael?"

"You're going to trust yourself," she says, her eyes boring into mine. "For the first time ever, you're going to do what you think is best. Not what your dad wanted. Not what's best for your man's career. You're going to do what's best for Hannah Farr."

I scratch my cheek. "Yeah, because the last time I trusted myself it worked out so well."

■ ■ ■ ■

It takes only twenty minutes to pack my office. Jade helps me gather just those things that matter; the rest they can pitch. I pull a half dozen awards from the wall. Jade wraps paper towels around framed pictures of Michael and me, along with the photo of my father. I remove a handful of items from my desk, and gather my personal files. Jade fastens the box with a ribbon of masking tape. Mission accomplished. No more tears, no sentimental keepsakes. That is, until I try saying good-bye to Jade.

We stare at each other, speechless, and then she opens her arms to me. I step inside and drop my head on her shoulder.

"I'm going to miss seeing this face every morning," she says.

"Promise me we'll stay friends."

She pats my back and whispers, "Forever and a day."

"I'm done. Nobody in this business will ever hire me."

"Don't be silly," she tells me. "You're Hannah Farr."

I step back and dab my eyes on my shirtsleeve. "The hypocrite who ruined her mother's life." I grab a tissue and blow my nose. "The thing is, Jade, I deserve this. I feel like this blow might finally even the score."

"That's why you did it, didn't you?"

I wonder if it's true. Like Dorothy, did I feel a need for a public flogging? No, I'm too private for that. I only know that this grievance was far too big to be exonerated by a Forgiveness Stone.

I glance at the makeup chair. "It'll be a whole lot easier getting Claudia ready for my show — her show."

"Yup. It'll be a cinch making her face beautiful. But it'll be a bitch trying to hide those dark spots on her heart." She gives me a fierce hug and whispers, "I've got some wasp repellant I can't wait for her to smell." She smiles and hands me the cardboard box. "I'll check on you later," she says, and blows me a kiss. "Stay in trouble."

I amble down the hall toward the elevator, praying nobody sees me. I punch the down button and bounce the box on my hip like a fussy toddler. *Please, just get me out of here.*

The elevator doors open and I descend to the lobby. I'm nearly to the double glass doors when I hear one of the five television monitors mounted on the lobby wall. It's tuned to *WNO News,* as usual. I pass it.

Then stop. Then backtrack.

On the screen, I watch Michael work his way up the steps of City Hall. He's back from Baton Rouge. He's wearing my favorite gray suit and the powder-blue tie I bought him at Rubensteins. Carmen Matthews, a WNO reporter, thrusts a microphone in his face. I notice the telltale crease in his forehead, and the back of my neck prickles.

"We've been good friends for over a year now," he says. "She's a very decent person."

My heart beats double-time. Are they talking about me? Am I the *good friend,* the *decent person* he's referring to?

"So you know about her past, that she'd falsely accused a man of rape?"

I gasp.

Michael scowls. "I don't believe legal charges were ever filed."

"But she did slander a man. He lost his job because of her. Were you aware of this?"

I stare at the screen. *C'mon, Michael, tell her. Work your magic. Your words can change everything. Tell her — and the city of New Orleans — that I've struggled with this for years now, that against your better judgment I insisted on coming clean — even though I'm not certain I was wrong! For God's sake, tell them I'm not a monster, that I was just a kid.*

He looks straight at the reporter. "I knew

she'd had a falling-out with her mother. But no, I had no idea she'd made up this false allegation."

Liar. You damn liar. It wasn't a false allegation! It was my *truth, and you know it's been haunting me.*

"What impact does this have on your future relationship?"

Michael looks confident and sure, the way he always does. But I know him. I see the way his lips are set and his head is cocked. He's quickly yet carefully weighing the aftermath of his options before choosing his words.

"I place a high value on honesty. Obviously, there's been a breach of trust."

My world goes black. "Bastard. You cowardly bastard."

"Hannah Farr is a very good friend of mine. You've seen us together at fund-raisers and social functions and whatnot. But I'm learning the details of Hannah's past right along with everyone else." He holds up a finger and speaks deliberately, each word distinct. "But let me be very clear. What she did or did not do in the past is something *she* needs to be held accountable for, not me."

The cardboard box slips from my hip and crashes to the floor.

Chapter 33

I stagger from the building, my entire career stuffed into a cardboard box. The clouds overhead boil and churn. I round the corner of St. Philip Street and get slapped by a gust from the northeast. But I don't turn away. Instead, I stare it down, daring it, welcoming the momentary catch of breath. I'm reminded of people who cut themselves out of desperation, simply to feel alive. For the first time, I almost understand. Emptiness is worse than pain.

It's lunchtime, and New Orleans' polished professionals, along with the usual throngs of tourists, are dashing off to lunch under black umbrellas. They're meeting clients, networking, enjoying the city — things I did just yesterday.

The sky opens up as I head east, bullets of rain pelting the already burdensome box. What possessed me to take the streetcar today? I should have known I was going to be canned. I should have driven. I see a taxi careening toward me, but I can't lift my arm for fear of dropping this damn box. The cab races past me, sending a blast of mud onto my khaki coat. "Bastard!"

I think of Michael, the real bastard, and seethe. How could he have betrayed me like this? My arms ache. I quickly calculate the trek: twelve more blocks until I reach the streetcar stop, and another block once I get off — all the while lugging this damn box like a vagabond.

Across the street, just inside Louis Armstrong Park, I spy a metal waste bin. Before I have time to reconsider, I step from the curb, landing ankle-deep in a puddle. The box lurches, and I'm fumbling to recover it when a Mercedes rounds the corner, nearly swiping me. "Shit!" I hoist the drenched box on my hip and manage a gangly half trot across the street.

The park feels dreary and abandoned today, the same way I feel. Affixed to a wooden fence, just above the trash bin, I see a sign telling me it's illegal to dump personal items. Wouldn't an arrest be just the perfect capstone on my day? I balance the soggy box on the edge of the bin and fish through the contents. Drops of rain cascade from my hair and eyelashes. I brush them away with my shoulder, but new drops instantly reappear. My fingers weave past files and paperweights, framed awards and desk calendars, and finally land on something hard and smooth. Yes! I yank it from the box and remove the paper-towel wrapping. I stare down at the photo of Michael and me sailing on Lake Pontchartrain, smiling into the camera like the happy couple I thought we were. I hurl it into the cavernous metal tank, taking enormous pleasure from the sound of shattered glass when it hits bottom.

At last I find the photo I've been searching for, the one of my dad and me, taken at the Critics' Choice Awards, just months before he died. He'd flown all the way from L.A. to escort me. I study the picture, beads of water forming on the glass. Yes, his nose is ruddy and his eyes glassy. Yes, he'd had too much to drink and made a fool of himself. But he's my father. I love him — the strongest, most broken man I ever knew. And dysfunctional though it was, he loved me, his selfishly generous daughter.

My salty tears mingle with the rain. I tuck the photo into my purse and search out one last item from the box, my Caran d'Ache limited edition fountain pen, the one Michael surprised me with when my show took second place in the Louisiana Broadcast Awards. Back when everyone thought I was the dynamic young upstart.

I tuck the pen into my coat pocket and heave the remaining contents into the bin, along with the cardboard box. "Good riddance," I say. The cover slams with a clang.

Lighter now, I continue down Rampart Street. Ahead of me, I see a teenage couple. The dark-haired boy holds a black umbrella over them with one hand and works the other into the back pocket of the girl's tight jeans. I wonder how he'll manage to get it out. It must hurt, stuck in that tiny square, the denim cutting into his pudgy fingers. Don't they realize how ridiculous they look, his big paw clutching her ass? But what do they care? They're young and they think they're in love. She doesn't know that in time, he'll betray her. She'll walk past a television monitor and hear him offer a disclaimer, as if she's nothing more than a faulty appliance.

I quicken my pace and follow the couple onto Canal Street. A homeless man sits on the wet concrete sidewalk in front of a vintage Walgreens pharmacy. A sheet of plastic covers his legs. He peers up at the duo in front of me and holds out a filthy Styrofoam cup. "Bless you," he says, extending his cup.

"What the fuck?" the boy says as he passes. "Even my dog knows to come in out of the rain."

The girl laughs and hits his arm. "You're so mean."

"Bless you," the man repeats as I pass, his dirty cup extended.

I give him a quick nod then turn my attention to the elegant Ritz-Carlton on the opposite side of the street. I'm nearly to the streetcar stop when I pause. I whirl around, bumping into a woman with dreadlocks.

"Excuse me," I say.

I weave in and out of bodies, a trout desperate to get upstream. I move quickly and accidentally step on the back of someone's sneaker. She curses back at me, but I don't care. I need to reach that man. I'm a half block away when our eyes meet. I slow my pace.

His eyes widen as I near, as if he's afraid of me. Does he think I'm coming back to belittle him? Has cruelty become his normal encounter?

I come up beside him and squat down. His eyes are rheumy, and up close I see crumbs in his snarled beard. I pull the fountain pen from my coat pocket and drop it into his cup. "Take it to a pawnshop," I tell him. "It's rose gold, eighteen-karat. Don't take less than three grand for it."

I rise, not waiting for a response, and slip back into the anonymous stream of people.

CHAPTER 34

It's after seven when the door buzzes.
Though I've been rehearsing this moment
all afternoon, my heart still pitches. I buzz
Michael up and stand beside the open door,
my arms akimbo. What can he possibly say
to justify his actions? Nothing! I refuse to
let him manipulate me. I will not allow him
to bullshit his way through this humiliation.

I hear the elevator's *ding* and watch the
doors slide open. Instead of Michael, Jade
steps out, wearing a pair of yoga pants and
pink hoodie.

"Hey!" I say, feeling a genuine smile light
my face for the first time all day.

She gives me a hug. Her dark hair is
heaped into a ponytail and not a stitch of
makeup masks her smooth caramel skin.
She's carrying a grocery bag from Langen-
stein's. "Marcus came over to the house to
watch the baseball game with Devon. I
thought you could use some company." She

raises the bag. "Sea-salt caramel ice cream."

"I adore you," I say, and pull her into my condo.

Before I have time to tell her I'm on my way out, the door buzzes again. "That's Michael," I say, and buzz him up. "We're supposed to go to dinner." I quickly tell her about the news spot.

"He's a rat fink. I realized it about eight months ago, when he stopped talking to you in future tense."

"Really? Why didn't you tell me?"

"A girl's gotta find out those things for herself. Just like I have to make my own decisions about Marcus."

I suck in a breath. She's right. I can't tell her what to do, regardless of how strongly I feel. I can only pray she'll make the right decision for her and Devon.

She puts the ice cream in the freezer. "I'll leave this for you."

"Don't go," I tell her. "Hang out here while I'm gone. Trust me, it's not going to be a late one."

"You sure you don't mind? I was hoping to avoid seeing Officer A-hole tonight. He's been putting the full-court press on me."

I smile. "I absolutely insist. Make yourself at home. The remote's on the coffee table and my laptop's in the bedroom."

"Thanks. I'll hide out in the bedroom until you're gone. Good luck."

She heads down the hall, closing the bedroom door behind her, and I reposition myself at my open door, just as before. This time, when the elevator opens, Michael steps out, still dressed in his gray suit and powder-blue tie. Damn. How does he manage to look so polished, even in today's tempest? I lift a hand to my hair, conscious that I'm two weeks overdue for a highlight. It feels limp and sticky, the unfortunate combination of my styling products and today's rain.

He catches sight of me and smiles, but I maintain my icy stare. I'm about to turn on my heels when another figure emerges from the elevator. What the hell? I look at Michael, my mouth agape, but he won't meet my eye. The coward's brought along his seventeen-year-old daughter as his shield.

"I thought we'd order in," Michael says. "It's nasty out there."

I clench my jaw and glare at him, but still he won't look at me.

"I want to go out tonight," I say, feeling my heart bat against my chest. "Unless, of course, you don't want to be seen with me."

He flashes me a nervous smile, then turns to Abby, as if making sure I'm aware of her presence.

I narrow my eyes at him and stand aside as Abby skulks toward my condo, staring into her cell phone as she types. She passes through the door in front of me without a hello.

"Hey, Abby," I say. What I'd like to say is, *Put your damn phone down, say hello, and then excuse yourself to the lobby for the next two hours so I can thoroughly lambaste your father.*

"Hey," she mumbles, passing through the foyer into my kitchen. She finally looks up from her phone when she spots the loaf of apple-crunch bread I'd made earlier. I watch her eyes light up for a split second before she catches herself admiring something I may have created. She returns to her text.

"Want a slice?" I ask, purposely ignoring Michael, who's perusing my wine rack for a bottle of red, as if tonight's just an ordinary date. "It's still warm."

She studies the loaf, then shrugs. "Why not?"

She says it as if she's doing me a favor, and I'm tempted to tell her never mind, that I don't give a whit whether she wants my bread, or my friendship. But that's simply not true. And I'm pretty sure she knows it.

I turn to the cabinet in search of my butter dish. Behind me, I hear a drawer open. By the time I land the butter and return to the island, Abby has carved a slice of bread using a dull butter knife. Damn! My oblong work of art is now torn and frayed. Abby watches me, and I swear she's hoping for a reaction.

"Butter?" I ask with false cheeriness, holding the dish in front of her. She sinks her knife smack-dab in the center of the butter stick. She spreads it on her bread, chews, and swallows, without so much as a thank-you or fuck-you.

I work to steady my breathing. *She's just a kid,* I repeat to myself.

I twist open a bottle of Voss and hand it to her, along with her favorite curlicue straw. Michael opens an Australian Shiraz. For a split second, I think of RJ and what I'd give to be sharing a bottle of wine with him tonight. Or would he, too, be horrified by my confession?

We three move to the living room. Outside, a blue-black shadow has captured the sky, and rain pelts my windowpane.

Rather than joining Michael on the sofa, I settle into a club chair, crossing my arms over my chest. Abby sits on the rug, her back against the coffee table. She twists around and plunks her water bottle on my mahogany coffee table, avoiding the coaster that's in plain sight. After swiping her buttery hands across my carpet, she grabs the remote and flicks through the channels, finally settling on a reality show about a houseful of models.

I stare blankly at the television screen, my anger mounting with each passing minute. I need to vent. I need to explain to Michael how hurt I am by his response to the reporter, how betrayed I feel. Finally, I can stand it no longer. I swivel my chair so that I'm facing him.

"How could you?" I ask, working to keep my voice steady and low.

He nods toward the back of Abby's head, as if to remind me that we're not alone here. Does he actually think I'd forgotten? My blood pressure soars and I refuse to turn away.

"Why?" I insist.

He shakes his head and whispers, "I was cornered."

"Bullshit," I say aloud. Abby spins around. I glare at her until she turns back to the TV, too angry to care if I'm being a bitch.

Michael slaps his thighs. "You girls ready to get some dinner? I'm starving."

"No," I say, at the same time Abby says yes.

Michael scowls at me, hesitates a moment, then says, "All right, then, Abs, let's roll."

I watch, stunned, as the two of them rise and move in unison toward the foyer. They're leaving. No. He can't go. He owes me an explanation, dammit!

"Why didn't you defend me, Michael?" I say, trailing him through the kitchen.

He reaches the island and wheels around, the first hint of hostility flickering in his eyes. "We'll talk about this later, Hannah."

His parental tone infuriates me. From over his shoulder, I catch sight of Abby. The message in her smug smile reads, *You lose.* Oh, hell no. This fight is just warming up, girlie.

"No," I say to Michael. "We'll talk about this now. I need answers. I need to know why you threw me under the bus, why you pretended not to know about my past, why you acted like I was nothing more than a friend."

"Um, maybe because that's what you are," Abby mumbles under her breath.

I whip around, adrenaline surging through my veins. Before I have time to open my mouth, Michael turns to her. "Sweetie, go down to the lobby, would you, please? I'll catch you in a minute."

A minute? He's giving me sixty-effing-seconds to vent? Damn him.

The moment Abby slams the door behind her, Michael's in my face. "Don't you ever talk to me like that in front of my daughter!"

I clench my teeth, wanting nothing more than to launch into a riff about his disrespectful, mean-spirited, bitch of a daughter, but I can't let him take me off-message. I pretend to be unfazed by his uncharacteristic burst of anger.

"Answer my question, Michael," I say, fighting to stay calm despite the hammering of my heart. "I walk past a television this morning and hear you telling the entire city that I'm your friend, that I need to be held accountable. Not one attempt to calm the fires? No, if anything, you fanned the flames!"

He runs a hand over his face and lets out a sigh. "This is tricky business. If I'm going to run for Senate —"

"Screw the Senate. I'm your girlfriend, dammit. Do you know how humiliating that was, hearing you call me a *decent person*? Your *good friend*?"

He lifts his shoulders. "It's not personal, darling."

"Well, it should be! You could have saved me, Michael. You have that power. Why didn't you use it?"

He fiddles with the button on his cuff. "It wasn't just my decision. Bill Patton had some strong opinions."

My head snaps backward. "What? You asked your campaign manager how to respond?"

"Sweetheart," he says, and reaches out to touch my arm. I jerk away.

"Don't touch me!"

"Listen to me, Hannah. Bill called an hour after the show aired. He knew we had to get in front of this." He grabs me by the arms and stares into my face. "I told you not to dredge up the past, didn't I? I knew you'd catch hell for it. And now you're blaming me for not protecting you."

I look away. It's true. He's right. He warned me, and I didn't listen. As he predicted, my actions put both our careers at risk. I blow out a stream of air, and with it, the last vestiges of my anger.

"What am I supposed to do now? I have no job. Everyone in this city hates me."

He loosens his grip and rubs my arms. "But elsewhere, you're a hot commodity. You'll be flooded with opportunities, mark my word. Lie low. In six months, a year, this city will have forgotten all about this fiasco. And so will I."

My heart begins to unclench. He's looking out for me. "Come here, babe," he
whispers, and opens his arms.

I wait a good five seconds before stepping
into them. I know I shouldn't give in so easily. But I just want to feel loved. My head
falls against his chest.

"Aw, sweetheart. You'll be fine." He kneads
the back of my neck. "You'll be better than
fine. You're going to land on your feet, I'm
sure of it. And just think, you won't have
Stuart to contend with." He leans back and
stares into my face, a sexy smile skimming
his lips. "Or your nemesis, Claudia *Can't-tell*
Campbell."

I tamp down a smile and step back. I cannot allow him to manipulate me. "I've lost
my health insurance. The COBRA they offered costs a fortune."

"It's only for the short term. Better suck
it up and pay it."

"With what? I'm unemployed. I have no
paycheck." We both know that's not entirely
true. Since my dad's death, I have plenty of
money. Luckily, Michael has enough tact
not to mention that now.

He nods, thoughtful. "Consider it done. I
know it's not much, but I'll pay for your
insurance." He cups my face and kisses my

forehead. "It's the one thing I can do for you."

My heart stutters. No. It's not *the one* thing. There is something else he could do. Something bigger and much more significant. A voice inside my head screams to me, *Now! Say it now!*

I step back and force myself to look directly into his blue eyes. "You could marry me, Michael. Then I could be on your insurance."

His hands fall to his side and he laughs, a jerky, nervous chuckle. "Well, I suppose that's true. And if I were one who acted impulsively, I might just accept your proposal." He taps his index finger on the tip of my nose. "Lucky for you, I don't make decisions under duress."

"Duress? We've been together almost two years! Remember last summer, when we were in Santa Barbara? You told me it was just a matter of time. You promised me one day I'd be your wife." I feel tears threaten and I blink them away. I refuse to become emotional. I must plow forward, before I lose my nerve. "When, Michael? When are you going to keep that promise?"

The air between us becomes thick. He chews the side of his cheek, staring at the tile floor. He sucks in a breath. Just when I think he's about to speak, I hear the door push open.

"C'mon, Dad. Let's go."

Shit! Abby's timing couldn't be worse. Michael's face floods with relief as she enters the kitchen. He smiles at his daughter-slash-savior and smooths her blond hair. "Sure thing, sweets."

All the affection drains from his face when he turns to me. "I'll call you later," he says, and strides to the door.

My vision blurs. He's walking out on me? But I'm no closer to having answers than I ever was.

"Go back downstairs, Abby," I say.

Abby wheels around, her head cocked. "Excuse me?"

I step in front of Michael and move to the door. "Go. Please," I repeat, my heart thumping as I open the door. "Your dad and I need to finish our conversation."

She looks at her dad for a rebuttal — or maybe protection. He pauses for a moment, then plants a hand on Abby's shoulder. "Now is not the time," he tells me, his voice but a feather. "I said I will call you later."

He nods to Abby, and she starts for the door.

"Now *is* the time," I say, my voice strong and fierce, foreign to me. It's as if someone has taken over my body. Someone capable and determined and confident. "Will you marry me, Michael?"

Abby snorts, mumbling something about having no pride. Michael glares at me, his face a portrait of disgust. He pats Abby's shoulder. "C'mon, sweetie. Let's go."

They pass in front of me as they walk out my door. I should let them go. I've said enough. But I can't. This arrow has left the bow. I'm hot on their heels, my voice louder, higher-pitched now. "What's wrong, Michael? Why can't you answer me?"

He doesn't look back. From somewhere behind me, I hear a door open. It's either Mrs. Peterson or Jade, and I picture two very different responses. Old Lady Peterson will be shaking her head, tut-tutting my outburst. But Jade? She'll be cheering me on, doing a little happy dance. I channel her energy and trail Michael toward the elevator.

"A simple yes or no," I say. "Just tell me."

Abby jabs at the elevator button. "Someone needs her meds."

"Be quiet, Abby."

She reaches for her phone, no doubt to text this scenario to her friends. In a split second I decide to go for the Hail Mary.

"You want something to text about, darling? I'll give you something text-worthy." I grab her father's coat sleeve. "Are you ever going to marry me, Michael? Or do you just enjoy the sex?"

Abby gasps. Michael's eyes cut to mine, steel-blue dry ice. The muscle in his jaw twitches, but he doesn't say a word. He doesn't have to. The elevator doors open. Abby and Michael step inside.

I stand before the open elevator, my breath jerky and ragged. What the hell have I done? Should I get on with them? Should I try to backtrack? Beg for forgiveness? Play it off as a joke?

Michael punches the button.

"That's it? You're leaving?"

He stares right through me, as if I'm invisible. The doors begin to slide shut.

"You fucking coward," I say. "Good riddance."

Just before the doors meet, I catch sight of Abby's face. She's smirking, as if she's won this contest. My anger peaks, reaching its crescendo. I let it flow, loud and strong, the final, climactic scene in an opera. "And that goes for you, too, you little bitch!"

CHAPTER 35

"Okay, doll, spill it. I need details." Jade perches on my kitchen counter while I walk in circles, hammering my forehead with my fist.

"Oh, damn! Oh, shit! I can't believe I did that. In the course of forty-eight hours, I've blown through two jobs and a boyfriend. Good-bye, hot commodity. Hello, hot mess."

I grab the open bottle of wine from my counter and drag another glass from the cupboard.

"It's like I was . . . out of control. I just kept pummeling and jabbing."

"I know. I heard. I couldn't believe that was you, Hannabelle. I had to sneak a peek, witness it with my own two eyes. You were brilliant!"

I feel my anger dissipating, humiliation and self-loathing quickly taking its place. I bury my head in my hands.

"What have I done, Jade? I blew it. Michael's never going to talk to me again." At once, I'm seized with panic. I grab my cell phone and frantically type a message to Michael. Before I have time to hit send, Jade leaps from the counter and snatches the phone from my clutches.

"Stop! Girl, you followed your instincts, and your instincts were right. You've been frustrated for months now. Trust me, if he wants you, he'll be back."

"No. I was out of line. I need to explain. I owe him an apology. Abby, too. How could I have said those things in front of Abby?" I close my eyes, allowing a wave of nausea to pass.

Jade grabs me by my shoulders. "You're blaming the victim, just like you accuse me of doing. Get ahold of yourself, Hannah. It was high time you had this conversation. You had every right to demand answers."

"But the way I did it. It was totally wrong. You should have heard the way I talked to Abby."

"Oh, I heard, all right. That little bitch was long overdue for a slap-down, and so was her daddy. So stop with the guilt."

I reach for the phone, but she drops it down the front of her sweatshirt. "I will not let you relapse. So you weren't the most eloquent. I'll give you that. Point is, you finally had your *come-to-Jesus* talk. You had the guts to ask him what you've been dying to know."

I let out a sigh. "And got the very answer I feared."

She smiles and whispers, "You burned down the house, doll."

"I did what?"

"You burned down the house," she repeats. "You went all-out, like a serial killer who sets the house on fire before turning the gun on himself. You passed the point of no return."

"Great. So now I'm being compared to a serial killer." I lean against my refrigerator and rub the bridge of my nose. "But you got one thing straight. I turned the gun on myself, all right."

She steps over to me, her blue-black pupils laser-focused. "People burn the house down for a reason, Hannabelle. It's a calculated move. They want to make sure there's no going back."

My back stiffens. Sure, I was frustrated in the relationship, but I wasn't ready to cut the cord, was I? "You think I *wanted* to ruin my relationship?"

The corners of Jade's mouth turn up. "Ever since you came back from Michigan, you're different." She lifts a lock of my hair. "I mean, look at you. It's like you've taken a holiday from Perfectionville."

I tuck my hair behind my ear. "Um, now might not be the best time to tell me that I look like hell."

"It's all good," she says. "You've got a mama now, and she loves you." Jade smiles at me. "And that vineyard guy . . . JR . . . RJ . . . whatever the hell his name is. Your eyes are happy when you tell me about him."

I shake my head. "That's never going to happen. Sure, he seemed like a great guy. But I barely know him. And he doesn't know me. He'd be just as repelled as everyone else if he knew what a fraud I was."

"*Was.* That's the operative word. But you aren't anymore. And if he's as decent as you claim he is, he's not going to give a shit what the thirteen-year-old Hannah did."

"It's no use. He's a thousand miles away."

She lifts her hands and looks around. "A thousand miles away from what?"

CHAPTER 36

It's 3:00 a.m. when I bolt from bed, my heart thrumming in my chest. I throw open the French doors, colliding with a wall of eighty-degree heat and 90 percent humidity. I stumble onto my balcony and suck in the air, but it's like breathing pudding. My nightshirt clings to my chest, and I grip the balcony rails, trying to steady the erratic pounding of my heart. I'm having a heart attack. I can't breathe! God, help me.

This will pass. It always does.

It's been six days since my show aired, and I haven't slept through the night since. Fiona and her damn stones! I took off my armor, and instead of the acceptance she promised, I've been rejected. By Michael. By my viewers. By my employers.

I want to go back to the life I had a week ago. I know it wasn't perfect, but it was so much easier than this lonely place of uncertainty. I'm in denial, I realize that. In

my fantasies, I imagine Michael calling —
or better yet, showing up at my door — to
apologize. He tells me he was wrong, and
that he respects my decision to confess. Or,
in a very private version tucked far into the
recesses of my consciousness, he tells me
he's thought about it. He loves me and he
wants to make me his wife.

But then I remember: I burned down the
house.

I think of Dorothy and the mess I've made
of her life. Damn these stones!

Without a moment to reconsider, I fly into
the condo and grab my phone. I plow
through my desk drawer until I find the
business card I'm looking for.

My hands shake as I punch in the
numbers. I don't care that it's the middle of
the night. She's on her fancy tour, raking in
millions.

*You've reached Fiona Knowles. Please
leave a message.*

All the pent-up anger and sadness comes
bearing down on me, and once again I'm
that young girl at Bloomfield Academy.
Except this time, I've found my voice. I grip
the phone so tightly my fingernails bite into
my palm.

"It's Hannah Farr. I'm wondering, Fiona,
do you even believe in these stones? Because

I think they're a load of crap. I lost my job, my boyfriend, my fans. My dear friend has lost her lifelong pal. And you're out there promoting this apology chain like it's some magic charm that'll wipe out all our sins and sadness. And that's bullshit. You don't get it. Sometimes 'I'm sorry' isn't enough." I clutch the phone, fully aware that I'm burning down yet another house. "What you did to me back in middle school? Well, it wasn't just me you hurt."

I close my eyes. "You broke up my family."

She won't know what the hell I'm talking about, but it's true. Fiona Knowles ransacked my world. Twice.

I lie on the wrought-iron chaise staring up at the heavens, until the first hint of blush colors the east. Then I pick up the phone and call my mother.

"Good morning, sweetheart."

My throat seizes up momentarily, the way it always does when I talk to her now. "Hello, Mom. How's everything?"

"That cold I told you about? Bob can't seem to shake it. But he's in good spirits. He done real good at elder care yesterday. And last night he ate an entire hot dog."

"I'm glad he's getting better." I silently

394

scold myself. I don't want to give her false hope. He may recover from his cold, but he's only going to deteriorate mentally.

"How about you, hon? Are things looking up?"

I close my eyes. "No. Last night I called Fiona Knowles and left a rant on her voice mail. I feel awful now."

"You got a lot on your mind. You're not yourself."

"You know, the sad thing is, I think I finally am myself. And still I disappoint."

"Oh, honey, you'll feel better when you get back to work. I'm sure it's just a matter of time before WNO calls you back from your leave."

Right. And Michael will leave politics and marry me and we'll have a dozen kids. I sigh, remembering that that's her way, always trying to be positive. "Thanks, Mom, but that's not going to happen. Remember I told you they're only calling it a leave. I've basically been canned."

"Do you need money until you find a new job? I can —"

"No. Absolutely not. But thank you." A knot of guilt tightens in my chest. My mother, who cleans houses, is offering me money. She doesn't know that I could be unemployed for a decade or more before

I'd run out of money, thanks to my father's inheritance . . . and his savvy divorce settlement years ago where he left his ex-wife penniless.

"I want you to remember," she says, "if things don't work out, you can always come home."

Home. Her home. The offer is spoken softly, as if she's asking a boy for a date and fears he'll say no. I pinch my nose and nod.

"Thank you, Mom."

"I'd love it," she says. "But I know how you feel about this place."

I picture her now, in her spotless kitchen with its handcrafted oak cabinets. In the next room, Bob sits in his recliner, working his puzzle. The place smells of wood and lemon polish and morning coffee. She's probably looking out the kitchen window at a pair of geese drifting on the lake. Maybe she sees Tracy next door, hanging sheets on the clothesline. They wave to each other, and later Tracy will walk over with the baby to sit and gab.

I compare it to my little world, here in this beautiful condo that won't grant me a night's sleep, where the only family photo is of my father, who's no longer alive.

How arrogant I'd been to judge her life.

"I was wrong," I say. "You've got a nice

place, Mom, a nice life."

"I think so. I thank my lucky stars, especially now that I got you."

What a lesson she is. I rub my throat. "I need to let you get to work. Thanks for . . ." I start to say *advice*, but unlike my father, she hasn't offered any. "Thanks for being there. Truly."

"Anytime, sweetheart. Day or night."

I hang up the phone. I go to my desk and retrieve my calendar. With the exception of a dentist appointment in three weeks, every square is empty. As Jade implied that night, what's keeping me here?

CHAPTER 37

Paris Parker Salon is abuzz with pretty young women Friday afternoon. It's Le Début des Jeunes Filles de la Nouvelle Orléans — the coming-out of sixty-five young debutantes. Tonight they'll be presented to an assembly of New Orleans' elite. Relationships will form, which will one day turn into engagements, and later elaborate weddings. That's the way it works in New Orleans — old wealth marries old wealth. I sit in the reception area, pretending to read an article in *Cosmopolitan,* TWENTY TIPS FOR LOOKING TEN YEARS YOUNGER. But all the while I'm peering over the magazine, waiting for Marilyn to arrive.

Like many southern women of her generation, Marilyn keeps a standing appointment each week for a shampoo and a style. But I'm beginning to wonder if she's canceled today.

I return to the magazine article. Where

was I? Ah, yes, *Tip #9. Camouflage your turkey neck with a scarf.*

I look up when I hear the door open, but it's just another pretty young woman. I gaze out at the salon floor. Young, hopeful beauties smile into mirrors, filled with dreams and possibilities. At once, I feel so very old. Have I missed my opportunity, my coming-out? Each year another batch of women enters the dating scene, younger, fresher, more exciting. How is a thirtysomething supposed to compete?

I startle when I spy Abby halfway across the room. Shit! She's standing at a styling station with two other girls, watching a redhead get an updo. Abby's friend must be a debutante. My heart quickens. Abby laughs at something the stylist says, then looks over at me, as if she knew I'd been watching her.

I cringe, replaying the awful scene I'd made when Michael and I broke up. I called her a bitch! What was I thinking? I manage to raise a hand and smile before hiding my face in my magazine. A moment later, I hear a voice in front of me.

"Hey, Hannah."

A volt of panic surges through me. Is Abby going to make a scene? Tell me off in front of the entire salon?

I peek up from my magazine. "Hi, Abby."

"Getting a haircut?" she asks.

In my entire courtship with her father, I don't think she'd ever asked me a personal question. What is she up to now? I set the magazine aside and stand, so that we're at eye level. If she starts yelling obscenities at me, I can make a run for it.

"No. I'm waiting for a friend." I gesture to the room. "Looks like y'all are having fun."

"Yeah. Deb season. It's crazy. I'm over it, though."

I nod, and an awkward silence comes over us. "Abby," I say, gripping my purse strap, "I'm really sorry for what I said last Friday night. I was wrong. You have every right to hate me."

She lifts her shoulders. "Honestly? For the first time, I actually liked you."

I stare at her, baffled, sure she's being sarcastic.

"You finally stood up for yourself. It's just . . . I know you're smart and all . . . but I could never understand why you didn't get it."

I wait, still not "getting it."

She looks me straight in the eye. "Hannah, my dad was never going to marry you."

I rear my head back, stung by her truth.

"It's true. His stock is way higher as a widower and single father than it would ever be as a married man."

I let the words sink in. I think of the way the media refer to Michael. *Mayor Payne, single father. Widower, Mayor Payne.* It's practically embedded in his title.

"Voters love that shit," Abby says. "So many times, I just wanted to strangle you, like that night at Broussard's when that couple got engaged and you sat there all teary-eyed. I couldn't believe you could be so stupid."

She's not being mean. For the first time, she's actually treating me like she cares. And what she's telling me makes sense. A single, devoted dad who lost his wife in a tragic accident. That's Michael's brand. I should have known, his brand means everything to him.

I rub my brow. "I feel like an idiot," I say, void of pretense or the desire to impress. "I cannot believe I never realized this."

"Hey, you made up for it last week. You were awesome, delivering those punches. Of course, my dad was ape-shit pissed, but I thought to myself, *Wow, the woman has a spine after all.*"

A ding comes from her cell phone and she glances at it. "Okay. Well, I guess I'll see you around."

"See you around, Abby. And thanks."

She walks away, then looks back at me. "Hey, you know that bread you make, especially that apple one with the crunchy stuff on top? You should, like, start a bakery or something. For real."

My smile fades when Marilyn walks into the salon. She's wearing a pink linen skirt and a cotton blouse, with a pale yellow sweater draped over her shoulders. She pauses at the reception table, and the redhead behind the desk smiles at her.

"Hello, Mrs. Armstrong. I'll let Kari know you're here. Can I get you some tea?"

"Thank you, Lindsay." She turns toward the waiting area and stops when she sees me.

"Hannah," she says, her voice cool.

I rise and meet her, rubbing the Forgiveness Stone in my hand. "Hello, Marilyn. I came here hoping to speak to you. It'll only take a minute. Please, can you sit down?"

She huffs. "Well, I don't suppose I have much choice, do I?"

I take her by the hand and we sit side by side. I tell her, once again, how foolish I'd been to let her and Dorothy on the show. And then I hand her a Forgiveness Stone.

"I was selfish. And wrong. You were blind-sided."

"You're right about that. You tricked me, that's why I'm so angry with you." She looks down at the stone in her hand. "But it wouldn't have mattered where Dorothy had made the confession. Truth is, it would have been devastating, regardless."

"It was a terrible decision," I say.

"Yes, as was your own on-air confession. I see you suffered a real beating. I was sorry to see that happened to you, Hannah."

How do I explain that Dorothy and I feel the same way? We deserved our come-uppance.

"I'm going to Michigan for a while. That's why I'm here. Dorothy will need a friend."

Marilyn raises her eyes. "How is she?" she asks quietly.

"Sad. Lonely. Heartbroken. She misses you terribly."

"Even if I were able to forgive, I'd never be able to forget."

"That old adage to forgive and forget is bullshit, if you ask me." I lift a hand. "I'm sorry for the profanity, Marilyn, but you aren't going to forget Dorothy's mistake. It would be impossible. And I promise you, Dorothy will never forget, either." I take one of her hands and squeeze, as if I can physically implant this message. "I'm no Fiona Knowles, but I believe forgiveness is even sweeter when it's granted with a vivid memory, when someone's fully aware of the pain the other person has caused, yet they make a choice to forgive anyway. Isn't that more generous than putting blinders on and pretending the grievance never happened?"

A pretty blonde dressed in a black approaches. "Mrs. Armstrong? Kari's ready for you."

Marilyn pats my hand. "I appreciate you coming, Hannah. But I can make no promises. My heart is broken, too."

I watch as she walks away, sad to think that two broken hearts have made a hole, rather than a whole.

CHAPTER 38

I'm in my bare feet kneading bread
Wednesday morning when my door buzzes.
I wipe my hands. Who's coming to visit on
a weekday morning? I thought I was the
only unemployed person in New Orleans.

I press the intercom. "Yes?"

"Hannah, it's Fiona. Can I come up,
please?"

I stare at the buzzer as if I'm being
punked. "Fiona Knowles?" I ask.

"How many Fionas do you know?"

I can't help but smile at her smart-aleck
reply. I buzz her up, and quickly toss a team
of measuring cups and spoons into the
kitchen sink. What's she doing here?
Another book event? And how did she get
my home address?

"Aren't you supposed to be on tour?" I
say when she steps off the elevator. It comes
out more of an accusation, and I tweak it.
"I'm surprised to see you, that's all."

"Last night was Nashville. Tonight I'm supposed to be at a bookstore in Memphis. I canceled and flew back here instead." She steps through the door. Her eyes shift and she glances about the foyer. She's nervous, like me. "Because you're right, Hannah. Sometimes 'I'm sorry' isn't enough."

She came all the way back for me? Her publisher must be footing the bill. I shrug and lead her into the kitchen. "Look, forget it. You caught me at a low point the other night."

"No. You were right. I owe you a sincere, face-to-face apology. And I need to know what I did to break up your family."

I glance at my coffeepot. It's half full. What the hell, it's going to be thrown out anyway. "Coffee?"

"Uh, sure. If it's not too much trouble. And if you have time."

"Time is the one thing I do have." I pull two mugs from the cupboard. "As I mentioned in my rant, I'm unemployed."

I fill the cups and we move into to the living room. We sit on opposite ends of the sofa, and she wastes no time getting to the point. Maybe she's hoping to get back to Memphis in time for tonight's gig.

"First, I know it's not enough, but I have to tell you how sorry I am for everything that's happened to you."

I lay a hand over my steaming cup. "Whatever. It's not like someone put a gun to my head. I made the confession with my own free will."

"I thought what you did was courageous."

"Uh-huh. You and maybe one or two other people. The rest of this city thinks I'm a hypocrite."

"I wish I could do something. I feel awful."

"Why did you hate me?" The words tumble from my mouth before I can catch them. In all the years that have passed, that insecure teen still wants answers.

"I didn't hate you, Hannah."

"Every day you made fun of me. The way I talked, the way I dressed, my low-rent family. Every damn day." I clench my jaw. She will not see me cry.

"Until one morning you decided I wasn't worth your time. And then I became invisible. Not just to you, to all your friends, too. That was even worse, eating alone, walking to class alone. I used to pretend I was sick, so I didn't have to go to school.

"I remember sitting in that cramped counseling office while my mom told Mrs. Christian how I got stomachaches every morning. She couldn't understand why I hated school. I wasn't about to tell on you. You would have crucified me."

Fiona hides her face in her hands and shakes her head. "I am so sorry."

I should stop, but I can't.

"After the meeting, she and Mrs. Christian were making small talk, trying to pretend they'd just had a productive meeting. My mom mentioned she wanted to have our kitchen remodeled." I pause, picturing the scene in the hallway, the two of them yammering on while I fiddled with someone's locker combination, wishing my mom would hurry up.

"Mrs. Christian recommended a construction worker. Bob Wallace, the wood-shop teacher at the public school."

Fiona's head falls back. "Don't tell me. The man she married?"

"That's right. If it hadn't been for you, my mother never would have met Bob."

As I spew the words, a dim picture takes shape in my mind. It's of my mother, smiling at Bob, her eyes full of love as she feeds him a forkful of spaghetti. I push the image away. Because right now I need to be angry at Fiona, not grateful.

"I could try to explain myself," Fiona says. "I could even spin a pretty sympathetic tale of a girl riddled with anxiety, who could never meet her mother's expectations." Her face is red and blotchy, and I have to force myself not to touch her arm, tell her it's okay. "But I'll spare you. The long and short of it is this: I was pissed off at the world. I was hurting. And people who hurt, hurt."

I swallow hard. "Who knew you were just as miserable as I was?"

"We do so much harm when we try to hide our pain. Because in one form or another, it always leaks out."

I offer a halfhearted smile. "Yours was more like a jet spray, actually."

The corners of Fiona's lips turn up. "No. It was a fucking geyser."

"There you go."

She lifts her hands in the air. "Even now, when I've created this bizarre forgiveness phenomenon, I feel like a fraud. Half the time I don't know what the hell I'm talking about."

I laugh. "Sure you do. You're the forgiveness guru. You wrote a book."

"Yeah, right. I'm flying by the seat of my pants. Truth is, I'm just a girl standing in front of an audience, hoping for forgiveness. An ordinary person, like everyone else, who just wants to be loved."

I feel my eyes sting and shake my head. "Isn't that the line Julia Roberts delivered to Hugh Grant at the end of *Notting Hill*?"

She smiles. "I told you I was a fraud."

It's been two days since the Memorial Day parade, and tiny American flags still line the sidewalk of the Garden Home. I enter the house, surprised to find Dorothy seated at an empty table in the dining room. Lunch won't be served for another thirty minutes. Someone has snapped a terry-cloth dish-towel-turned-bib around her neck. I want to fling it off her, remind these people that this woman has dignity, but I realize the bib is innocent. The caregivers are covering her from a mess that she might make. I wish I'd had a bit of protection when I made my mess.

I pull the loaf from my tote as I approach the table.

"I smell Hannah's bread," she says. Her voice is chipper today. Maybe time is working its magic. Or better yet, maybe she's heard from Marilyn.

"Good morning, Dorothy." I bend down to hug her. The smell of Chanel perfume, the feel of her thin arms around my neck, makes me sentimental today. Or maybe it's the fact that I'll be leaving next week. For whatever reason, I cling to her more tightly this morning. She pats my back as if she senses my emotional frailty.

"You're okay, Hannah Marie. Now come, sit down and tell me your story."

I drag a chair from the next table and tell her about my visit from Fiona. "I was shocked that she actually came all the way here just to apologize again."

"Lovely. And do you feel better?"

"I do. But I'd say the jury's still out on whether shedding our shame is a good thing or a foolish thing. Take us, for example. Will our lives ever get back to normal?"

"Dear, don't you know? Confessing freed us. But next time, we need to take more care when we expose those fragile pieces of our hearts. Tenderness is meant to be shared only with those who'll provide a soft landing."

She's right. Claudia Campbell wasn't a worthy confidant. My mind travels to Michael. No, he didn't provide a soft landing, either.

"I'm glad you're so optimistic."

"I am. We have everything now." She lays a hand on my arm. "We finally have ourselves."

I mull it over for a moment. "Yeah? Well, let's hope that's enough. So tell me, how's life? How's Patrick?"

"Dandy." She pulls a letter from her

pocket and hands it to me.

I smile. "He wrote you a love letter?"

"It's not from Paddy. It's a response to my stones."

Marilyn has forgiven her! Fantastic! But then I see the return address.

"New York City?"

"Go ahead, read it. Aloud, please. I'd like to hear it again."

I unfold the letter.

Dear Mrs. Rousseau,

I was stunned to receive your letter of apology. As you can see, I'm returning the stone to you, but please know, your apology was never necessary. I sincerely regret that you carried such guilt for losing contact with me after that day in class.

It's true, I never returned to Walter Cohen High. And no doubt you thought you'd lost me. I wish you'd known, all these years, that you were the very person who saved me. It sounds cliché, but I walked into your classroom that June day a troubled boy, and I walked out a man. And what's more, a man I actually liked.

I remember that morning so clearly. You'd called me up to your desk to look

at your grade book. Nothing but I's —
incompletes. I hadn't turned in a single
project that semester. You were
apologetic and explained that you had
no choice but to fail me. I wouldn't
graduate.

It wasn't exactly a surprise. All
semester you'd been on my case. I can't
recall exactly how many times you called
me at home, and once, you even showed
up on my doorstep. You begged me to
come to school, you pleaded with my
mother. I was six credits shy of graduat-
ing, which meant I had to pass all my
classes that semester. And you were hell-
bent on helping me get them. Not just
your English credit, either. You'd talked
to my other teachers, too. But I didn't
make it easy for you. I had a million
excuses, and yes, some of them were
even valid. But bottom line was, you
couldn't give a credit to a kid who came
to class but once a week, at best.

So yes, we both remember that day.
But I'm not sure if you remember the
rest of that class.

Before you began the day's lesson, you
asked Roger Farris to put his Walkman
away. He groaned and stashed it under
his desk. Halfway through the hour,

Roger announced that his Walkman was missing. He pitched a fit, sure someone had stolen it.

Kids started pointing fingers. Some suggested you search us. You wouldn't hear of it.

Very calmly, you told the class that someone had made a mistake. You claimed that one of us in the room was having serious regrets and wanted very much to do the right thing. Then you walked over to your little cement-block office attached to the classroom and turned out the light. You announced that every student in class would spend twenty seconds alone in the dark room. We were to take our backpacks and purses. The person in possession of the tape player would leave it behind in the office, you were certain.

We all moaned and whined. What a load of crap, making us feel like thieves. Everyone knew it was Steven Willis. He was the poor kid who smoked a lot of weed. It was shocking that he was even in school that day. Most of the time he was truant.

Why not just confront him, search his backpack and spare the rest of us? He'd never give up Roger's Walkman, now that he had it. We tried to convince you that people didn't operate that way, that you were naïve.

But you insisted. You said we were all, by nature, good. That the person who had "accidentally" taken the Walkman was struggling right now, wishing they could have a do-over.

So reluctantly, we obliged you. One by one, we stepped into the blackness of your tiny cubicle. Gina Bluemlein kept time, tapping on the door to let us know when our twenty seconds had elapsed. By the end of class, we'd all spent our allotted time alone in the dark office.

And then the moment of truth arrived. We huddled at the door as you entered the office. By then, we were as anxious as you to see the results of your experiment. You flipped on the lights. It took a minute before we spotted it. But there it was, on the floor beside your file cabinet. Roger Farris's Walkman.

The class was stunned. We erupted in cheers and high fives. The entire class left that day feeling a newfound optimism for humanity.

And me? That single event changed my life. You see, just as everyone suspected, I took the Walkman. The class was right

— I had no intention of giving it back. I'd wanted a Walkman, but my old man was out of a job. And Roger was an asshole, anyway. What the hell did I care?

But your profound belief in my goodness changed my entire mind-set. When I laid that Walkman beside the cabinet and walked out of that office, it was as if I had shed my old skin. That layer of callousness, the feeling that I'd been victimized all my life and the world owed me, peeled away. For the first time I ever remember, I felt like I was worth a damn.

So you see, Mrs. R., your apology was unwarranted. I left your class and went straight to the Adult Ed office. Six weeks later, I'd completed my GED. The thought that I might actually be good, that you believed in me, completely changed my way of thinking. The kid whose parents knocked him around, who blamed the world for his shitty fate, began to take control. I wanted to prove you right. Your lesson that final day of high school served as a catalyst for everything I did thereafter.

Please know that I, for one, am forever grateful that you saw the goodness in me and allowed me to act on it.

Sincerely yours,
Steven Willis, Attorney at Law
Willis and Bailey Law Firm
149 Lombardy Avenue
New York, NY

I blot my eyes on my shirtsleeve and turn to Dorothy. "You must be so proud."

"Another candle is lit," she says, and swipes her eyes on her terry-cloth bib. "My room is getting brighter."

For every candle that we blow out, we light another. What a journey of trial and error this human experience is. The shame and guilt we carry are tempered by moments of grace and humility. In the end, we can only hope that the light we cast outshines the darkness we create.

I squeeze Dorothy's hand. "You are an incredible woman."

"Yes, she is."

I spin around and see Marilyn standing behind me. Just how long she's been there, I'm not sure.

Dorothy's eyes widen. "Is that you, Mari?"

Marilyn nods. "It's me." She bends down to kiss her friend's forehead. "And for the record, Dottie, your room is not getting brighter. It has always been ablaze with light."

It's one o'clock when I get back home, feeling lighter for having witnessed the reunion of my two friends — and for having found a letter from RJ in my mailbox. My hands shake as I slide my finger under the seal.

Dear Hannah,
Thank you for your letter. I wasn't sure I'd hear from you again. No need to apologize. It makes sense that a woman as impressive as you would be in a committed relationship. I respect your honesty and integrity.

I pace the kitchen, staring at the words *committed relationship*. But I'm not in a committed relationship anymore. I can see you now, guilt-free!

Please stop by next time you're in "the Mitten" with or without your mom — or your boyfriend. I promise I'll behave like a gentleman this time. And as always, when you tire of your current situation, I want to be at the top of your dance card.
Yours,
RJ

I lean against the refrigerator and reread the letter. RJ's obviously infatuated with the woman he thinks I am. I've never told him the truth about my past, and after the horrible fallout here, why would I? Like everyone else, he'd be horrified to learn of the girl I once was.

I'd love to see him again, but can I go back to pretending? Can I return to the same kind of superficial affair I had with Michael, or Jack, and once again try to stuff those old demons behind the trapdoor? I remember Jack's parting line: *No wonder it's so easy to let me go, Hannah. Fact is, you never really let me in.*

No. I can't.

I practically sprint to my desk. I pick up my pen and grab a sheet of stationery.

Dear RJ,
    My dance card is empty.

Fondly,
Hannah

CHAPTER 39

My car is fully fueled, and I had the oil changed last week, after taking Marilyn and Dorothy out for lunch. Two suitcases are perched at my front door, along with a tote stuffed with power bars and nuts and water and fruit. I'm all set to leave for Michigan, first thing tomorrow morning. I'm sound asleep when I get the call at 2:00 a.m.

"He's gone, Hannah!"

Jesus, Bob's dead. I swing my legs over the side of the bed. "I'm so sorry, Mom. What happened?"

"I got up to use the bathroom. He wasn't in bed. He's not in the house. He's gone, Hannah. I've been outside searching for him, but I can't find him anywhere!"

I let out a sigh. He's not dead. That's good, I tell myself. But deep inside I can't help but think Bob's death would give my mother new life, though I know she wouldn't see it that way.

She speaks so quickly I can't understand her. "Can't find him. Looked everywhere."

"Slow down, Mom. He's okay." But I don't believe it. Bob has no survival skills. And with the woods so close to the house, and the lake, and the cold nighttime temperatures . . .

"I'm on my way. Call the police. We'll find him, I promise."

She lets out a breath. "Thank goodness you're coming."

Finally, her daughter will be there for her in her time of need. And what she needs is her husband.

I call the house every half hour but only reach her answering machine. I'm ten miles outside of Memphis when she picks up.

"The police found him, huddled in the bottom of his boat."

The boat. The old fishing boat I reintroduced him to last month. I must have triggered a memory that day when I took him for a boat ride. God, even my good intentions go bad.

"Oh, Mom, I'm sorry. How is he?"

"Suffering from hypothermia. He was lying in three inches of cold water. The paramedics came. Wanted to take him to Munson for a checkup. But he'd had enough. I got him to eat some hot cereal and tucked him into bed."

"I should be there by seven tonight."

"I'll have dinner for you."

"No. That's okay. I'll grab something."

"I insist. And, Hannah?"

"Yes?"

"Thank you. You can't imagine what a comfort you are to me."

I think about it all the way to Michigan. Perhaps I'm a fool, not having learned my lesson after all I've lost. The thought terrifies me, but I must. There's no question about it. I have two more apologies to make, this time to Bob's son and daughter, before it's too late.

I've never met Anne and Bob Junior. They were adults when their father became involved with my mother. How they found out about my accusation, I'm not sure. But they know. My mother tells me she and Bob have very little contact with Anne and Junior. I can only guess that I'm responsible for their distance. Our old neighbor Mrs. Jacobs told the school district, and surely people talked. Bob's ex must have known. But would she have been cruel enough to tell her children? Apparently so.

I stare ahead at an endless string of traffic

along I-57. Anne, the older of the two, must be in her late forties, not much younger than my mother. She was already married and living in Wisconsin during that summer of '93. Junior was in college, I think.

Will they come alone or bring their families? I'm not sure which would be worse, facing their wrath in a small group or large.

My stomach knots. I crank up the volume of my iPod. Lifehouse sings, "I'm halfway gone and I'm on my way . . ." The song seems to mimic my journey. I'm halfway there. Just a few more apologies to make. I've come a long way but still not far enough. I've removed the hood on my cloak of darkness, but the collar is still choking me.

My head falls against the headrest. How can I possibly face them? If someone told me they'd falsely accused my father of sexual molestation I would despise them, probably more fiercely than my father would. And no apology, no matter how sincere, can make up for lost time.

I could sugarcoat the accusation, offer my excuses, try to explain that I was just a young girl, holding fast to a silly fantasy that my parents might reunite. I could even tell them the truth, that to this day I can't be certain whether the touch was accidental. But that seems insincere, as if I'm hedging. No, if I'm going to do this, I'm going to accept 100 percent culpability, not 50 percent, or even 99 percent. I'm all in.

The sun has disappeared behind the lake when I pull into the driveway. I turn off the ignition and spy my mother standing on the porch stoop, as if she'd been waiting for me all day. If I didn't know better, I'd think she was the one with Alzheimer's. Her hair is piled in a haphazard ponytail, and she's wearing a pair of glasses that are dated and too big for her thin face. Her jacket is unbuttoned, revealing faded sweatpants and a T-shirt beneath. From a distance, she looks like a twelve-year-old girl.

They come back to me now, all those comments we'd get, people mistaking us for sisters. A thought strikes me before I can strike it. Was that what Bob found attractive, that my mother looked like a child?

I run to her. "Mom!"

She looks up, as if she were startled to see me. "Hannah." She meets me in the damp grass and pulls me into a hug, tighter today, almost desperate.

"How is he?" I ask.

"Been sleeping on and off all day." She

puts a hand to her mouth. "I was so care-less. I've been meaning to put a bell on the bedroom door. You should've seen him, Hannah. He was soaked through and shiver-ing like a wet puppy."

I cup my mother's face, as if she's the child and I'm the parent. "He's okay now. And it's not your fault, Mom. You've found him. You've got him back."

I think about the metaphor for my mother's life. Losing the ones she loves, hav-ing them slip away, leaving her to wonder where they are or if they'll survive.

It's been twenty-two years since I've spent a night in this cabin. I wonder if it could ever feel like home. I stand at the threshold of their tiny bedroom, listening to my mother sing to Bob the same song she used to sing to me.

"Like a bridge over troubled water. I will lay me down." Her voice is husky and slightly off-key, and a lump rises in my throat.

She smooths Bob's hair and kisses his cheek. Just before she turns out the light, I notice a photo on Bob's nightstand.

"What's this?" I ask, and wander over to it.

"Bob's favorite picture," she tells me.

I lift the oak frame and see my teenage self, standing at the end of the dock with Tracy. We're looking over our shoulders at the camera, as if he'd just yelled, "What are you boys up to?" and we'd spun our heads as he snapped the photo. I squint at the picture. The left leg of my bathing suit has risen a bit, exposing the flesh of my white buttock in contrast with my tan thigh.

I set the photo back down. An uneasiness comes over me. Of all the pictures, why has he chosen this one to keep on his bedside table?

As quickly as my suspicions flare, I squelch them. I was in my swimsuit nearly every day that summer. Of course that's what I'd be wearing in a picture.

I turn out the lamp, remembering what I told Marilyn. *Forgiving doesn't always require forgetting.* But in my case, I think it does. That fuzzy snapshot of my truth is impossible to bring into focus. If I'm going to forgive, I need to forget.

My mother and I sit on the back deck sipping lemonade. The night air is cool, punctuated with chirping crickets and honking bullfrogs. She lights a citronella candle to keep the mosquitoes away and tells me about the fancy homes she cleans.

She leaves for a moment to check on Bob. When she returns to her seat on the glider, she smiles at me. "Where were we?"

Where were we? It's as if she's skipped over all those bad years, the years I'd hurt her and refused to see her. Her love for me seems as strong as it ever was, as if she's completely forgiven my cruelty. This is the sweet forgiveness that Fiona is talking about.

"I want to apologize."

"Oh, honey, stop. We forgave you years ago."

"No. My apology to Bob was too late." I take a deep breath. "I want to apologize to his kids."

For several seconds she just stares at me. "Hannah, no."

"Please, Mom. I've been thinking about this, about how they grew estranged from their dad. It's my fault."

"You don't know that, sweetie."

"Can you arrange a meeting with Anne and Junior? Please?"

The candle's flame illuminates the lines in her face. "It's been years since we seen the kids. It's likely to open a can of worms. You sure you want to do this?"

No, I'm not the least bit sure. In fact, I'd like to avoid Bob's kids for the rest of my life. But I can't. I owe it to them, and to the man whose reputation I ruined.

"Yes. Please. I need to do this, Mom."

Her face turns toward the darkness. "What if they won't come?"

"Tell them it's urgent. Tell them whatever you need to. They must hear this, from me. Anything less would be cowardly."

"When?"

"Can we arrange it for Saturday? Please?"

She nods, and I'm certain she thinks I'm hoping to be absolved. But I'm not. I'm hoping they absolve Bob.

Chapter 40

I settle myself on a stool, forcing myself to eat a tuna sandwich while my mom rinses cherries for her pies. I check my watch for the umpteenth time. They'll be here in three hours. My stomach pitches, and I toss my sandwich onto my plate.

My mother stands in profile, running water over the metal colander. She's wearing a pair of white capris and a sleeveless blouse.

"You look pretty, Mom."

She spins around and smiles. "I thought you'd like this."

"I do." I notice the perfect piecrust rolled out on the counter. "You've always loved to bake, haven't you?"

She looks over at her crust. "Nothing fancy, like you got in New Orleans. Just good old-fashioned fruit pies and cookies and cakes. The stuff my mama used to make."

She uses her shoulder to push a stray lock of hair from her face.

"I hope they like cherry pie. Once, years ago, they came for Christmas. Staci — that's Junior's ex-wife — she ate two slices." She glances up at the clock above the stove. "Anne was planning to leave Wisconsin at eight, which should put her here around three. Junior promised he'd come around the same time. I got a spaghetti casserole for dinner. And a salad, of course." She talks quickly, without breaking for dialogue. I notice her hands are shaking.

"Mom, are you okay?"

She looks up. "Honestly? I'm a wreck." She pours the cherries into a bowl, then tosses the colander in the sink. The metal clang startles me.

I stand and go to her, holding her by the arms. "What is it?"

She shakes her head. "It's been a long time since they seen Bob. They don't know what they're in for. And Anne? She's going through another divorce. She snapped at me when I called, let me know I was putting her out by asking her to come."

I close my eyes. "I'm so sorry, Mom. This is my fault."

She glances toward the bedroom where Bob naps and lowers her voice, as if he might overhear and comprehend the conversation. "I told her it might be the last time she'd see him."

I suck in a breath. She might be right. Bob hasn't spoken since they pulled him wet from the boat Wednesday. And his cough is getting worse, not better. Again, I feel culpable. Would he have wandered out to the boat if I hadn't insisted on taking him for that ride last month?

"I'm sorry, Mom. You've got a lot on your plate, and I'm piling on more."

She swallows hard and holds up a hand, as if she can't talk about it now. "And Junior, he's always polite, but I could tell he wasn't too happy."

"I've done so much damage."

For the first time my mother's facade breaks. "Yes. Yes, you have. I'll give you that. I just hope it's not too late. I hope Bob recognizes them."

A cloud comes over me. This is a mistake. My mother and I both have unrealistic expectations.

She pours a cup of sugar over the cherries. "Maybe, just maybe Bob will understand that he's been forgiven."

Forgiven? The hair on the back of my neck rises. How odd that my mom uses the word *forgiven.* How can he be forgiven when he's done nothing wrong?

She stands at the living room window, checking her watch every few minutes. At 2:40, a van pulls into the drive.

"Anne's here," my mom says, grabbing her lipstick from her pocket and dabbing her lips. "Should we go greet her?"

My heart pounds. From the window, I watch a middle-aged woman climb from a van. She's tall, with graying shoulder-length hair. From the passenger side, a girl who looks to be about nine steps out.

"She brought Lydia," my mother says.

I'm flooded with emotions, everything from sadness to terror to relief. I'm going to be crucified by this woman. And I deserve it.

The van is followed by another vehicle, this one a white pickup truck. It reminds me of RJ's truck, and I'm comforted by the fact that, regardless of the outcome here today, I'll see him on Monday. I'll tell him everything about my past, create a fresh, clean slate. Somehow, I know he'll understand.

The truck crawls to a stop behind the van. Anne and Lydia wait, their synchronized arrival clearly planned.

My heart picks up speed. I need air. I turn

away and step to where Bob has been staged in his velour recliner. My mother and I managed to get him out of bed this morning. I combed his hair, and my mother shaved his face. He's awake now, but the newspaper she positioned in his lap is askance, and he's far more interested in his reading glasses. He turns them in his hands, picking at one of the plastic nosepieces.

I remove the paper from his lap and smooth down the wisps of gray hair on his head. He coughs, and I grab him a tissue.

"So good of you to come," I hear my mother call through the open door.

They're walking into the house now. The tiny room is closing in on me. I want to run.

"Thanks, Suzanne," a male voice says.

I spin around. And that's when I see him. RJ.

CHAPTER 41

For a moment it doesn't register. What's RJ doing here? How did he find me? I smile and take a step toward him, but the look on his face stops me cold. He's already put the puzzle pieces together. And I do, too.

Oh, dear God. RJ is Robert Junior, Bob's son.

"You're Hannah," he says. It's not a question. It's more of a plea. His eyes are heavy, and he looks down at his feet. "Jesus. I am so sorry."

"RJ," I say, but I'm at a loss for words. He thinks I'm the girl his father molested. In a moment he'll learn the truth. But right now I can't speak.

He crosses an arm over his chest, and puts one hand to his mouth. He stares at me and shakes his head. "Not you." The grief in his eyes shatters my heart.

"You know Junior?" my mother asks.

My throat is so tight I can barely breathe.

I must nod, because she doesn't repeat the question. Time rolls in on itself. Of course. Why didn't I see it? It all makes sense now. He grew up near Detroit. His parents divorced when he was in college. He'd never forgiven his dad — for what, he didn't say. It seemed too personal to ask at the time, but now I know. All these years, RJ thought his father was a monster.

My mother introduces me to Anne, and RJ steps behind me, over to where his father sits.

I search for a nickel of warmth in Bob's daughter's blue-gray eyes but find nothing but ice. My hand shakes when I offer it. Anne takes it perfunctorily. She doesn't bother to introduce me to her daughter, so I do it myself.

"I'm Hannah," I say to the thin girl wearing denim shorts and a tank top.

She coughs, the same deep cough I hear from Bob. "I'm Lydia," she croaks. She stares up at me. If it's true that children see people for who they really are, then I'd say Lydia is the exception. She's gazing up at me as if I'm a star, when really I'm a misguided missile who has decimated her family.

Anne glances at her father in the chair but makes no attempt to go to him. I force myself to touch her arm. I speak loudly, so that RJ hears, too.

"I asked my mother to gather you here." I stop and take a deep breath, clenching and unclenching my fists. *I can do this. I must do this.* "I have something I need to tell you."

"Can I get anyone a drink?" my mother asks. She's smiling, as if she's hosting a holiday, but I can hear the tremor in her speech. She's terrified. "I got tea, lemonade. Or Lydia, maybe you'd like a Coke?"

Lydia starts to reply, but Anne cuts her off. "Let's get on with it," she says, as if she already knows why she's here and what I'm about to say. "We need to get back." She puts a hand on her daughter's shoulder. "Go outside, now."

They're going back tonight? It's a seven-hour drive back to Madison. No. They must have a motel in town, or maybe they're staying with RJ. I think of the meal my mother prepared, and her tactful request that I sleep on the sofa tonight so Anne could have the tiny guest room. I helped her change the sheets, and watched her cut peonies from the garden to place on the dresser. One more disappointment for the woman who wants to be accepted. Maybe my father was right when he said the key to happiness was having low expectations.

After Lydia goes outside, Anne sits on the sectional, my mother perches on the arm of Bob's recliner. RJ takes the oak chair my mother brought out earlier from the kitchen table.

I lift the two pouches of stones I'd positioned on the coffee table earlier.

"I have an apology to make," I say, standing before them. "I came here a month ago, hoping to make peace with your father. You see, when I was thirteen years old, not much older than Lydia, I decided an accidental touch was a deliberate one. I lied."

It's the first time I've called it a lie. Was it a slip of the tongue, or am I finally willing to admit it? For the life of me, I still don't know. But for today, it was a lie. Without proof, that's the only way I can call it.

"Maybe you've heard about these Forgiveness Stones. I've given one to my mother and one to your father. Now I want to offer one to each of you."

RJ plants his elbows on his knees, his chin resting on his folded hands. He stares at the floor. Anne says nothing. I glance over at Bob. He's sleeping now, his head fallen back on the cushion, his reading glasses cockeyed. My chest tightens.

"I thought that by giving your father a stone, it would ease my shame, or at least some of it. But the fact is, I haven't really made peace. Because I still need to apologize to you two."

I take a stone from each pouch. "Anne," I say, stepping toward her. "Please forgive me for what I did to you and your family. I know I can never give you back the time you lost. I am so sorry."

She stares at the stone in my outstretched hand, and I wait, trying to keep my hand steady. She's not going to accept it. And I don't blame her. Just as I'm about to pull back my hand, she reaches out. For the briefest moment, her eyes flicker to mine. She plucks the stone from my palm and jabs it into her pocket.

"Thank you," I say, and finally breathe. But I know this is just a step. She may have accepted the stone, but that doesn't mean it'll be returned to me with a pretty bow and a letter declaring her forgiveness. But it's a start, as much as I can hope for today.

One down and one to go. I move to RJ.

He continues to stare at the floor. I look down at him, wishing I could touch those unruly brown waves. His hands are folded as if in prayer. Suddenly he seems so pure to me. RJ is the perfect man, while I'm the sinner. How could such an unequal pairing ever flourish?

Please, God, help me do this. Help me get through to him. My intention today was to soften their hearts, to pave the way for them to bid a final loving farewell to their father. But now everything's changed. I love this man. And I need his forgiveness.

"RJ," I say, my voice wavering. "I am so, so sorry. Whether you find it in your heart to forgive me, I hope it's not too late to heal your feelings for your father." I extend the stone, my palm flat. "Please accept this as a symbol of my remorse. If I could turn back —"

He raises his head and looks at me. His eyes are shot with red. His hand rises to meet mine, as if in slow motion. A surge of relief washes over me.

I hear the crack before I feel the blow. The stone rockets across the room, pelting the picture window.

Tears spring to my eyes. I clutch my stinging hand and watch as RJ rises from the chair and moves to the door.

"Junior," my mother says, leaping to her feet.

The screen door slams shut behind him. From the window, I see him march toward his truck. I can't let this happen. I have to make him understand.

"RJ!" I say, running out the door and

439

down the porch steps. "Wait!"

He throws open his truck door. Before I reach the driveway, his truck peels away. I watch until the billowing cloud of dust settles into the dirt road, a scene reminiscent of the day my mother was left standing at the end of the driveway, pebbles flying from my father's car tires.

It's only five o'clock when we four sit down to eat. Bob was still in his room napping when the baked spaghetti came out of the oven, and Anne insisted we not wake him. I could see the relief in my mother's face. The afternoon seemed to take its toll on everyone, including Bob. Mealtime wouldn't be easy today, with strangers at the table. She probably wanted to spare Bob his dignity.

We sit at the table, finishing our cherry pie. I pretend to eat, but I only move the cherries around on my plate. Swallowing is impossible. My throat aches every time I think of RJ and the hurt and disgust in his eyes.

Anne is just as silent as I am. My mom tries to compensate by passing around the ice-cream carton, offering another slice of pie.

Did we actually expect that the six of us

would dine together, maybe open a bottle of wine, laugh, and chat? It seems impossible in hindsight. How stupid of me. RJ and Anne aren't my siblings. They have no reason to forgive me. The fact that Anne is still here is a wonder. Perhaps some part of her feels guilty about her brother's reaction. Or maybe she took pity on my mother when she found out she had prepared a meal.

Thankfully, Lydia breaks the awkward silence. She chatters about her bout of bronchitis and a horse named Sammy and her best friend, Sara. "Sara can do a back handspring. She took gymnastics. I can only do a front handspring. I'll show you if you want, Hannah."

I smile, grateful for Lydia's youthful oblivion. If she only knew all the pain I've caused her mother. I push back my chair and toss my napkin onto the table. "Sure. Let's see what you've got."

"Five minutes," Anne says to Lydia. "We need to get going."

"But I need to say good-bye to Grandpa."

"Make it snappy."

I follow Lydia from the kitchen. Behind me, I hear my mother. "Another piece of pie, Anne? A cup of coffee?"

"You're sweet to your grandpa," I say as Lydia and I traipse to the backyard.

"Yeah. I only seen him a couple times." Lydia kicks off her yellow flip-flops. "I always wanted one, though — a grandpa, I mean."

I've robbed her of Bob, too. And poor Bob, never having known his grandchild. Lydia dashes across the yard, flipping herself with a perfect landing. I clap and whoop, though my heart isn't in it. All I can think about is the mess I've made of so many lives.

"Bravo! I'm thinking summer Olympics, 2020."

She coughs and slides her feet into her flip-flops. "Thanks. Actually, I just want to make the dance team. In two years I'll be in middle school. My mom wants me to do soccer, but I suck at that."

I look down at this carefree spirit, with her long legs and the slightest hint of breasts. Such undisguised beauty. When, exactly, do we begin to cover our glory?

"Be yourself," I tell her, "and you won't go wrong." I take her arm. "C'mon, let's go say good-bye to your grandpa."

Bob lies atop the bed, beneath an orange-and-yellow afghan. His pink skin shines, and tufts of hair seem to pull in every direction, making him look like a little boy. My heartstrings tug. His eyes flutter open when he hears Lydia's honking cough.

"Sorry, Grandpa." She crawls onto the bed, throwing off the afghan and snuggling up beside him.

As if it's instinctual, he pulls his arm up and wraps it around her. She curls her little body to his.

I hand Lydia Bob's favorite wooden puzzle and kiss his grisly cheek. He looks up at me, and for a second I swear he knows me. But then his eyes glaze over and he stares blankly at the puzzle piece.

"Look closely," Lydia tells him, pointing to the wooden airplane. "See how this piece has a corner here?"

I turn to leave when Anne appears at the door. She peers into the room. I watch as her gaze lands on the bed, where her daughter and father lie together.

Her face sets. In two swift strides, she marches across the room. "Get away from him!" She grabs Lydia's arm and yanks. "How many times have I told you —"

"Anne," I interrupt, and start toward her. "It's okay. I told you —"

I stop when I see her face, wounded and aching. She turns to me, and our eyes meet. *Did he hurt you? Were you molested?* I don't put voice to the questions. I don't have to.

She reads them in my face.

From across the room, she nods her head,
ever so slightly.

CHAPTER 42

I lie in my mother's guest bed, staring at the ceiling. It all makes sense. Anne's difficulty with male relationships, her distance from her father, even before I came into the picture. She's kept it hush all her life, and there I was, making it public. She didn't want anyone to know her secret. And that apology I offered? She saw right through it.

I feel a quickening of my pulse. A bizarre mix of disgust and vindication comes over me. I was right, all those years ago. I didn't make a false accusation. I've been acquitted. I can go back to New Orleans and reclaim my reputation! I can let my mother know that after all we've been through, I was right! I'll send RJ a letter — no, I'll drive to the vineyard. First thing tomorrow morning! I'll tell him that I was right, let him know I wasn't some evil child trying to ruin his father's life.

But Anne is gone now. What if nobody

believes me? I have no proof. What if I mistook an innocent nod for confirmation of a heinous act?

But that look on her face, the horror and the pain. I know what she was telling me with that slight nod of the head.

I throw an arm over my pillow. I cannot spend the rest of my life second-guessing myself. If only I had a piece of evidence to prove to RJ — and to myself — that I was right.

I bolt upright. But I do have evidence. And I know exactly where to find it.

The crescent moon creates a silver trail on the lake's surface. I race toward it, my bare feet slipping on the wet grass, the beam of the flashlight bouncing like a jackrabbit. My body is trembling when I reach the boat. I prop the flashlight against a life jacket, and grab the tackle box.

I work to fit the tiny key into the padlock. The lock is corroded with rust, refusing the key's entry. I try again, poking and jabbing at the rusty lock.

"Damn you!" I say through clenched teeth. I pry the latch with my bare hands until they ache. But it's futile.

I push the hair from my brow and drop my head. There, at the bottom of the boat, I spy an old screwdriver. I place one knee on the tackle box and slide the screwdriver beneath the metal latch. With all my might I pull.

"Open, goddammit." My fingers cramp as I strain to break the lock. It's no use. The lock won't budge.

I glare at the box as if it's human. "What are you hiding, huh?" I give it a kick. "Girlie magazines? Kiddie porn?" I hiss at it, then try one more time. This time the tiny key slides into the lock as if it were brand-new.

Fusty smells of mold and tobacco assault me when I lift the metal lid. I raise the flashlight, both dreading and anticipating what I'll find within. But the trays are empty. No bobbers or fishing lures. Just a deck of cards and a half-filled pack of Marlboro Reds. I lift the damp package. And there, at the bottom of the tackle box, I see a plastic sandwich bag, bulging at the seams.

I aim my flashlight at the bag, my heart banging against my chest. It's zip-locked, and stuffed with what looks like photos . . . glossy magazine photos. My stomach lurches and I think I'm going to be sick. Pornography, I'm certain. Maybe even a written confession. I lunge for it like it's my salvation.

Just as my fingers meet the bag, I freeze. I hear Dorothy's words, as clearly as if she were sitting at the helm shouting them to me. *Learn to live with ambiguity. Certainty is a fool's comfort.*

I lift my head to the heavens. "No!" I whimper. "I'm so tired of ambiguity."

I gaze out at the flat gray lake and think of RJ. This bag could clear my reputation. RJ would learn the truth, once and for all. Surely he'd forgive me now.

But he would never forgive his father. That scar that would never fade.

I drop my head in my hands. Fiona is right. We lie and cover up for two reasons: to protect ourselves or to protect others. Alzheimer's has rendered Bob harmless now. I no longer need protection from him. But those who love him do. I need to protect *their truth.*

I slam the lid shut. No one needs to know the truth. Not RJ. Not my mother. Not my old fans or former employers. Not even me. I will learn to live with ambiguity.

My hands tremble as I reattach the padlock and snap it shut. Before I have time to change my mind, I remove the tiny key from the fob. With all my might, I hurl it into the lake. It waffles atop the moonlit water for a moment, then sinks.

Chapter 43

For the next four days, I mourn. I mourn the loss of RJ's friendship and all the possibilities I'd imagined. I mourn the diminishing life of the man in the next room, struggling for each breath as the woman at his side sings him comfort. I mourn the loss of two decades with my mother, and the superhero I thought was my father.

In time I'll come to accept that we are not so different from one another. We are each of us flawed human beings, filled with fears and desperate for love, foolish people who chose the comfort of certainty. But for now, I grieve.

My mother wakes me at 4:30 a.m. "He's gone."

This time there's no mistaking her message. Bob is dead.

It's surprising how much one learns about

a person at his funeral, and how many unanswered questions will be buried alongside him. At my father's memorial two years ago, I learned that my dad dreamed of being a pilot, something he never realized, though I'm not sure why. Today, as I stand before Bob's grave site listening to his fellow AA members recount Bob's struggle, I learn that Bob was a foster child. I discover that he ran away at age fifteen and was homeless for a year before a restaurant owner took him under his wing, offering him a job in the kitchen and a room upstairs. It took him six years, but he put himself through college.

What happened in that foster home that drove him to the streets? And what demon was he fighting in that twelve-step program? Alcoholism, as he claimed, or something even more destructive?

I hold my mother's hand and bow my head as the preacher says a final prayer, asking for God's forgiveness. From the corner of my eye, I see RJ's stoic profile, where he stands on the other side of my mom. I close my eyes. *Please forgive Bob, and me. And please, please soften RJ's heart.*

The preacher makes the sign of the cross, and Bob's casket is lowered into the ground. One by one, the crowd disappears. A man walks over to my mother. "Your husband was a good man," he says.

"The best," she says. "And he'll be rewarded." If Dorothy were here, she'd be pleased. Hope is wishing he'd be rewarded. Faith is knowing that he will be.

I squeeze her arm and turn toward the car, allowing her a few final minutes alone to say good-bye to the love of her life. When I do, I come face-to-face with RJ.

He's wearing a dark suit and white shirt. For a quick moment, our eyes lock. I can't be certain what I see there. It's no longer the disdain I saw a week ago. It's more of a disappointment, or longing. I imagine he, too, grieves the loss of what might have been.

I startle when I feel a pair of arms around my waist. I look down and see Lydia. She buries her face in my dress, and her shoulders quake.

"Hey, sweetheart," I say, kissing the top of her head. "You okay?"

She squeezes me tighter. "I killed him."

I pull away. "What are you talking about?"

"I gave him that pneumonia. I got too close to him."

Slowly, her mother's words come back to me. *Get away from him!*

I squat down and take her by the arms.

451

"Oh, honey, you didn't hurt your grandpa."

She sniffles. "How do you know?"

"Because I did." I swallow hard. "Your grandpa snuck off to his boat, all because I took him on a boat ride. They found him cold and wet the next morning. That's when he got sick. And he never got better."

I dig around in the dirt with my shoe until I find two stones. I offer one to her, then take her other hand in mine. Together we walk to his grave.

"But if you think you've done something wrong, whisper it to the Forgiveness Stone, like this." I cup the stone next to my mouth and say, "I am sorry, Bob."

Her face is skeptical when she looks at the stone in her hand, but she cups it to her mouth anyway. "I'm sorry if I gave you my bronchitis, Grandpa. But maybe it really was Hannah, because she's the one who took you on the boat ride and all."

I smile. "Okay, on the count of three, we toss our stones into the grave, and Grandpa will know we're sorry. One. Two. Three."

Her stone lands on the casket. Mine lands beside it.

"I hope that worked," she says.

"Hope is for wussies," I say, and take her hand. "You've got to have faith."

■ ■ ■ ■

Two cars remain on the narrow cemetery lane, my mother's Chevrolet and RJ's truck. They're parked thirty yards from each other. A light mist begins to fall. Beneath a plaid umbrella, I walk arm in arm with my mother. To our right, Lydia spins circles with her hands outstretched, either oblivious to the sprinkles or enjoying them. I glance behind me. RJ walks with Anne. Her head is close to his, as if they're deep in conversation. I need to say something to him. This may be the last time I ever see him.

We're nearly to her car when my mother stops.

"Get in, honey. It's open. I'm going to invite the kids back to the house."

I hand her the umbrella and watch as she traipses over to her stepchildren, two adults she never really knew. They won't be coming to the house; I already know it. And it's not because of her; it's because of me.

A moment later, she turns back toward me, her clouded face telling me I was right.

I stand in the sleet, watching RJ move farther and farther away from me. My heart aches. This is my last opportunity. I need to say something. But what? *I'm sorry? I still don't know what happened that night? I'm learning to live with ambiguity, can you?*

They've reached the truck now. Lydia runs over and hops in the backseat. Anne steps into the passenger seat. RJ grabs hold of his door handle. Instead of opening it, he turns around. Through the misty air, his eyes find mine, as if he sensed I'd been watching him.

My heart trips. He lifts his head, a simple, neutral gesture of acknowledgment. But it's not simple to me. It ignites a tiny flicker of optimism. I let go of my mother's arm and raise my hand.

Slowly, I move toward him, terrified he'll bolt if I move too quickly. My heel gets stuck in the grass, and I nearly trip. There go the last vestiges of grace. I regain my balance and trot, faster now, desperate to reach him.

I stand before him, drops of rain falling from my hair and eyelashes.

"I am so sorry," I say, my breath heavy. "Please believe me."

He reaches out and touches my arm. "I do." He turns toward his truck. "You take care."

Once more, I watch as RJ gets in his truck and drives away.

■ ■ ■ ■

My mother and I spend the following week and a half cleaning out Bob's closets and drawers. She keeps his robe, a flannel shirt, and three sweaters. She won't part with his shaving kit or his hairbrush.

"My husband passed two weeks ago," she tells me as she tapes the flaps of a cardboard box. "But Bob has been gone for five years."

She sets aside two small piles of mementos for Anne and RJ. "I'll pack Anne's and send them to her. But I thought maybe Junior would like to come over for —"

"No, Mom. He's not going to come here until I leave."

"Then let's the two of us take this stuff to the vineyard. I never been there. Bob was already too far gone when Junior moved home."

"He won't see me." It strikes me that the man who refuses to see me is perhaps the only man who ever did. He saw the face without makeup, the klutzy girl with flat hair and a torn dress. He's aware of the surly teen who thought she knew it all. RJ knows every ugly side of me I've tried to keep hidden. And unlike Fiona's fairy-tale version of forgiveness, he's not able to love the ugly.

■ ■ ■ ■

By the third week, it's clear my mother is strong enough to be alone again. It's also clear I'm not going to hear from RJ. I tell her of my plans before I have a chance to change my mind.

The first Monday in July, I load my suitcase in my trunk, struck again by the almost nonexistent footprint I leave these days. I still talk to Dorothy and Jade every day, but I have no job, no boyfriend or husband or child to kiss good-bye or worry about. It's both liberating and horrifying, knowing how easily I can disappear. I put the key in the ignition and buckle my seat belt, hoping to drive the ache from my heart.

"You be careful," my mother says, leaning in to kiss my cheek one more time. "Call when you get there."

"You sure you don't want to join me?"

She nods. "I like it here. You know that."

I pull the diamond-and-sapphire necklace from my purse and hand it to her. "This belongs to you," I say, tucking the platinum chain into her hand.

She stares at the sparkling stones, and I see the recognition flicker. "I — I can't take this."

"Sure you can. I had it appraised. It's only a fraction of what you deserve."

I drive away and picture her returning to her empty house, her heart heavy. She'll think I forgot something when she finds the papers on the kitchen counter. I imagine her, staring down at the official appraisal, covering her mouth when she sees the figure. And then she'll open my letter, and learn about the money I've transferred into her account. At last, she will have received the settlement from my father that she should have gotten two decades ago.

I ease onto I-94 and turn on the radio. John Legend streams through the speakers, belting out a bittersweet ballad completely incongruent with the glorious July day. I crack my window and try to focus on the cloudless blue sky instead of the heartbreaking song that reminds me of RJ. Did I really think he'd call, after all I've put his family through?

I fight back tears and turn to another station. Terry Gross is interviewing a new novelist. I punch the cruise control and drift along with the traffic, listening to Terry's soothing voice, feeling the monotonous hum of the road beneath my tires. Just how long has it been since I've taken a road trip?

I smile, remembering the time Julia and I drove my old Honda from L.A. to New Orleans, a three-day trip that spanned almost two thousand miles. I scowl, trying to recall why my dad couldn't make it. *Julia can take you,* he'd said. *She's got nothing better to do.* Was that true? Because now it seems utterly disrespectful.

I picture Julia, singing along to Bon Jovi, her blond ponytail bouncing to the rhythm. Did my dad appreciate her? Did he know how loyal she was to him, how loyal she'd be even after he was gone?

I make a mental note to send her a Forgiveness Stone. I know Julia, and those hidden letters must be weighing heavily on her mind. She needs to hear that I was no different, that I, too, protected my father at all costs, including my integrity.

The streets of Chicago sizzle with energy and the summer's heat. It's four o'clock when I find the old brick building on Madison Street. I take the elevator to the third floor, and wander down the narrow hallway, searching for Suite 319. The handmade sign on the door tells me I've arrived.

Forgiveness Stones Reunion
Headquarters

I peer through the glass door, the large room like a hive of swarming bees. And there she is, the queen bee, perched behind a desk with her nose in the computer screen and a phone at her ear. I open the door.

She doesn't see me until I'm standing in front of her. When she looks up, a flashbulb of fear goes off, and I know it's still there, her burden that I have yet to lift.

I place a stone on her desk.

"This is for you."

Fiona rises and comes to my side of the desk. We stand facing each other like two awkward teens. "You are absolutely and totally forgiven. And this time, I mean it."

"But I ruined your life." Her response is half statement, half question.

"My old life," I say. "And maybe that's a good thing." I step back and glance about the room. "Need another pair of hands?"

CHAPTER 44

I pay a fortune for a one-month rental apartment in Streeterville, though I'm rarely there. During the next four weeks, I spend most every waking hour at headquarters with Fiona and a couple dozen other volunteers, or at Chicago City Hall picking up permits, or meeting with vendors or officials from Millennium Park. At night, we gather at Fiona's apartment for pizza and beer, or at the Purple Pig for happy hour.

We're at Sweetwater Tavern when Fiona orders me her new favorite drink, a Grant Park Fizz.

"It's a delicious concoction of gin, ginger simple syrup, lime, soda, and cucumber. I challenge you to drink slowly."

"Oh, God," I say between sips. "Best thing these lips have tasted in months."

She smiles and slings an arm around my shoulder. "You do realize, don't you? We're actually becoming friends."

"Yeah, well, don't blow it this time," I say, and clink her glass with mine.

"Any news?" she asks.

She's talking about RJ and the final two stones I'm hoping to get.

"Nothing from him," I say. "But I did get a stone back from his sister, Anne."

"The one you suspect . . ."

"Uh-huh. Her message was short and cryptic. Something like, *Enclosed is your stone. Your apology is accepted. It happened once, long ago. I hope we can let it be now.*"

"So he did molest her! Only one time, but still."

"Maybe. Or perhaps she's referring to the one time it happened to me."

Fiona sighs. "Oh, for Christ's sake! She hasn't really told you a thing. You need to ask her —"

I lift a hand. "She's told me enough. She forgives me. And she's right. It's time we let it go."

Rain by seven, done by eleven. We're all counting on the old wives' tale today. It's 6:00 a.m. and we're at headquarters, loading boxes of T-shirts and paraphernalia in a downpour.

"Hand me that box," my mother tells Brandon, an adorable twentysomething

461

volunteer. "There's room in that van for one more."

"Sure thing, Ma."

Since her arrival on Thursday, Fiona and the gang of volunteers have taken to calling my mother "Ma." She smiles every time they do. I imagine that single word is like a symphony to her after years of being deaf.

The clouds break just after nine, an hour before the event officially opens. Already people are milling about, wearing T-shirts that say STONE ME, THE CONFESSION OBSESSION, or STONED AND ATONED. But mine simply says STONED. I can't pretend that I've been forgiven, or even that I've properly atoned. I'm not sure that's even possible. As Fiona says, forgiveness, like love and life, is complicated.

I turn my attention to the day, the celebration I've been looking forward to for weeks. In the smallest corner of my mind, I fantasize that RJ comes today. But I keep the thought backstage. My father taught me long ago to avoid expectations.

Fiona and I scurry from table to table, from vendor to vendor, making sure everything's in order. But it's just nervous energy. Everything's on autopilot now. My mother busies herself checking out the baked goods offered by the local vendors.

"Six dollars for a slice of pie," she tells me. "Can you imagine? I'm in the wrong business."

It's eleven when I spot Dorothy and her entire entourage. She's sandwiched between Marilyn and Patrick, clutching both their arms. I grab my mother's hand and we run over to them.

"Hello, guys! I want you to meet my mother. Mom, these are my dear friends Dorothy and Marilyn and Mr. Sullivan."

"Paddy," he says, correcting me.

Dorothy offers her hand. "You've got a beautiful daughter."

"Don't I, though?" my mother says. "Now, if you'll please excuse me, I got some T-shirts to sell."

We wave her good-bye, and Marilyn turns to me. "Oh, Hannah, thank you for making this possible."

"No. Thank *Dorothy* for making this possible. I would've taken a shortcut with these stones, but she wouldn't let me."

Coming up behind them, I spy Jackson, his arm slung around a pretty brunette with a very pregnant belly. "Hannah, meet my wife, Holly."

I feel a brief stab of envy. What I wouldn't give to be married and pregnant. Could I ever have truly forgiven Jack? I like to think

I'm softer now, that the new me could get over his betrayal. But in truth, I think Jack was right. He wasn't the one.

I take Holly's hand. "It's really nice to meet you, Holly. Congratulations on your marriage, your baby."

She looks up at her husband with pure adoration. "I'm a lucky girl." She turns back to me. "Hey, I hear you're responsible for a whole slew of Rousseau apologies."

I smile, thinking of the Chain of Forgiveness, from me to Dorothy, to Marilyn, to Jackson. "Well, it's actually Dorothy — your mother-in-law — who's responsible."

Jackson shakes his head. "That's not what she says." He clamps the shoulder of a short, silver-haired gentleman. "Hey, you remember my father, Stephen Rousseau."

"Of course." I take the hand of Dorothy's ex-husband, the man who left her after breast surgery. I wonder how Dorothy feels about having him here today.

"I'm happy to say my dad returned my stone," Jack says. "I was once a selfish kid who thought my happiness was more important than his. Hard to believe, I know." He grins, the same happy, lopsided grin I thought I'd stolen.

"And I sent my stone on to Dot," Mr. Rousseau says, and glances at his ex-wife.

"I wasn't the most sensitive husband."

I study Dorothy. She keeps her head high and doesn't crack a smile. But there's a peace in her face now that had been missing.

"Nonsense," she says, and quickly turns to me. "We're meeting Steven Willis here today. My old student who's living in New York. Remember, Hannah?"

"Yes. How could I forget your brilliant scheme with the stolen Walkman?" I pat Dorothy's hand. "Y'all have fun. I'll catch up with you later. I'm off to meet Jade at Crown Fountain."

I head down the cement path. I'm about thirty feet away when I hear someone call my name. "Hannah!"

I wheel around and see Jack, trotting over to me.

"Hey, my mom told me about what happened in Michigan, and how the vineyard owner hasn't forgiven you. She said you really loved the guy."

My heart shreds, and I want to disappear. I roll my eyes, feeling my face heat. "Love? C'mon. I hardly knew him."

His face becomes tender. "It's okay, Hans. You can be soft."

Tears well in my eyes, and I bat them away. "This is ridiculous." My laugh curdles,

465

and I hide my face. "I'm so sorry."

"It's none of my business," he says. "But don't blow it, Hans. If you really love this guy, fight for him."

He squeezes my arm and turns away.

Thoughts of RJ invade my mind, as if the guard I'd hired to keep him at bay just walked out on the job. How is he? Does he ever think of me? *You never give up on someone you love.* Have I given up on RJ? No. I tried. He gave up on me.

Jade stands beside her father's wheelchair, the two of them clearly entertained by the fountain. She's pointing to a teenage boy whose face is a digital projection on a giant water screen. A cascade of water spurts from his mouth. Jade's father laughs.

"Hannabelle!" Jade shouts when she sees me. I throw my arms around her, then bend down to hug her father.

"How are you feeling, Pop?"

He's gaunt, with crescents of black beneath his eyes. But he's smiling, and his embrace is strong.

"Better than I have in months."

"Dad and his brothers have been tearing it up this weekend, haven't you, Dad?"

While Mr. Giddens enjoys the fountain, I

pull Jade aside. "How is he? And how are you?"

She smiles, but her eyes are heavy. "He's exhausted, but happy. We're talking weeks now, not months. I don't want to let him go, but if I have to, at least I know he's proud of me."

"And all of your righteous wrongdoings." I squeeze her arm. "How are things back home?"

"Marcus brought me roses last week. Told me he's sorry for the umpteenth time. Swore he'd be the perfect husband if I'd just give him one more chance."

All my hard edges return. I suck in a breath and remind myself not to judge. "Okay. That's sweet. What'd you tell him?"

She slaps my arm with the back of her hand. "Don't get all soft on me now, Hannabelle. What do you think I told him? I told him to bugger off. There's no way in hell he's coming back. In my book, it's one strike, you're out!"

I laugh out loud and spin her in a circle. "Good for you! Sometimes 'I'm sorry' just doesn't cut it."

I glance at my watch. It's almost noon. From the direction of Pritzker Pavilion I hear a band playing Pharrell Williams's "Happy."

467

"Is he here?" Jade asks.

She's talking about RJ. Like me, she thought maybe, just maybe, he'd come.

"No," I say. "He's not coming." And at this moment, I'm sure of it. That old cloak of darkness threatens to trap me. And just like that, I make a split-second decision.

"He's not coming here . . . which is why I'm going there, to Michigan, to his vineyard."

Jade squeals. "Go! Get out of here!"

As I dash away, I hear her calling to me. "Stay in trouble!"

My mother claps a hand over her mouth when I tell her I'm leaving. "Oh, honey, are you sure that's a good idea? He knows you're here. I told him all about this reunion when I took Bob's things over to him last week."

I deflate. My mother is afraid I'll be humiliated again. She knows RJ will never forgive me. I look into her eyes and see a woman whose life has been dictated rather than created. The only time she's ever gone after what she wanted was when she refused to leave Michigan, and Bob. Whether that was a good decision or a poor one, I honestly couldn't say.

"Do you want to come with me?"

She looks around at the crowd, and I can almost read her mind. It's been years since she's been out of Harbour Cove, since she's been free to roam and explore and be responsible for only herself. "If you'd like me to."

"Or you can stay at the apartment, take the train back Wednesday, just like you'd planned."

She brightens. "Would you mind?"

"Of course not. I'll call you tonight. If it doesn't go well, I'll drive back tomorrow."

She gives me a hug before I leave. "Good luck, sweetie," she says, and pats down my hair. "I'm here for you. You know that, right?"

I nod. We've come a long way since that mother-daughter pair in Chicago all those years ago. Gone are the anger and judgment and the need for certainty. But our relationship isn't perfect, either. It's clear that the mother-daughter bond of my dreams is just that — a dream. We won't have long discussions about politics and philosophy and books and art. We won't share a love of wine and restaurants and films. My mother isn't a wise and savvy woman who's going to dole out life-changing advice or pearls of wisdom.

Instead, she offers something better. She

469

gives my heart and all its fragile pieces a soft place to land.

CHAPTER 45

Except for the distant screeching of sparrows in the orchard, it's quiet when I pull into the vineyard just after four o'clock. I look around for RJ's truck, but it's nowhere in sight. I hurry across the parking lot and groan when I see the sign on the door. CLOSED.

Damn! I knock on the door anyway and peer up at the apartment window overhead. But the curtains are drawn. It's just as deserted as the rest of the place.

I collapse onto a bench on the patio. It's too late. I shouldn't have come. The voice of doubt creeps in, telling me I'm unworthy, that I'm crazy to think someone like RJ would ever love me. *Leave. Just go, right now, before you make a fool of yourself again.*

No. This time I'm not giving up. I will fight for RJ. Maybe I'll lose, but in the end, I'll know I haven't left it to chance.

To kill time, I wander out beyond the

main building, glancing at my watch every five minutes. *C'mon, RJ! I need to see you.*

I roam past a tractor parked on the hill, in front of a wooden shed. Beneath the eaves of the shed, I run my hand along a workbench hosting an assortment of tools. I pick up a hammer, a pair of pliers, a screwdriver. Each bears the initials RW etched into its handle. Robert Wallace. Bob's carpenter tools. My mother's gift to RJ.

My foot hits against something hard. I step back and squint. There's a box wedged under the workbench. The hairs on my arms rise. No. It can't be.

Slowly, I lower myself to a squatting position and peer beneath the bench. I gasp and clutch my throat. Bob's red metal tackle box.

I look around. Nobody's in sight. I move cautiously, as if I'm wading into roiling waters that threaten to drown me, once again, in the quest for certainty.

My heart pounds. Is the reappearance of this box a sign? Am I supposed to see the contents?

With both hands, I drag the rusty old box from its hiding place. It weighs almost nothing. In an instant, I make a decision. I'll put it in my trunk. Later, I'll pitch it in a trash container, sparing RJ from ever discovering the plastic bag of photos inside.

The minute the metal box slides into daylight, I see it. I gasp. The lid hangs open now, like the gaping mouth of a croc. I stare down at it.

The only thing inside is a rusty padlock, its hook severed with a hacksaw. Someone — RJ, no doubt — has finally solved the mystery.

The orchard disappears behind night's shadow, taking with it the day's warmth. I find a sweater in my car and wrap it around me, then move to a picnic table. I make a tent of my arms and rest my head on the table. Gazing out at the army of cherry trees barely visible in the dusk, I focus on a slew of twinkling lights somewhere far out in the vineyard, until my eyelids become heavy.

I startle when I feel a tap on my shoulder. It's pitch-black. I blink, and finally my eyes adjust. I can make out his face.

"RJ."

I sit up, suddenly embarrassed. He must think I'm a nut, asleep here on his property. Or worse yet, a psycho stalker.

Every instinct tells me to run. This man doesn't want to see me. He's not going to forgive. What was I thinking? But I can't. I won't. I've come too far and lost too much.

He takes the spot beside me, his legs facing the opposite direction as mine so that we're shoulder to shoulder, our faces inches apart.

I put a hand to my chest, trying to calm my racing heart, and force myself to look him in the eyes.

"Please," I say. "Feel this." My hand trembles as I take his hand and place it on my thundering heart. "That's me," I say, "terrified of you." He tries to pull his hand away, but I keep it there, above my heart. "I'm asking you, begging you, RJ, to please forgive me." I close my eyes. "And I'm scared to death, because you have the power, right now, to either crush this fractured heart, or help it heal."

I release his hand and it falls to his side. He stares at me, his jaw muscle clamped tight. I turn away, wishing I could disappear. That's it. It's over. I've exposed my heart and still he's silent. Tears spring to my eyes, and I rise. I need to get out of here before he sees me cry.

My breath catches when I feel his hand clutch my wrist, pulling me back down. I turn to him. His eyes are soft now. He smiles and reaches out to graze his knuckles across my cheek. "I've traveled all the way to Chicago and back, and that's the best you can do?"

I lift a hand to my mouth. "You went to Chicago? Today? To find me?"

He nods. "A girl I know once told me, 'When you love someone, you never give up on them.' "

"The very reason I came here," I say.

He cups my face in his hands and leans in. His lips are soft when they meet mine, and my eyes fall shut. The moment is everything I'd hoped for — no, everything I'd *believed* it would be.

I pull the stone from my pocket. It's smooth and soft, and after so many months I almost mistake it for a comfort. But it's not. It's a weight.

"I tried to give you this once, at my mother's house. I'm asking you again, RJ, will you please forgive me?"

He takes the stone from me. "Yes, I forgive you." His gaze penetrates mine, and he runs a hand down the side of my hair. "You're a good person, Hannah. A truly good person."

My throat squeezes shut and I close my eyes. This simple validation is what I've been longing to hear all my life — what everyone longs to hear. "Thank you."

"I'm sorry it took me so long." He turns

the stone over in his hand. "When you can't forgive yourself, it's hard to forgive someone else."

I hold my breath, waiting for him to tell me about what he found in the tackle box.

"I never told you the true reason I've taken Zach and Izzy under my wing."

I blink. "They're yours," I say, without judgment.

"No." He chews his bottom lip. "Their dad used to work for me. After one too many times of showing up drunk and at least a dozen warnings, I fired him. He begged for another chance, but I wouldn't hear him out."

"You did what you had to do," I say.

He rolls the stone in his palm. "Yeah, well, I didn't really have to do it. Russ bought a handle of Jack Daniel's on his way home. Fell asleep on the kitchen floor and never woke up."

I close my eyes. "Oh, RJ."

"The man needed help, and I turned my back."

I take his hand and squeeze. "Let it go. Forgive yourself. The way I see it, it's the only choice we have."

We sit in silence for a minute, our hands intertwined, and then he rises. "Come," he says, pulling me to my feet. "I have something to show you."

He grabs a flashlight and leads me through the parking lot and down a gravel path. I'm relieved when we pass the shed and he doesn't mention the tackle box.

He holds my hand as we move through the shadowy orchard, and tells me how he found my mom at the reunion. "I couldn't believe it when she told me you'd left. I told her I was going back, and made her promise not to call you. I wanted it to be a surprise. I drove ninety miles an hour all the way home. I was so afraid you'd be gone when I got here."

"I wouldn't have left," I tell him. "I would have waited forever."

He lifts my hand and kisses it.

"I still can't believe you closed the vineyard on a Saturday," I say. "I know how precious summer weekends are up here."

"Believe it or not, we're on track to have the best year yet, which isn't saying a whole hell of a lot." He grins down at me. "Now, if only I could find a good baker, I'd be golden. Know of anybody?"

"As a matter of fact, I do. But she comes as a set — a mother-daughter duo."

"Really?" He squeezes my hand. "You're hired. Both of you."

We walk another hundred yards when he

stops at the base of a giant maple tree.

"It's all yours," he says, patting the trunk and gazing up. "We've been waiting for you."

The wooden tree house sits about twelve feet above us, surrounded by twinkling leaves and branches. I stare at RJ through a haze of tears. "You . . . This is for me?"

He nods.

I throw my arms around him and kiss his mouth, his cheeks, his forehead. He laughs and spins me around. When he sets me back on my feet, I grab hold of the ladder.

"Oh, no, you don't," he says, blocking my entrance. "You can't get in without the secret password."

I cock my head. "Okay. And what's the secret password?"

"You know it. You're the one who told me. Think about it."

I smile, and think back to the evening at dinner, the night I told him about my dream of the tree house. When he asked the secret password, I blurted out, *I have a boyfriend, RJ.*

"C'mon," he says, his eyes dancing. "You remember."

I hesitate. "I . . . have . . . a boyfriend?"

He grins. "That's right. And the next sentence?"

It takes me a second. "RJ?"

He nods. "Two sentences, not one."

My voice breaks when I repeat the password. "I have a boyfriend. RJ."

"How does that sound?" he whispers.

"Perfect."

It's foggy the next morning when we walk along the bay. My hair is pulled into a ponytail, and my face is pink from RJ's harsh soap. I'm wearing one of his old shirts and the leggings I had on yesterday. He drapes an arm around my shoulder and we walk in contented silence.

I didn't ask him about the tackle box last night. And I never will. The way I see it, one of two things happened since that confession nine weeks ago in my mother's living room. RJ has either discovered my accusation was valid, or he has learned to forgive me. I don't need to know which.

We stop along the shore, and he pulls the stones from his pocket. He keeps one in his left hand and places the other in my palm, the one that tells me I'm forgiven. He looks at me, and together we throw our stones — and the weight they symbolize — into the lake. We stand hand in hand, watching the ripples multiply and spread. Slowly, they merge again and finally disappear com-

pletely, so that nobody except RJ and me
would ever know the stones, or the ripples
in their wake, ever existed.

ACKNOWLEDGMENTS

Thomas Goodwin said it best when he said, "Those blessings are sweetest that are won with prayer and worn with thanks." I give thanks every day, and still the sentiment feels grossly inadequate. Having a novel published was a dream; having a second novel published seems downright fanciful. And if it weren't for the enthusiasm, conviction, and gentle prodding by my fabulous agent, Jenny Bent, I may still be tapping away on this one.

I'm thrilled to have, along with Jenny, a publishing dream team led by Clare Ferraro and my extraordinary editor, Denise Roy. Denise, I can't begin to thank you for your keen eye and insight, your remarkable accessibility, and your uncanny ability to create urgency and calmness simultaneously. My sincere thanks and admiration to Ashley McClay, Courtney Nobile, Rachel Bressler, John Fagan, Matthew Daddona, and the entire sales force at Penguin/Plume. And I cannot forget the gem of a woman behind the scenes, Victoria Lowes. You wear each of your many hats beautifully.

My deepest love and gratitude to my incredible husband, Bill. A better writer would have the words to tell you what you mean to me. Thank you to my loving parents, who are my biggest cheerleaders, my wonderful aunts, cousins, stepchildren, and siblings, especially my sister, Natalie Kiefer, who continues to rally friends for nearly every book event.

A special thank-you to David Spielman, my talented brother-in-law and NOLA consultant. The phone calls, e-mails, and personalized maps were invaluable. Thank you to the lovely broadcast journalists who generously offered their expertise: Sheri Jones, Rebecca Regnier, and Kelsey Kiefer. A heap of praise to my dear friend and fellow teacher, Gina Bluemlein, for her brilliant scheme with the stolen Walkman (actually a stolen phone), and allowing me to use it in my book. Additional thanks to Sarah Williams Crowell for inviting me to my very first book club and sharing the white carpet story. I knew I wanted to include it in my novel, a tribute to your beautiful spirit as well as to your parents, Don and Nancy Williams.

My love and appreciation to my wonderful friends, for every kind word and show of support. Humongous and heartfelt thanks to my generous, self-appointed assistant, Judy Graves. Every writer should be so lucky to have a friend like you.

To my early readers, Amy Bailey Olle and Staci Carl, your notes and suggestions were invaluable. And Amy, you're the best writing partner a gal could have.

To all the booksellers, bloggers, and book clubs who have graciously hosted me or promoted my book, it's been a thrill and an honor. Special thanks to Kathy O'Neil of the R Club, and to the Fairview Adult Foster Care Home — the lovely and spunky Marilyn Turner, in particular. And to my dear friend, Dorothy Silk, your spirit still shines.

For me, the biggest perk of writing has been the new reader and author friends I've made, including Julie Lawson Timmer and Amy Sue Nathan. Being able to share insecurities and celebrate with you, along with Kelly O'Connor McNees and Amy Olle, has saved me oodles in therapy.

And to you, my dear reader, for investing your precious time and entrusting me to tell you a story. I am humbled and honored, and I thank you from the bottom of my heart.

And finally, having written a book about forgiveness, I'd be remiss if I didn't say I'm sorry. Because I am. Truly.

ABOUT THE AUTHOR

Lori Nelson Spielman lives in Michigan with her husband. *Sweet Forgiveness* is her second novel. She is currently on leave from her teaching job while she works on her third. Please visit Lori's website at www .LoriNelsonSpielman.com.

The employees of Thorndike Press hope you have enjoyed this Large Print book. All our Thorndike, Wheeler, and Kennebec Large Print titles are designed for easy reading, and all our books are made to last. Other Thorndike Press Large Print books are available at your library, through selected bookstores, or directly from us.

For information about titles, please call:
  (800) 223-1244

or visit our Web site at:
  http://gale.cengage.com/thorndike

To share your comments, please write:
Publisher
Thorndike Press
10 Water St., Suite 310
Waterville, ME 04901